ANDOLFO · GOY · BROCCARDO · NOSENZO

DEEP BEYOND™

VOLUME 02

DEEP BEYOND, VOL. 2. First printing. March 2022. Published by Image Comics, Inc. Office of publication: PO BOX 14457, Portland, OR 97293. "Deep Beyond" is created by Mirka Andolfo, David Goy, Andrea Broccardo, and Barbara Nosenzo. Copyright © 2022 Arancia Studio s.n.c. All rights reserved. Contains material originally published in single magazine form as DEEP BEYOND #7-12. "Deep Beyond," its logos, and the likenesses of all characters herein are trademarks of Arancia Studio s.n.c., unless otherwise noted. "Image" and the Image Comics logos are registered trademarks of Image Comics, Inc. No part of this publication may be reproduced or transmitted, in any form or by any means (except for short excerpts for journalistic or review purposes), without the express written permission of Arancia Studio s.n.c., or Image Comics, Inc. All names, characters, events, and locales in this publication are entirely fictional. Any resemblance to actual persons (living or dead), events, or places, without satiric intent, is coincidental. Printed in Canada. For international rights, contact: licensing@aranciastudio.com. ISBN: 978-1-5343-2115-1.

DEEP BEYOND is proudly produced at Arancia Studio, Torino, Italy • #weArancia
ARANCIA STUDIO S.N.C. • **Davide G.G. Caci**: Chief Executive Officer • **Andrea Meloni**: Chief Creative Officer • **Mirka Andolfo**: Art Director • **Giulia Dell'Accio**: Executive Assistant • **Fabrizio Verrocchi**: Marketing, Design, and Communication Guru • **Fabio Amelia**: Editorial Production Manager • **Antonio Solinas**: Talent Relations Manager • **Luca Blengino**: Senior Editor • **Damiano Tessarolo**: Junior Editor • **Daniele Mittica**: Project Manager

DEEP BEYOND

created by
MIRKA ANDOLFO - DAVID GOY
ANDREA BROCCARDO - BARBARA NOSENZO

MIRKA ANDOLFO and DAVID GOY writers

ANDREA BROCCARDO artist   BARBARA NOSENZO colorist

MAURIZIO CLAUSI letterer - ROSSANO BRUNO editor

ANTONIO SOLINAS associate editor - ANDREA MELONI color editor

DAMIANO TESSAROLO editor assistant - FABRIZIO VERROCCHI designer

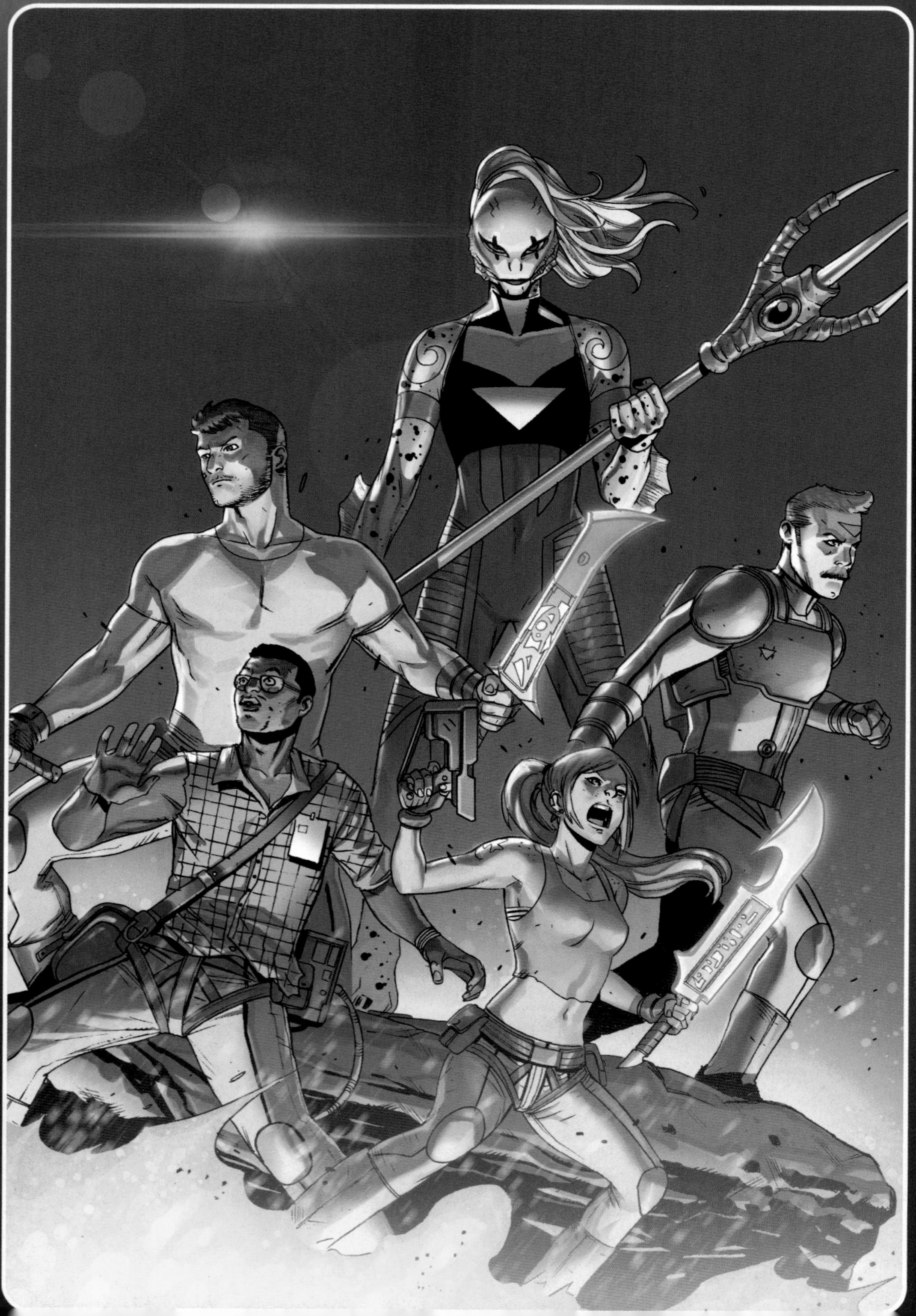

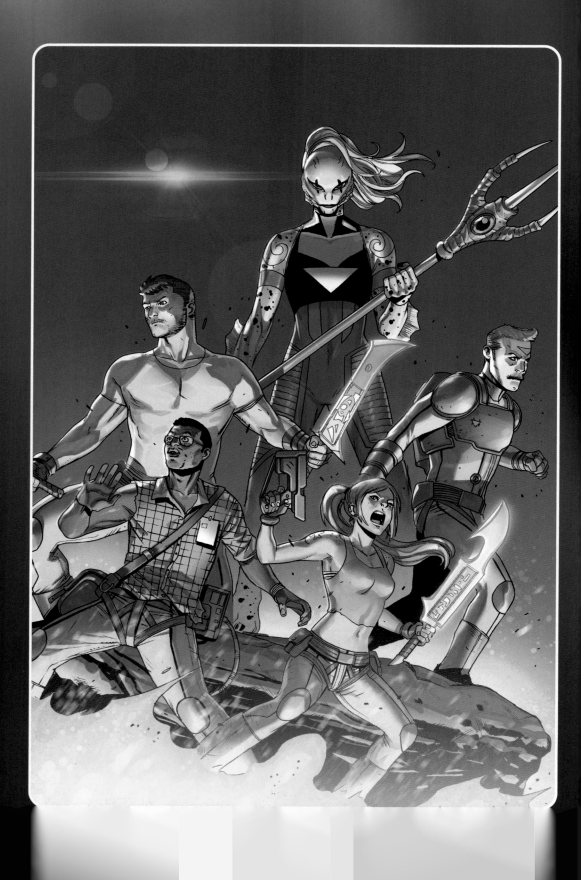

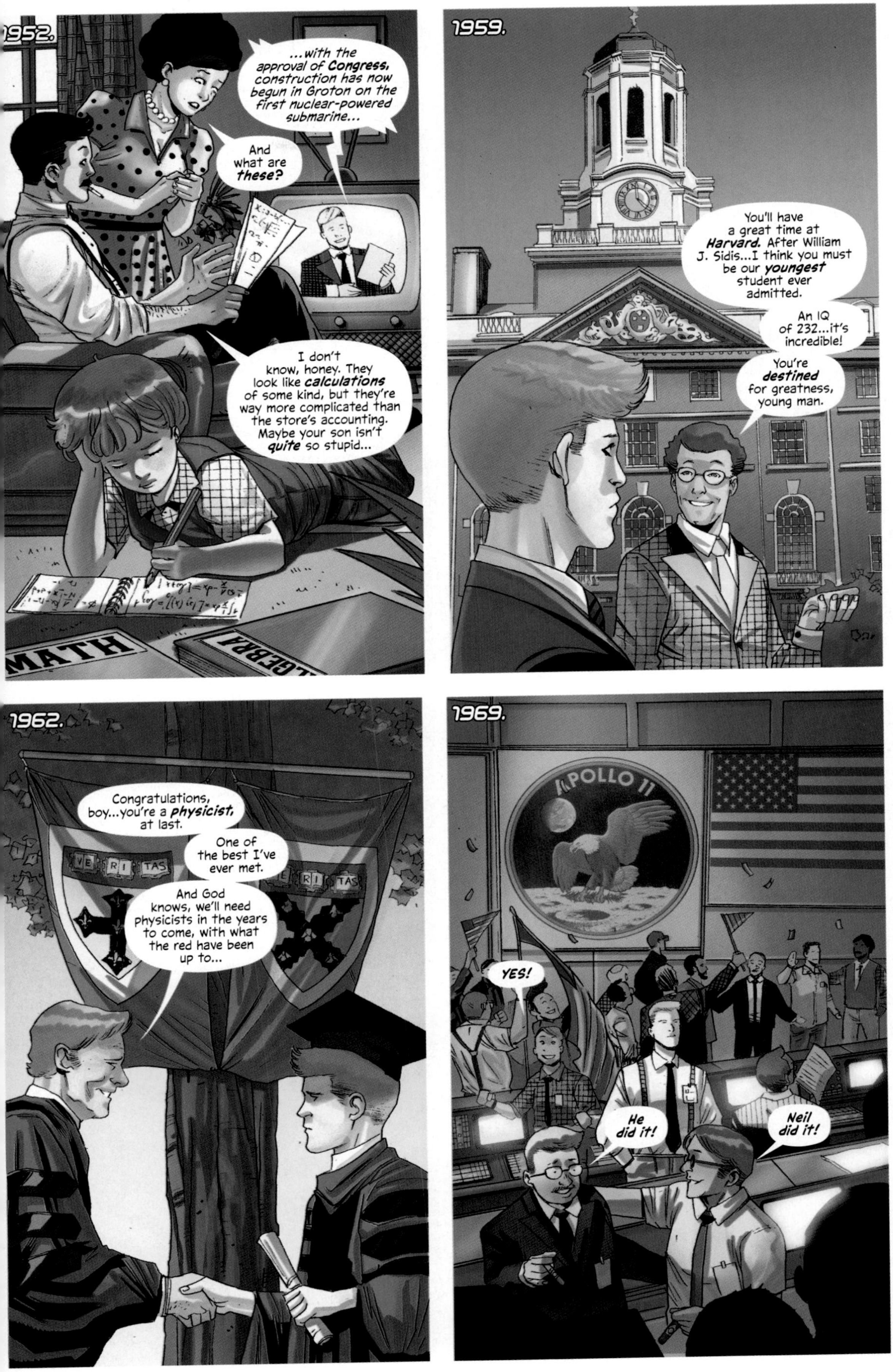
1952.
...with the approval of Congress, construction has now begun in Groton on the first nuclear-powered submarine...
And what are these?
I don't know, honey. They look like calculations of some kind, but they're way more complicated than the store's accounting. Maybe your son isn't quite so stupid...
MATH
ALGEBRA
1959.
You'll have a great time at Harvard. After William J. Sidis...I think you must be our youngest student ever admitted.
An IQ of 232...it's incredible!
You're destined for greatness, young man.
1962.
Congratulations, boy...you're a physicist, at last.
One of the best I've ever met.
And God knows, we'll need physicists in the years to come, with what the red have been up to...
VE RI TAS
VE RI TAS
1969.
APOLLO 11
YES!
He did it!
Neil did it!

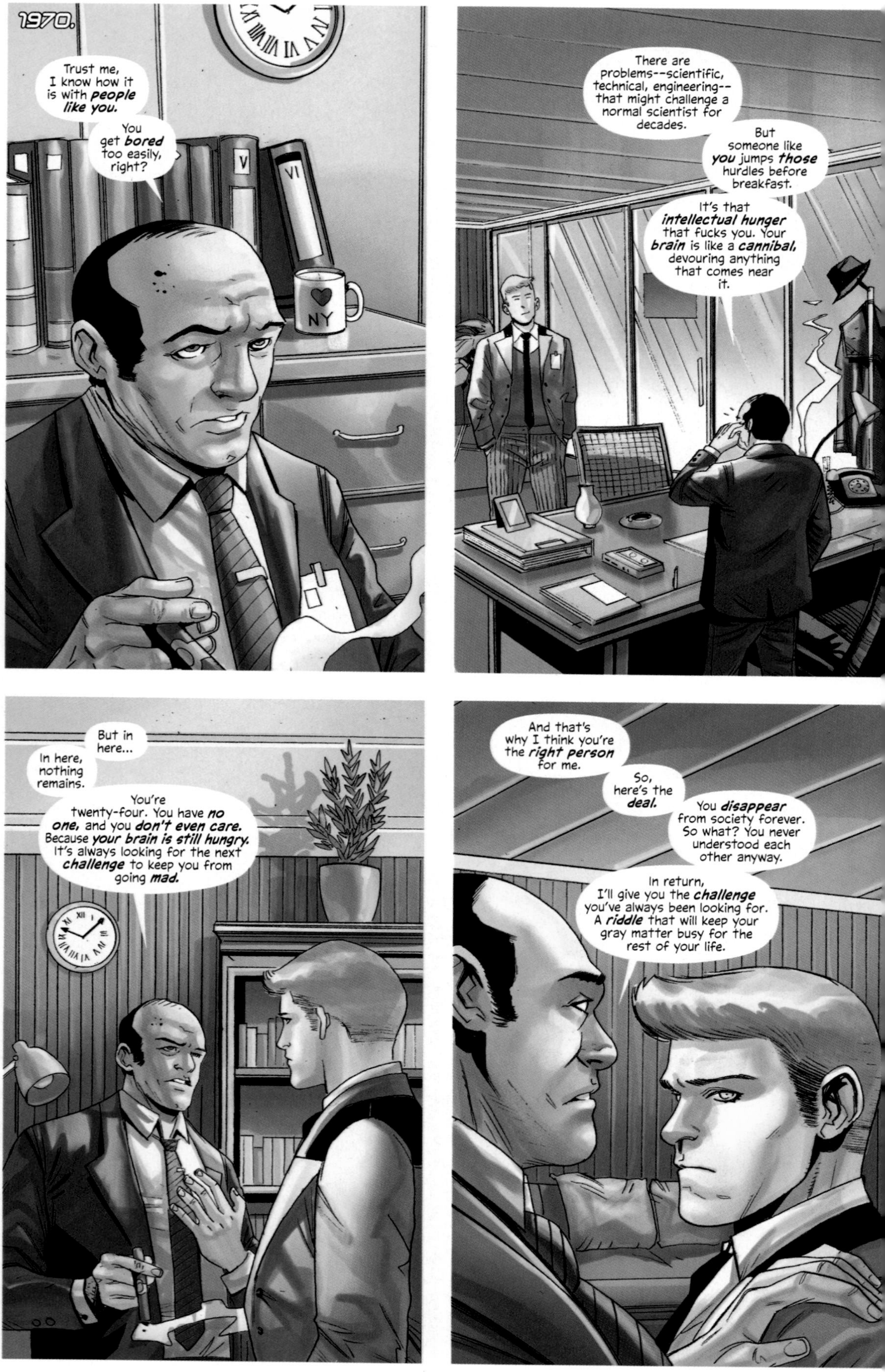
1970.
Trust me, I know how it is with *people like you.*
You get *bored* too easily, right?
There are problems--scientific, technical, engineering--that might challenge a normal scientist for decades.
But someone like *you* jumps *those* hurdles before breakfast.
It's that *intellectual hunger* that fucks you. Your *brain* is like a *cannibal,* devouring anything that comes near it.
But in here...
In here, nothing remains.
You're twenty-four. You have *no one,* and you *don't even care.* Because *your brain is still hungry.* It's always looking for the next *challenge* to keep you from going *mad.*
And that's why I think you're the *right person* for me.
So, here's the *deal.*
You *disappear* from society forever. So what? You never understood each other anyway.
In return, I'll give you the *challenge* you've always been looking for. A *riddle* that will keep your gray matter busy for the rest of your life.

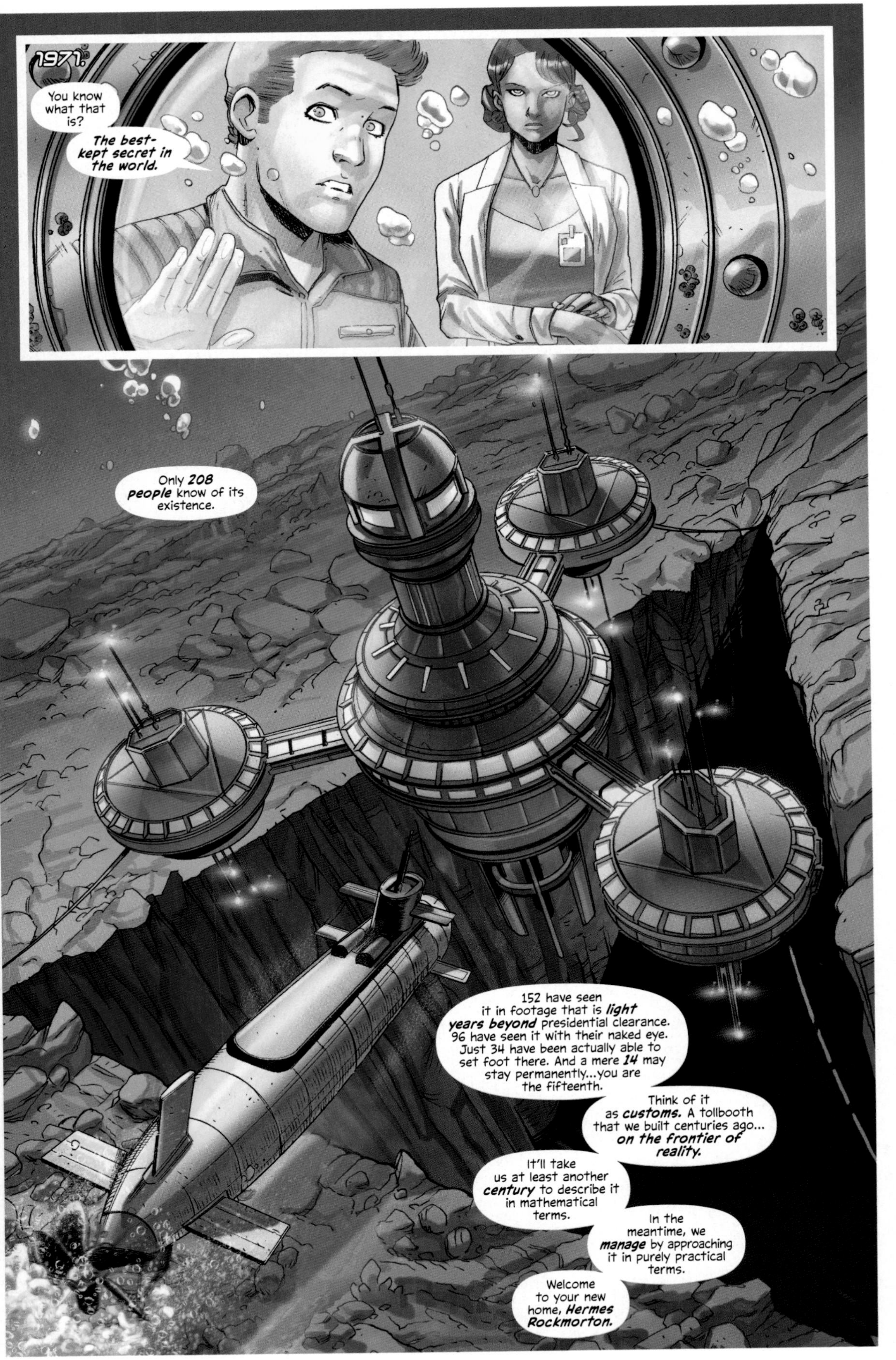
1971.
You know what that is?
The best-kept secret in the world.
Only 208 people know of its existence.
152 have seen it in footage that is light years beyond presidential clearance. 96 have seen it with their naked eye. Just 34 have been actually able to set foot there. And a mere 14 may stay permanently...you are the fifteenth.
Think of it as customs. A tollbooth that we built centuries ago... on the frontier of reality.
It'll take us at least another century to describe it in mathematical terms.
In the meantime, we manage by approaching it in purely practical terms.
Welcome to your new home, Hermes Rockmorton.

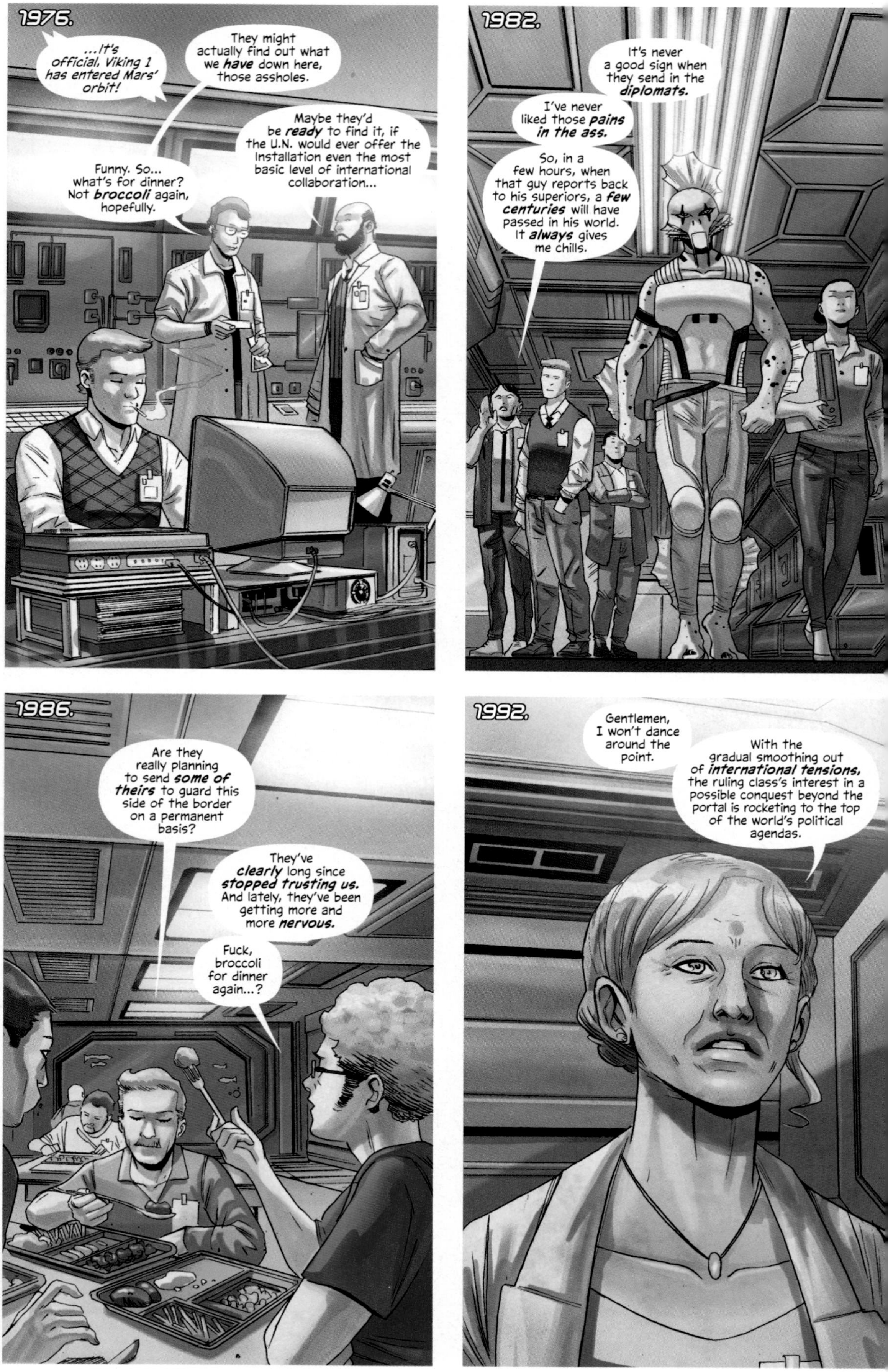
1976.
...It's official, Viking 1 has entered Mars' orbit!
They might actually find out what we *have* down here, those assholes.
Maybe they'd be *ready* to find it, if the U.N. would ever offer the Installation even the most basic level of international collaboration...
Funny. So... what's for dinner? Not *broccoli* again, hopefully.
1982.
It's never a good sign when they send in the *diplomats.*
I've never liked those *pains in the ass.*
So, in a few hours, when that guy reports back to his superiors, a *few centuries* will have passed in his world. It *always* gives me chills.
1986.
Are they really planning to send *some of theirs* to guard this side of the border on a permanent basis?
They've *clearly* long since *stopped trusting us.* And lately, they've been getting more and more *nervous.*
Fuck, broccoli for dinner again...?
1992.
Gentlemen, I won't dance around the point.
With the gradual smoothing out of *international tensions,* the ruling class's interest in a possible conquest beyond the portal is rocketing to the top of the world's political agendas.

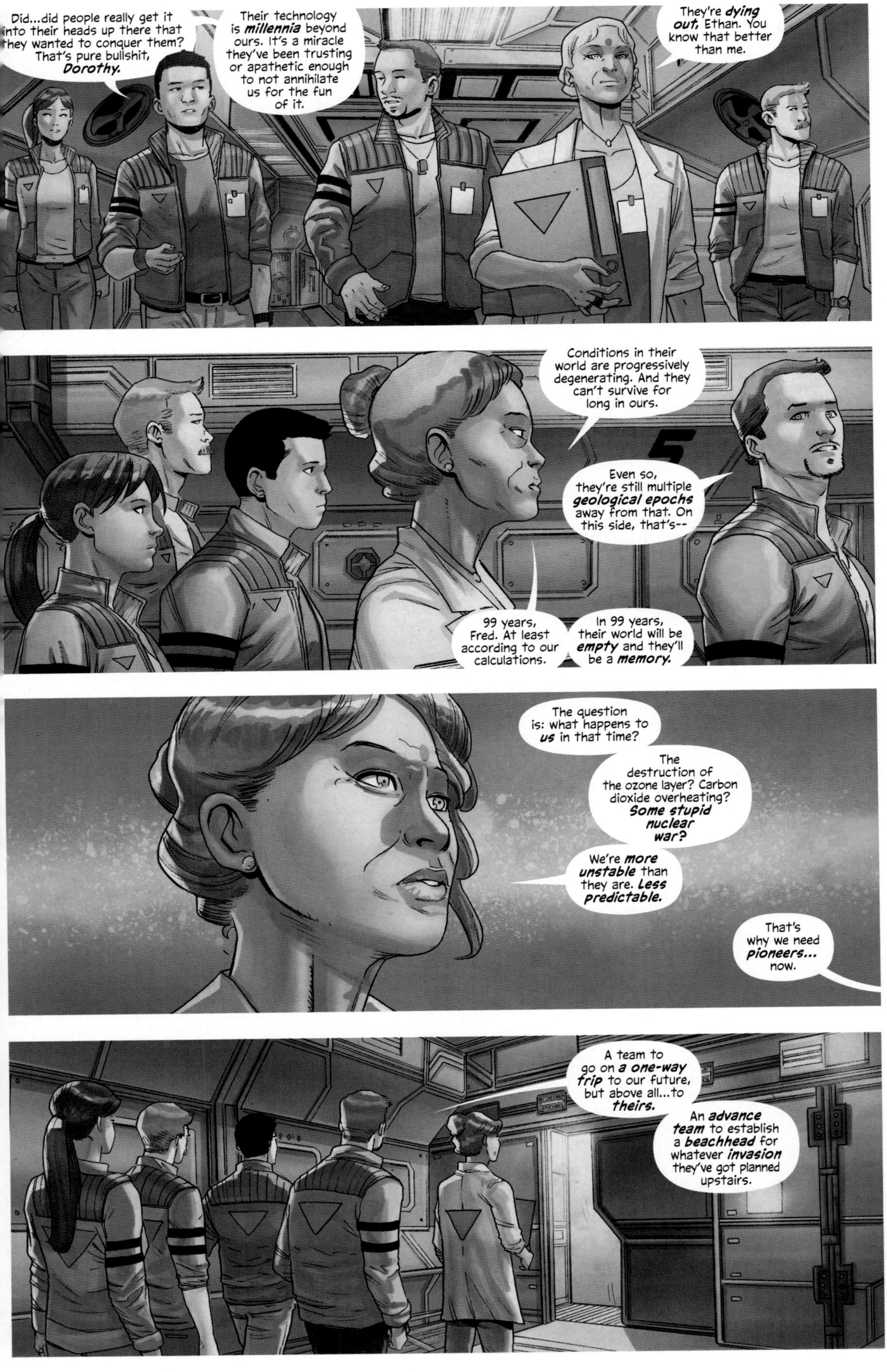
Did...did people really get it into their heads up there that they wanted to conquer them? That's pure bullshit, **Dorothy.**
Their technology is ***millennia*** beyond ours. It's a miracle they've been trusting or apathetic enough to not annihilate us for the fun of it.
They're ***dying out,*** Ethan. You know that better than me.
Conditions in their world are progressively degenerating. And they can't survive for long in ours.
Even so, they're still multiple ***geological epochs*** away from that. On this side, that's--
99 years, Fred. At least according to our calculations.
In 99 years, their world will be ***empty*** and they'll be a ***memory.***
The question is: what happens to ***us*** in that time?
The destruction of the ozone layer? Carbon dioxide overheating? ***Some stupid nuclear war?***
We're ***more unstable*** than they are. ***Less predictable.***
That's why we need ***pioneers...*** now.
A team to go on ***a one-way trip*** to our future, but above all...to ***theirs.***
An ***advance team*** to establish a ***beachhead*** for whatever ***invasion*** they've got planned upstairs.

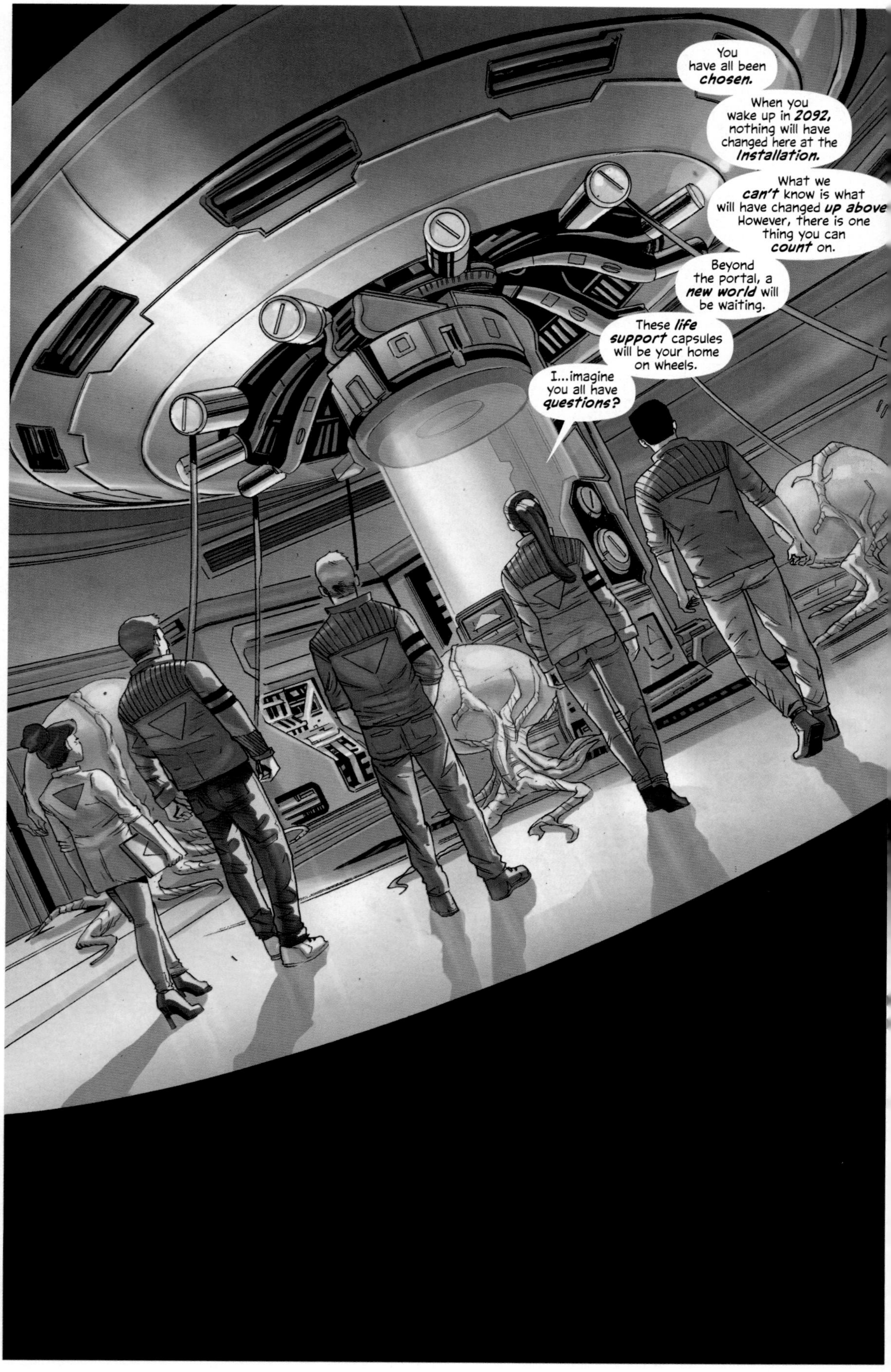
You have all been chosen.
When you wake up in 2092, nothing will have changed here at the Installation.
What we can't know is what will have changed up above. However, there is one thing you can count on.
Beyond the portal, a new world will be waiting.
These life support capsules will be your home on wheels.
I...imagine you all have questions?

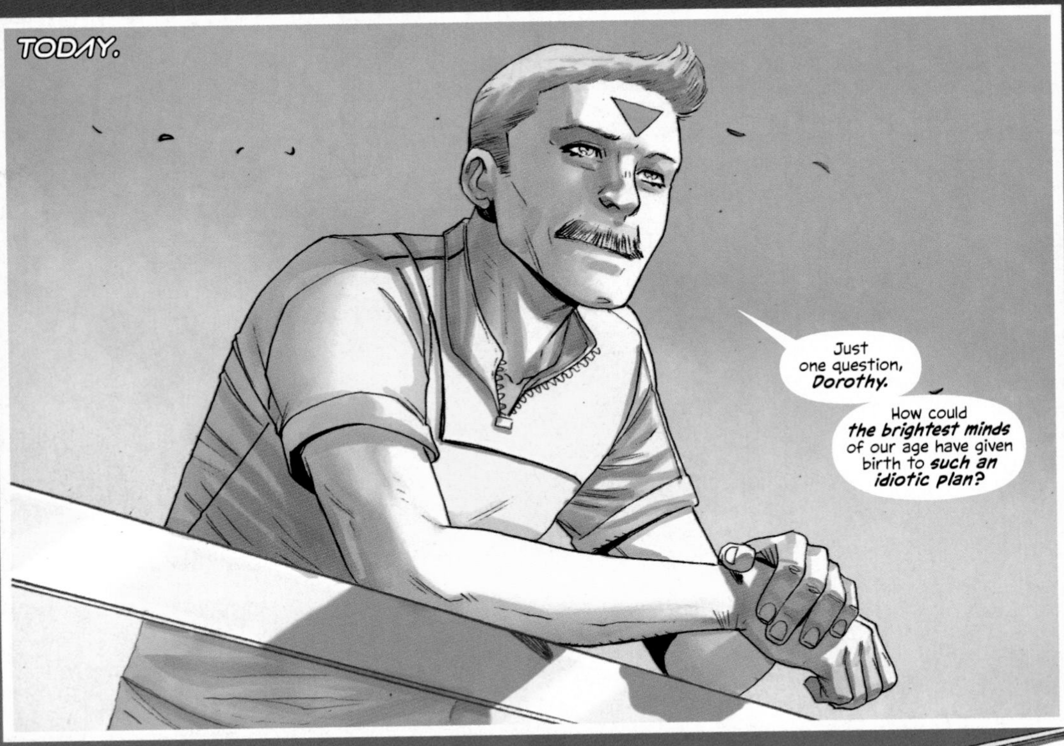
TODAY.
Just one question, *Dorothy.*
How could ***the brightest minds*** of our age have given birth to ***such an idiotic plan?***

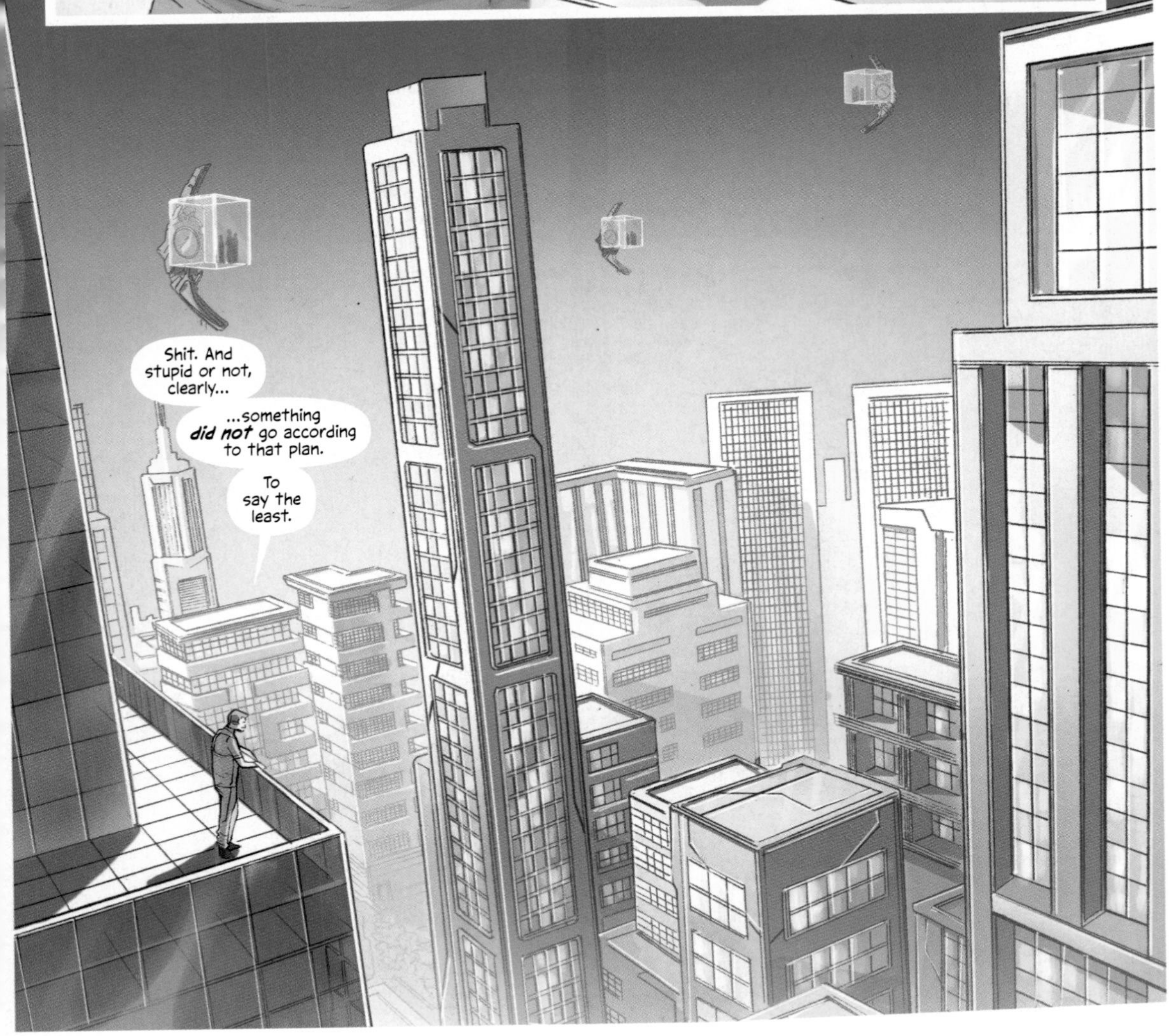
Shit. And stupid or not, clearly...
...something ***did not*** go according to that plan.
To say the least.

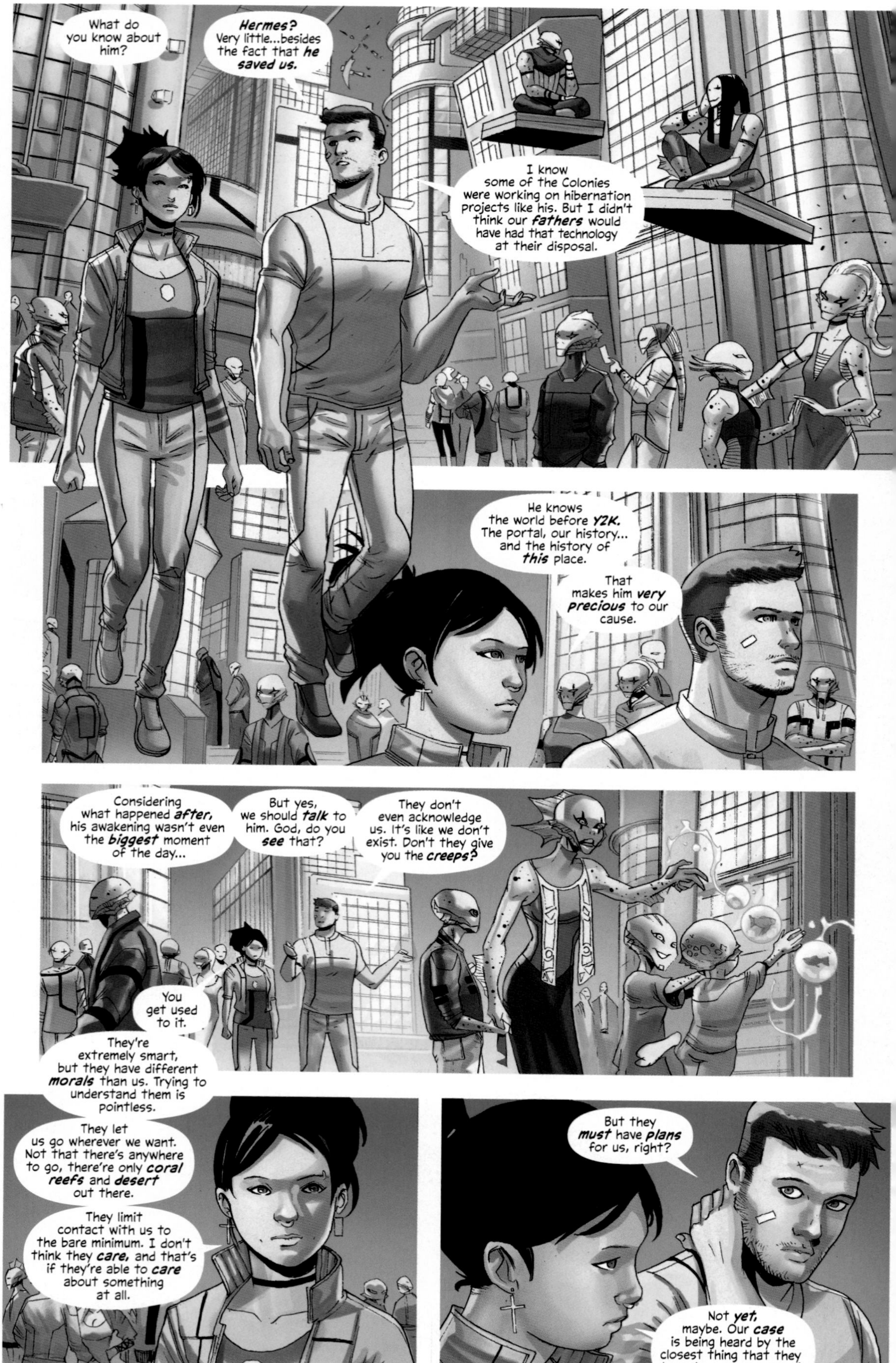

What do you know about him?
Hermes? Very little...besides the fact that he saved us.
I know some of the Colonies were working on hibernation projects like his. But I didn't think our fathers would have had that technology at their disposal.
He knows the world before Y2K. The portal, our history... and the history of this place.
That makes him very precious to our cause.
Considering what happened after, his awakening wasn't even the biggest moment of the day...
But yes, we should talk to him. God, do you see that?
They don't even acknowledge us. It's like we don't exist. Don't they give you the creeps?
You get used to it.
They're extremely smart, but they have different morals than us. Trying to understand them is pointless.
They let us go wherever we want. Not that there's anywhere to go, there're only coral reefs and desert out there.
They limit contact with us to the bare minimum. I don't think they care, and that's if they're able to care about something at all.
But they must have plans for us, right?
Not yet, maybe. Our case is being heard by the closest thing that they have to a government.

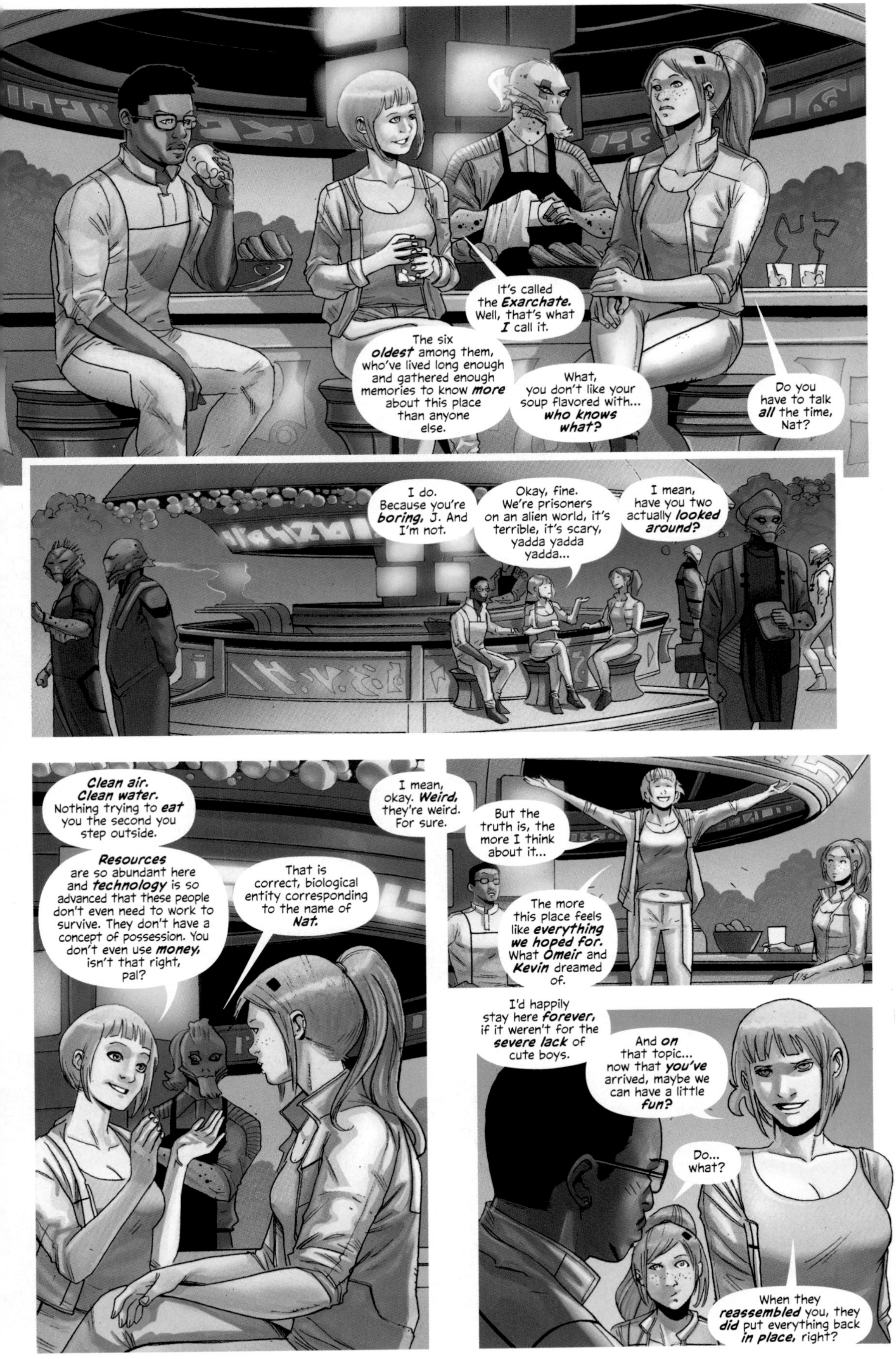
It's called the *Exarchate.* Well, that's what *I* call it.
The six *oldest* among them, who've lived long enough and gathered enough memories to know *more* about this place than anyone else.
What, you don't like your soup flavored with... *who knows what?*
Do you have to talk *all* the time, Nat?
I do. Because you're *boring,* J. And I'm not.
Okay, fine. We're prisoners on an alien world, it's terrible, it's scary, yadda yadda yadda...
I mean, have you two actually *looked around?*
Clean air. Clean water. Nothing trying to *eat* you the second you step outside.
Resources are so abundant here and *technology* is so advanced that these people don't even need to work to survive. They don't have a concept of possession. You don't even use *money,* isn't that right, pal?
That is correct, biological entity corresponding to the name of *Nat.*
I mean, okay. *Weird,* they're weird. For sure.
But the truth is, the more I think about it...
The more this place feels like *everything we hoped for.* What *Omeir* and *Kevin* dreamed of.
I'd happily stay here *forever,* if it weren't for the *severe lack* of cute boys.
And *on* that topic... now that *you've* arrived, maybe we can have a little *fun?*
Do... what?
When they *reassembled* you, they *did* put everything back *in place,* right?

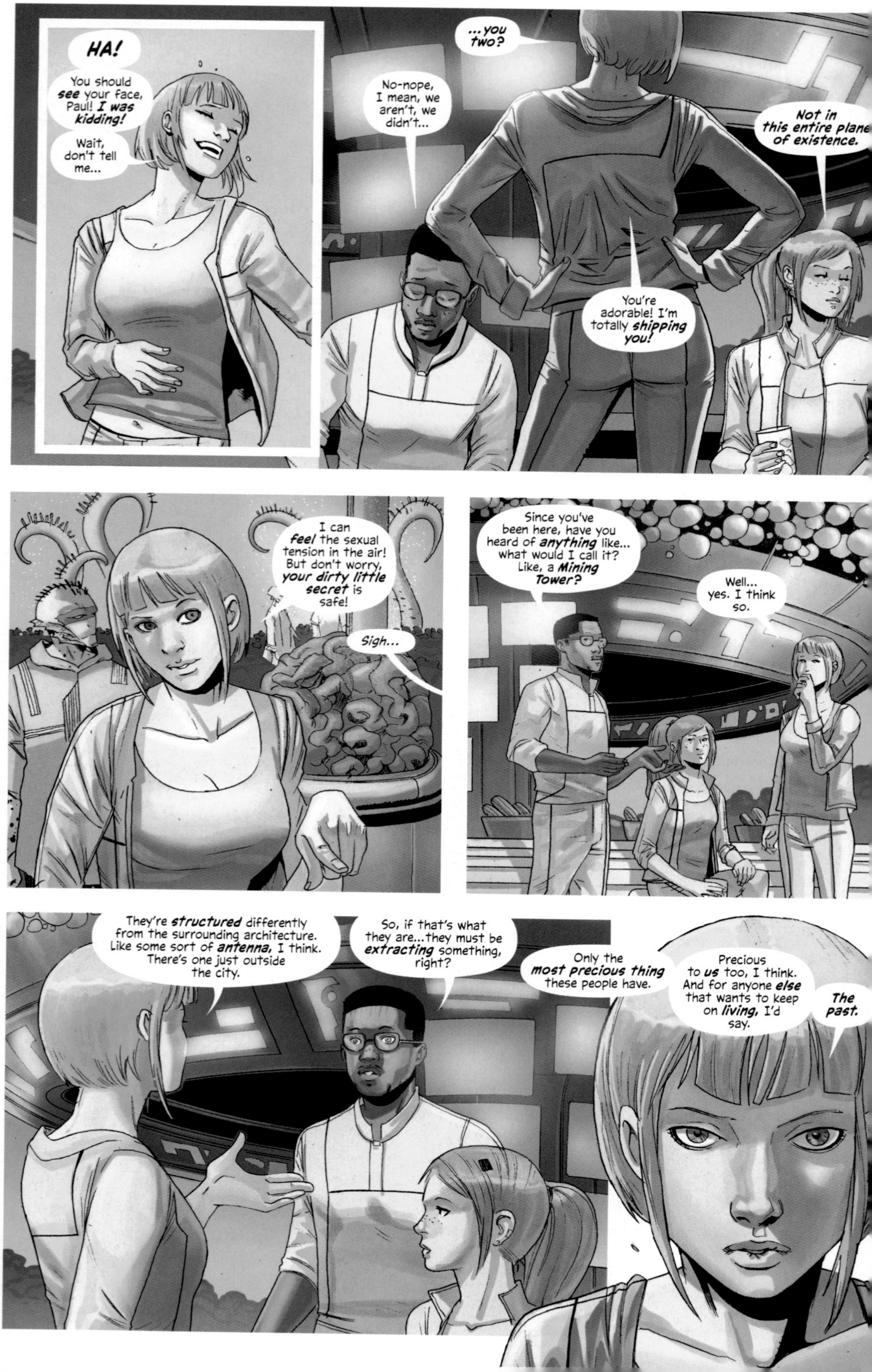
HA!
You should see your face, Paul! I was kidding!
Wait, don't tell me...
No-nope, I mean, we aren't, we didn't...
...you two?
Not in this entire plane of existence.
You're adorable! I'm totally shipping you!
I can feel the sexual tension in the air! But don't worry, your dirty little secret is safe!
Sigh...
Since you've been here, have you heard of anything like... what would I call it? Like, a Mining Tower?
Well... yes. I think so.
They're structured differently from the surrounding architecture. Like some sort of antenna, I think. There's one just outside the city.
So, if that's what they are...they must be extracting something, right?
Only the most precious thing these people have.
Precious to us too, I think. And for anyone else that wants to keep on living, I'd say.
The past.

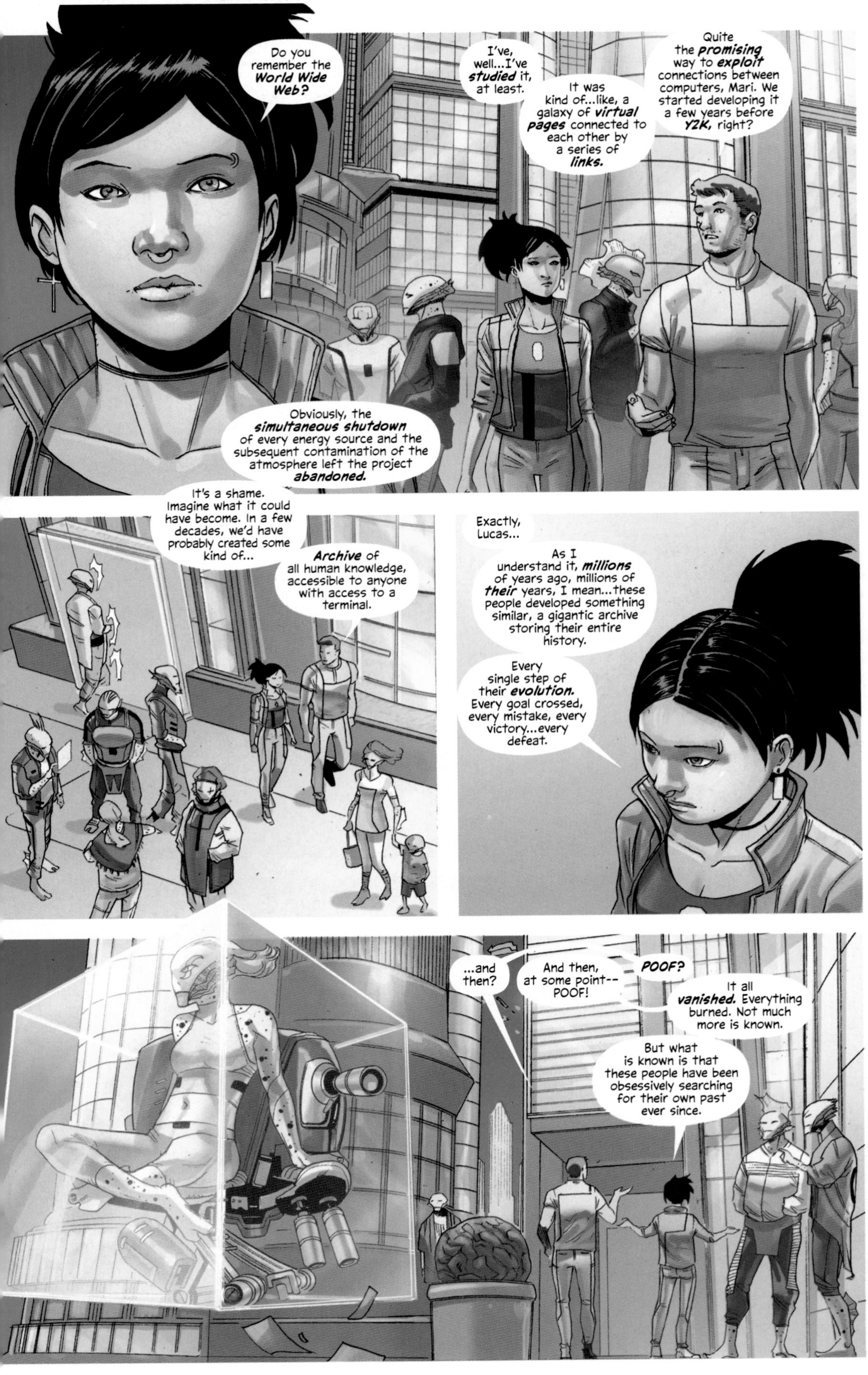
Do you remember the World Wide Web?
I've, well...I've studied it, at least.
It was kind of...like, a galaxy of virtual pages connected to each other by a series of links.
Quite the promising way to exploit connections between computers, Mari. We started developing it a few years before Y2K, right?
Obviously, the simultaneous shutdown of every energy source and the subsequent contamination of the atmosphere left the project abandoned.
It's a shame. Imagine what it could have become. In a few decades, we'd have probably created some kind of...
Archive of all human knowledge, accessible to anyone with access to a terminal.
Exactly, Lucas...
As I understand it, millions of years ago, millions of their years, I mean...these people developed something similar, a gigantic archive storing their entire history.
Every single step of their evolution. Every goal crossed, every mistake, every victory...every defeat.
...and then?
And then, at some point--POOF!
POOF?
It all vanished. Everything burned. Not much more is known.
But what is known is that these people have been obsessively searching for their own past ever since.

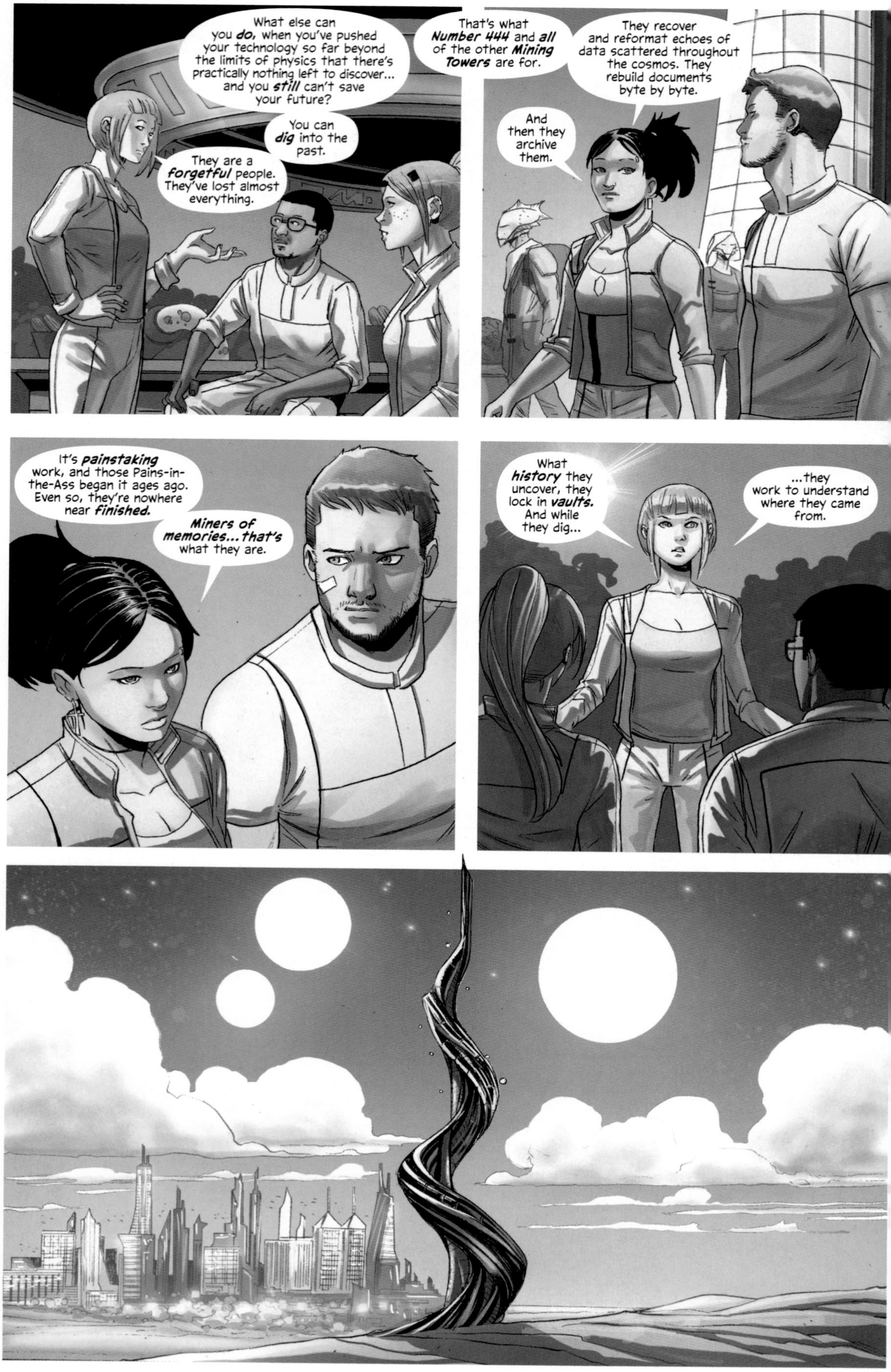

What else can you do, when you've pushed your technology so far beyond the limits of physics that there's practically nothing left to discover... and you still can't save your future?
You can dig into the past.
They are a forgetful people. They've lost almost everything.
That's what Number 444 and all of the other Mining Towers are for.
They recover and reformat echoes of data scattered throughout the cosmos. They rebuild documents byte by byte.
And then they archive them.
It's painstaking work, and those Pains-in-the-Ass began it ages ago. Even so, they're nowhere near finished.
Miners of memories...that's what they are.
What history they uncover, they lock in vaults. And while they dig...
...they work to understand where they came from.

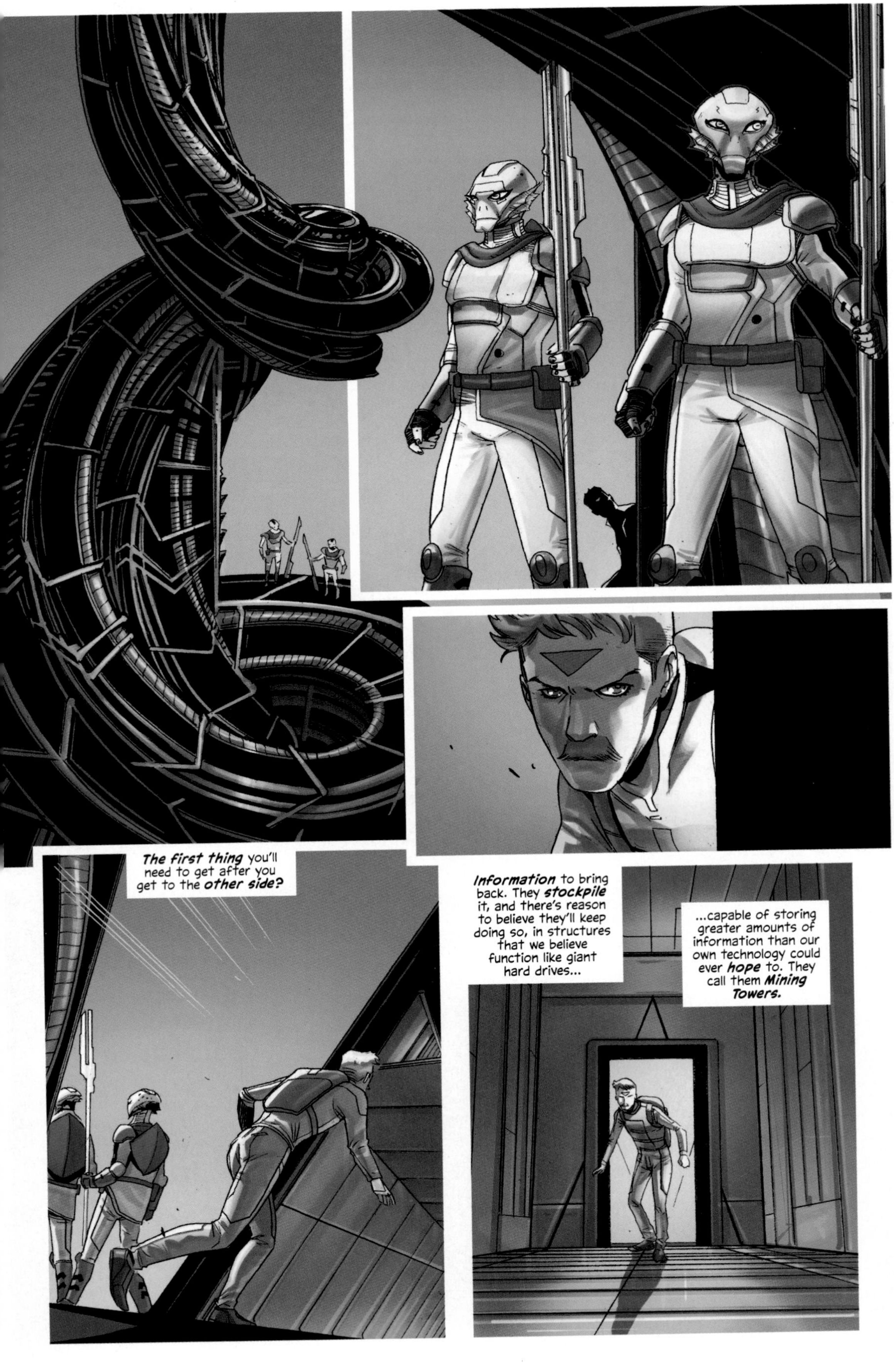

The first thing you'll need to get after you get to the *other side?*
Information to bring back. They *stockpile* it, and there's reason to believe they'll keep doing so, in structures that we believe function like giant hard drives...
...capable of storing greater amounts of information than our own technology could ever *hope* to. They call them *Mining Towers.*

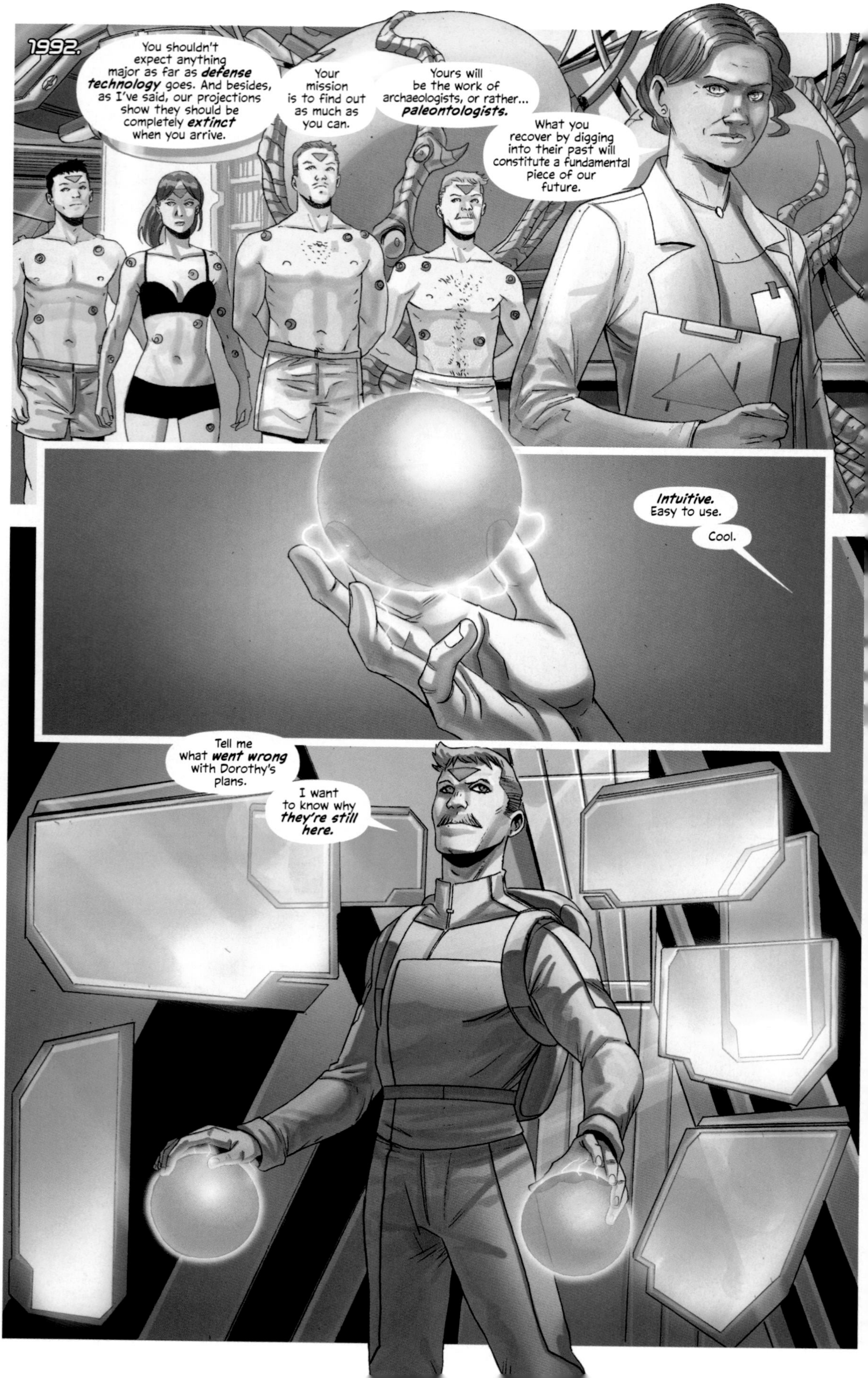
1992.
You shouldn't expect anything major as far as defense technology goes. And besides, as I've said, our projections show they should be completely extinct when you arrive.
Your mission is to find out as much as you can.
Yours will be the work of archaeologists, or rather... paleontologists.
What you recover by digging into their past will constitute a fundamental piece of our future.
Intuitive. Easy to use.
Cool.
Tell me what went wrong with Dorothy's plans.
I want to know why they're still here.

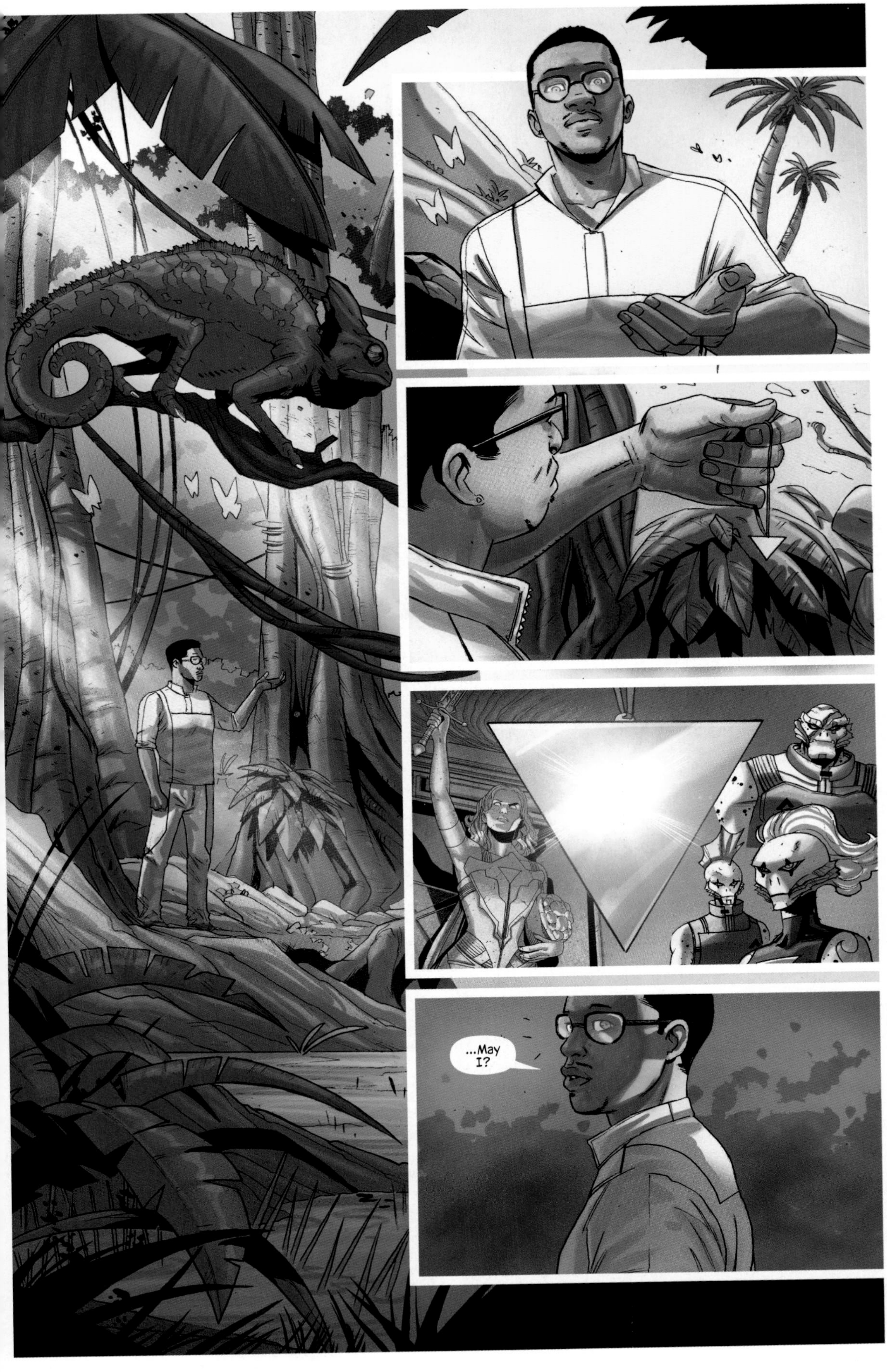
...May I?

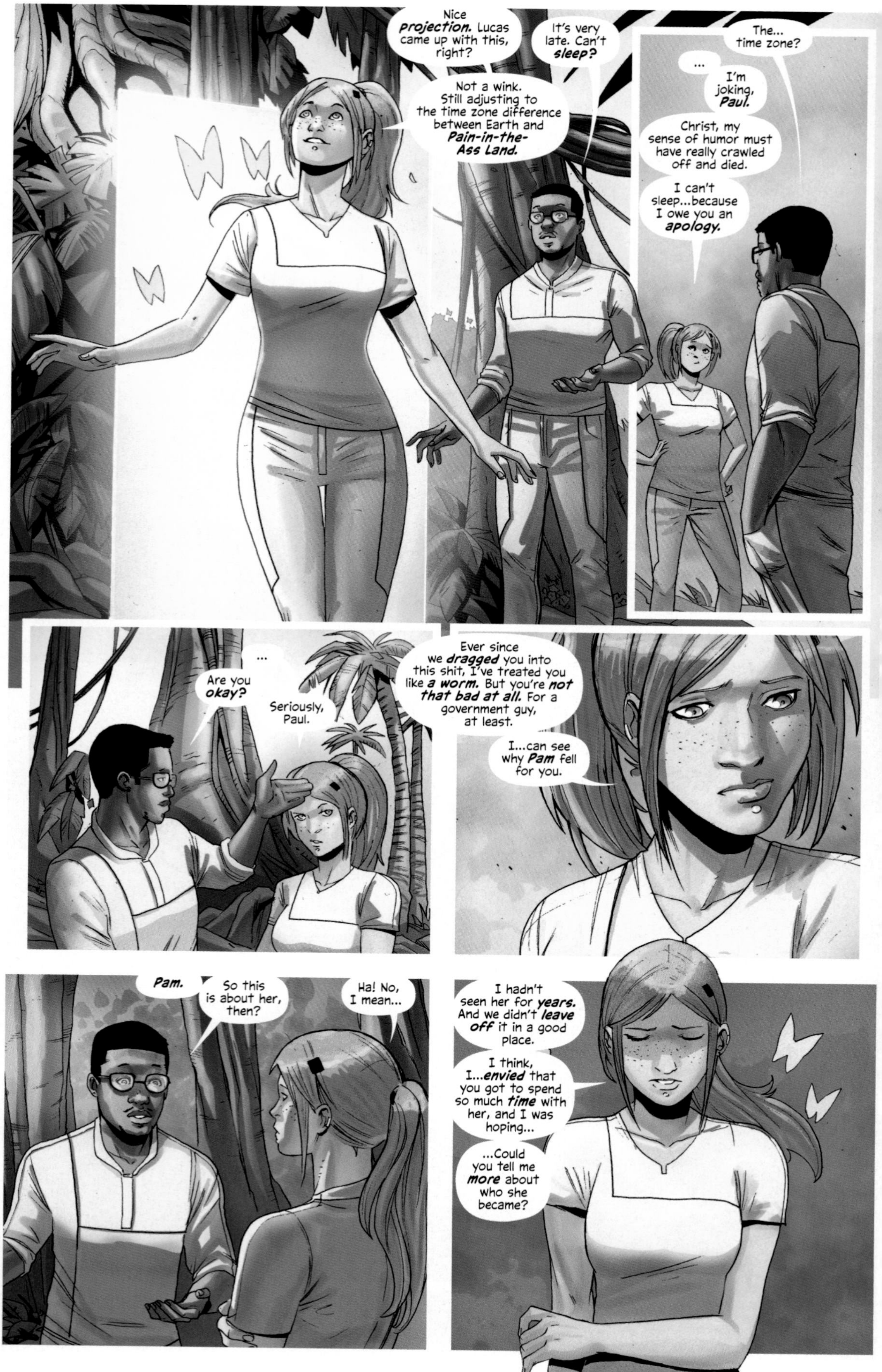
Nice *projection.* Lucas came up with this, right?
It's very late. Can't *sleep?*
Not a wink. Still adjusting to the time zone difference between Earth and *Pain-in-the-Ass Land.*
The... time zone?
...
I'm joking, *Paul.*
Christ, my sense of humor must have really crawled off and died.
I can't sleep...because I owe you an *apology.*
...
Are you *okay?*
Seriously, Paul.
Ever since we *dragged* you into this shit, I've treated you like *a worm.* But you're *not that bad at all.* For a government guy, at least.
I...can see why *Pam* fell for you.
Pam.
So this is about her, then?
Ha! No, I mean...
I hadn't seen her for *years.* And we didn't *leave off* it in a good place.
I think, I...*envied* that you got to spend so much *time* with her, and I was hoping...
...Could you tell me *more* about who she became?

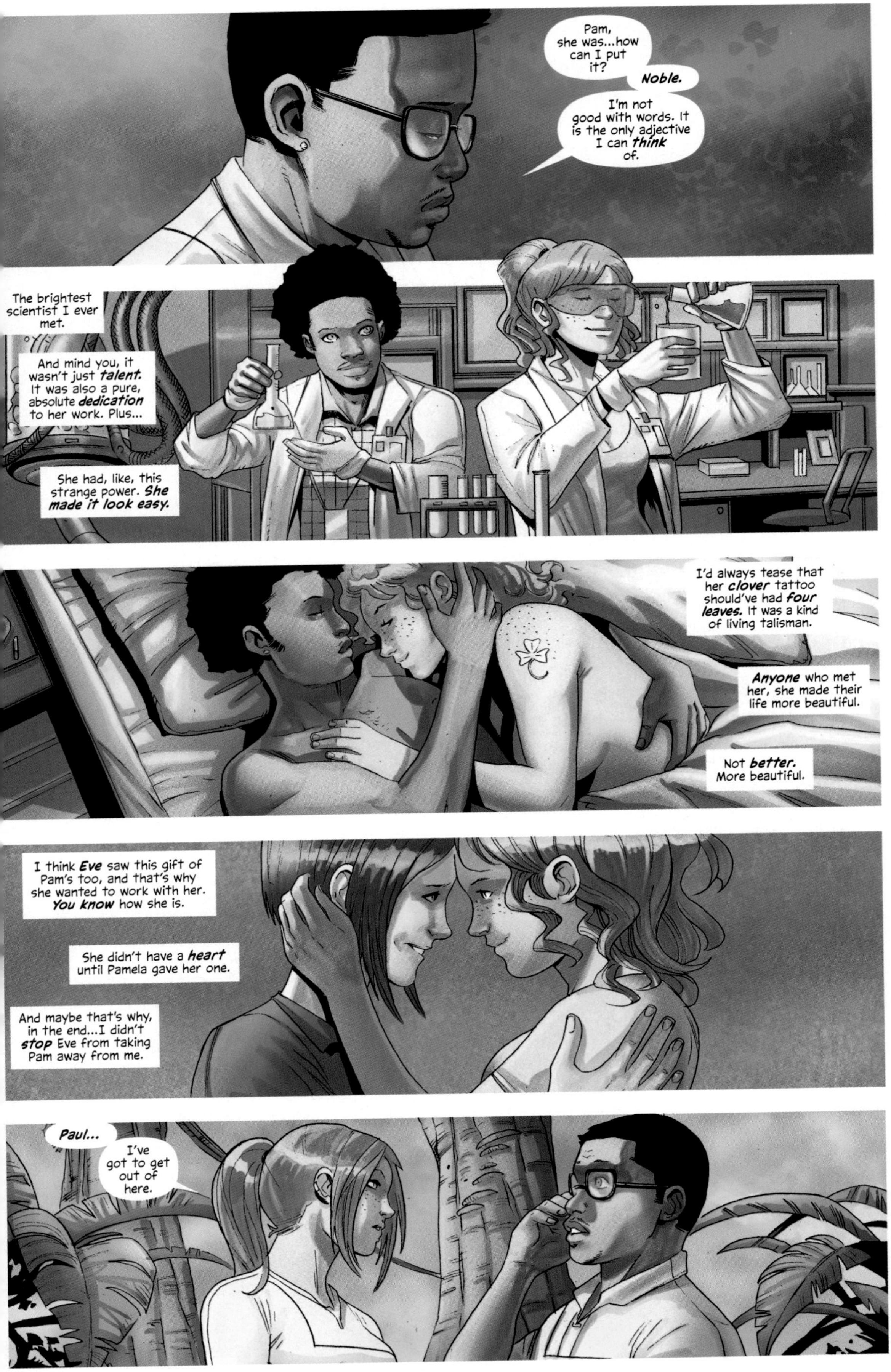
Pam, she was...how can I put it?
Noble.
I'm not good with words. It is the only adjective I can think of.
The brightest scientist I ever met.
And mind you, it wasn't just talent. It was also a pure, absolute dedication to her work. Plus...
She had, like, this strange power. She made it look easy.
I'd always tease that her clover tattoo should've had four leaves. It was a kind of living talisman.
Anyone who met her, she made their life more beautiful.
Not better. More beautiful.
I think Eve saw this gift of Pam's too, and that's why she wanted to work with her. You know how she is.
She didn't have a heart until Pamela gave her one.
And maybe that's why, in the end...I didn't stop Eve from taking Pam away from me.
Paul...
I've got to get out of here.

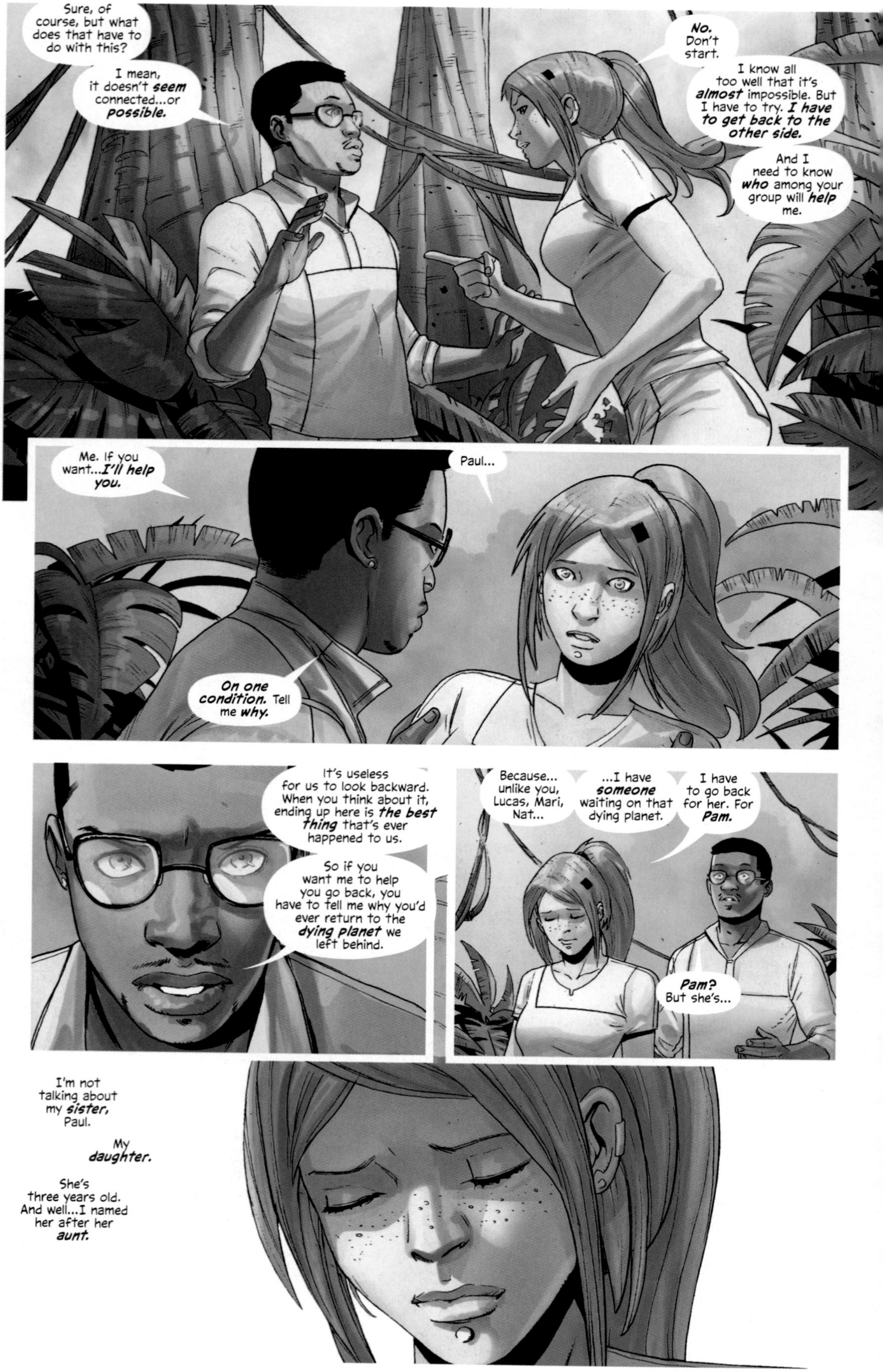

Sure, of course, but what does that have to do with this?
I mean, it doesn't *seem* connected...or *possible.*
No. Don't start.
I know all too well that it's ***almost*** impossible. But I have to try. ***I have to get back to the other side.***
And I need to know ***who*** among your group will ***help*** me.
Me. If you want...***I'll help you.***
Paul...
On one condition. Tell me ***why.***
It's useless for us to look backward. When you think about it, ending up here is ***the best thing*** that's ever happened to us.
So if you want me to help you go back, you have to tell me why you'd ever return to the ***dying planet*** we left behind.
Because... unlike you, Lucas, Mari, Nat...
...I have ***someone*** waiting on that dying planet.
I have to go back for her. For ***Pam.***
Pam? But she's...
I'm not talking about my ***sister,*** Paul.
My ***daughter.***
She's three years old. And well...I named her after her ***aunt.***

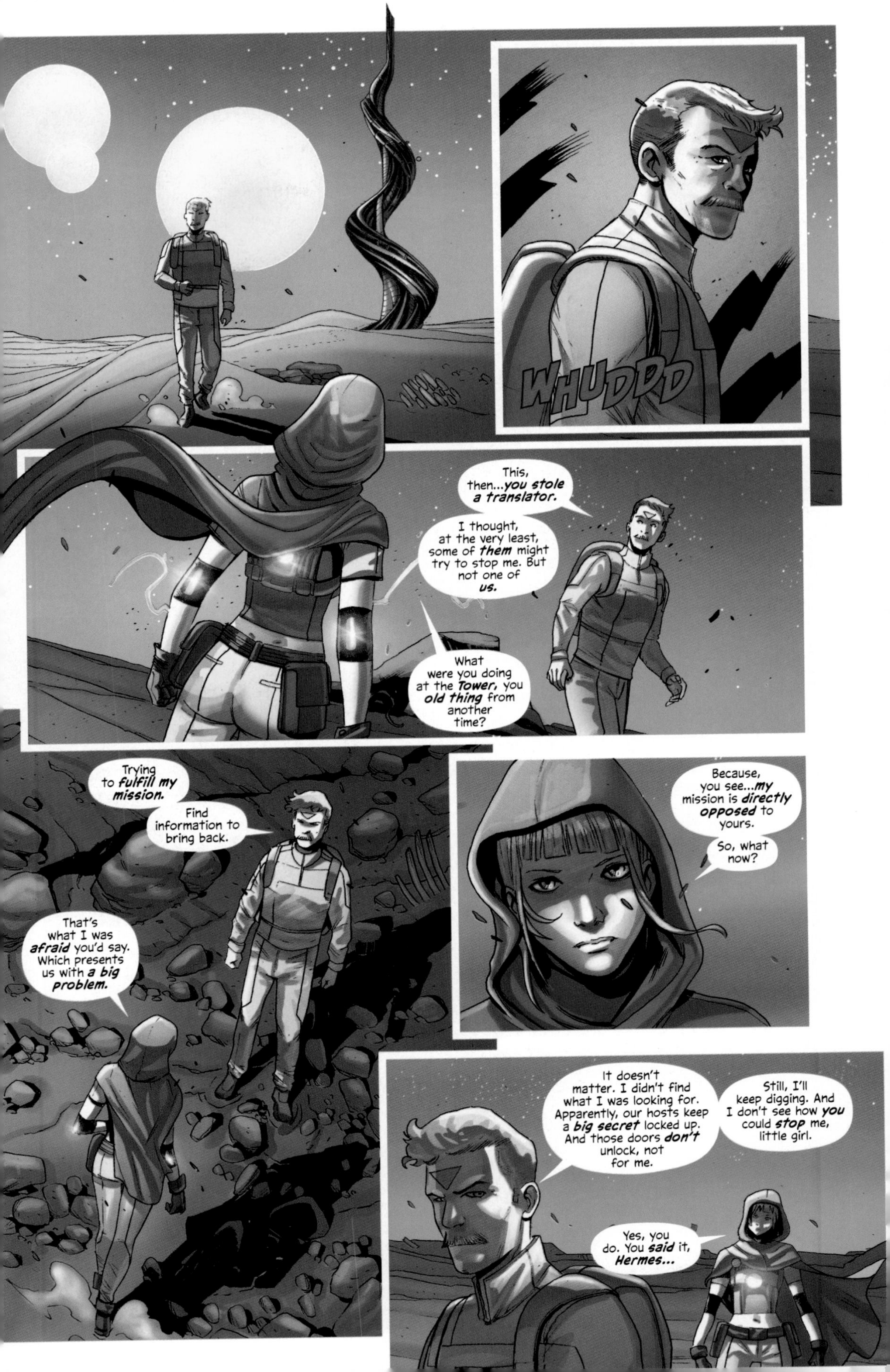
WHUDDD
This, then...you stole a translator.
I thought, at the very least, some of them might try to stop me. But not one of us.
What were you doing at the Tower, you old thing from another time?
Trying to fulfill my mission.
Find information to bring back.
Because, you see...my mission is directly opposed to yours.
So, what now?
That's what I was afraid you'd say. Which presents us with a big problem.
It doesn't matter. I didn't find what I was looking for. Apparently, our hosts keep a big secret locked up. And those doors don't unlock, not for me.
Still, I'll keep digging. And I don't see how you could stop me, little girl.
Yes, you do. You said it, Hermes...

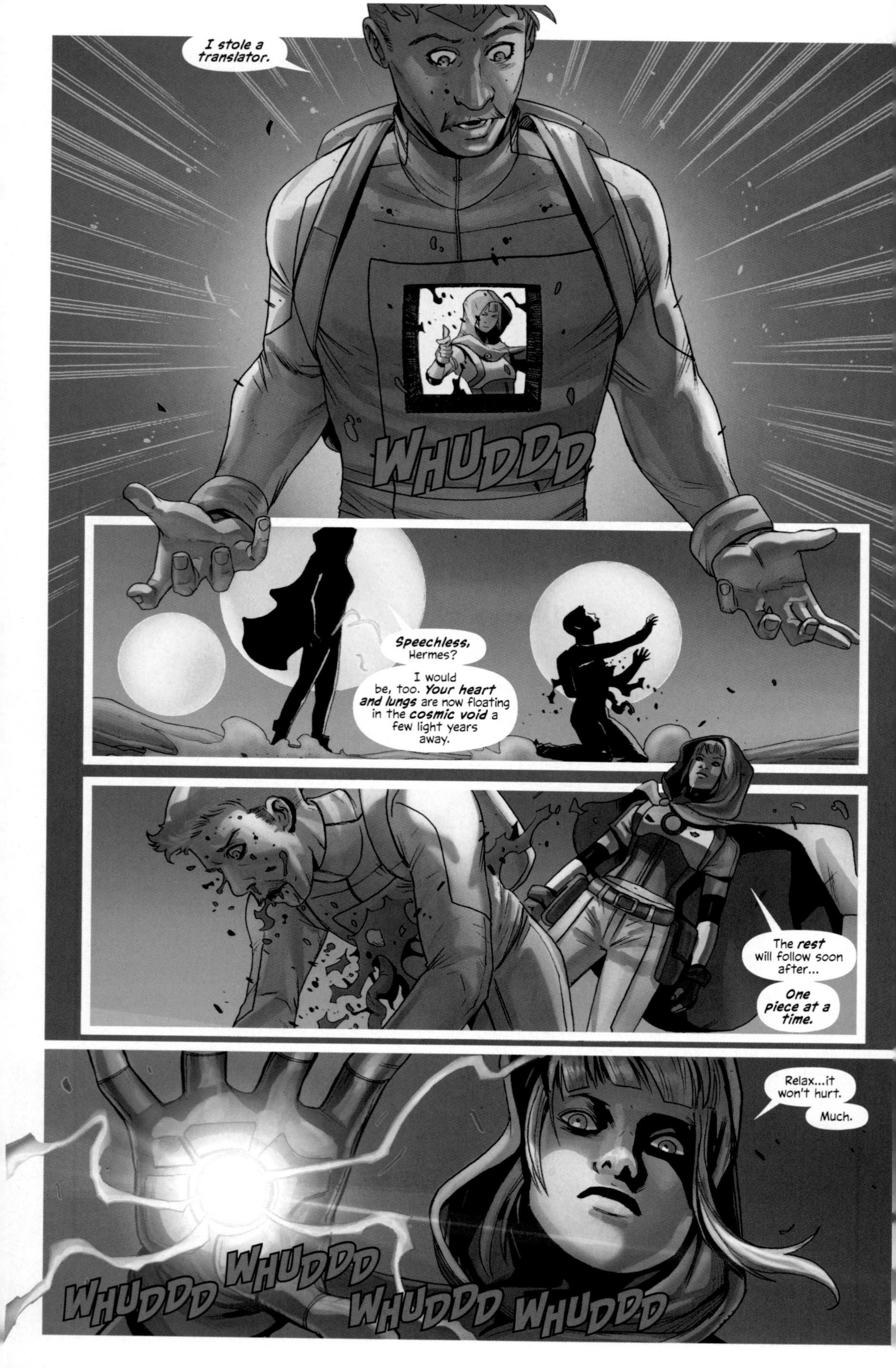
I stole a translator.
WHUDDD
Speechless, Hermes?
I would be, too. Your heart and lungs are now floating in the cosmic void a few light years away.
The rest will follow soon after...
One piece at a time.
Relax...it won't hurt.
Much.
WHUDDD WHUDDD WHUDDD WHUDDD

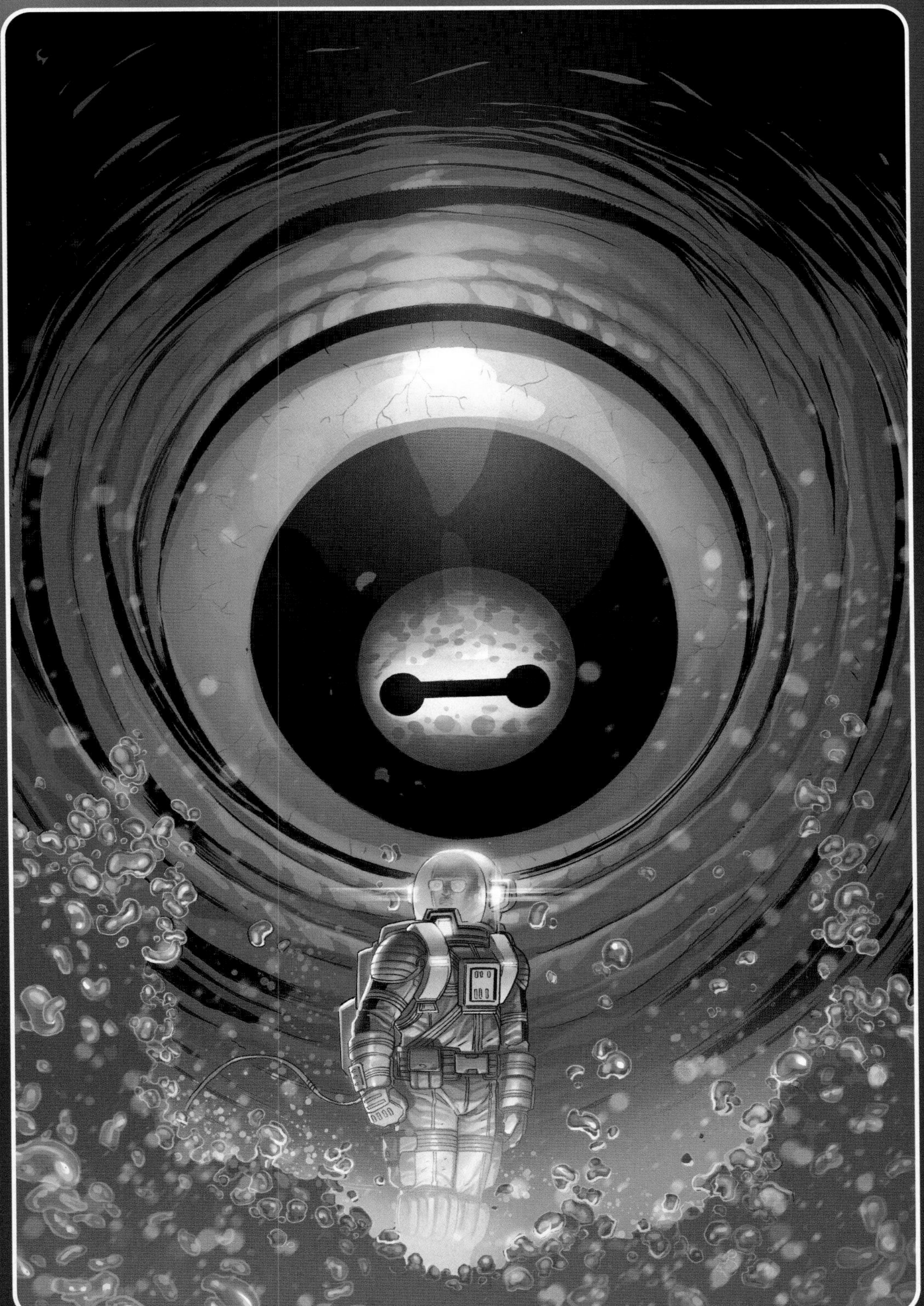

CHAPTER 08

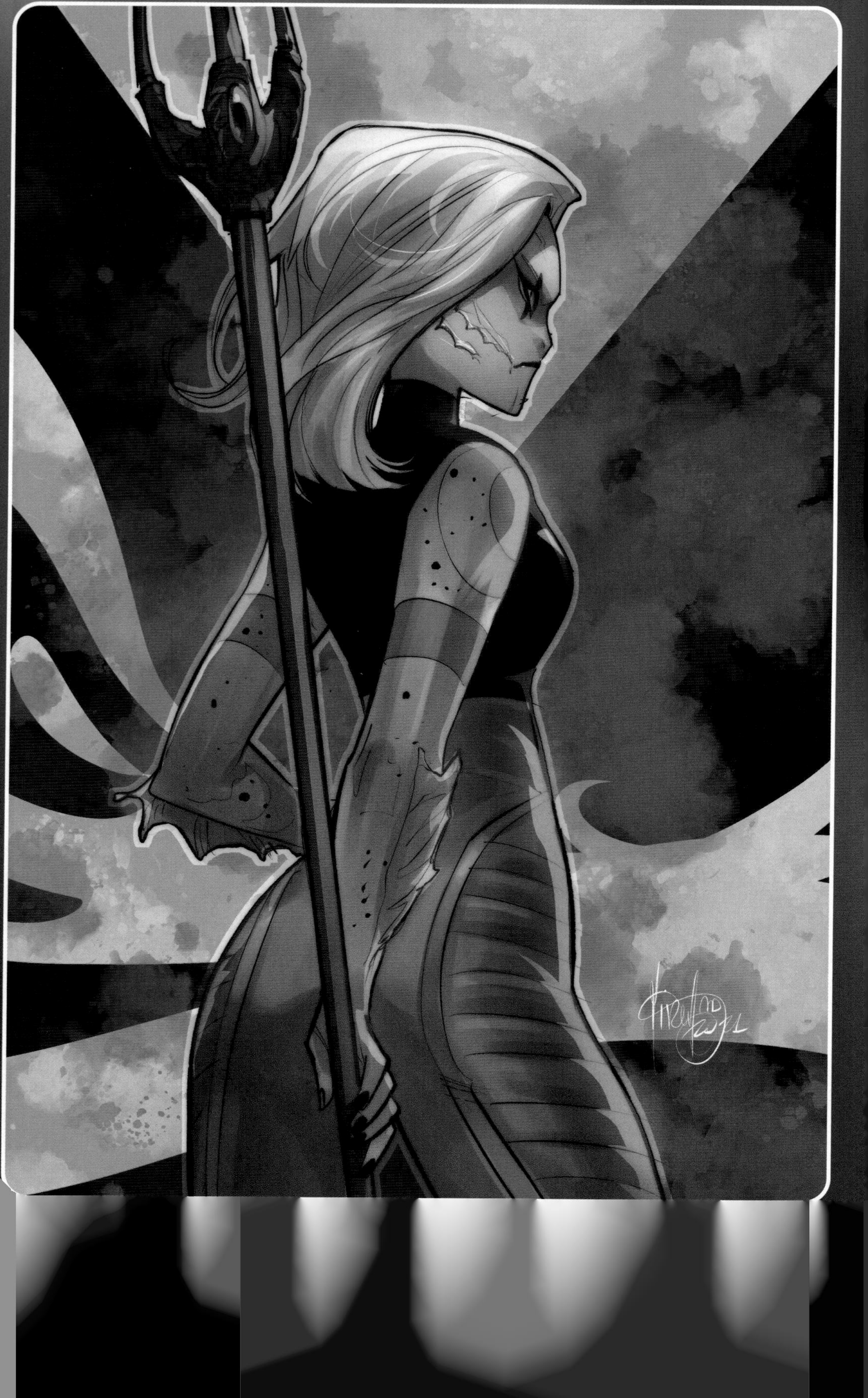

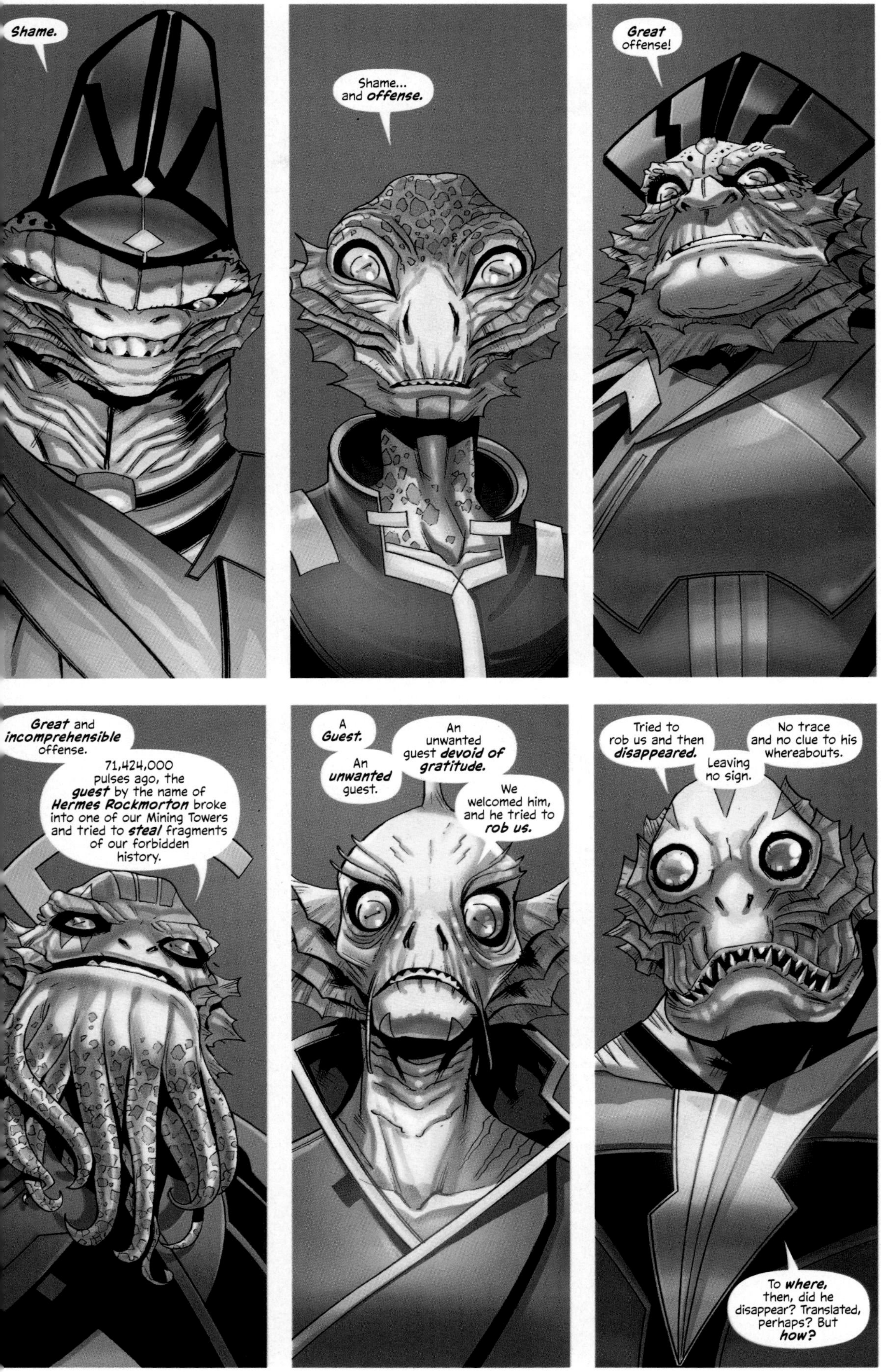
Shame.
Shame... and offense.
Great offense!
Great and incomprehensible offense.
71,424,000 pulses ago, the guest by the name of Hermes Rockmorton broke into one of our Mining Towers and tried to steal fragments of our forbidden history.
A Guest.
An unwanted guest.
An unwanted guest devoid of gratitude.
We welcomed him, and he tried to rob us.
Tried to rob us and then disappeared.
Leaving no sign.
No trace and no clue to his whereabouts.
To where, then, did he disappear? Translated, perhaps? But how?

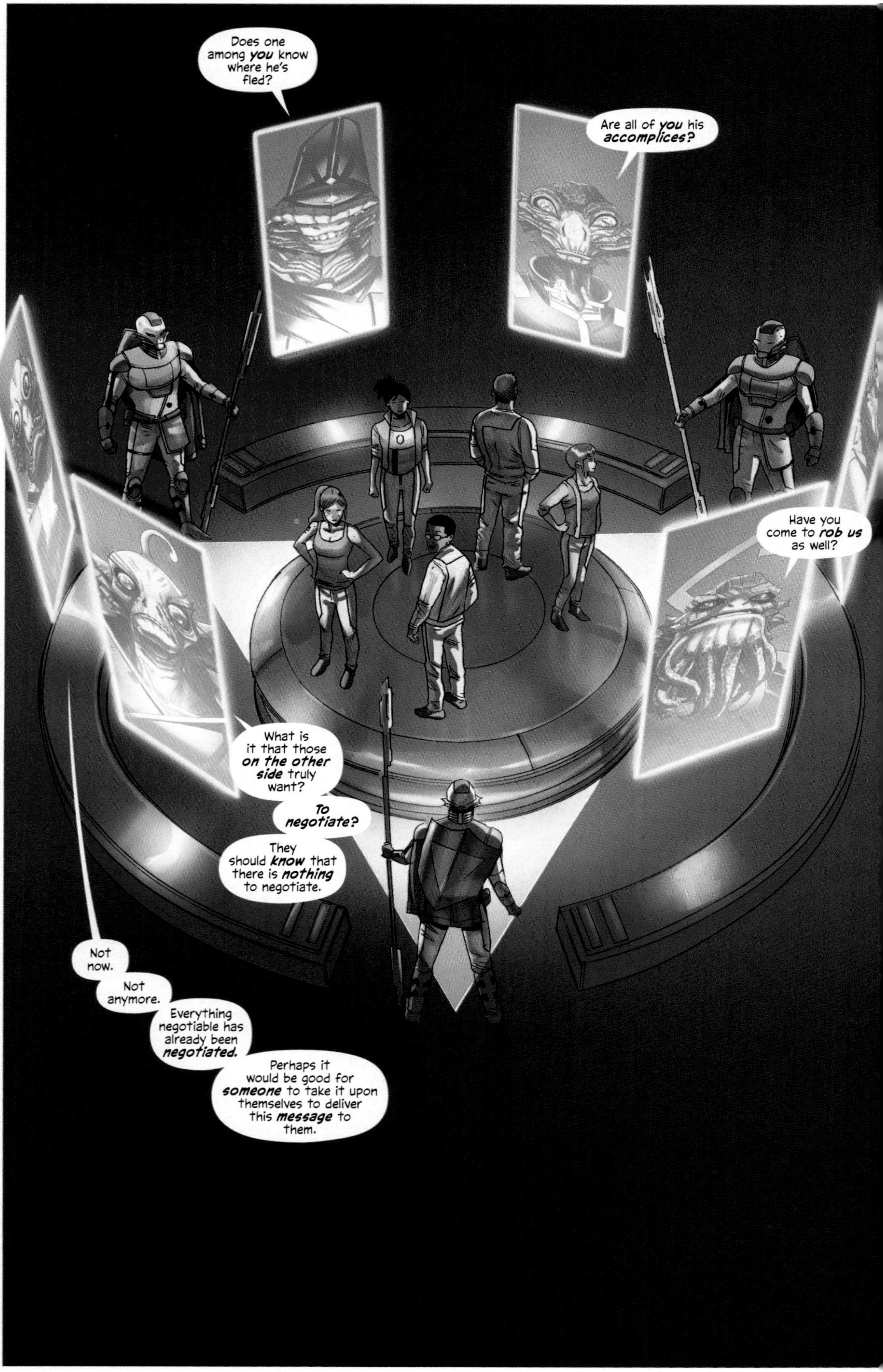
Does one among you know where he's fled?
Are all of you his accomplices?
Have you come to rob us as well?
What is it that those on the other side truly want?
To negotiate?
They should know that there is nothing to negotiate.
Not now.
Not anymore.
Everything negotiable has already been negotiated.
Perhaps it would be good for someone to take it upon themselves to deliver this message to them.

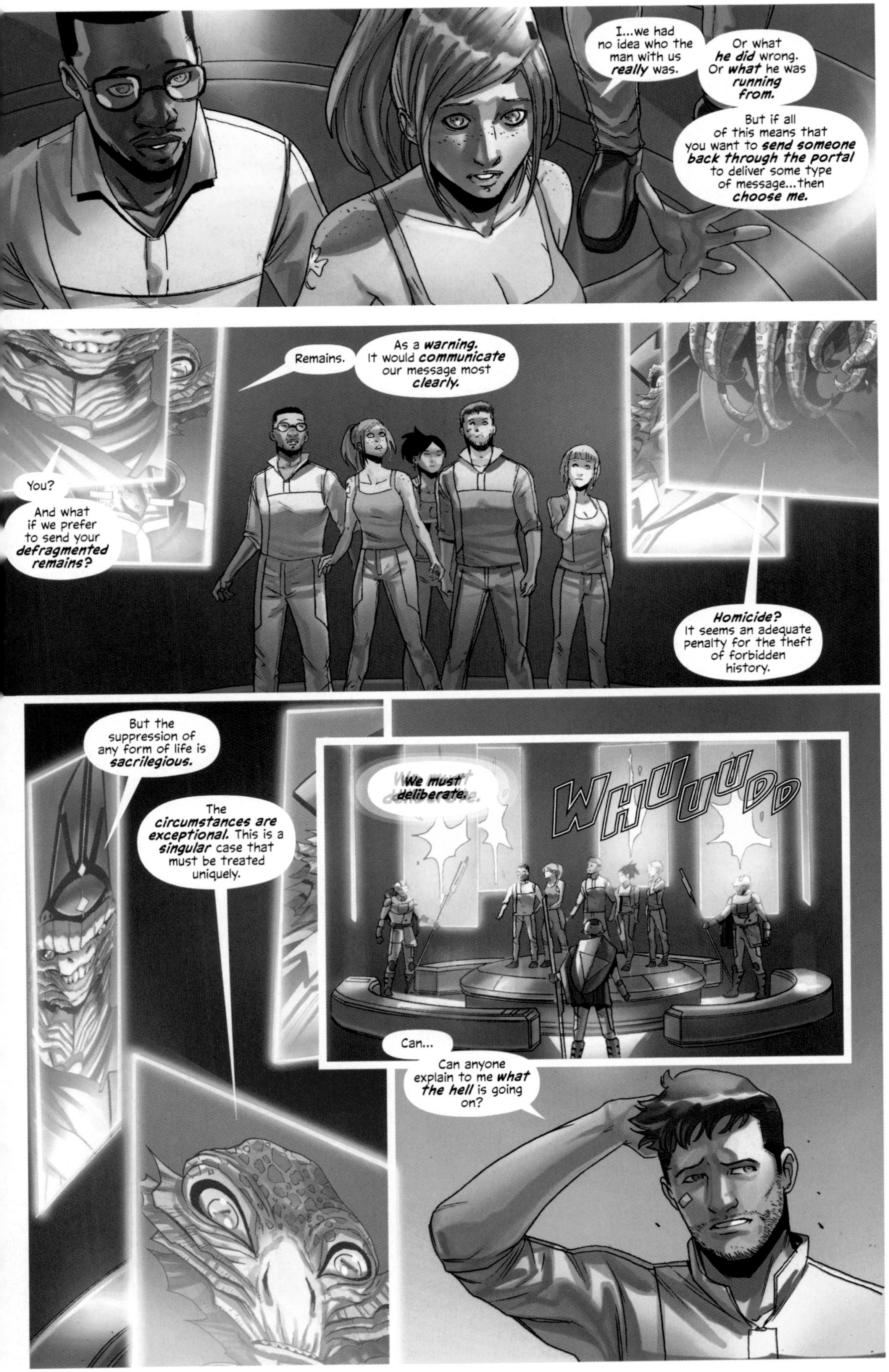
I...we had no idea who the man with us really was.
Or what he did wrong. Or what he was running from.
But if all of this means that you want to send someone back through the portal to deliver some type of message...then choose me.
You?
And what if we prefer to send your defragmented remains?
Remains.
As a warning. It would communicate our message most clearly.
Homicide? It seems an adequate penalty for the theft of forbidden history.
But the suppression of any form of life is sacrilegious.
The circumstances are exceptional. This is a singular case that must be treated uniquely.
We must deliberate.
WHUUUDD
Can...
Can anyone explain to me what the hell is going on?

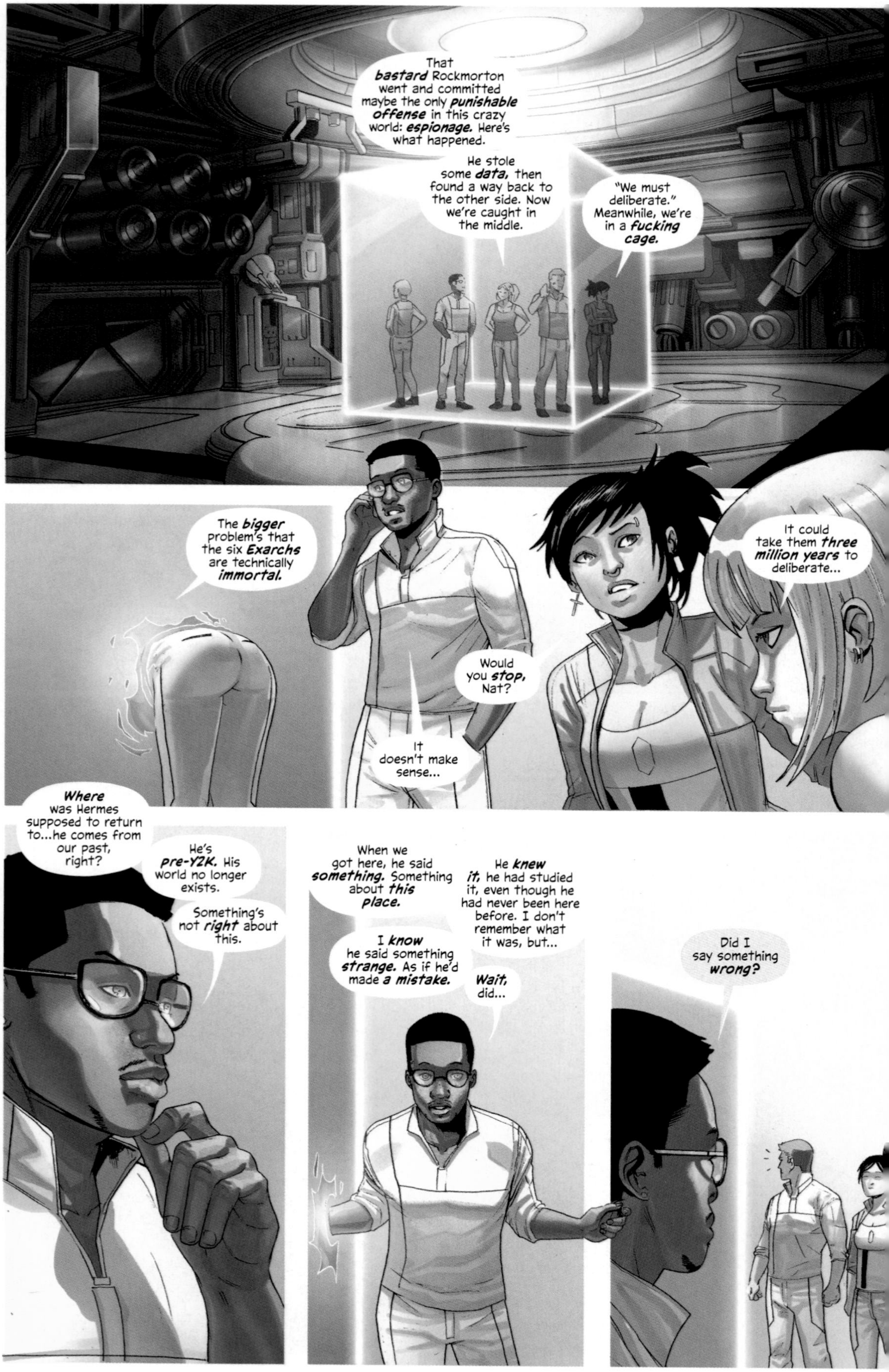
That bastard Rockmorton went and committed maybe the only punishable offense in this crazy world: espionage. Here's what happened.
He stole some data, then found a way back to the other side. Now we're caught in the middle.
"We must deliberate." Meanwhile, we're in a fucking cage.
The bigger problem's that the six Exarchs are technically immortal.
It could take them three million years to deliberate...
Would you stop, Nat?
It doesn't make sense...
Where was Hermes supposed to return to...he comes from our past, right?
He's pre-Y2K. His world no longer exists.
Something's not right about this.
When we got here, he said something. Something about this place.
I know he said something strange. As if he'd made a mistake.
He knew it, he had studied it, even though he had never been here before. I don't remember what it was, but...
Wait, did...
Did I say something wrong?

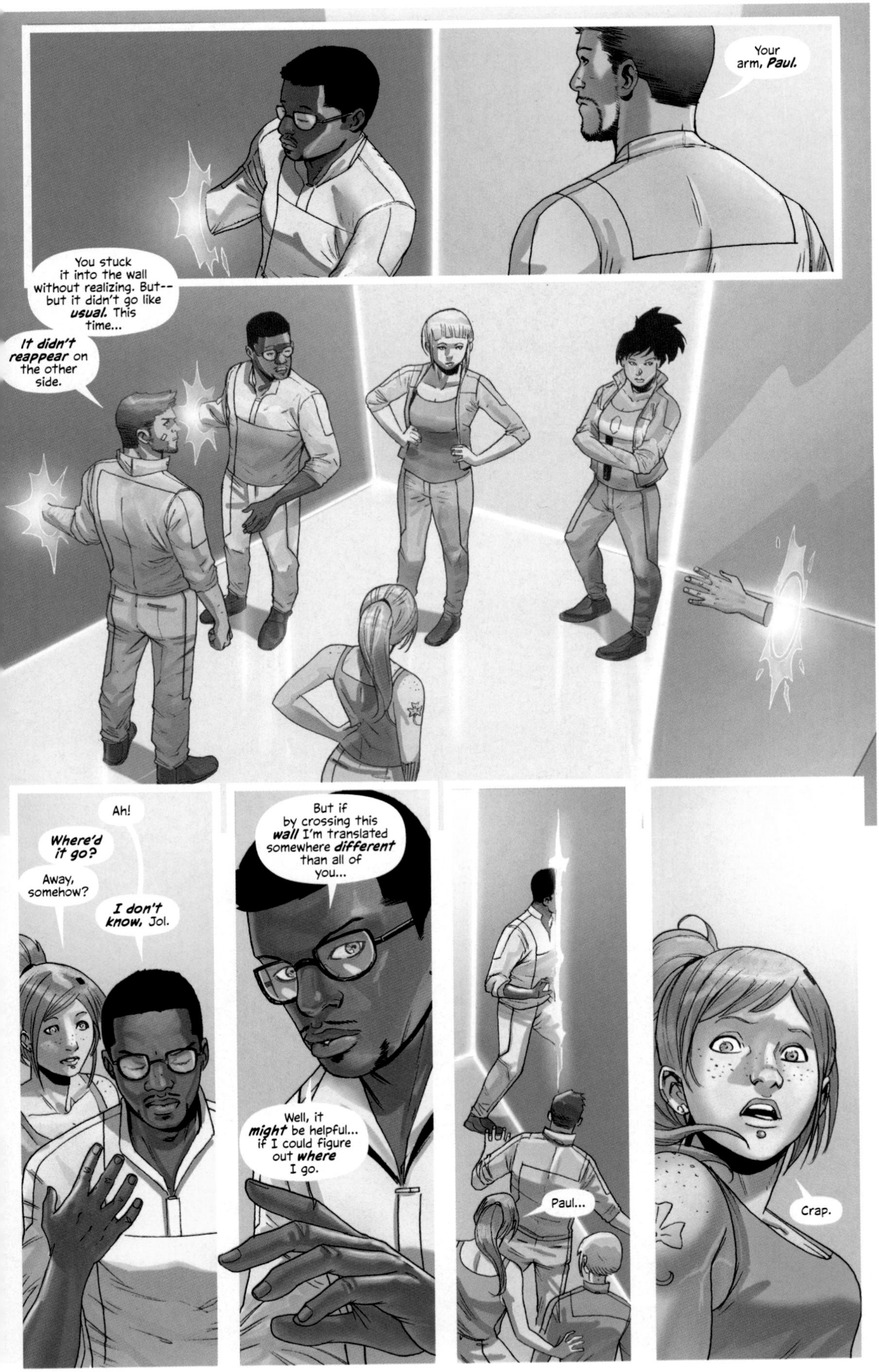
Your arm, *Paul.*
You stuck it into the wall without realizing. But--but it didn't go like *usual.* This time...
It didn't reappear on the other side.
Ah!
Where'd it go?
Away, somehow?
I don't know, Jol.
But if by crossing this *wall* I'm translated somewhere *different* than all of you...
Well, it *might* be helpful... if I could figure out *where* I go.
Paul...
Crap.

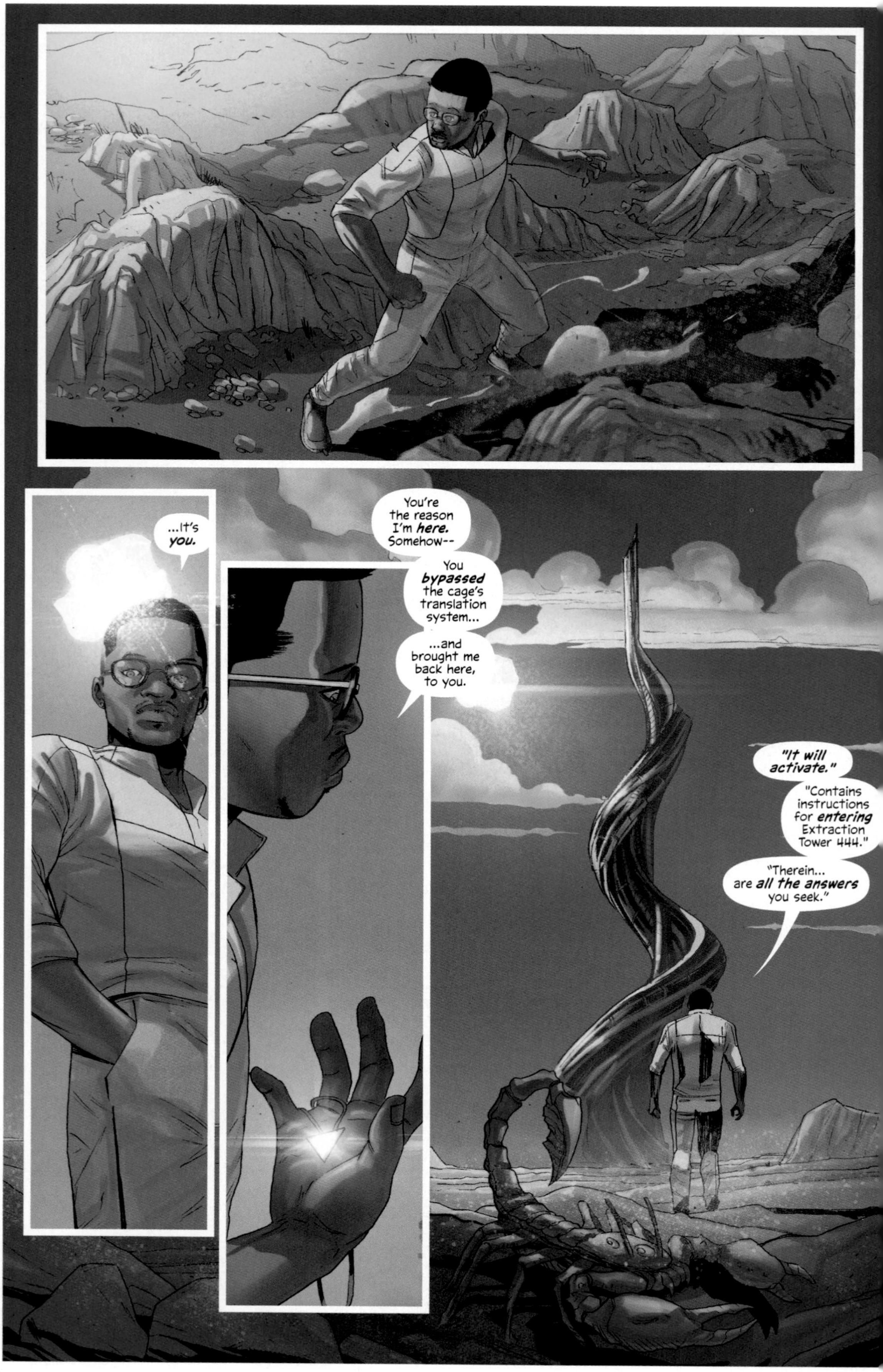
...It's you.
You're the reason I'm here. Somehow--
You bypassed the cage's translation system...
...and brought me back here, to you.
"It will activate."
"Contains instructions for entering Extraction Tower 444."
"Therein... are all the answers you seek."

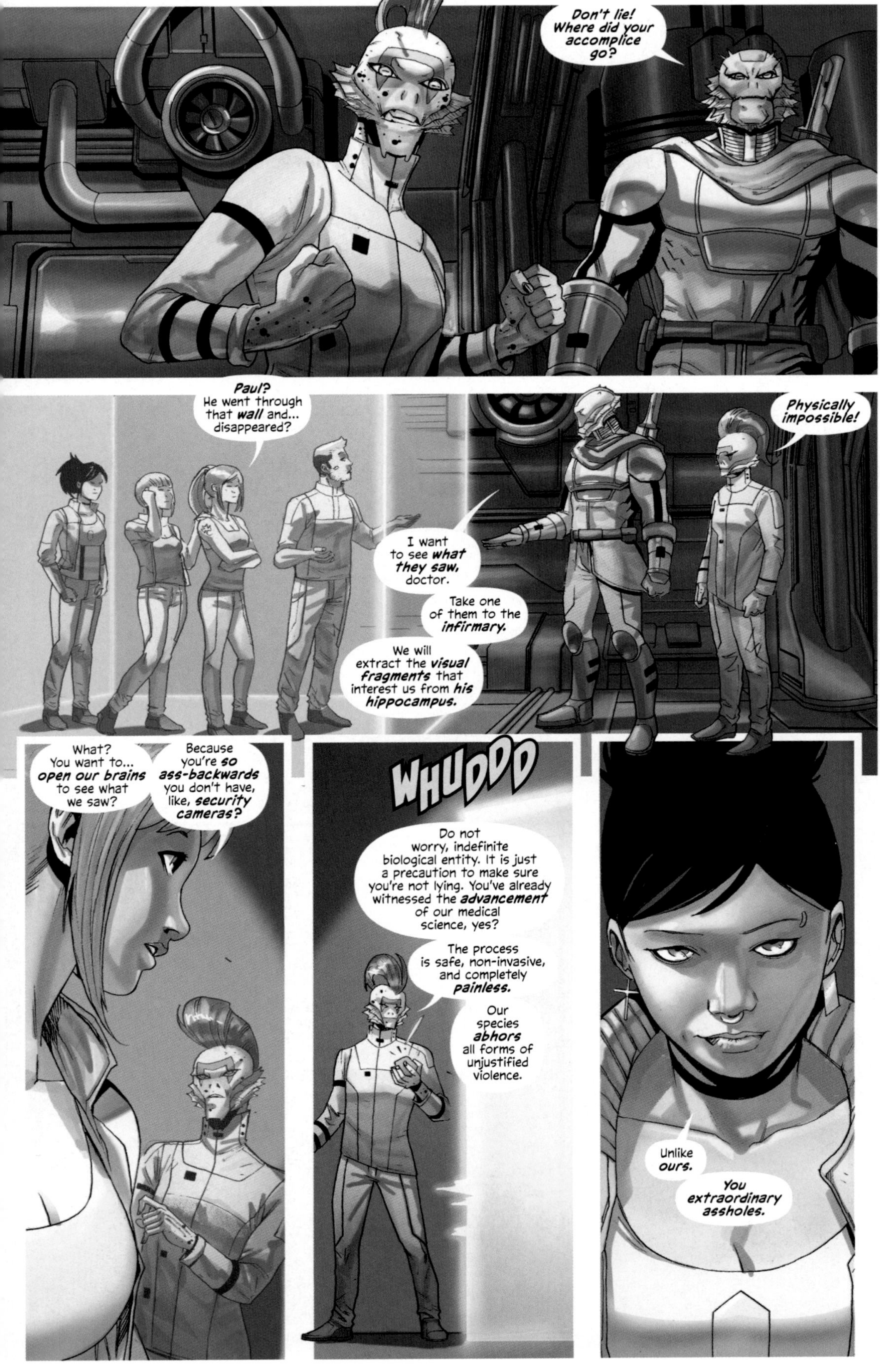

Don't lie! Where did your accomplice go?
Paul? He went through that wall and... disappeared?
Physically impossible!
I want to see what they saw, doctor.
Take one of them to the infirmary.
We will extract the visual fragments that interest us from his hippocampus.
What? You want to... open our brains to see what we saw?
Because you're so ass-backwards you don't have, like, security cameras?
WHUDDD
Do not worry, indefinite biological entity. It is just a precaution to make sure you're not lying. You've already witnessed the advancement of our medical science, yes?
The process is safe, non-invasive, and completely painless.
Our species abhors all forms of unjustified violence.
Unlike ours.
You extraordinary assholes.

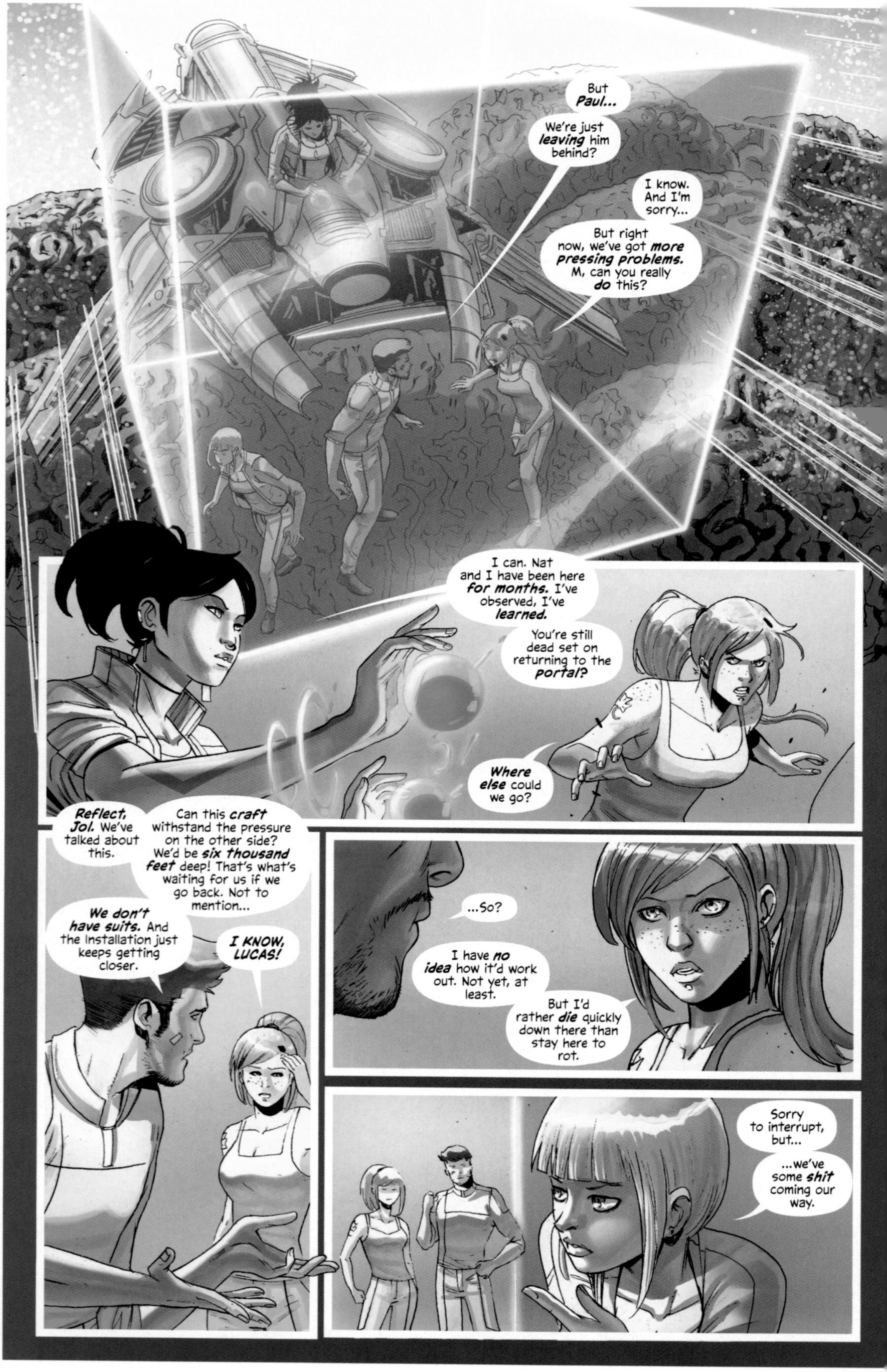
But Paul...
We're just leaving him behind?
I know. And I'm sorry...
But right now, we've got more pressing problems. M, can you really do this?
I can. Nat and I have been here for months. I've observed, I've learned.
You're still dead set on returning to the portal?
Where else could we go?
Reflect, Jol. We've talked about this.
Can this craft withstand the pressure on the other side? We'd be six thousand feet deep! That's what's waiting for us if we go back. Not to mention...
We don't have suits. And the Installation just keeps getting closer.
I KNOW, LUCAS!
...So?
I have no idea how it'd work out. Not yet, at least.
But I'd rather die quickly down there than stay here to rot.
Sorry to interrupt, but...
...we've some shit coming our way.

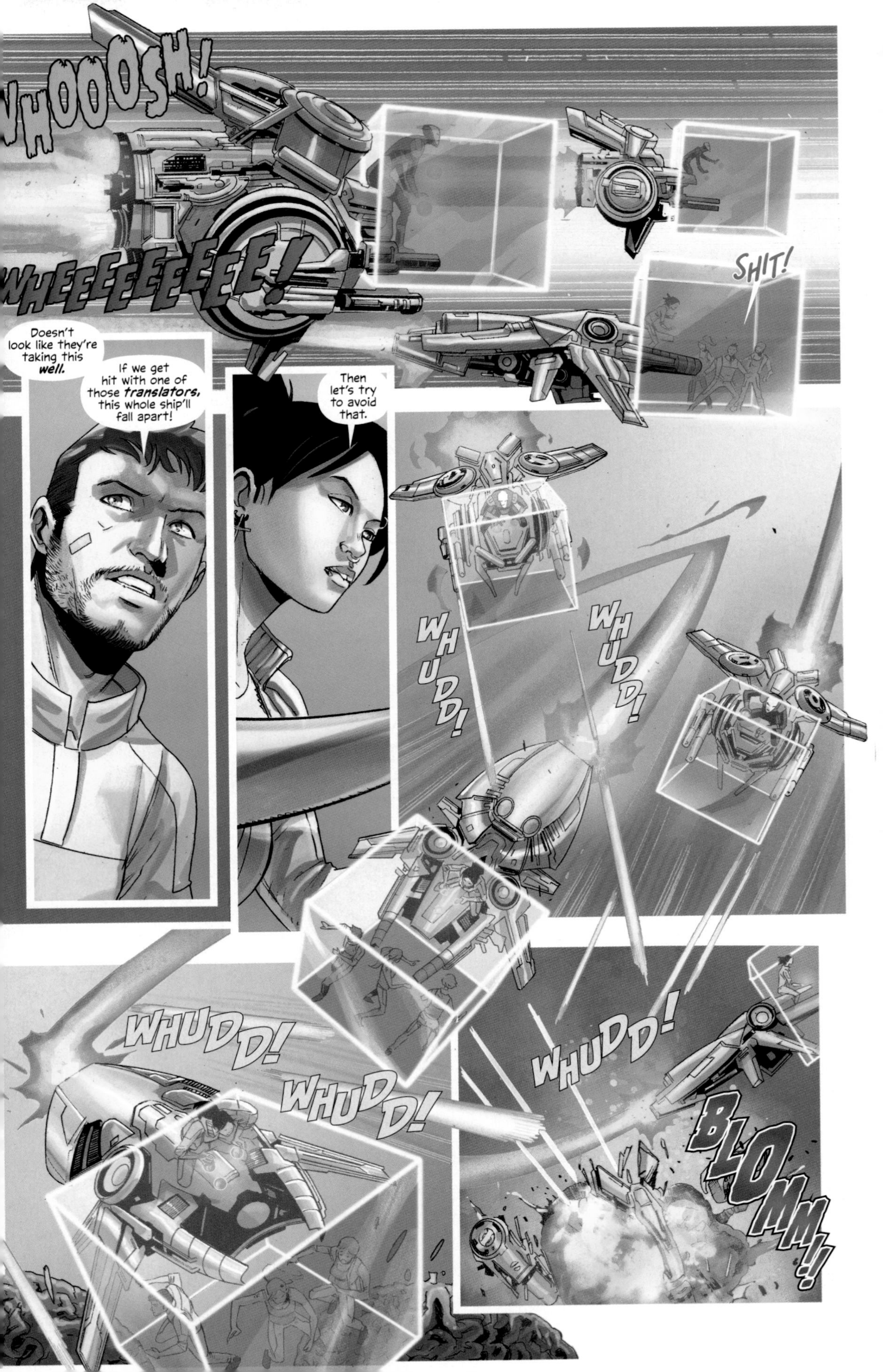
WHOOOSH!
WHEEEEEEEEEE!
SHIT!
Doesn't look like they're taking this *well.*
If we get hit with one of those *translators,* this whole ship'll fall apart!
Then let's try to avoid that.
WHUDD!
WHUDD!
WHUDD!
WHUDD!
WHUDD!
BLOMM!!

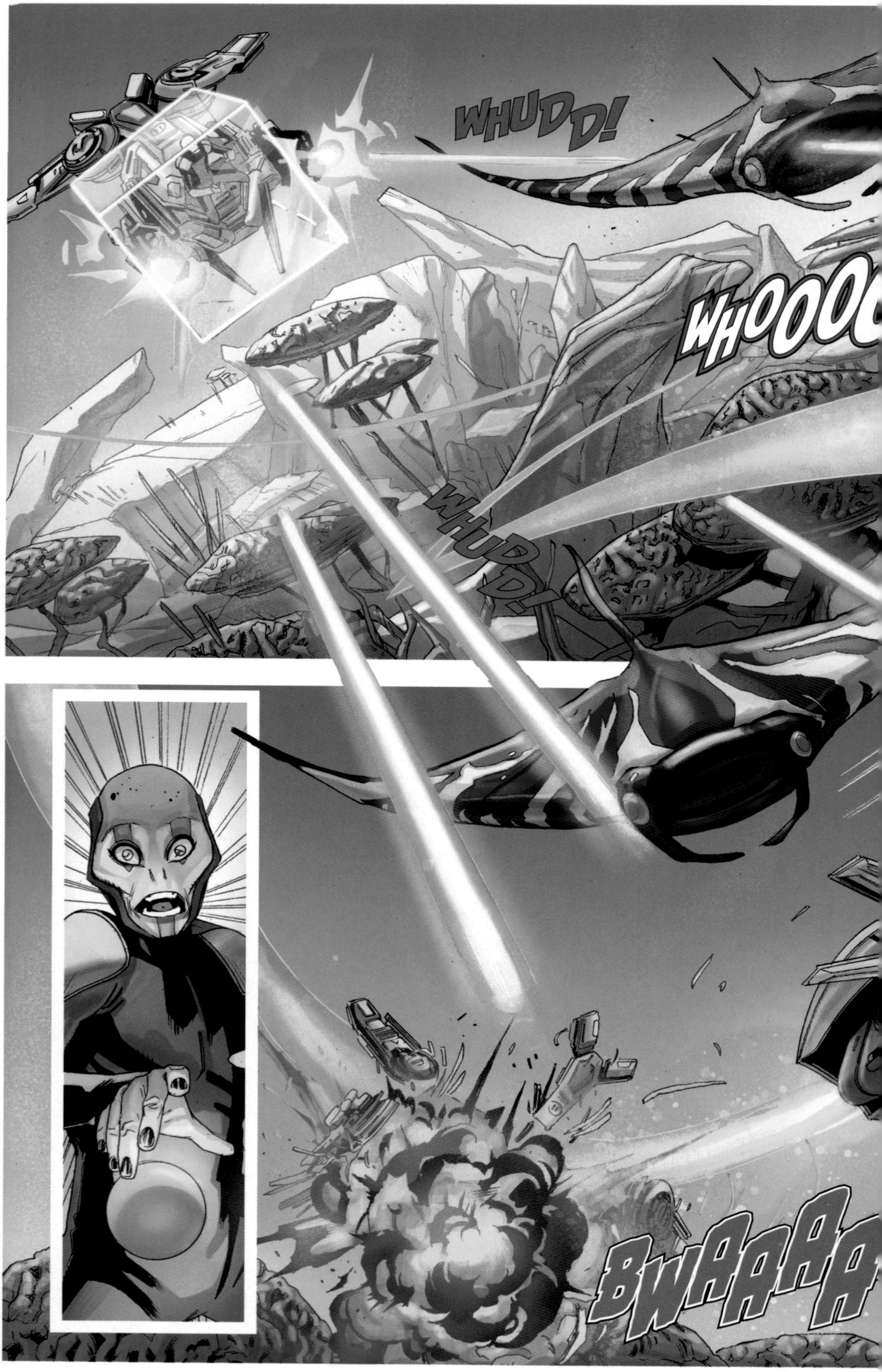
WHUDD!
WHOOOO
WHUDD!
BWAAAA

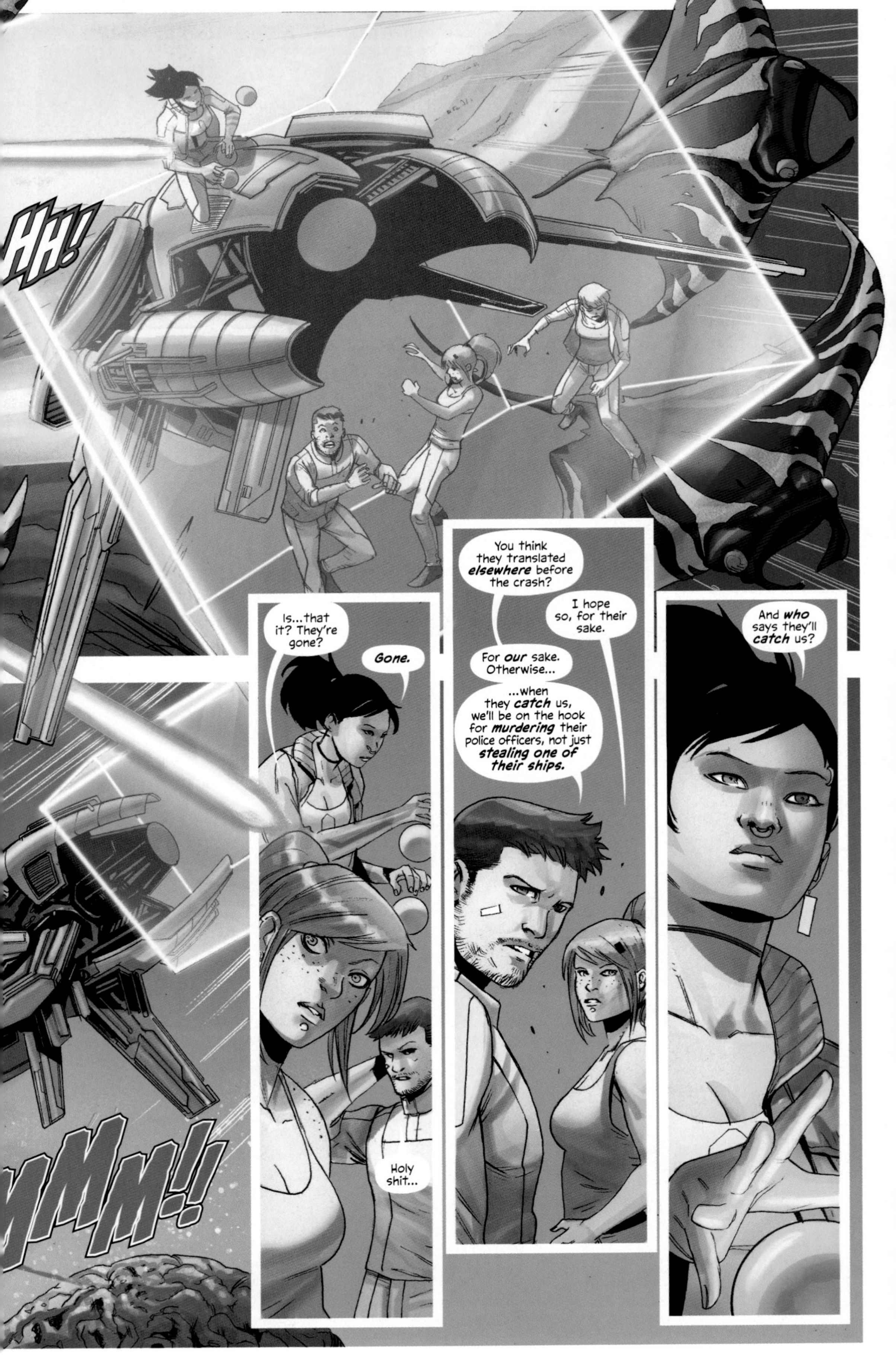

HH!
MMM!!
Is...that it? They're gone?
Gone.
Holy shit...
You think they translated elsewhere before the crash?
I hope so, for their sake.
For our sake. Otherwise...
...when they catch us, we'll be on the hook for murdering their police officers, not just stealing one of their ships.
And who says they'll catch us?

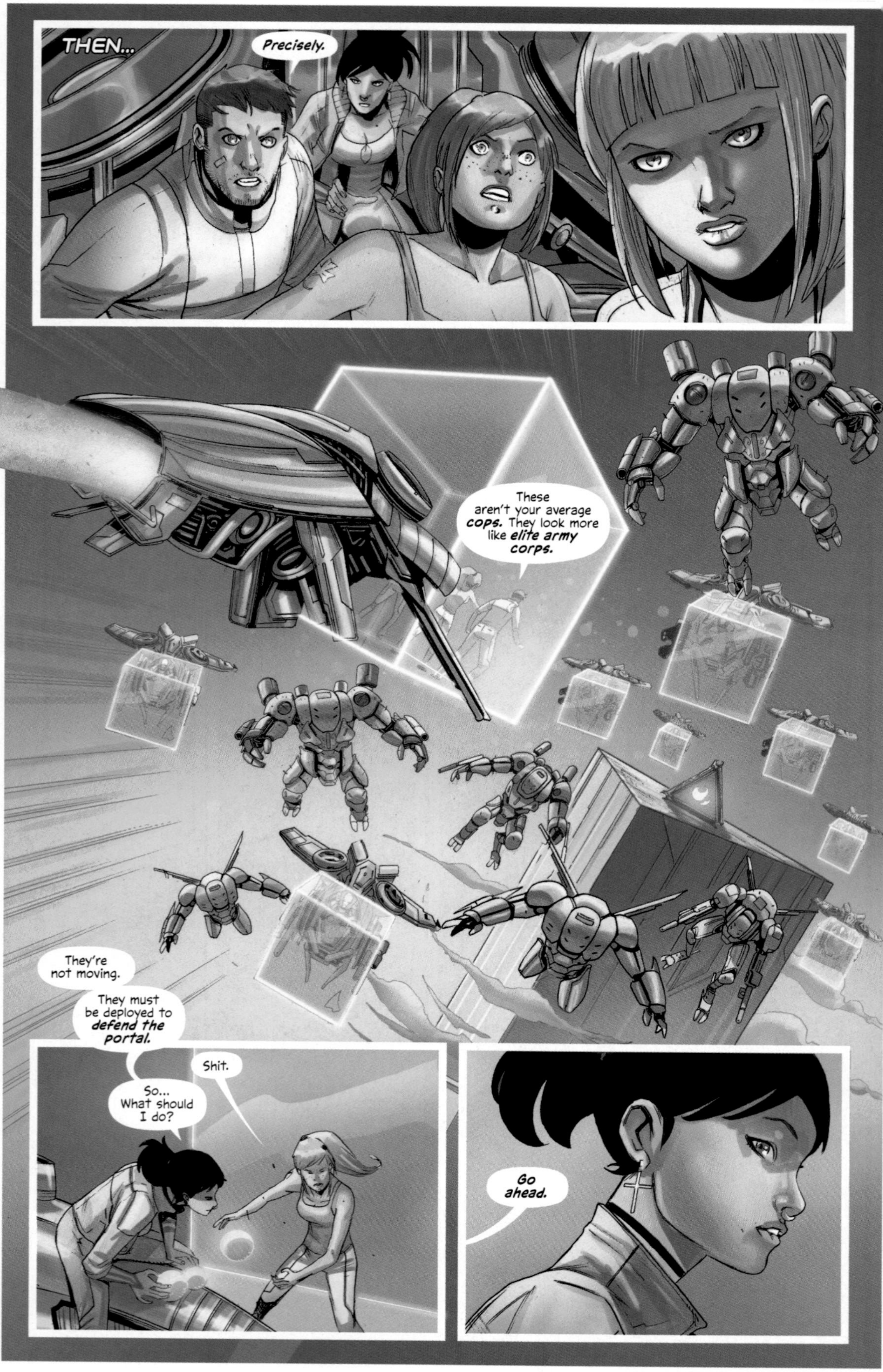
THEN...
Precisely.
These aren't your average cops. They look more like elite army corps.
They're not moving.
They must be deployed to defend the portal.
Shit.
So... What should I do?
Go ahead.

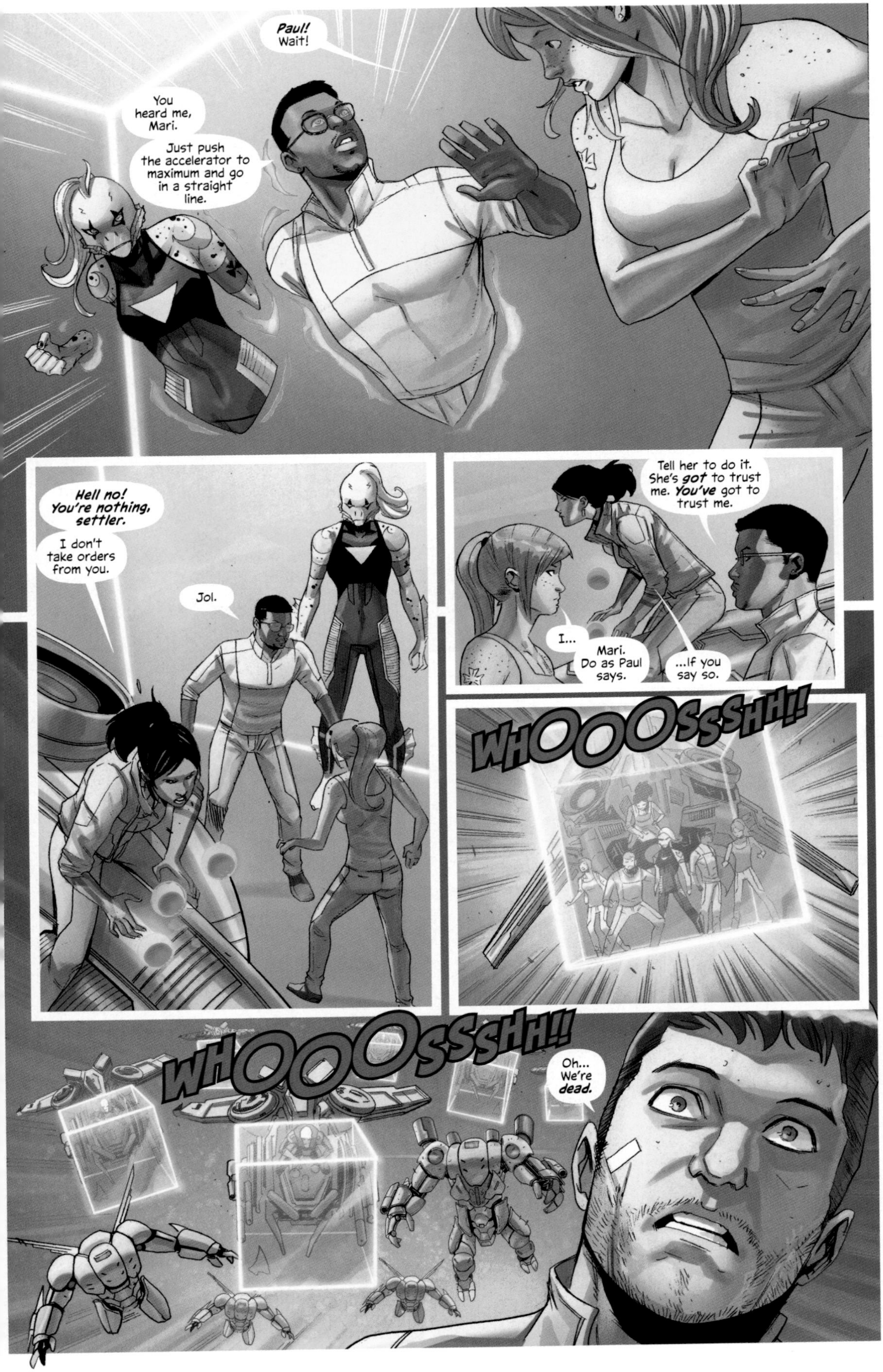
You heard me, Mari.
Just push the accelerator to maximum and go in a straight line.
Paul! Wait!
Hell no! You're nothing, settler.
I don't take orders from you.
Jol.
Tell her to do it. She's got to trust me. You've got to trust me.
I...
Mari. Do as Paul says.
...If you say so.
WHOOOSSSHH!!
WHOOOSSSHH!!
Oh... We're dead.

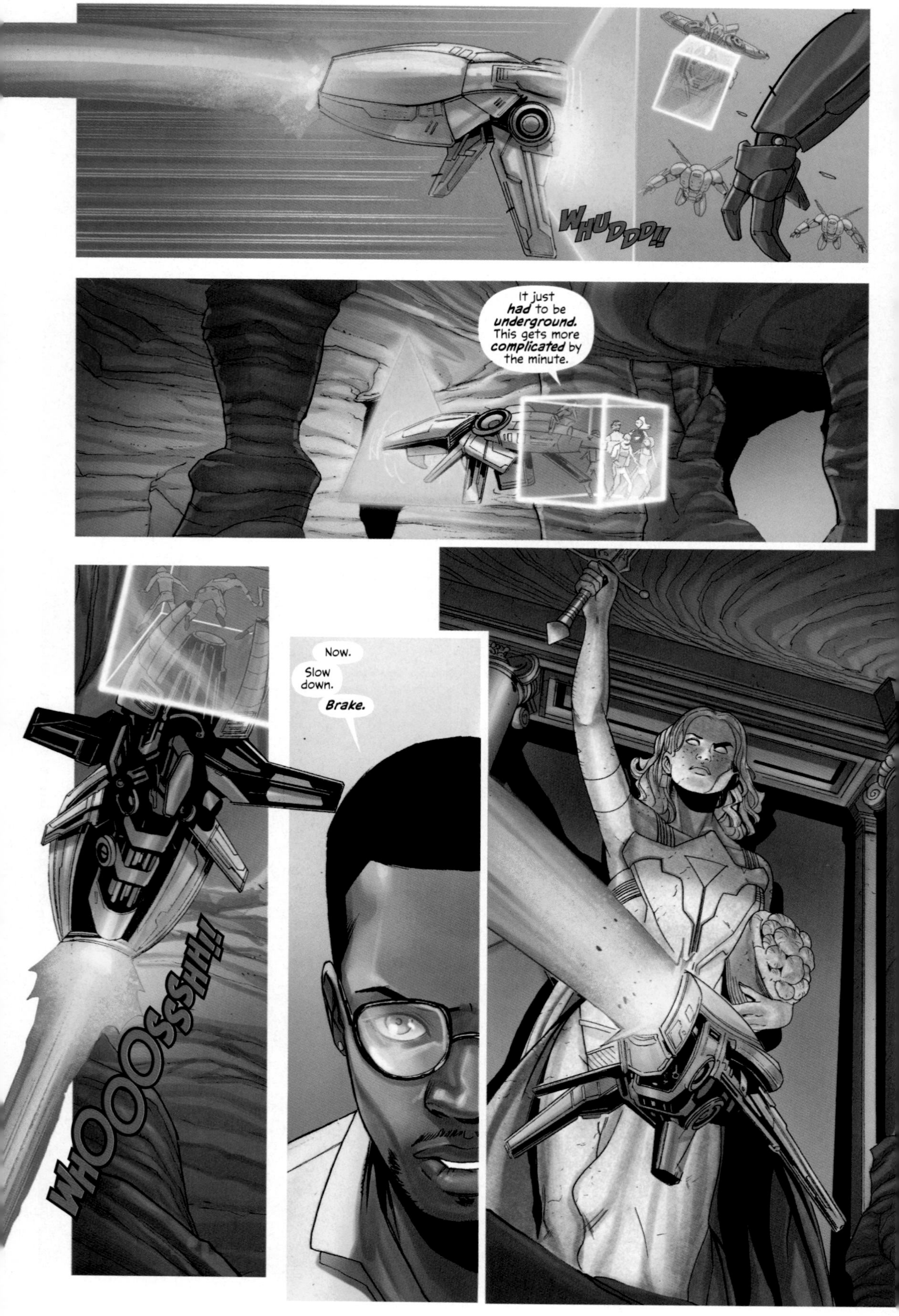
WHUDDD!!
It just had to be underground. This gets more complicated by the minute.
Now.
Slow down.
Brake.
WHOOOSSSHH!!

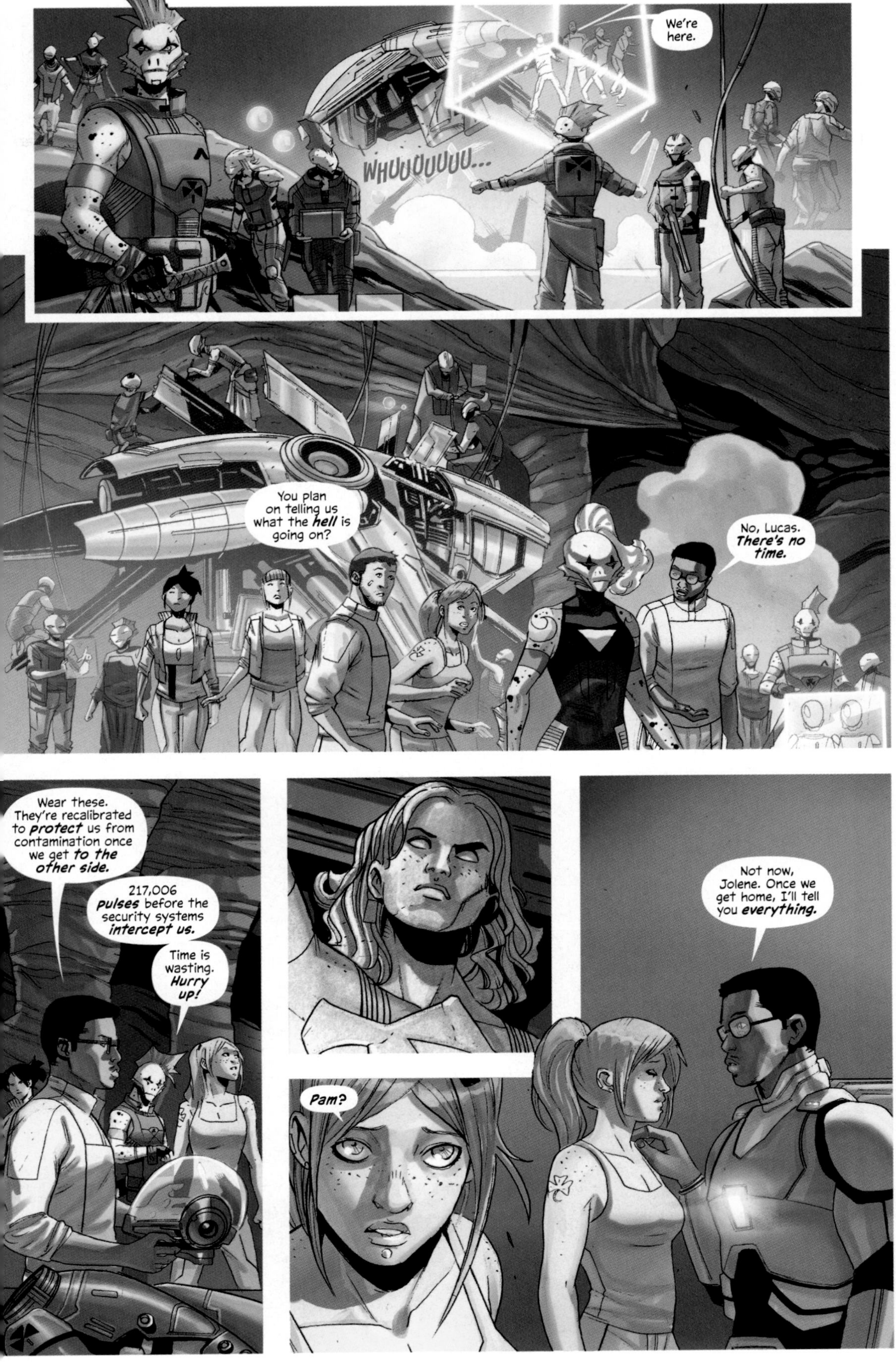
We're here.
WHUUUUUUU...
You plan on telling us what the *hell* is going on?
No, Lucas. *There's no time.*
Wear these. They're recalibrated to *protect* us from contamination once we get *to the other side.*
217,006 *pulses* before the security systems *intercept us.*
Time is wasting. *Hurry up!*
Pam?
Not now, Jolene. Once we get home, I'll tell you *everything.*

What are they doing?

To help us **get back.**

They have a side-shift stable enough--or at least I hope--to prevent the **craft** from being crushed like a can of beans once we're 20 atmospheres deep.

Are...are you coming with us?

Lucas. Mari. **Come on.**

I'll explain it all later, okay?

Translator **positioned.**

It **should** have enough power...

Enough at least to help you break through into your gaseous atmosphere.

Let's go!

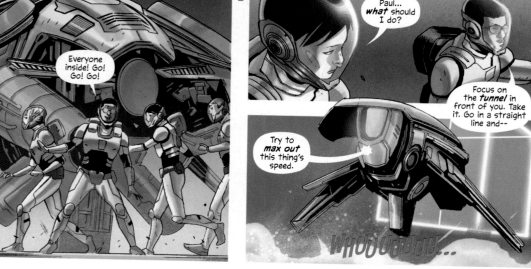

Everyone inside! Go! Go! Go!

Paul... **what** should I do?

Focus on the **tunnel** in front of you. Take it. Go in a straight line and--

Try to **max out** this thing's speed.

WHUDDDDDDDD...

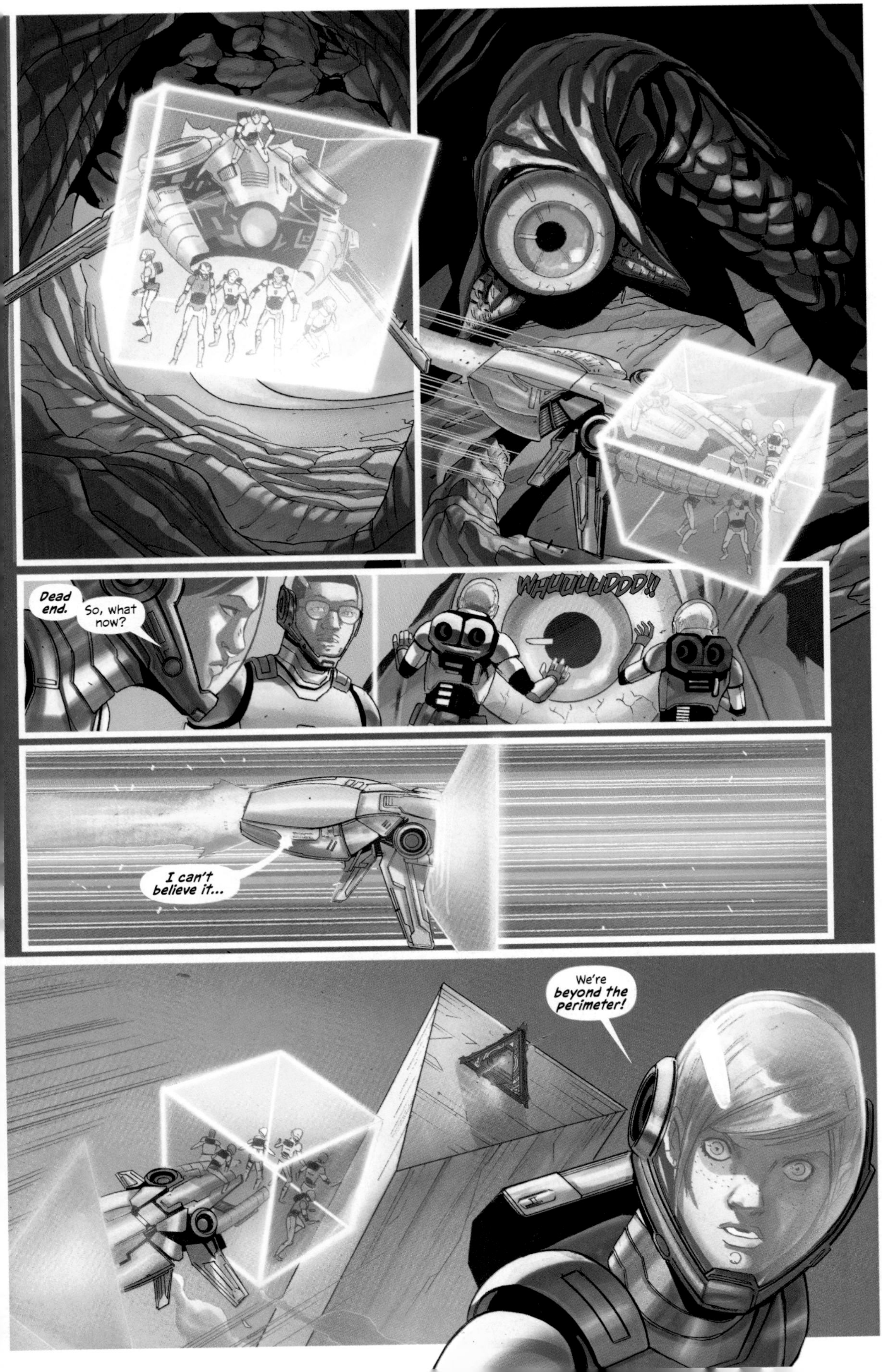

Dead end.
So, what now?
WHUUUUDDD!!
I can't believe it...
We're beyond the perimeter!

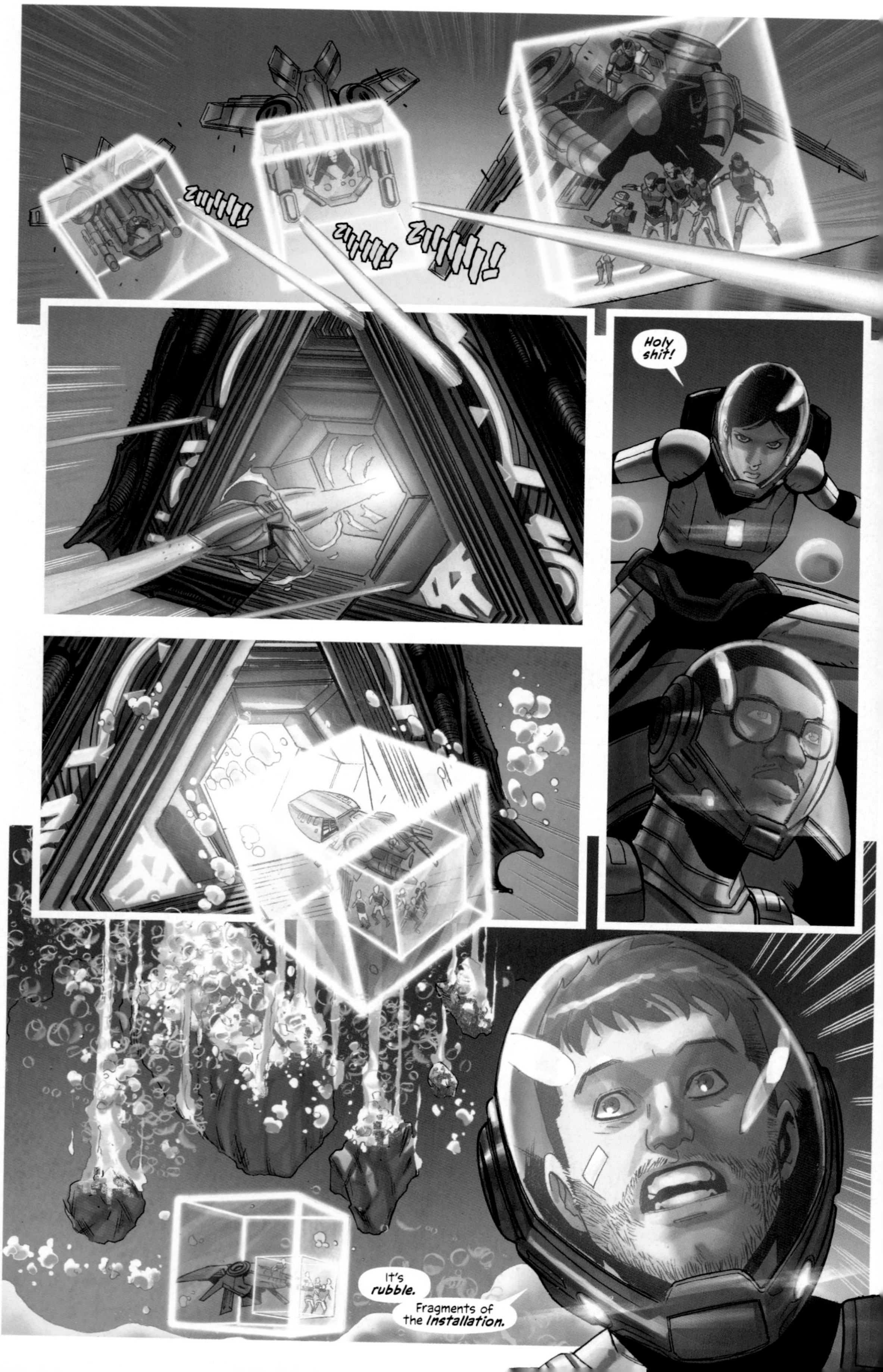
ZWHHZ!
ZWHHZ!
ZWHHHHZ!
Holy shit!
It's *rubble.*
Fragments of the *Installation.*

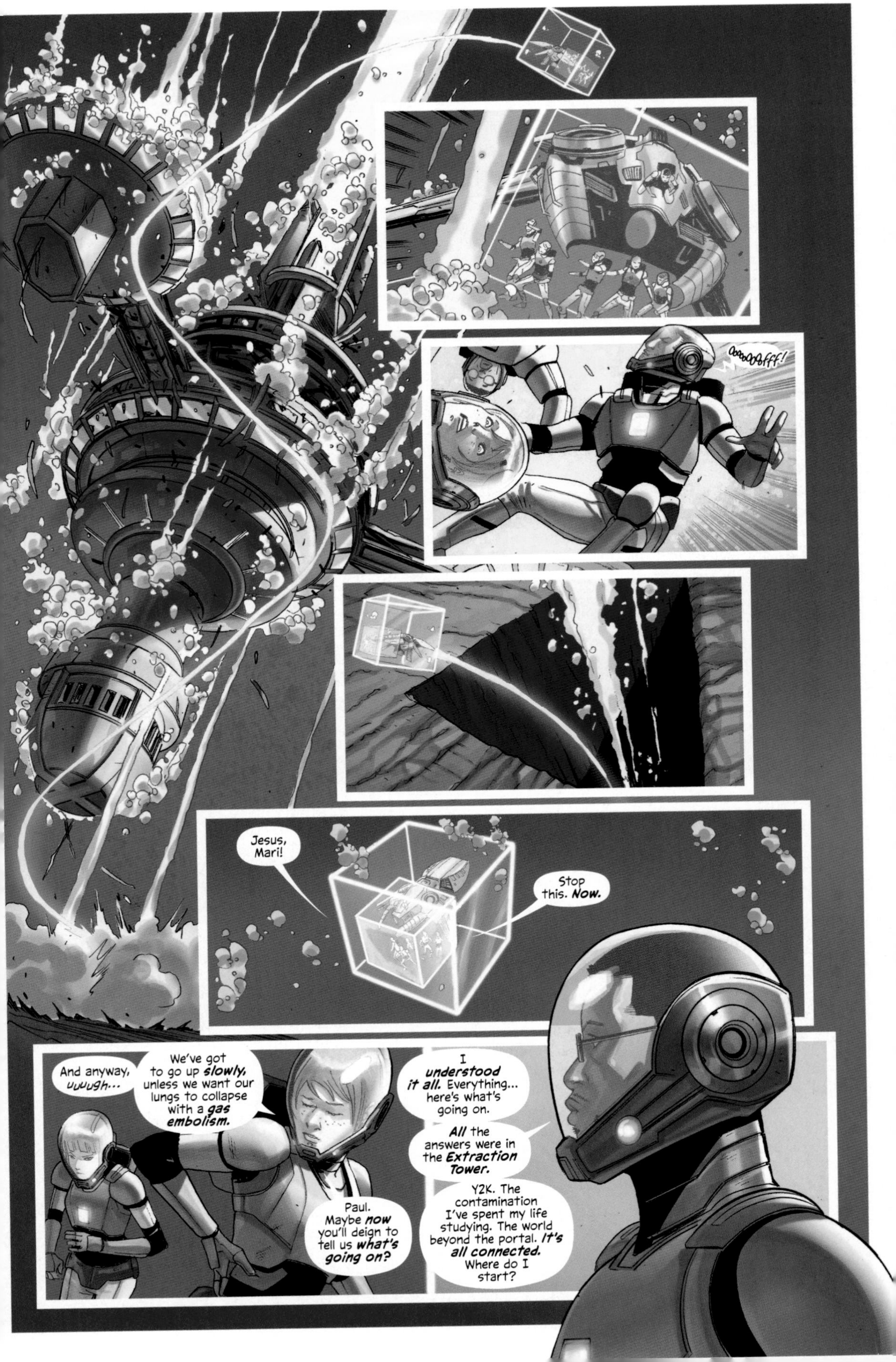

aaaaaaaaffff!
Jesus, Mari!
Stop this. Now.
And anyway, uuuugh...
We've got to go up slowly, unless we want our lungs to collapse with a gas embolism.
Paul. Maybe now you'll deign to tell us what's going on?
I understood it all. Everything... here's what's going on.
All the answers were in the Extraction Tower.
Y2K. The contamination I've spent my life studying. The world beyond the portal. It's all connected. Where do I start?

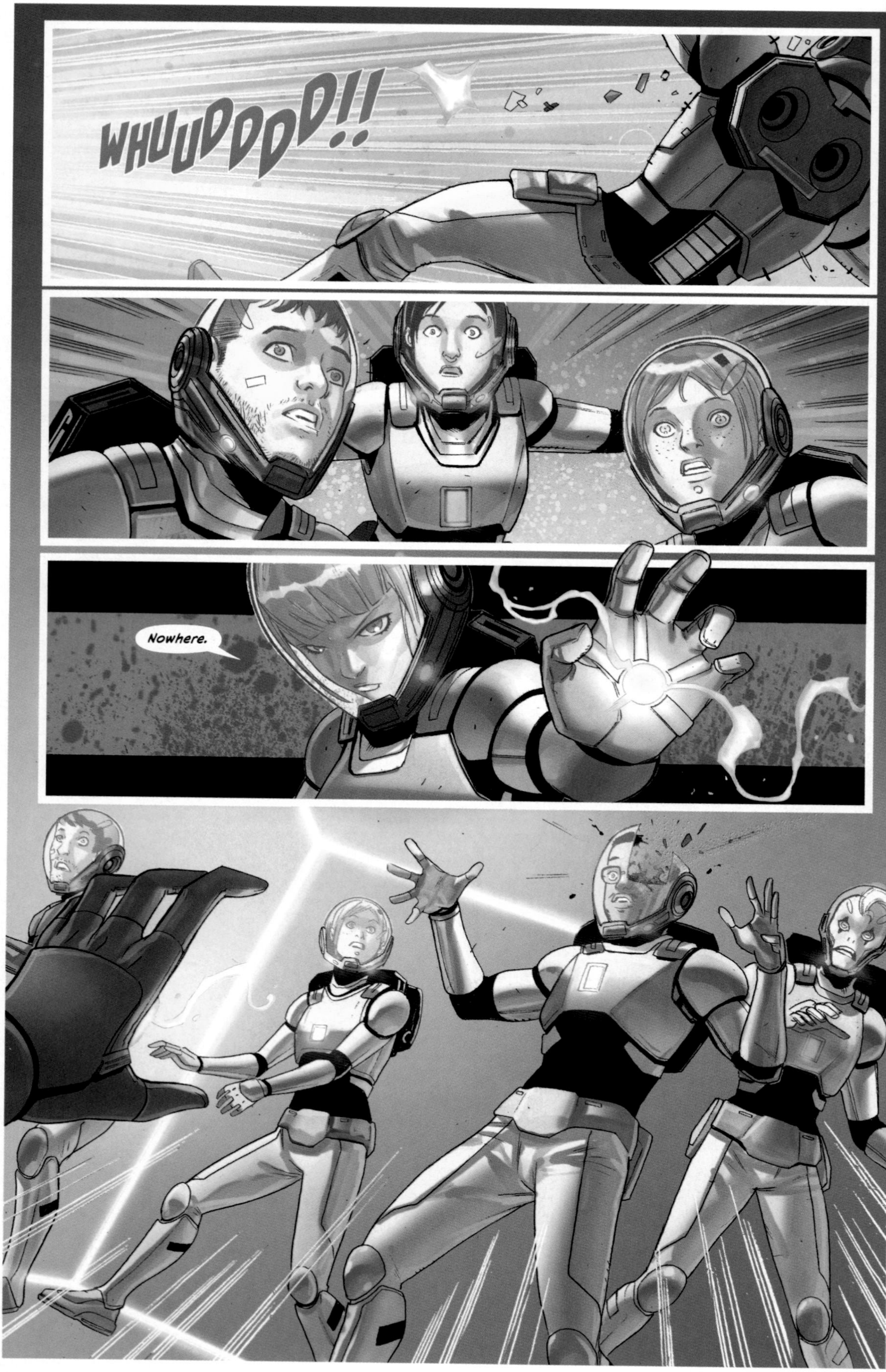
WHUUDDDD!!
Nowhere.

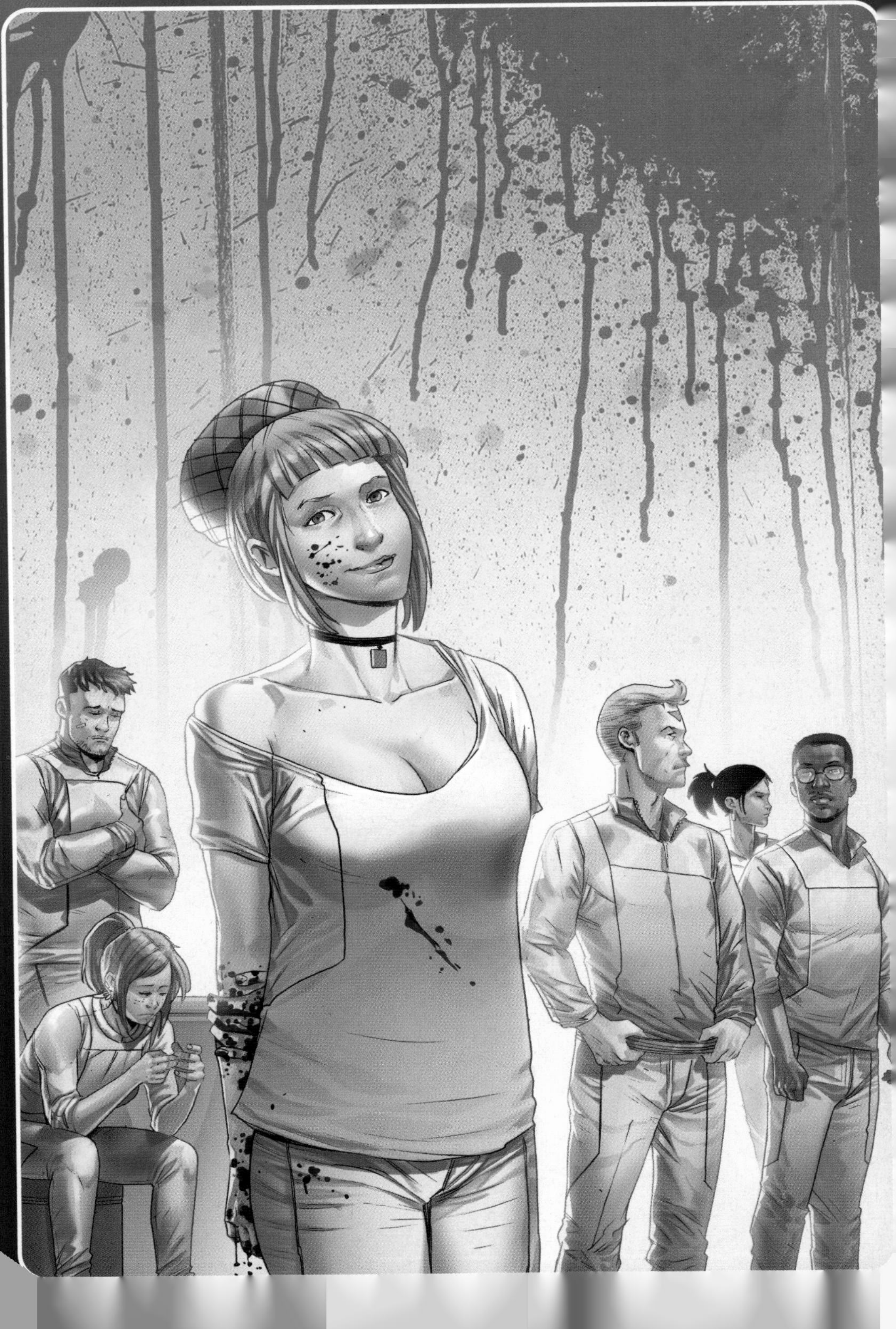

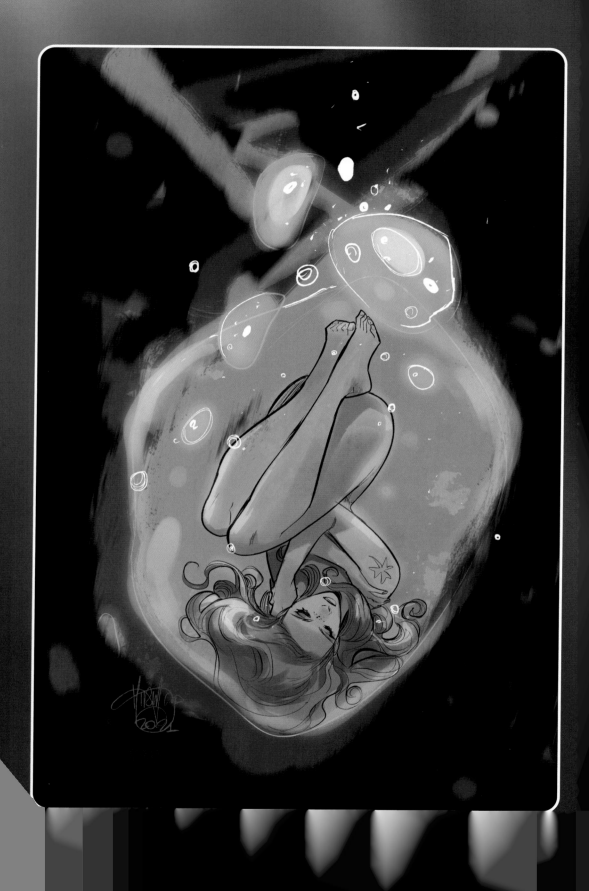

Let's take stock of the situation.
My name is Paul Bailey. I'm 29, and I've always considered myself a loser.
Seven days ago, I was sitting alone in my hole, gulping down cheap vodka and crying to myself...
Thinking about the fact that the only woman I've ever loved was dead... due to her own actions.
Now, here I am, in that fraction of a second between this moment and my final exit from the scene, contemplating something that may be...
...if my astronomical knowledge isn't too rusty...
...the elliptical dwarf galaxy of Canis Major.
Yeah...not exactly a normal way to pass on.

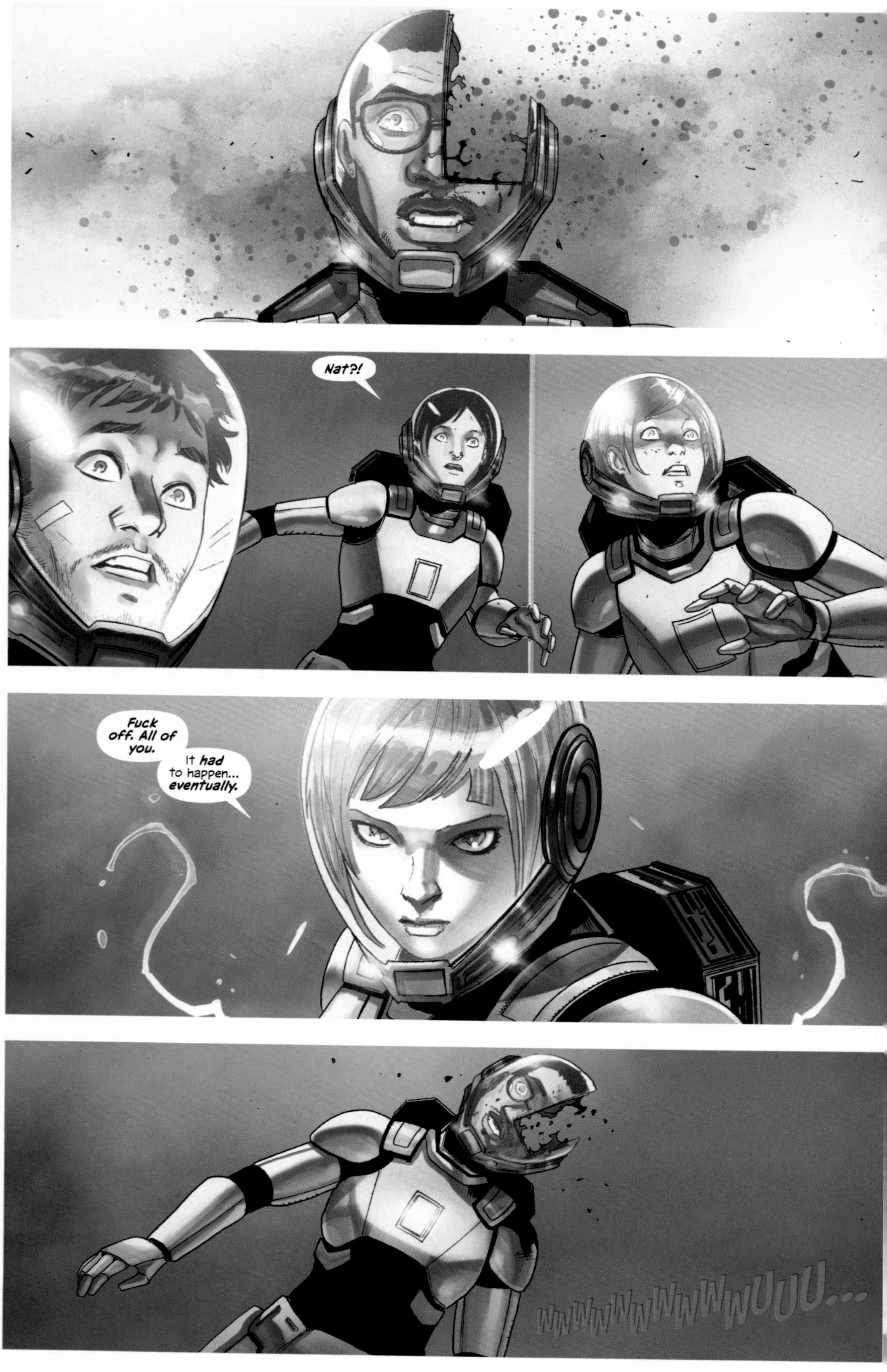
Nat?!
Fuck off. All of you.
It had to happen... eventually.
WWWWWWWWWWWWUUU...

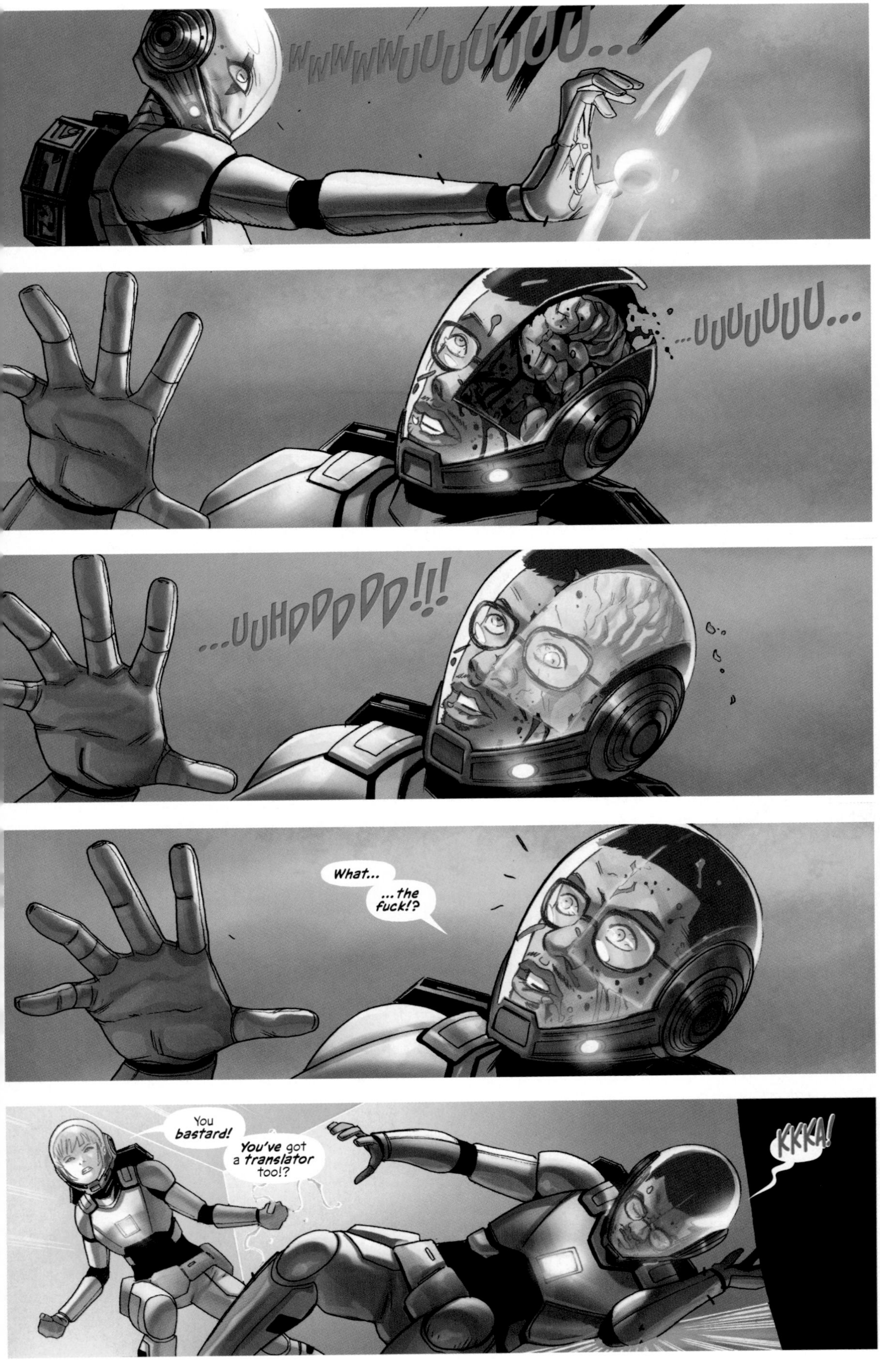
WWWWWUUUUUU...!
...UUUUUUU...
...UUHDDDDD!!!
What...
...the fuck!?
You bastard!
You've got a translator too!?
KKKA!

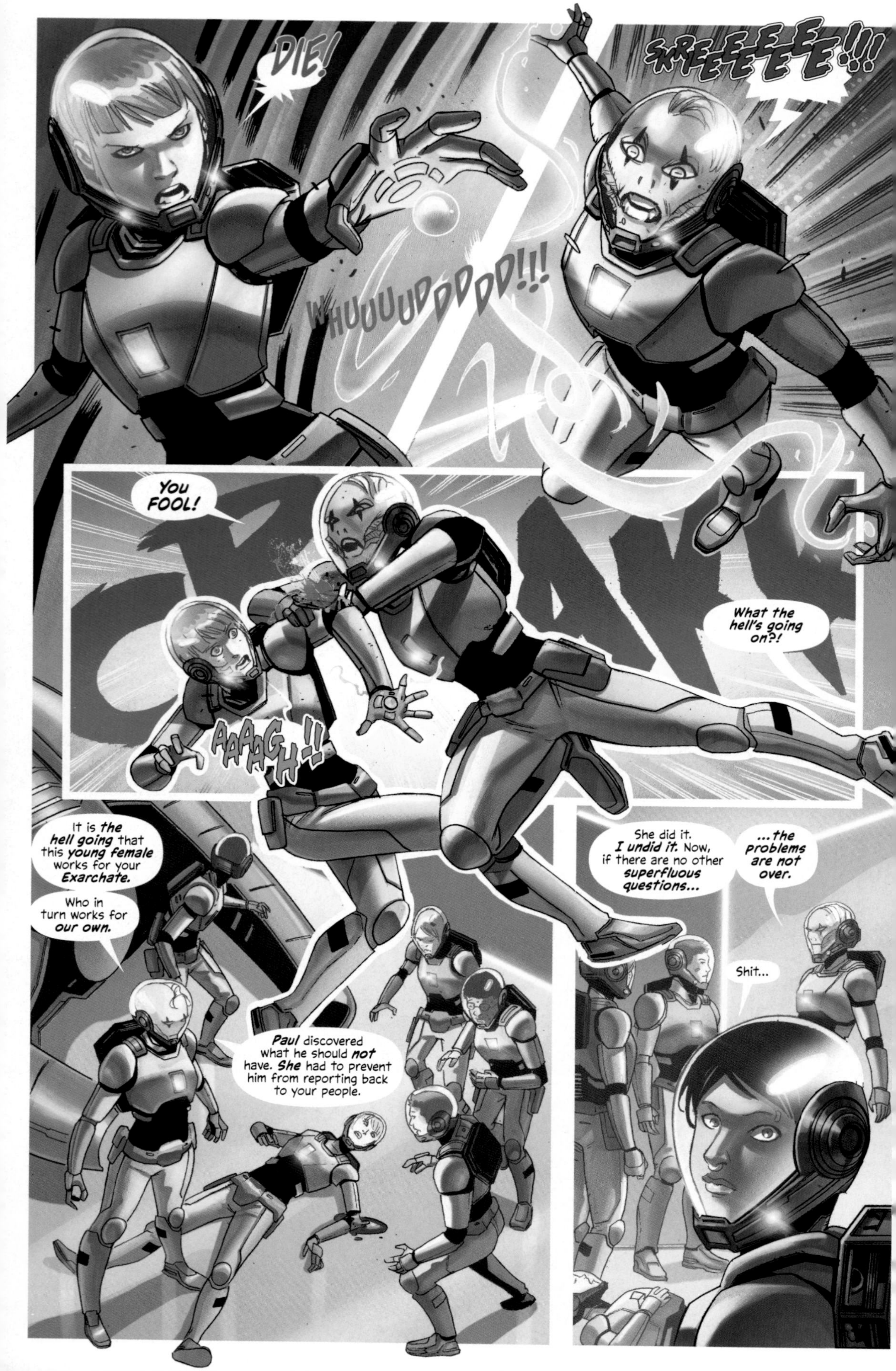

DIE!
SKREEEEEEEE!!!
WHUUUUDDDDD!!!
You FOOL!
AAAAGH!!
What the hell's going on?!
It is the hell going that this young female works for your Exarchate.
Who in turn works for our own.
Paul discovered what he should not have. She had to prevent him from reporting back to your people.
She did it. I undid it. Now, if there are no other superfluous questions...
...the problems are not over.
Shit...

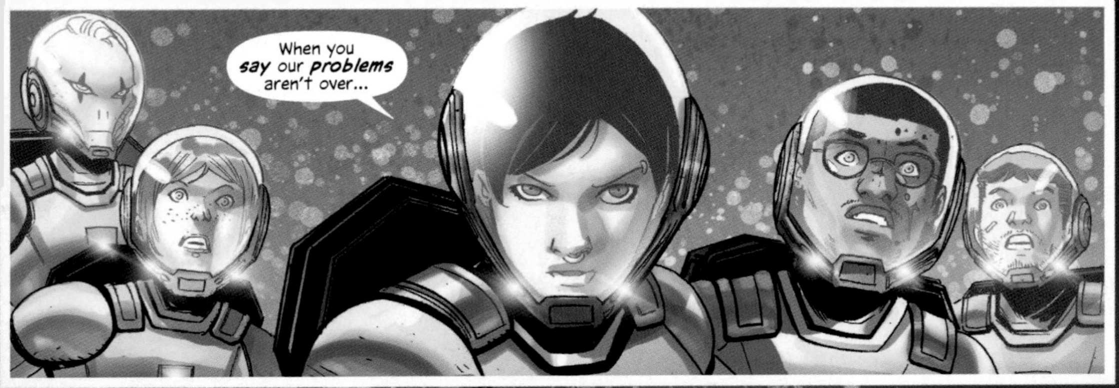
When you *say* our *problems* aren't over...

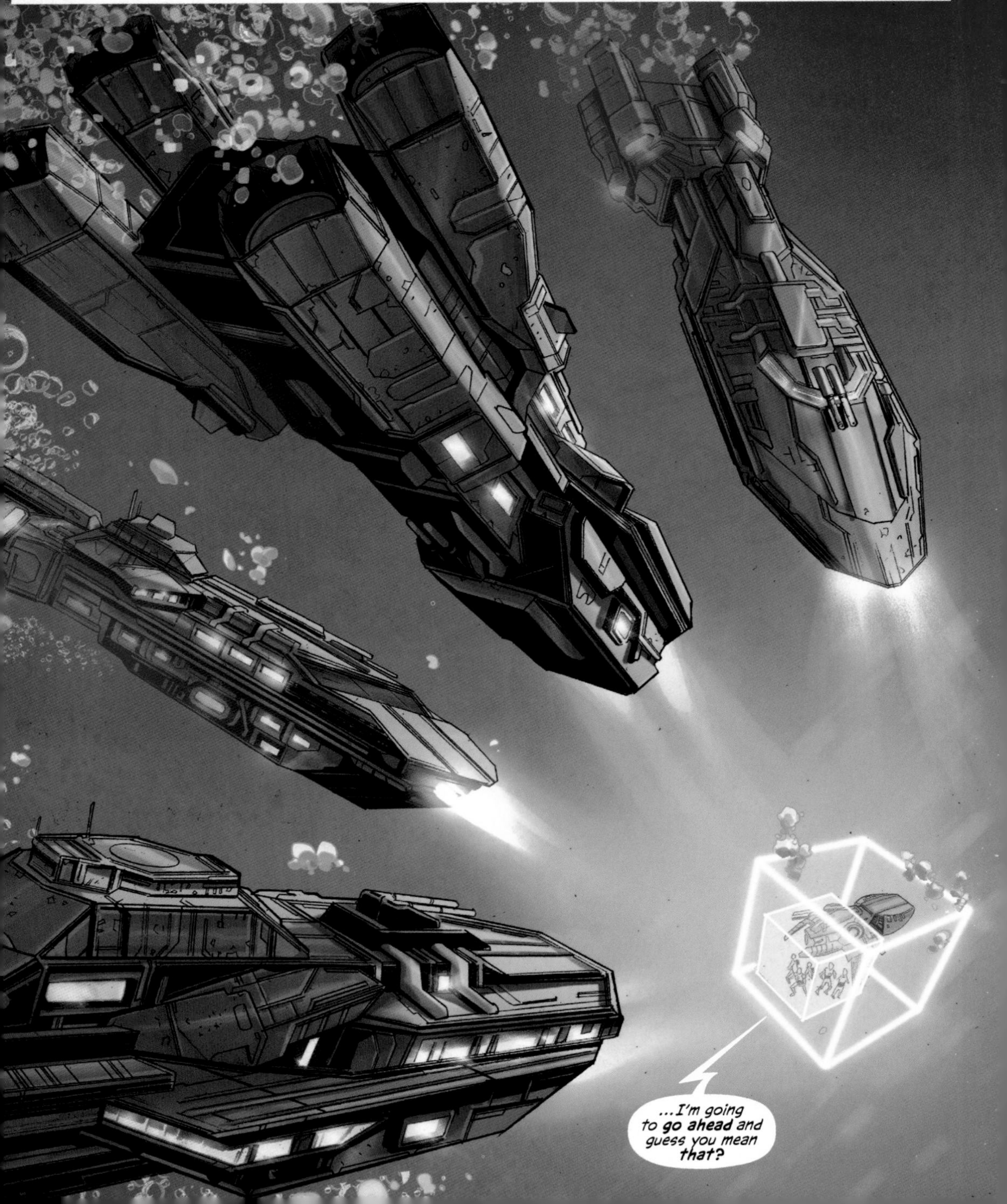
...*I'm going to **go ahead** and guess you mean **that?***

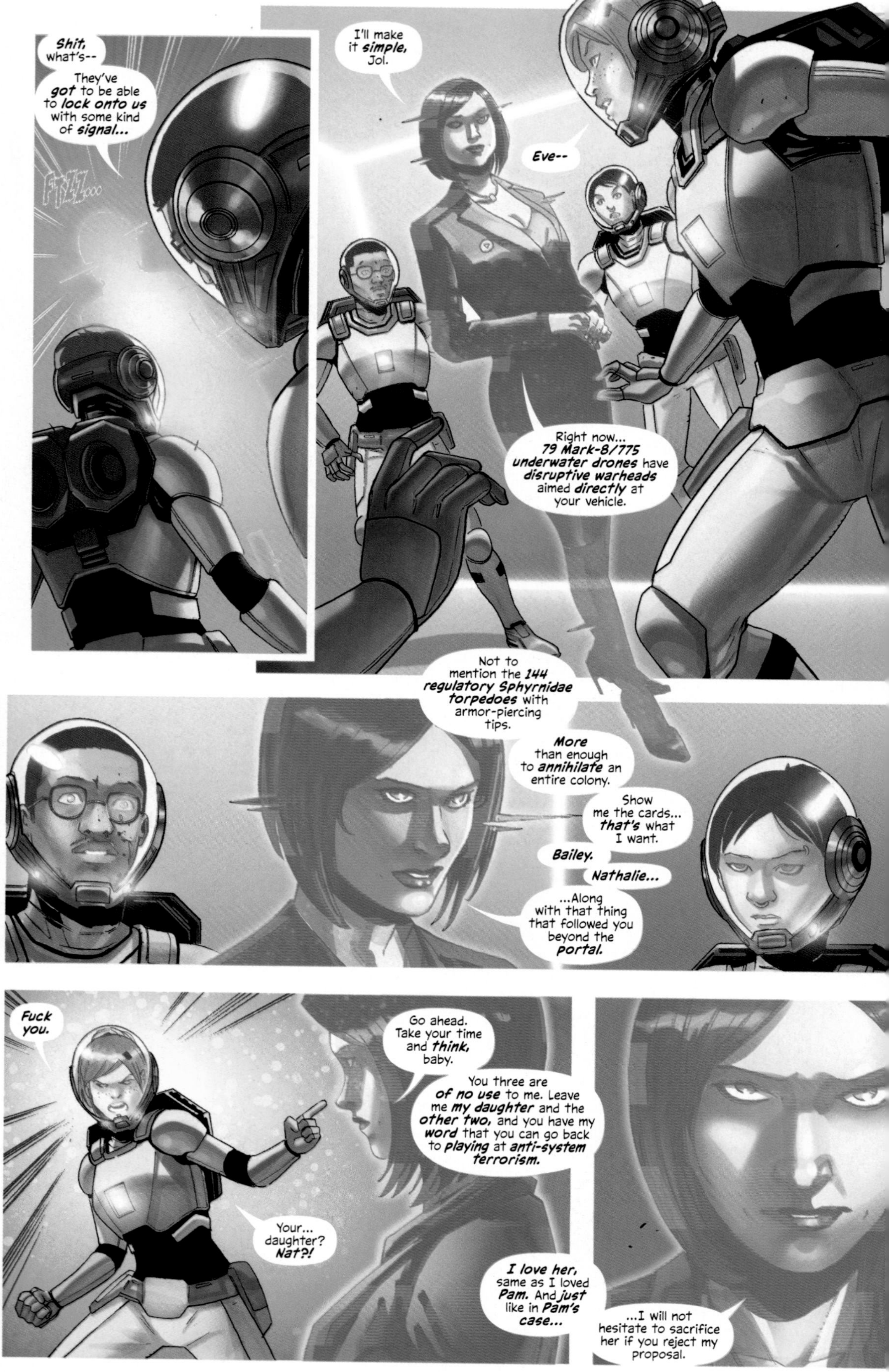
Shit, what's--
They've got to be able to lock onto us with some kind of signal...
I'll make it simple, Jol.
Eve--
Right now... 79 Mark-8/775 underwater drones have disruptive warheads aimed directly at your vehicle.
Not to mention the 144 regulatory Sphyrnidae torpedoes with armor-piercing tips.
More than enough to annihilate an entire colony.
Show me the cards... that's what I want.
Bailey.
Nathalie...
...Along with that thing that followed you beyond the portal.
Fuck you.
Go ahead. Take your time and think, baby.
You three are of no use to me. Leave me my daughter and the other two, and you have my word that you can go back to playing at anti-system terrorism.
Your... daughter? Nat?!
I love her, same as I loved Pam. And just like in Pam's case...
...I will not hesitate to sacrifice her if you reject my proposal.

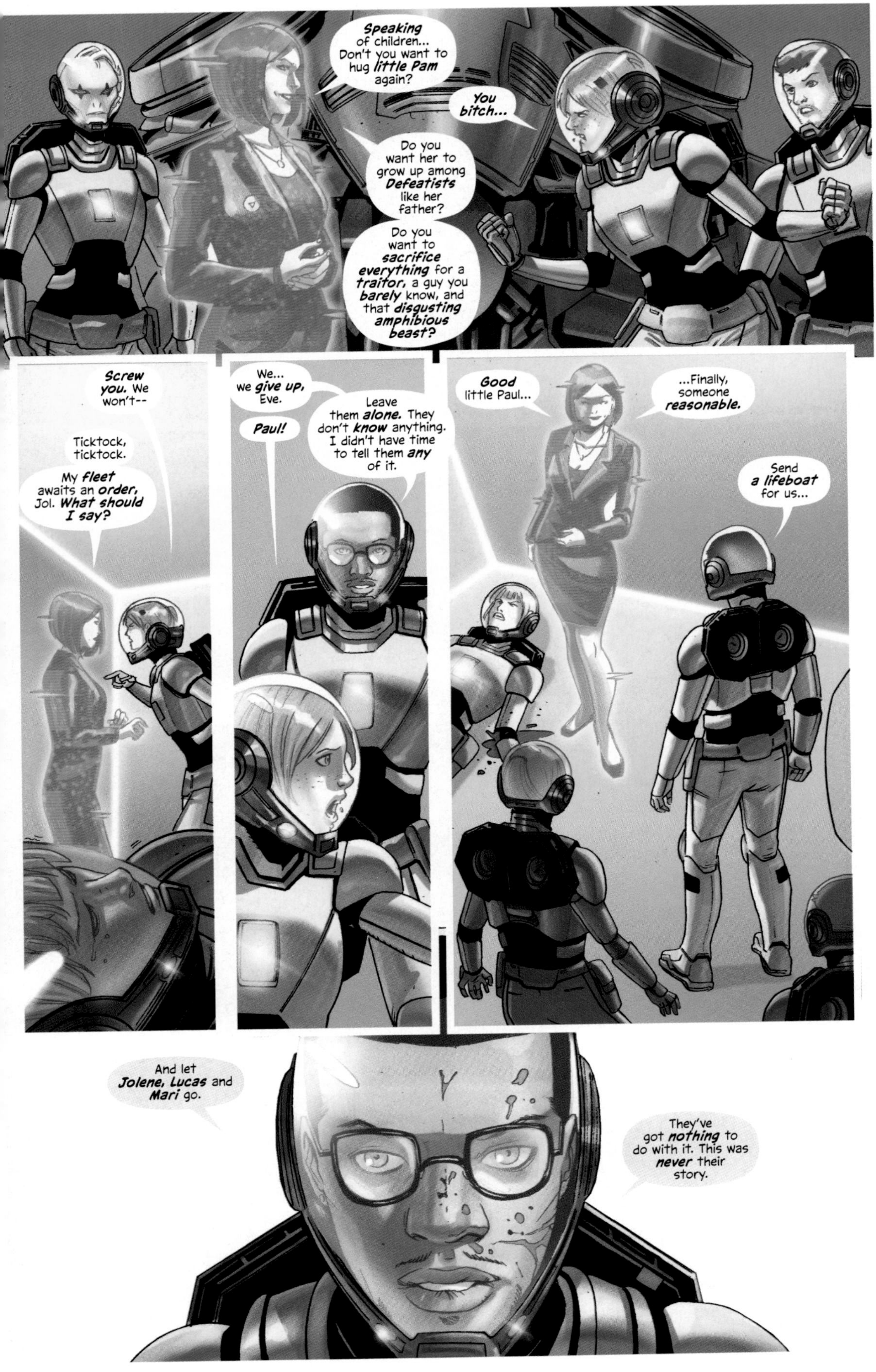
Speaking of children... Don't you want to hug little Pam again?
You bitch...
Do you want her to grow up among Defeatists like her father?
Do you want to sacrifice everything for a traitor, a guy you barely know, and that disgusting amphibious beast?
Screw you. We won't--
Ticktock, ticktock.
My fleet awaits an order, Jol. What should I say?
We... we give up, Eve.
Paul!
Leave them alone. They don't know anything. I didn't have time to tell them any of it.
Good little Paul...
...Finally, someone reasonable.
Send a lifeboat for us...
And let Jolene, Lucas and Mari go.
They've got nothing to do with it. This was never their story.

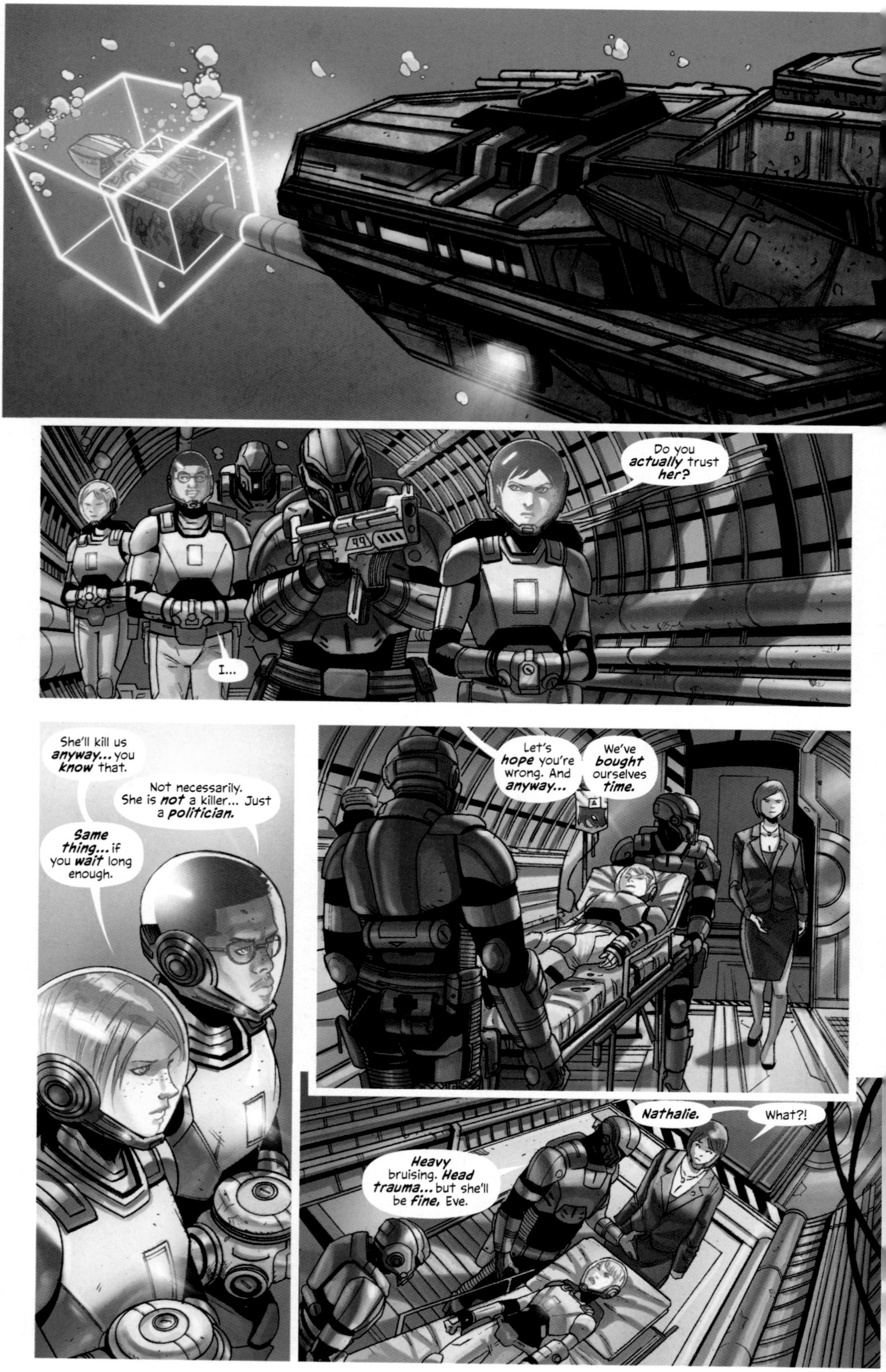

Do you actually trust her?
I...
She'll kill us anyway... you know that.
Not necessarily. She is not a killer... Just a politician.
Same thing... if you wait long enough.
Let's hope you're wrong. And anyway...
We've bought ourselves time.
Nathalie.
What?!
Heavy bruising. Head trauma... but she'll be fine, Eve.

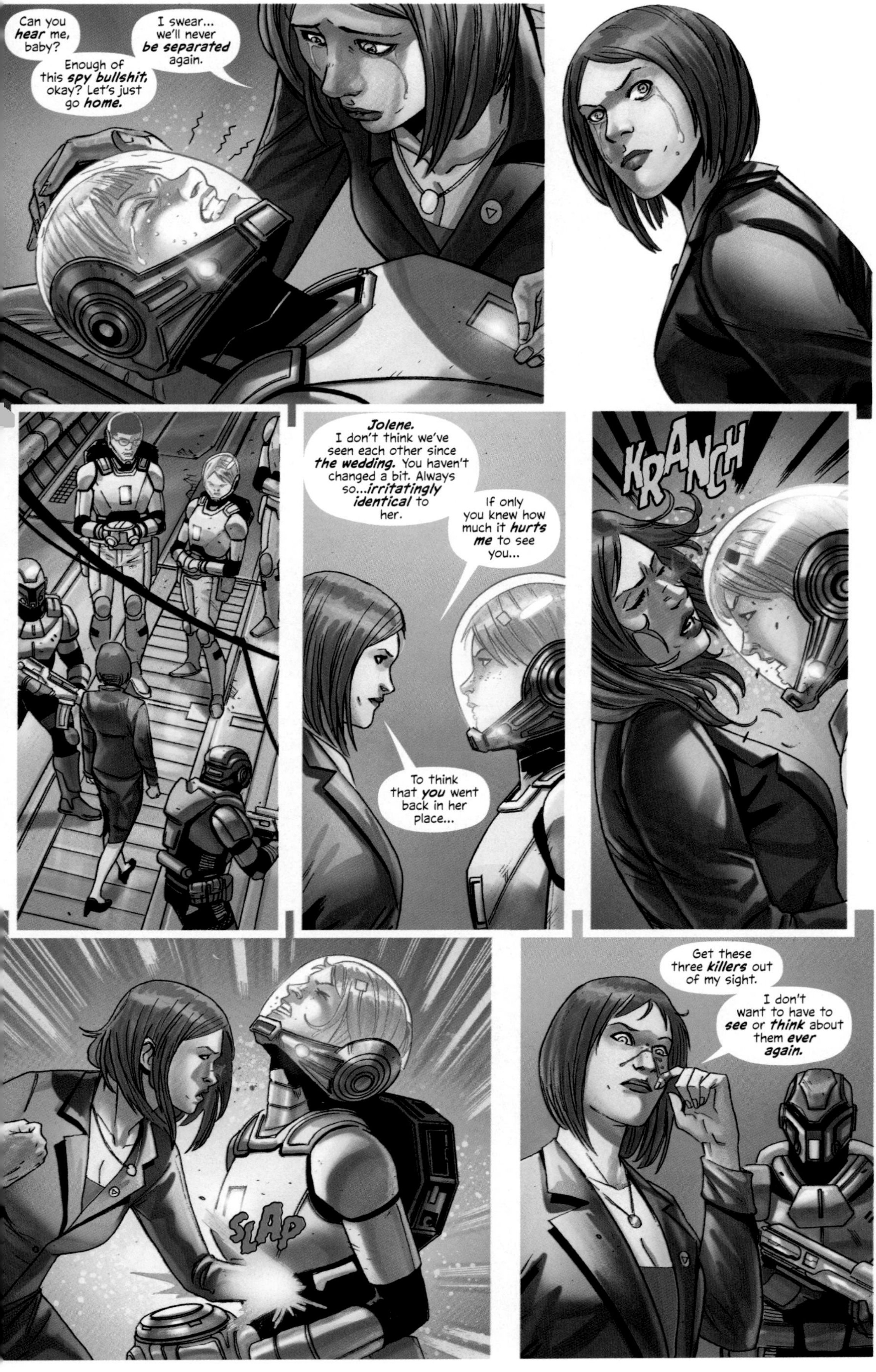
Can you hear me, baby?
Enough of this spy bullshit, okay? Let's just go home.
I swear... we'll never be separated again.
Jolene. I don't think we've seen each other since the wedding. You haven't changed a bit. Always so...irritatingly identical to her.
If only you knew how much it hurts me to see you...
To think that you went back in her place...
KRANCH
SLAP
Get these three killers out of my sight.
I don't want to have to see or think about them ever again.

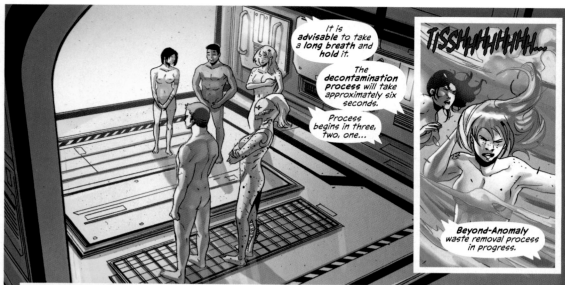

It is **advisable** to take a **long breath** and **hold it.**

The **decontamination process** will take approximately **six seconds.**

Process begins in **three, two, one...**

TISSHHHHHHH...

Beyond-Anomaly waste removal process in progress.

You three!

Grab **overalls** from the locker **behind** you and **suit up.**

Any **Beyond-Anomaly** artifacts, including the **survival systems** you came with, will be **destroyed.**

Where're you **taking** us?

You'll be **transported** by emergency unit to **Quadrant 387.** On the **coast.** There, you'll be given a fast land vehicle, oxygen, and fuel enough to **return to your base...**

...or **wherever else you** want.

Not like **we** care...as long as it's not **here.**

What about **Paul?** And...**her?**

I'm not **authorized** to **answer** that.

Paul...

It's fine, **Jol.** It's all good.

I'm **glad** you'll be able to go home. It's been a **nice** trip.

...but it **was** nice to be doing it **with** you all.

Well, maybe **nice** isn't the right word...

With **you,** I mean.

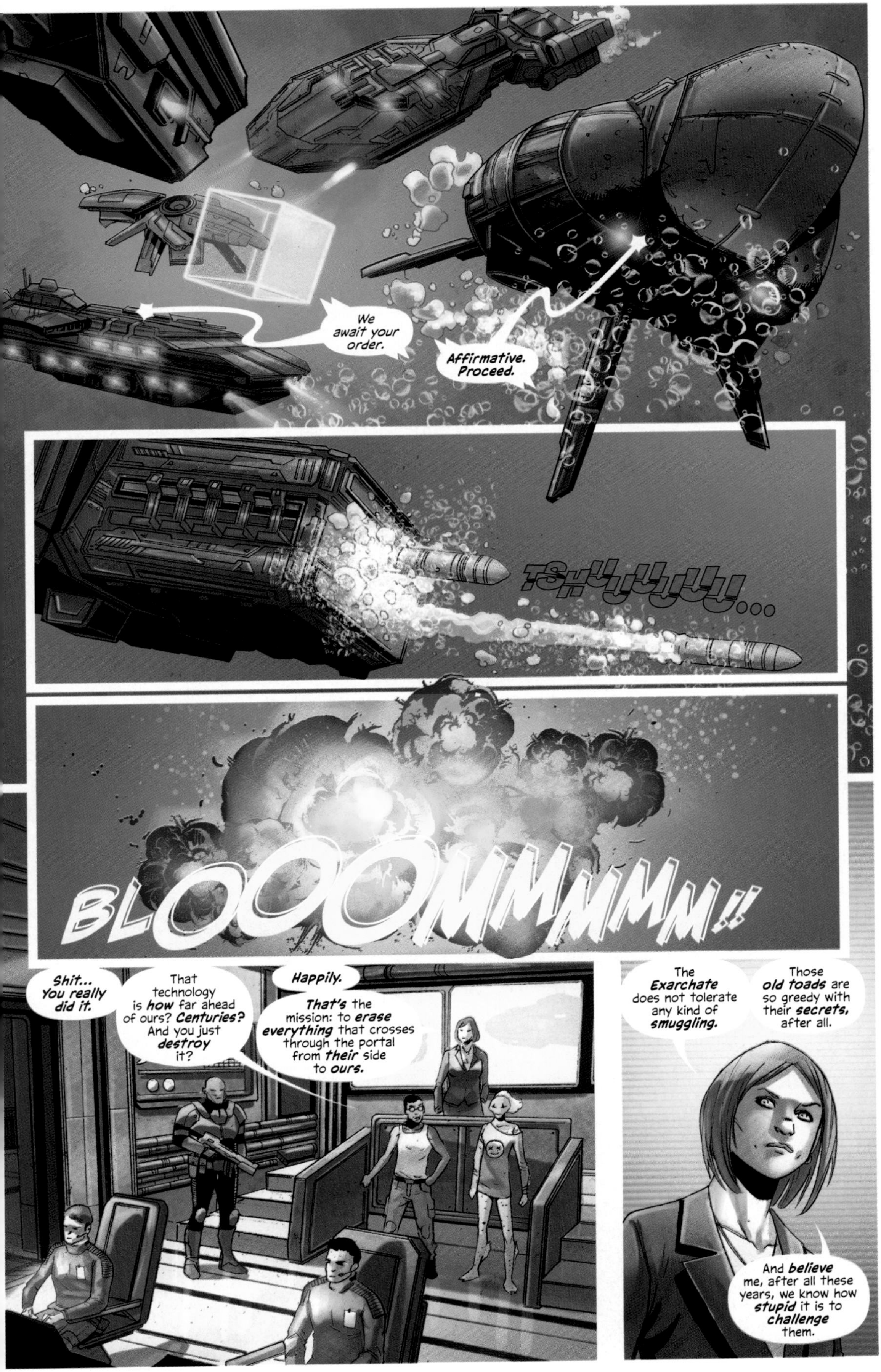

We await your order.
Affirmative. Proceed.
TSHUUUUUUU...
BLOOOOMMMMMM!!
Shit... You really did it.
That technology is how far ahead of ours? Centuries? And you just destroy it?
Happily.
That's the mission: to erase everything that crosses through the portal from their side to ours.
The Exarchate does not tolerate any kind of smuggling.
Those old toads are so greedy with their secrets, after all.
And believe me, after all these years, we know how stupid it is to challenge them.

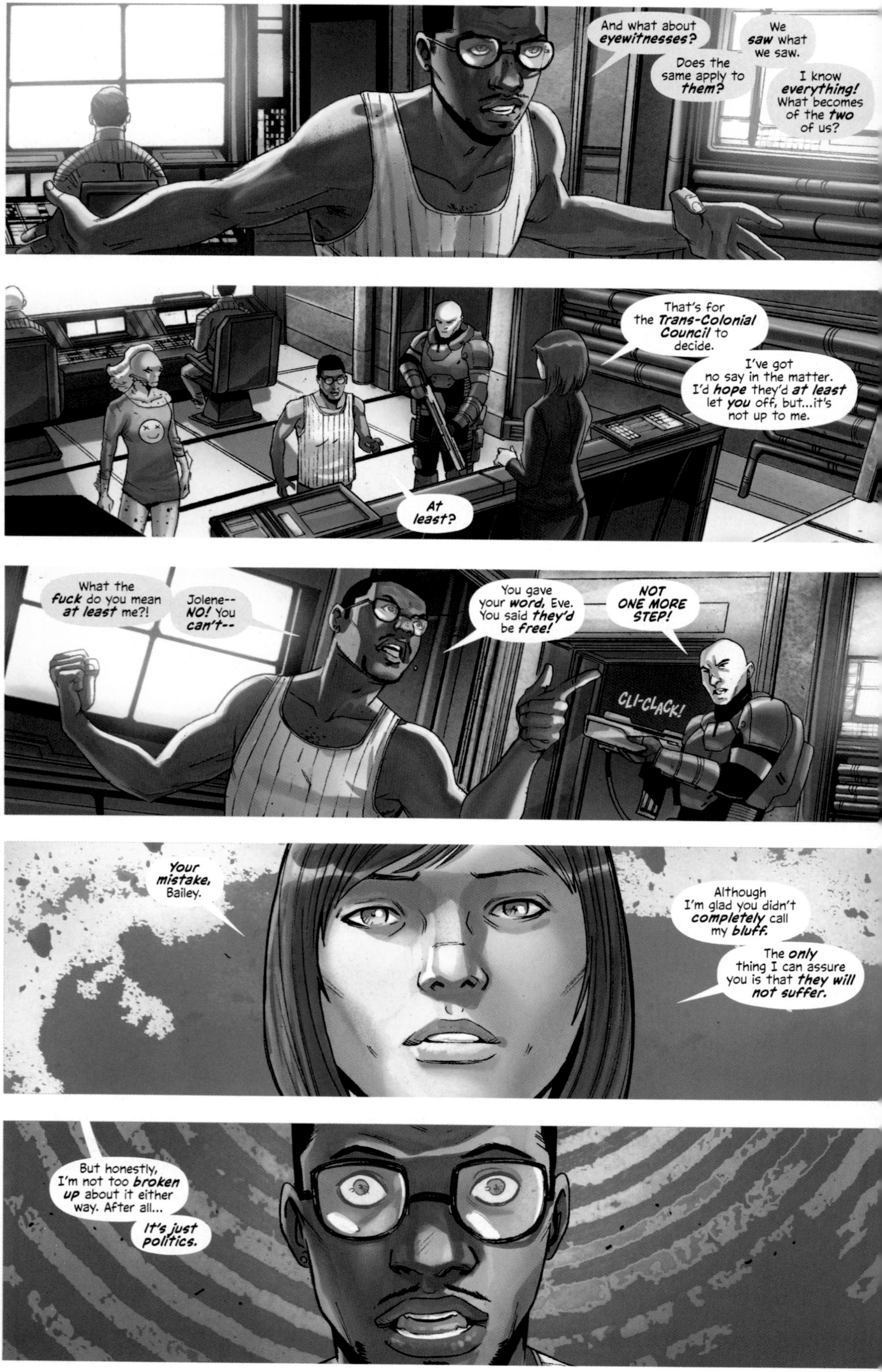

And what about eyewitnesses?
Does the same apply to them?
We saw what we saw.
I know everything! What becomes of the two of us?
That's for the Trans-Colonial Council to decide.
I've got no say in the matter. I'd hope they'd at least let you off, but...it's not up to me.
At least?
What the fuck do you mean at least me?!
Jolene-- NO! You can't--
You gave your word, Eve. You said they'd be free!
NOT ONE MORE STEP!
CLI-CLACK!
Your mistake, Bailey.
Although I'm glad you didn't completely call my bluff.
The only thing I can assure you is that they will not suffer.
But honestly, I'm not too broken up about it either way. After all...
It's just politics.

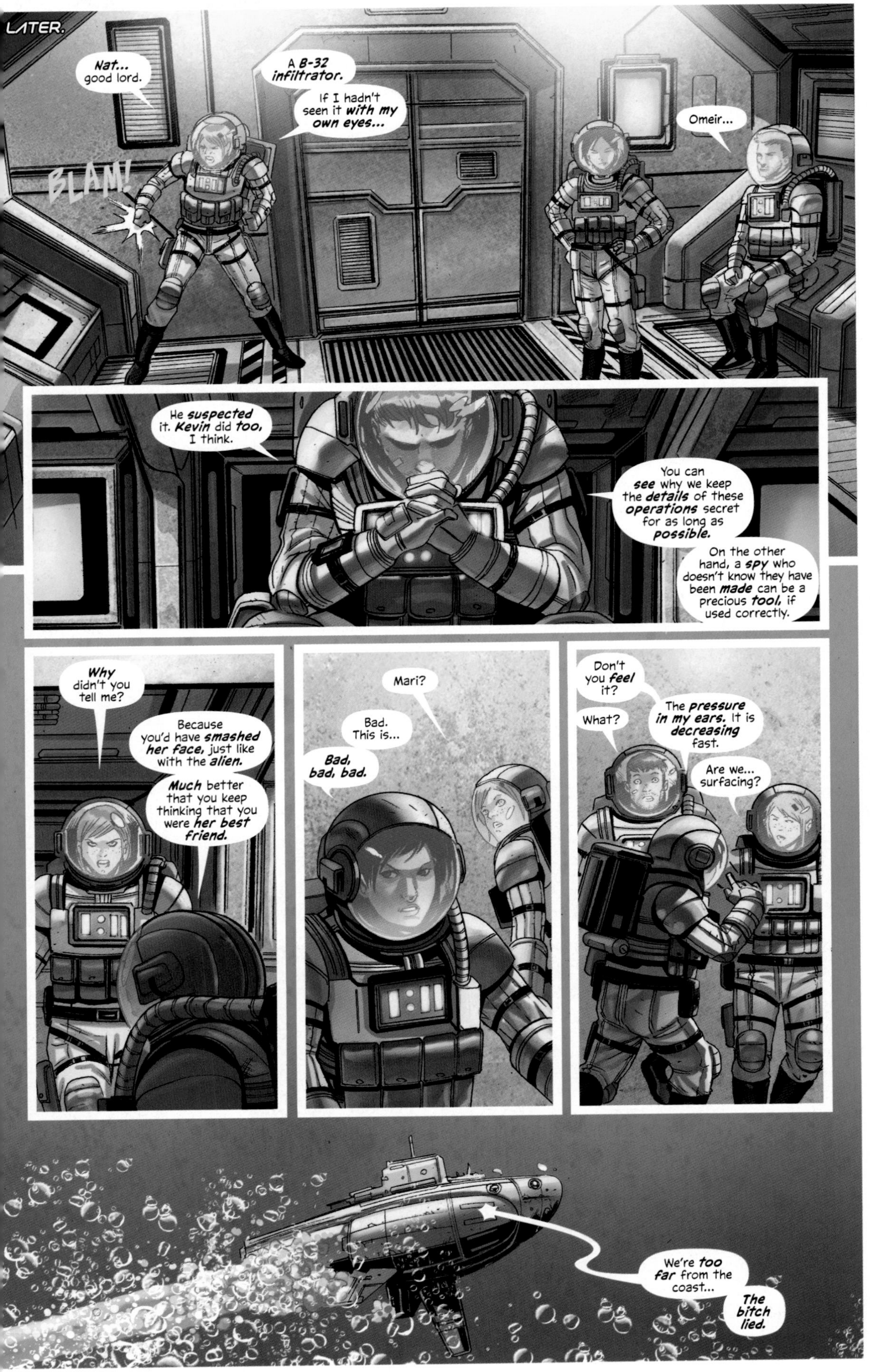
LATER.
Nat... good lord.
A B-32 infiltrator.
If I hadn't seen it with my own eyes...
BLAM!
Omeir...
He suspected it. Kevin did too, I think.
You can see why we keep the details of these operations secret for as long as possible.
On the other hand, a spy who doesn't know they have been made can be a precious tool, if used correctly.
Why didn't you tell me?
Because you'd have smashed her face, just like with the alien.
Much better that you keep thinking that you were her best friend.
Mari?
Bad. This is...
Bad, bad, bad.
Don't you feel it?
What?
The pressure in my ears. It is decreasing fast.
Are we... surfacing?
We're too far from the coast...
The bitch lied.

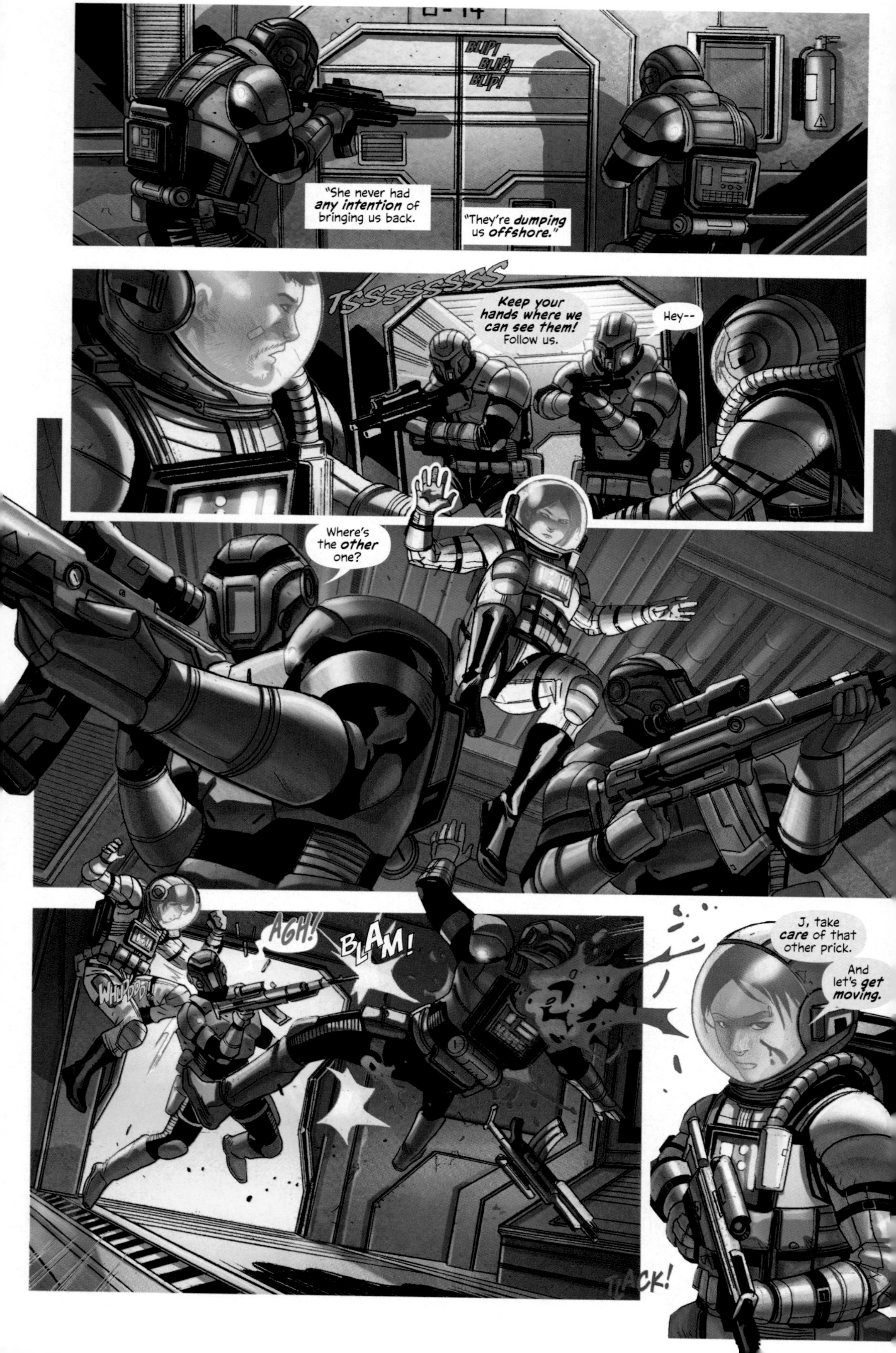
B-14
BLIP!
BLIP!
BLIP!
"She never had any intention of bringing us back.
"They're dumping us offshore."
TSSSSSSSSS
Keep your hands where we can see them! Follow us.
Hey--
Where's the other one?
AGH!
BLAM!
WHUDDD!
J, take care of that other prick.
And let's get moving.
TIACK!

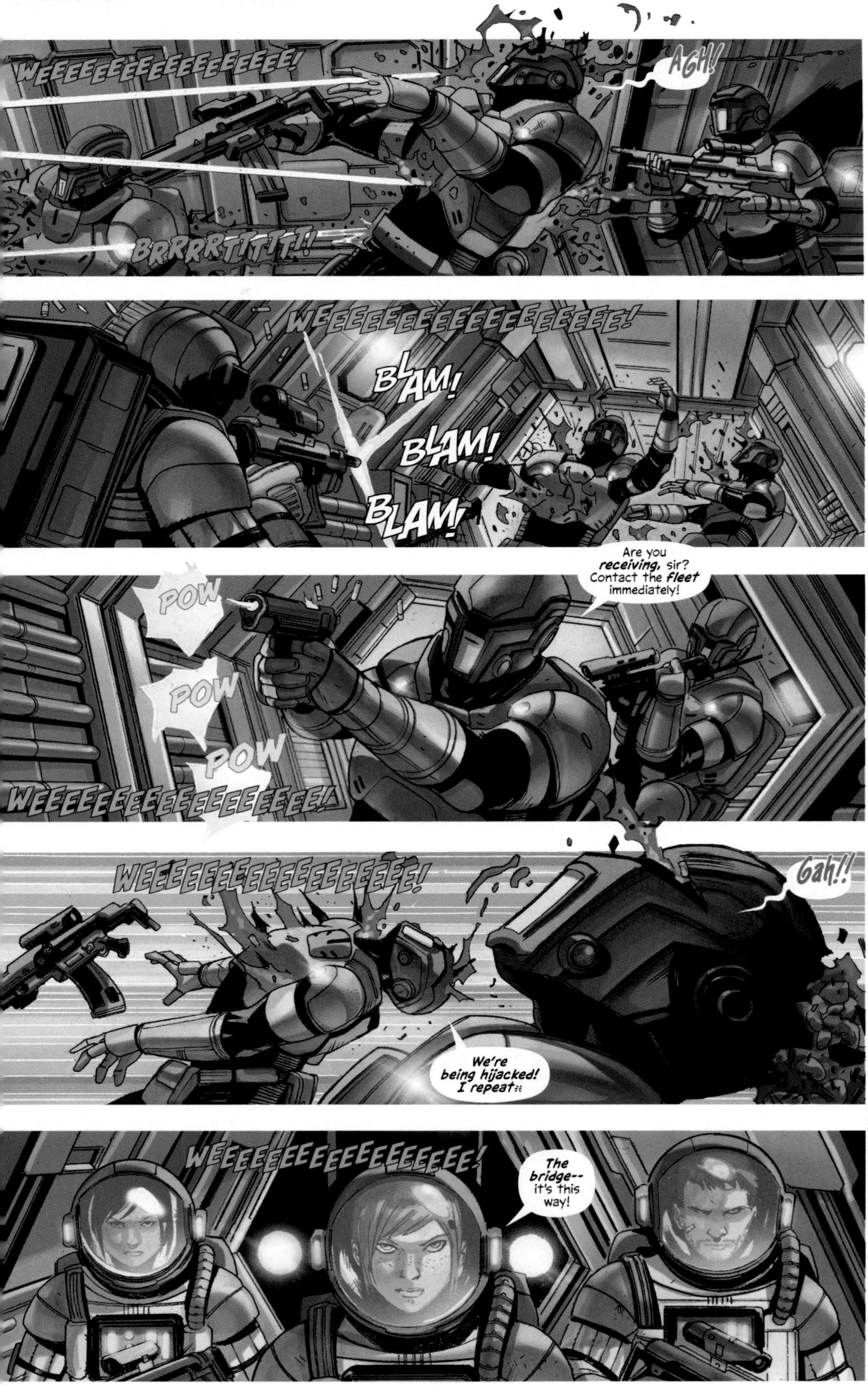
WEEEEEEEEEEEEEEEEE!
AGH!
BRRRRTTTTT!
WEEEEEEEEEEEEEEEEEEE!
BLAM!
BLAM!
BLAM!
POW
POW
POW
WEEEEEEEEEEEEEEEEEE!
Are you receiving, sir? Contact the fleet immediately!
WEEEEEEEEEEEEEEEEEE!
Gah!!
We're being hijacked! I repeat--
WEEEEEEEEEEEEEEEEEE!
The bridge-- it's this way!

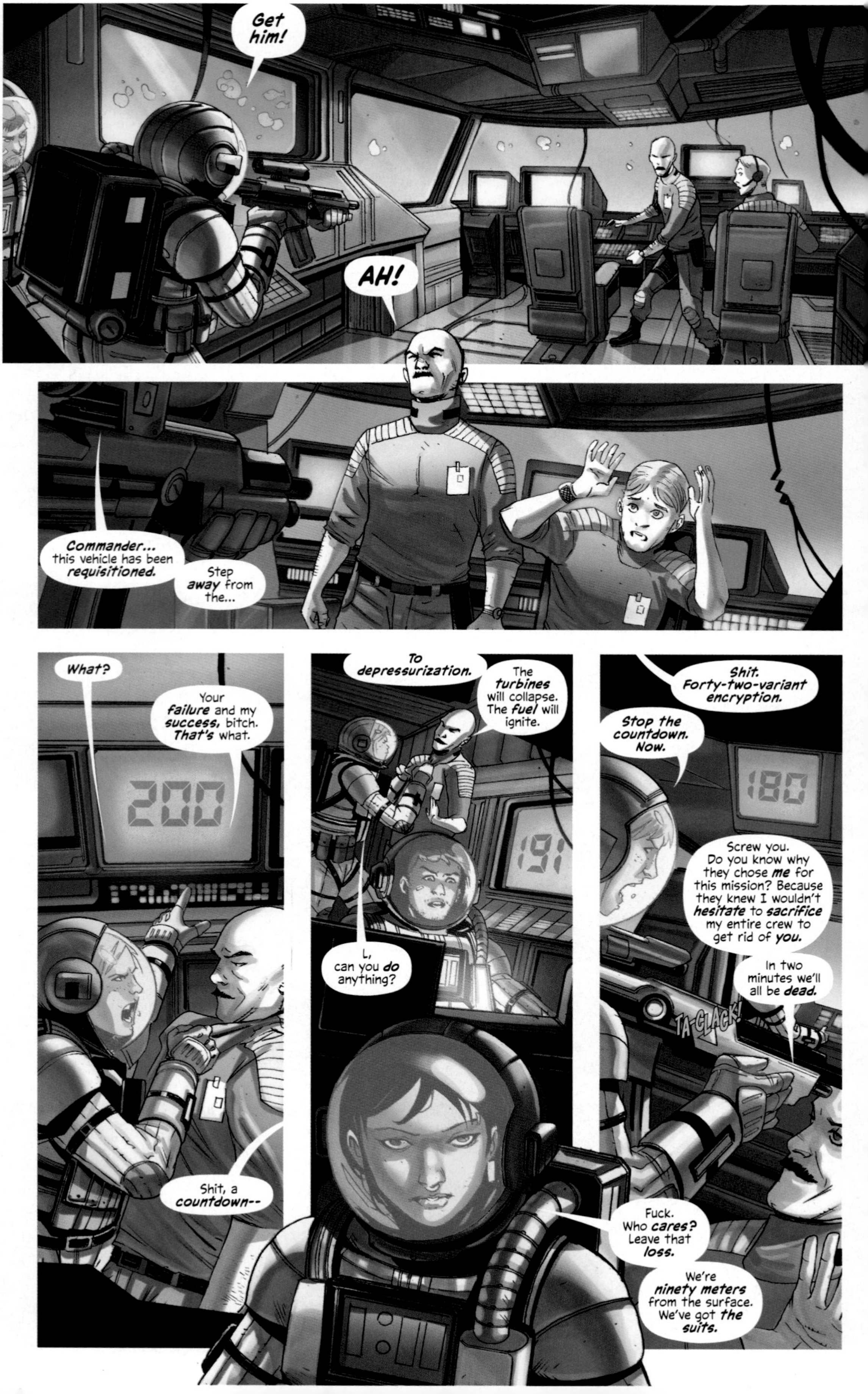
Get him!
AH!
Commander... this vehicle has been requisitioned.
Step away from the...
What?
Your failure and my success, bitch. That's what.
200
Shit, a countdown--
To depressurization.
The turbines will collapse. The fuel will ignite.
191
L, can you do anything?
Fuck. Who cares? Leave that loss.
We're ninety meters from the surface. We've got the suits.
Shit. Forty-two-variant encryption.
Stop the countdown. Now.
180
Screw you. Do you know why they chose me for this mission? Because they knew I wouldn't hesitate to sacrifice my entire crew to get rid of you.
In two minutes we'll all be dead.
TA-CLACK!

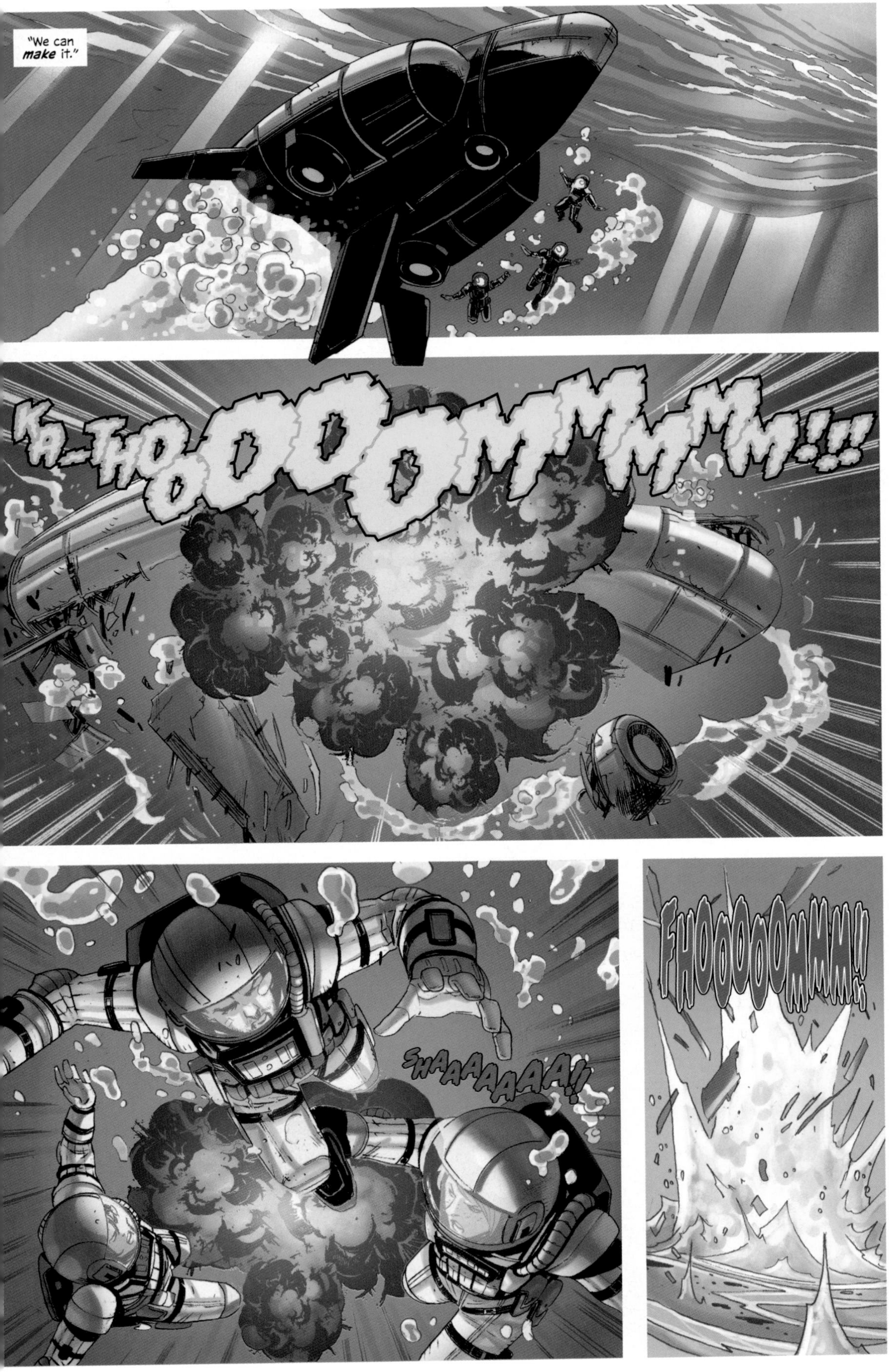
"We can make it."
KA-THBOOOOMMMM!!!
SHAAAAAAA!!
FHOOOOOMMM!!

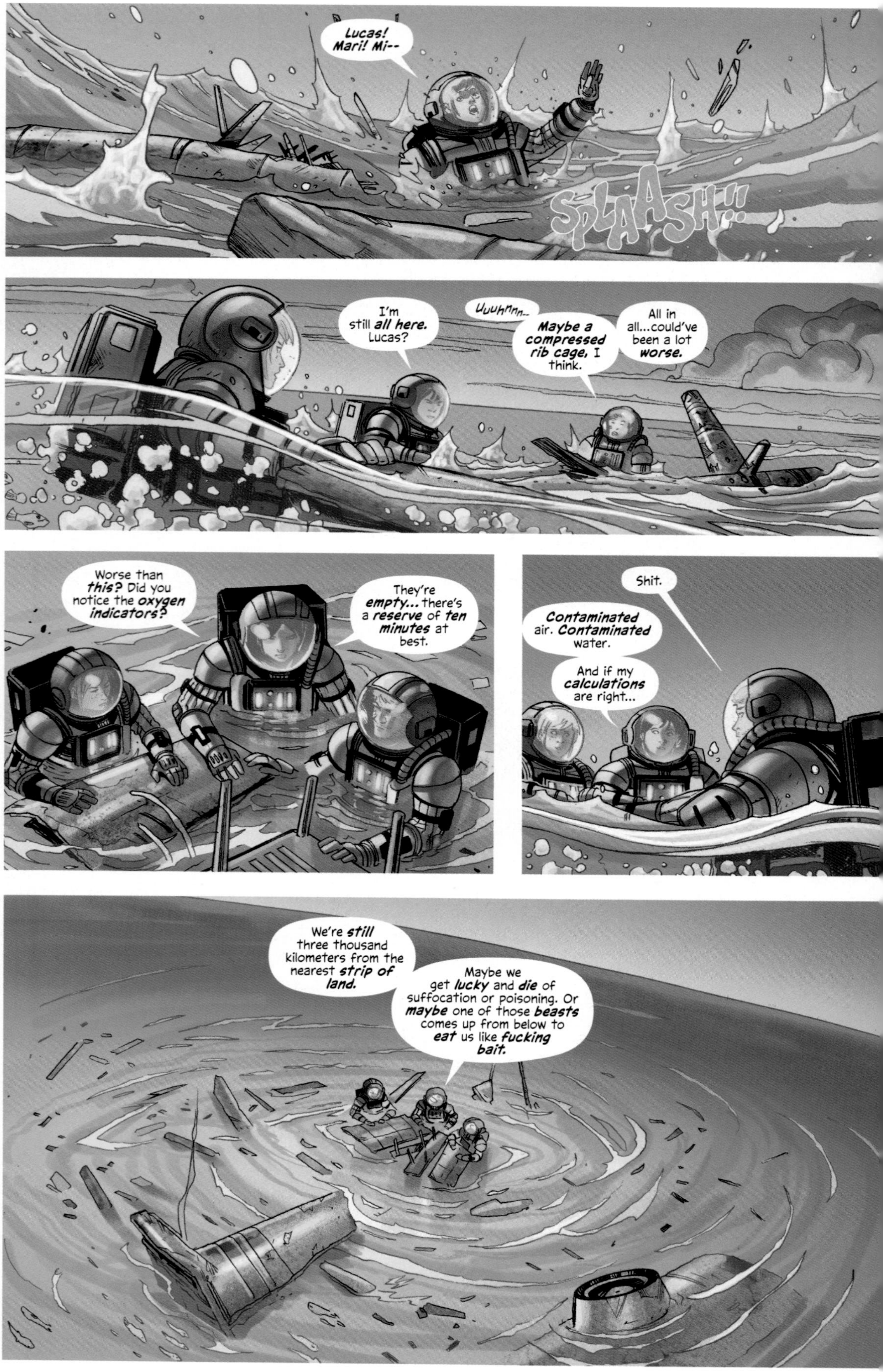
Lucas! Mari! Mi--
SPLAAASH!!
I'm still all here. Lucas?
Uuuhnnn...
Maybe a compressed rib cage, I think.
All in all...could've been a lot worse.
Worse than this? Did you notice the oxygen indicators?
They're empty... there's a reserve of ten minutes at best.
Shit.
Contaminated air. Contaminated water.
And if my calculations are right...
We're still three thousand kilometers from the nearest strip of land.
Maybe we get lucky and die of suffocation or poisoning. Or maybe one of those beasts comes up from below to eat us like fucking bait.

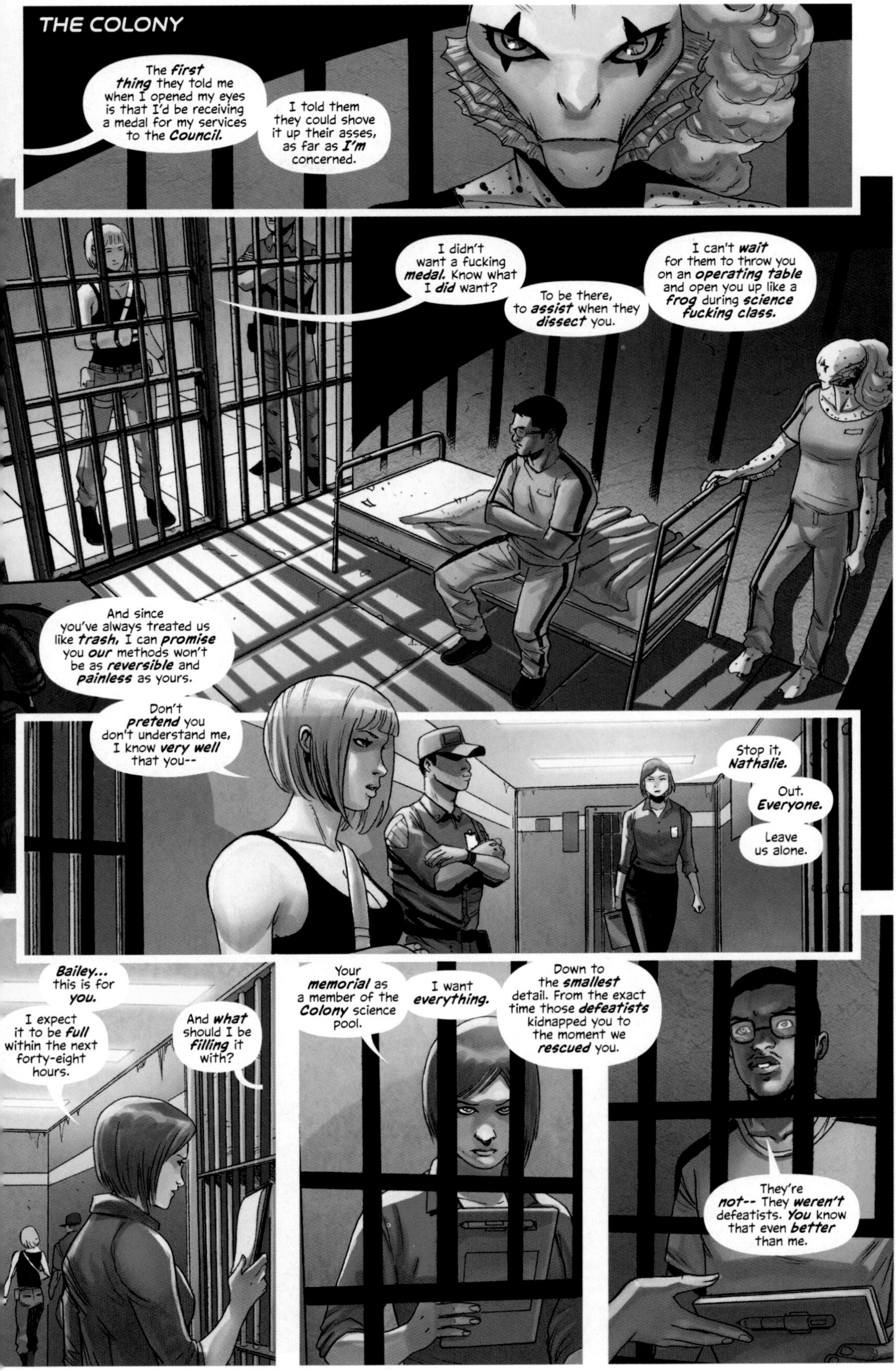
THE COLONY
The first thing they told me when I opened my eyes is that I'd be receiving a medal for my services to the Council.
I told them they could shove it up their asses, as far as I'm concerned.
I didn't want a fucking medal. Know what I did want?
To be there, to assist when they dissect you.
I can't wait for them to throw you on an operating table and open you up like a frog during science fucking class.
And since you've always treated us like trash, I can promise you our methods won't be as reversible and painless as yours.
Don't pretend you don't understand me, I know very well that you--
Stop it, Nathalie.
Out. Everyone.
Leave us alone.
Bailey... this is for you.
I expect it to be full within the next forty-eight hours.
And what should I be filling it with?
Your memorial as a member of the Colony science pool.
I want everything.
Down to the smallest detail. From the exact time those defeatists kidnapped you to the moment we rescued you.
They're not-- They weren't defeatists. You know that even better than me.

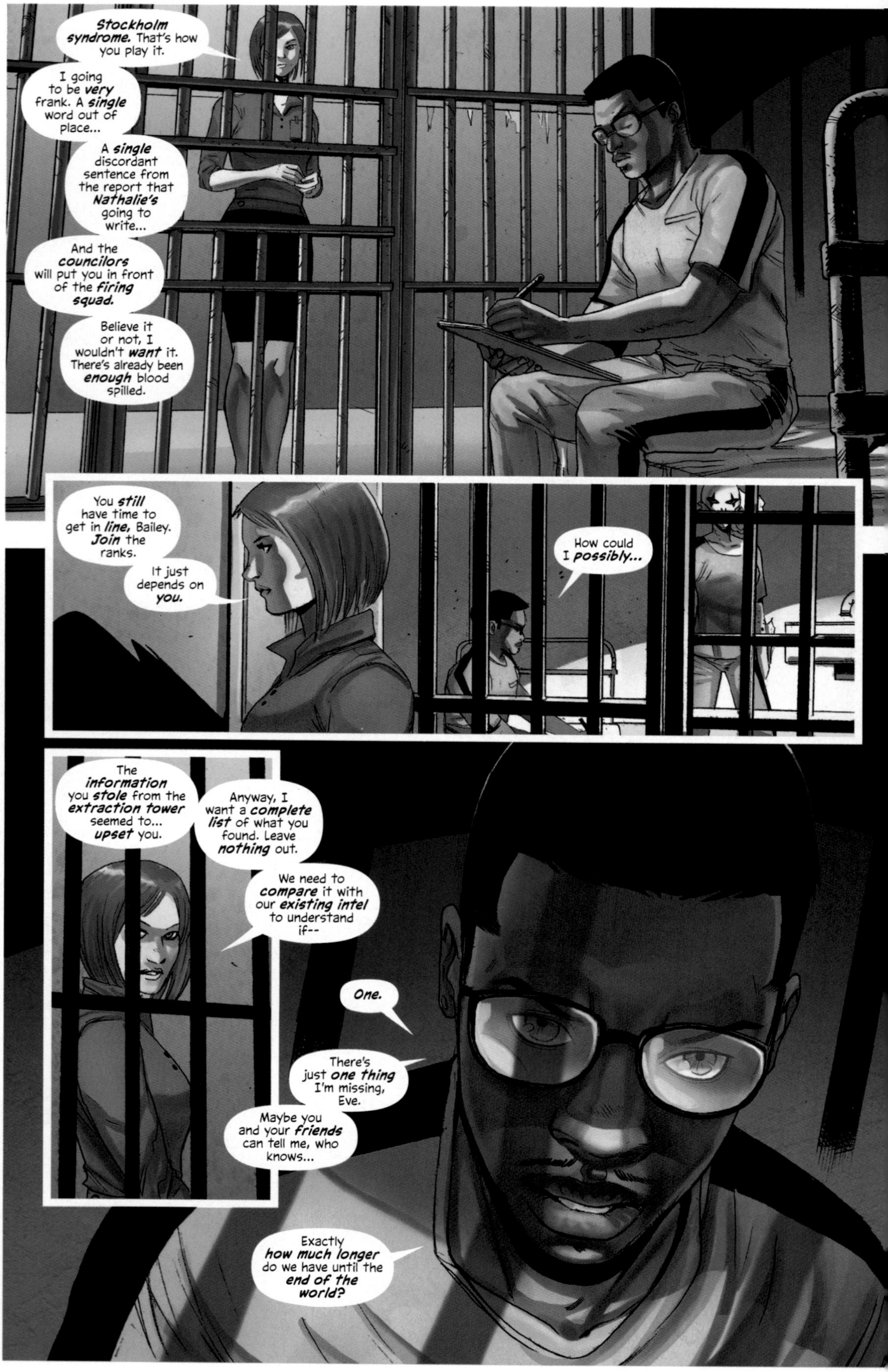
Stockholm syndrome. That's how you play it.
I going to be very frank. A single word out of place...
A single discordant sentence from the report that Nathalie's going to write...
And the councilors will put you in front of the firing squad.
Believe it or not, I wouldn't want it. There's already been enough blood spilled.
You still have time to get in line, Bailey. Join the ranks.
It just depends on you.
How could I possibly...
The information you stole from the extraction tower seemed to... upset you.
Anyway, I want a complete list of what you found. Leave nothing out.
We need to compare it with our existing intel to understand if--
One.
There's just one thing I'm missing, Eve.
Maybe you and your friends can tell me, who knows...
Exactly how much longer do we have until the end of the world?

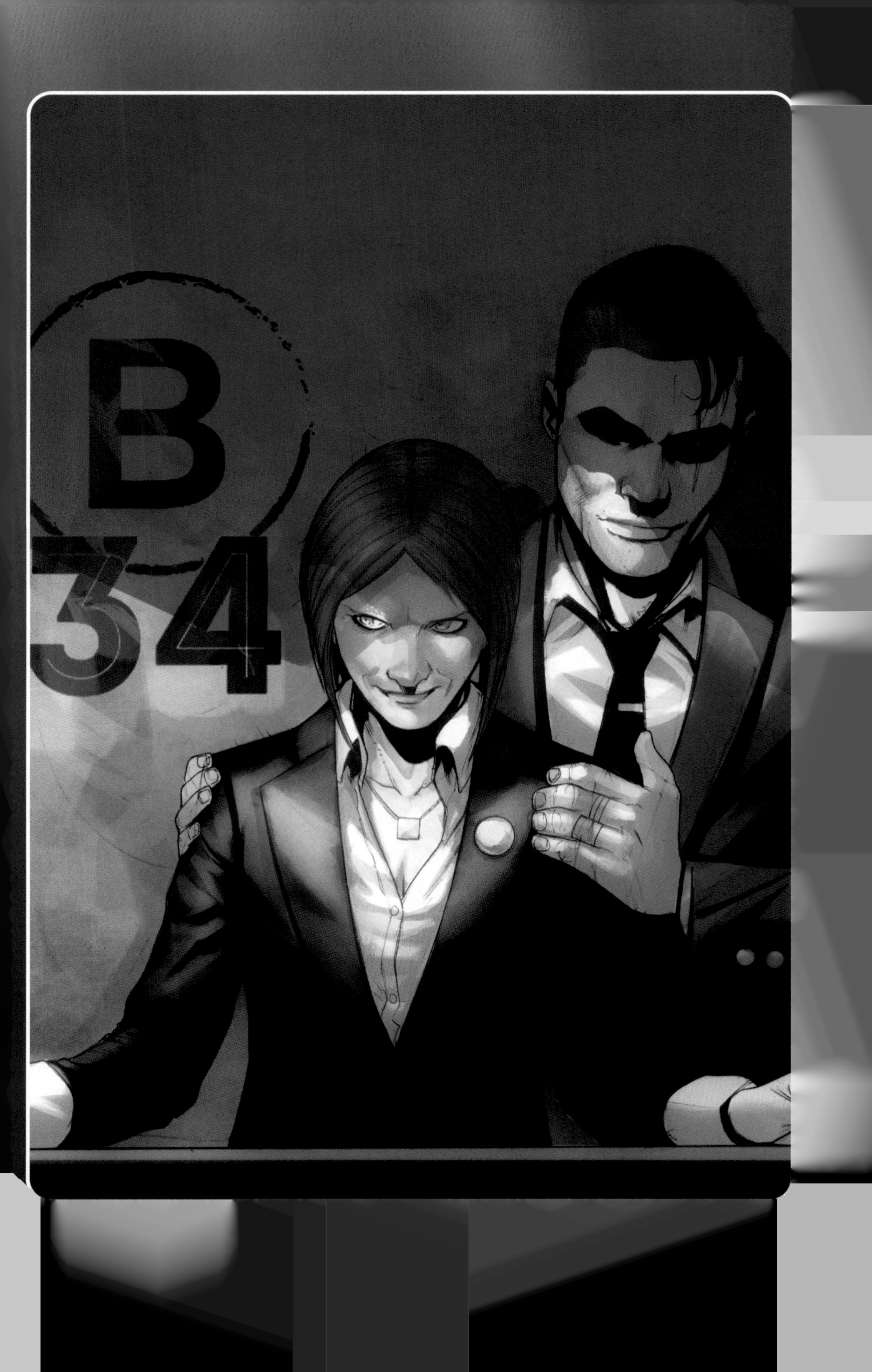
B
34

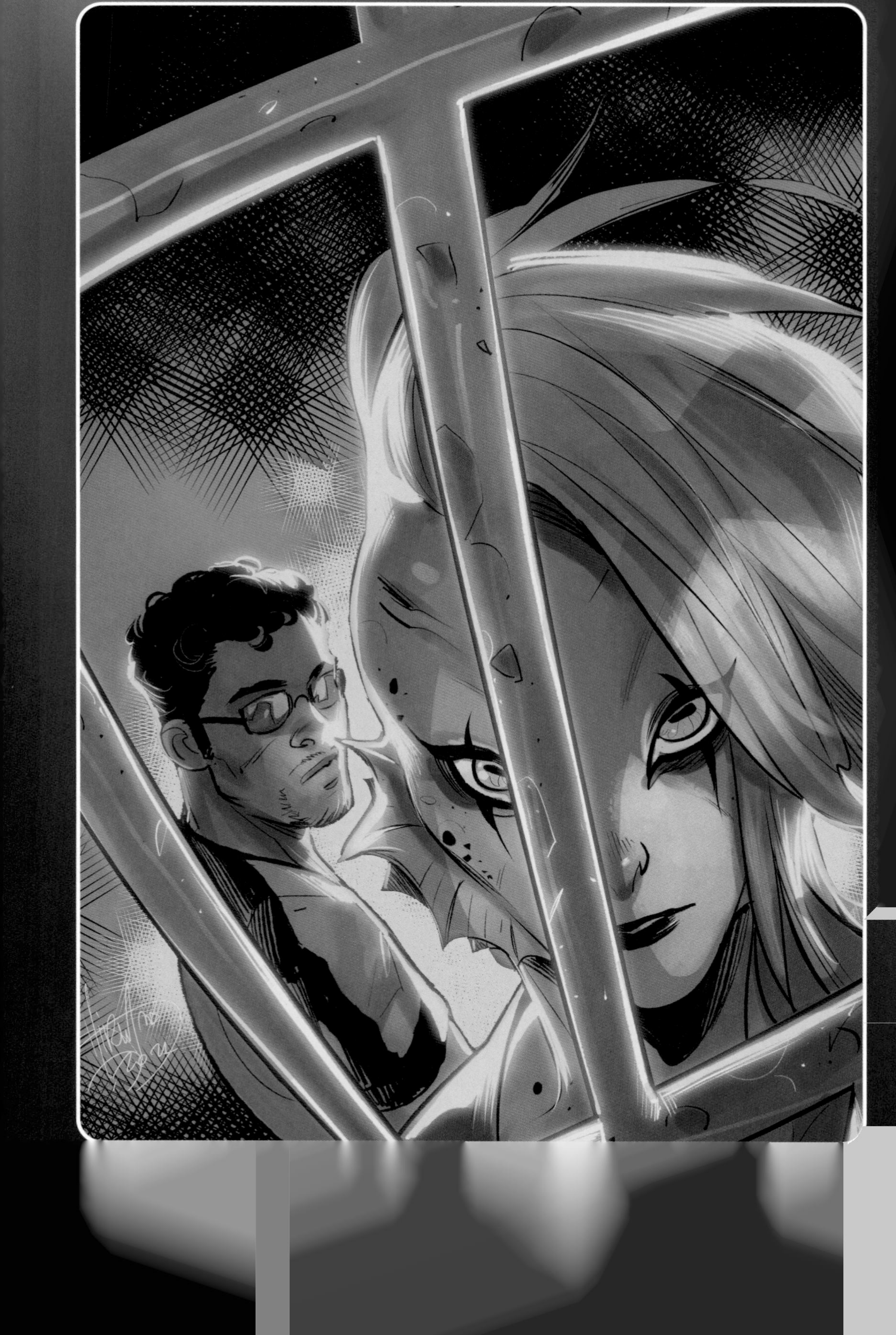

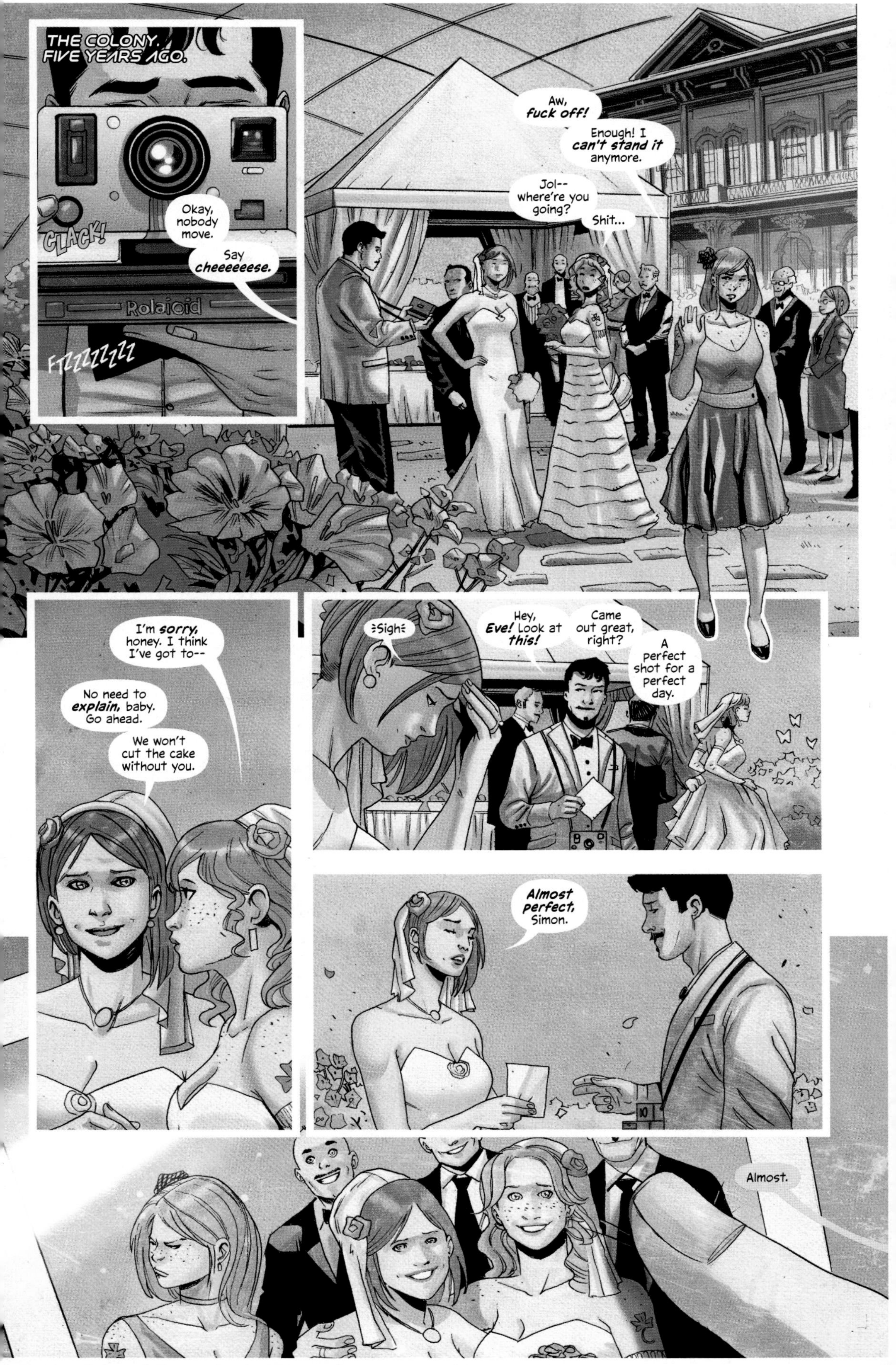
THE COLONY. FIVE YEARS AGO.
Okay, nobody move.
Say cheeeeeese.
CLACK!
Rolaioid
FTZZZZZZZ
Aw, fuck off!
Enough! I can't stand it anymore.
Jol-- where're you going?
Shit...
I'm sorry, honey. I think I've got to--
No need to explain, baby. Go ahead.
We won't cut the cake without you.
Sigh
Hey, Eve! Look at this!
Came out great, right?
A perfect shot for a perfect day.
Almost perfect, Simon.
Almost.

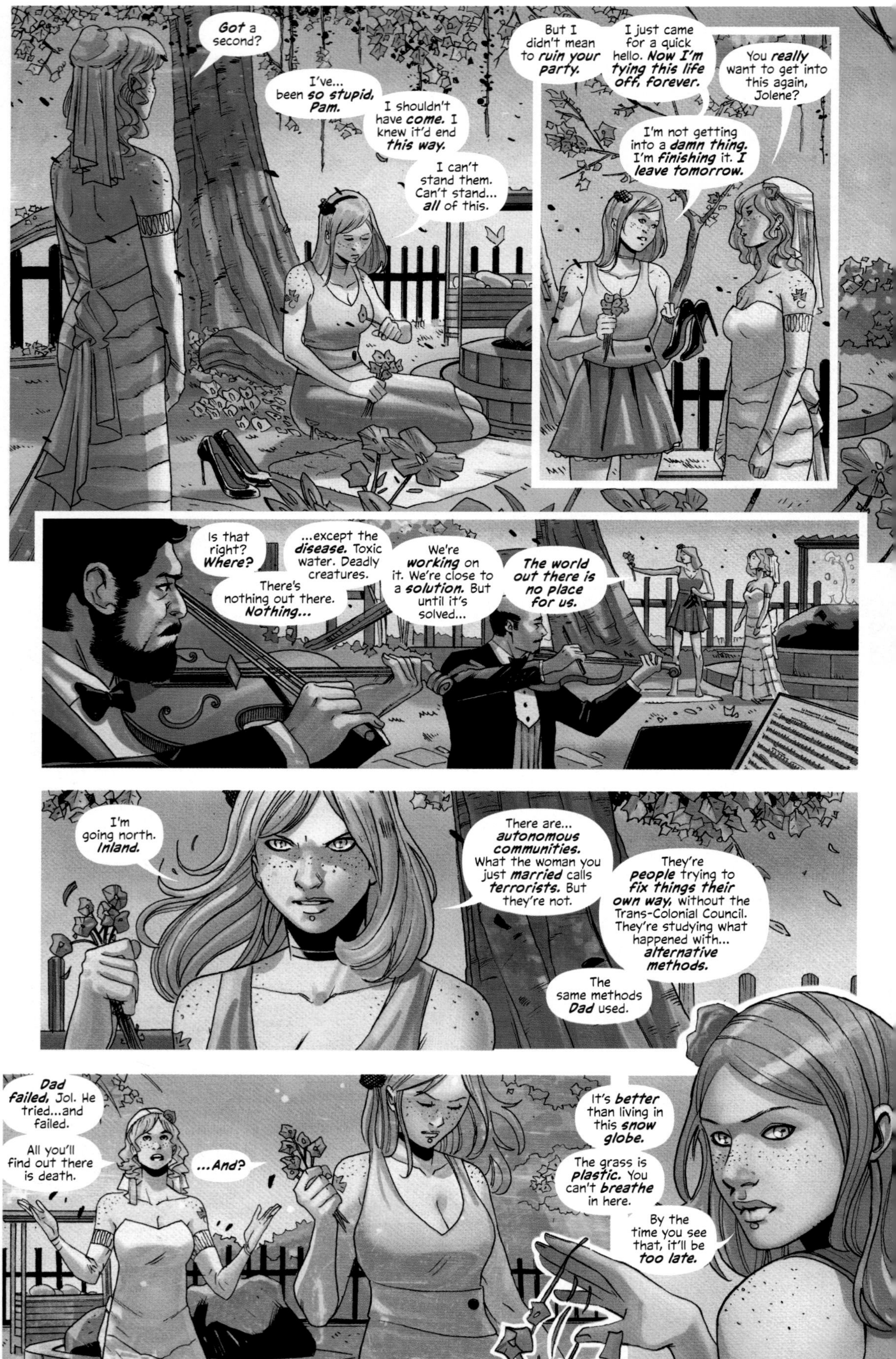
Got a second?
I've... been so stupid, Pam.
I shouldn't have come. I knew it'd end this way.
I can't stand them. Can't stand... all of this.
But I didn't mean to ruin your party.
I just came for a quick hello. Now I'm tying this life off, forever.
You really want to get into this again, Jolene?
I'm not getting into a damn thing. I'm finishing it. I leave tomorrow.
Is that right? Where?
There's nothing out there. Nothing...
...except the disease. Toxic water. Deadly creatures.
We're working on it. We're close to a solution. But until it's solved...
The world out there is no place for us.
I'm going north. Inland.
There are... autonomous communities. What the woman you just married calls terrorists. But they're not.
They're people trying to fix things their own way, without the Trans-Colonial Council. They're studying what happened with... alternative methods.
The same methods Dad used.
Dad failed, Jol. He tried...and failed.
All you'll find out there is death.
...And?
It's better than living in this snow globe.
The grass is plastic. You can't breathe in here.
By the time you see that, it'll be too late.

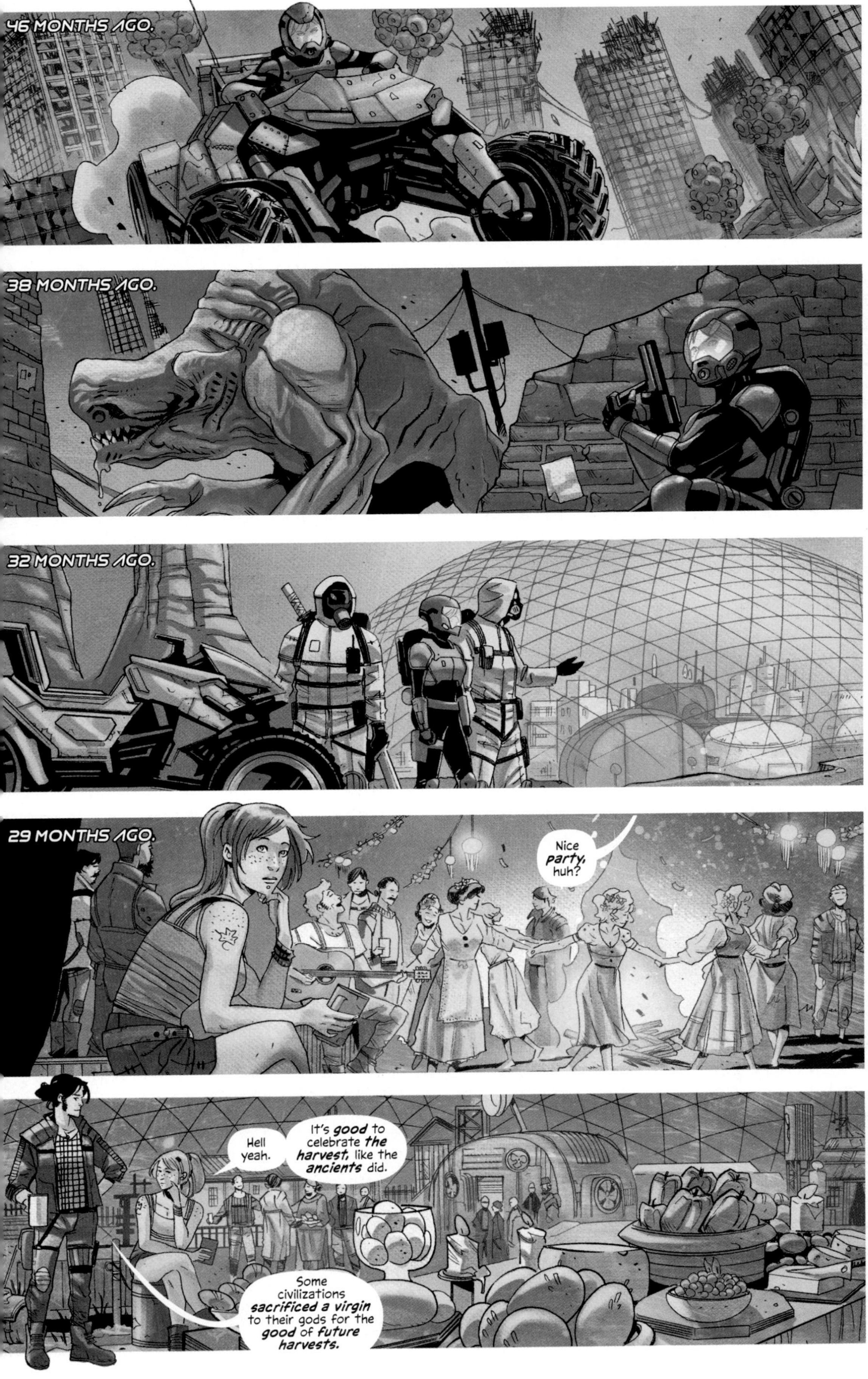
46 MONTHS AGO.
38 MONTHS AGO.
32 MONTHS AGO.
29 MONTHS AGO.
Nice party, huh?
Hell yeah.
It's good to celebrate the harvest, like the ancients did.
Some civilizations sacrificed a virgin to their gods for the good of future harvests.

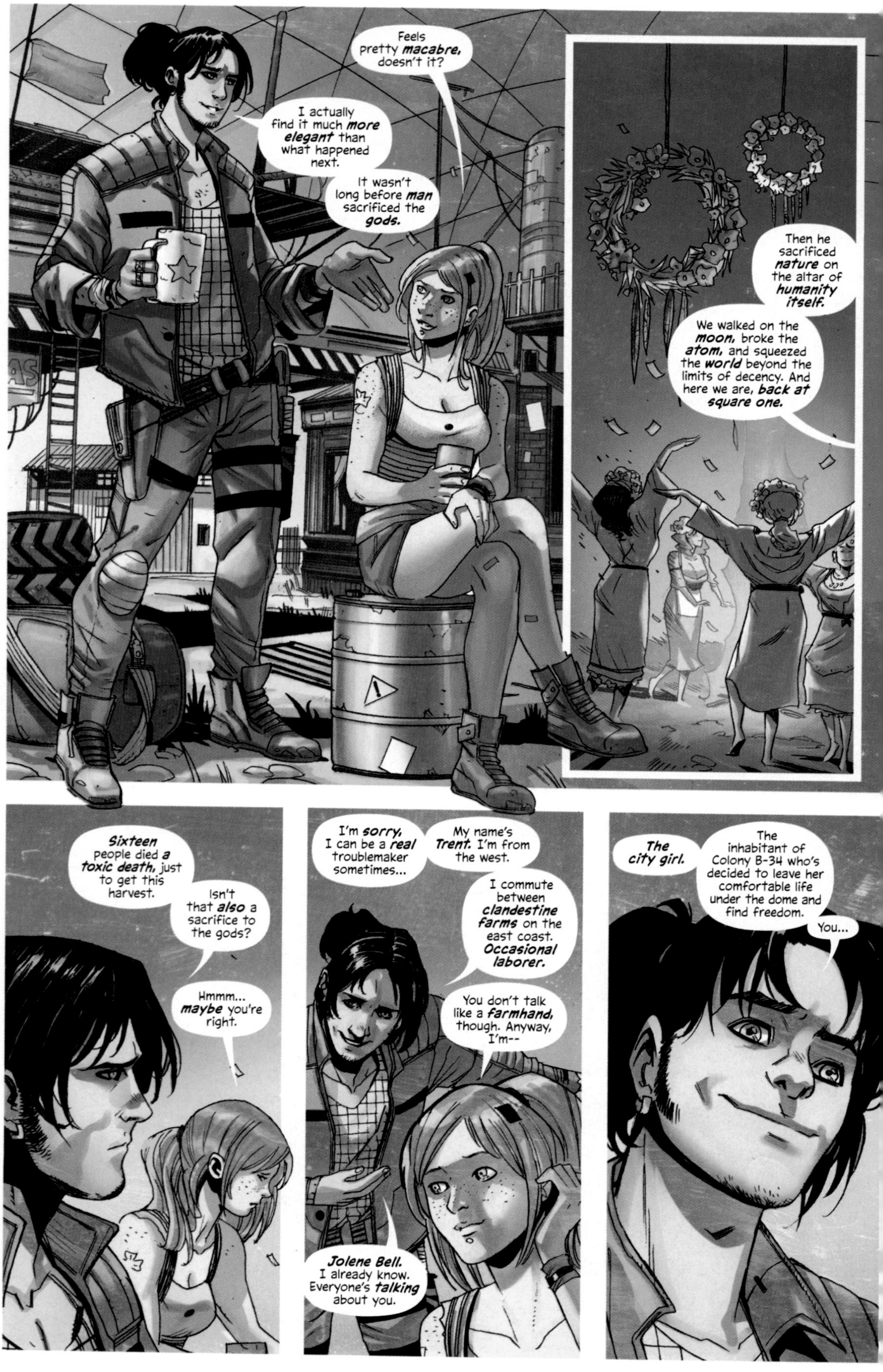
Feels pretty *macabre,* doesn't it?
I actually find it much *more elegant* than what happened next.
It wasn't long before *man* sacrificed the *gods.*
Then he sacrificed *nature* on the altar of *humanity itself.*
We walked on the *moon,* broke the *atom,* and squeezed the *world* beyond the limits of decency. And here we are, *back at square one.*
Sixteen people died *a toxic death,* just to get this harvest.
Isn't that *also* a sacrifice to the gods?
Hmmm... *maybe* you're right.
I'm *sorry,* I can be a *real* troublemaker sometimes...
My name's *Trent.* I'm from the west.
I commute between *clandestine farms* on the east coast. *Occasional laborer.*
You don't talk like a *farmhand,* though. Anyway, I'm--
Jolene Bell. I already know. Everyone's *talking* about you.
The city girl.
The inhabitant of Colony B-34 who's decided to leave her comfortable life under the dome and find freedom.
You...

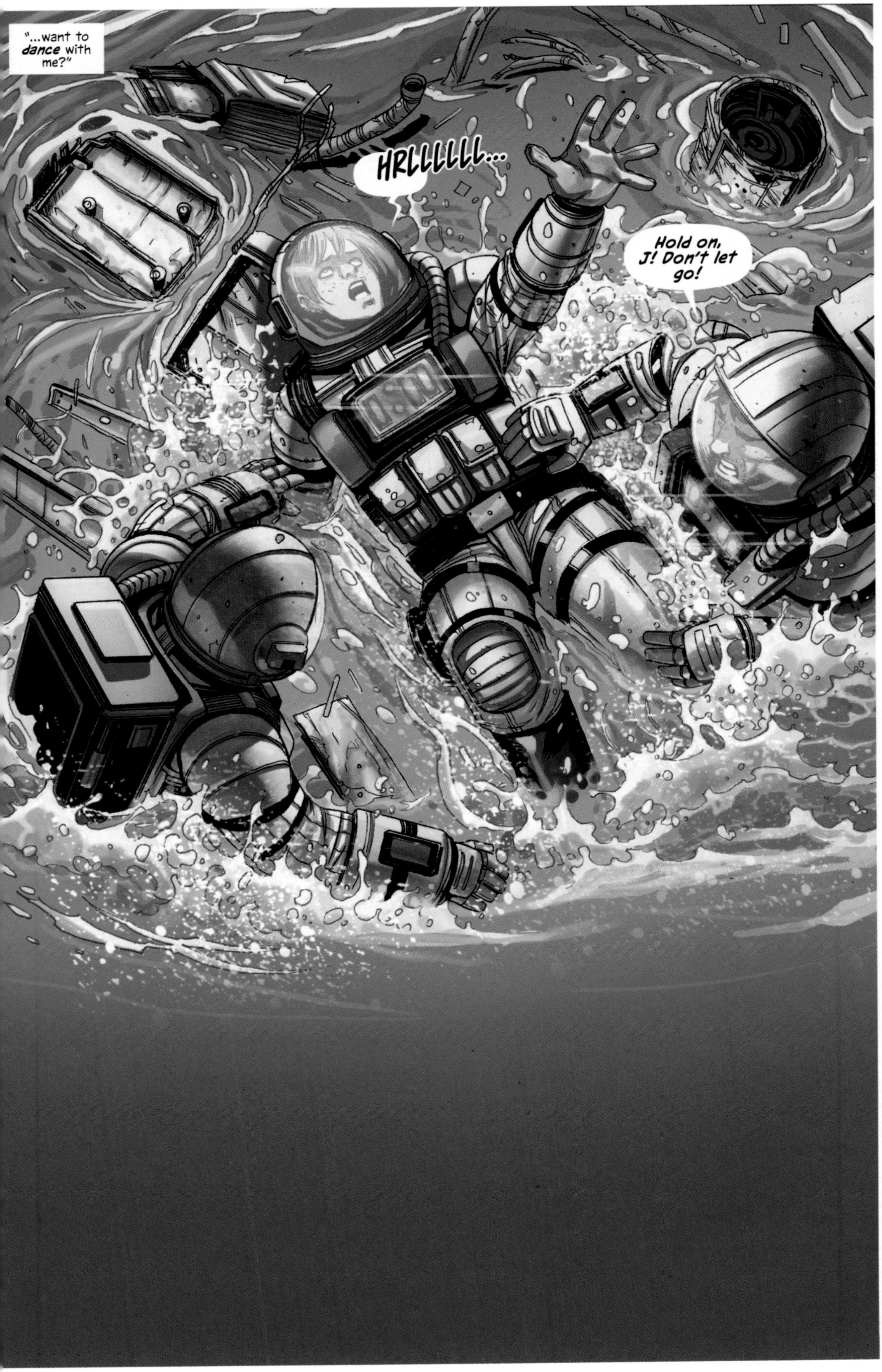
"...want to *dance* with me?"
HRLLLLLL...
Hold on, J! Don't let go!

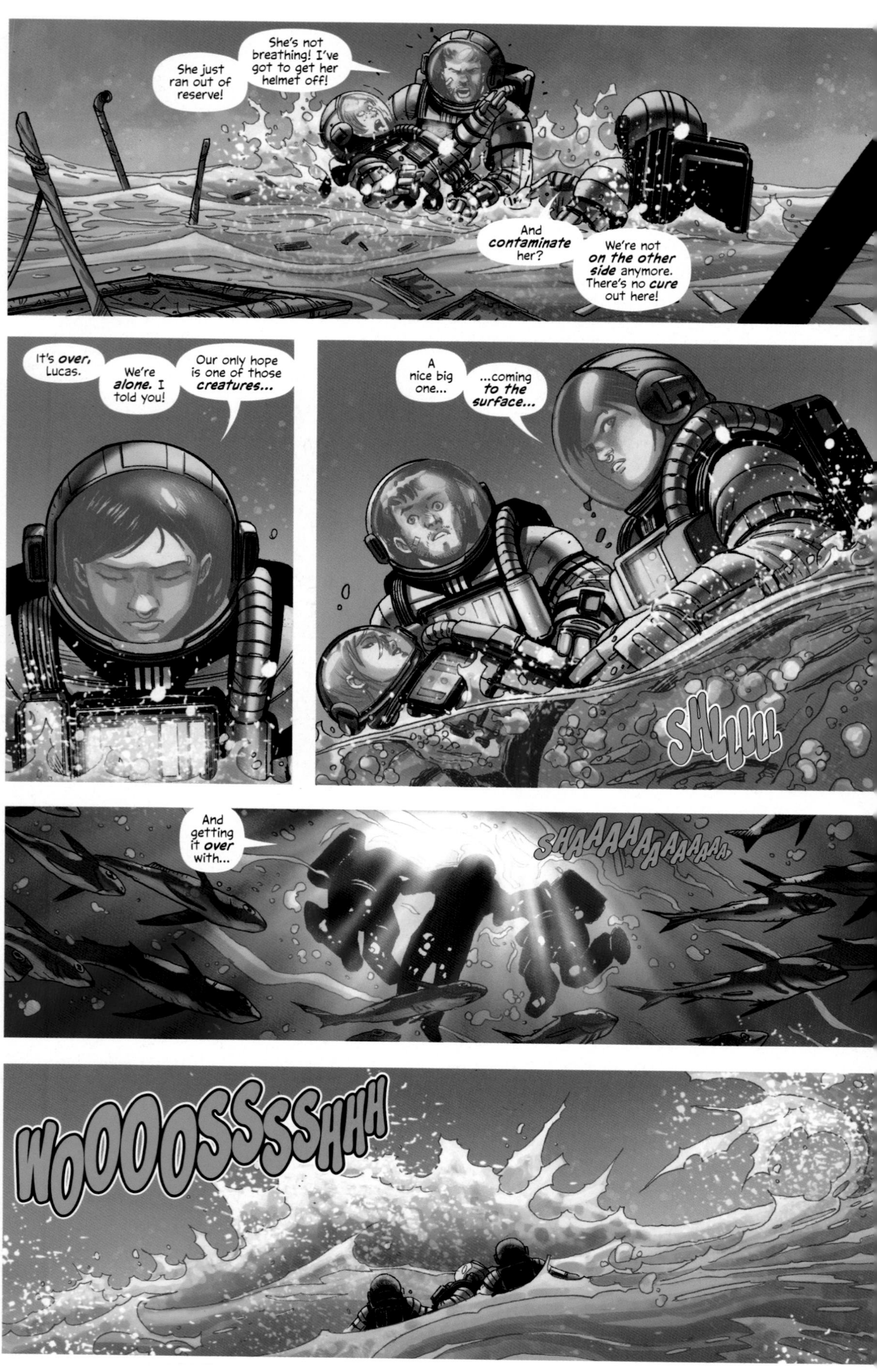
She just ran out of reserve!
She's not breathing! I've got to get her helmet off!
And contaminate her?
We're not on the other side anymore. There's no cure out here!
It's over, Lucas.
We're alone. I told you!
Our only hope is one of those creatures...
A nice big one...
...coming to the surface...
SHLLLLL
And getting it over with...
SHAAAAAAAAAAAA
WOOOOSSSSHHH

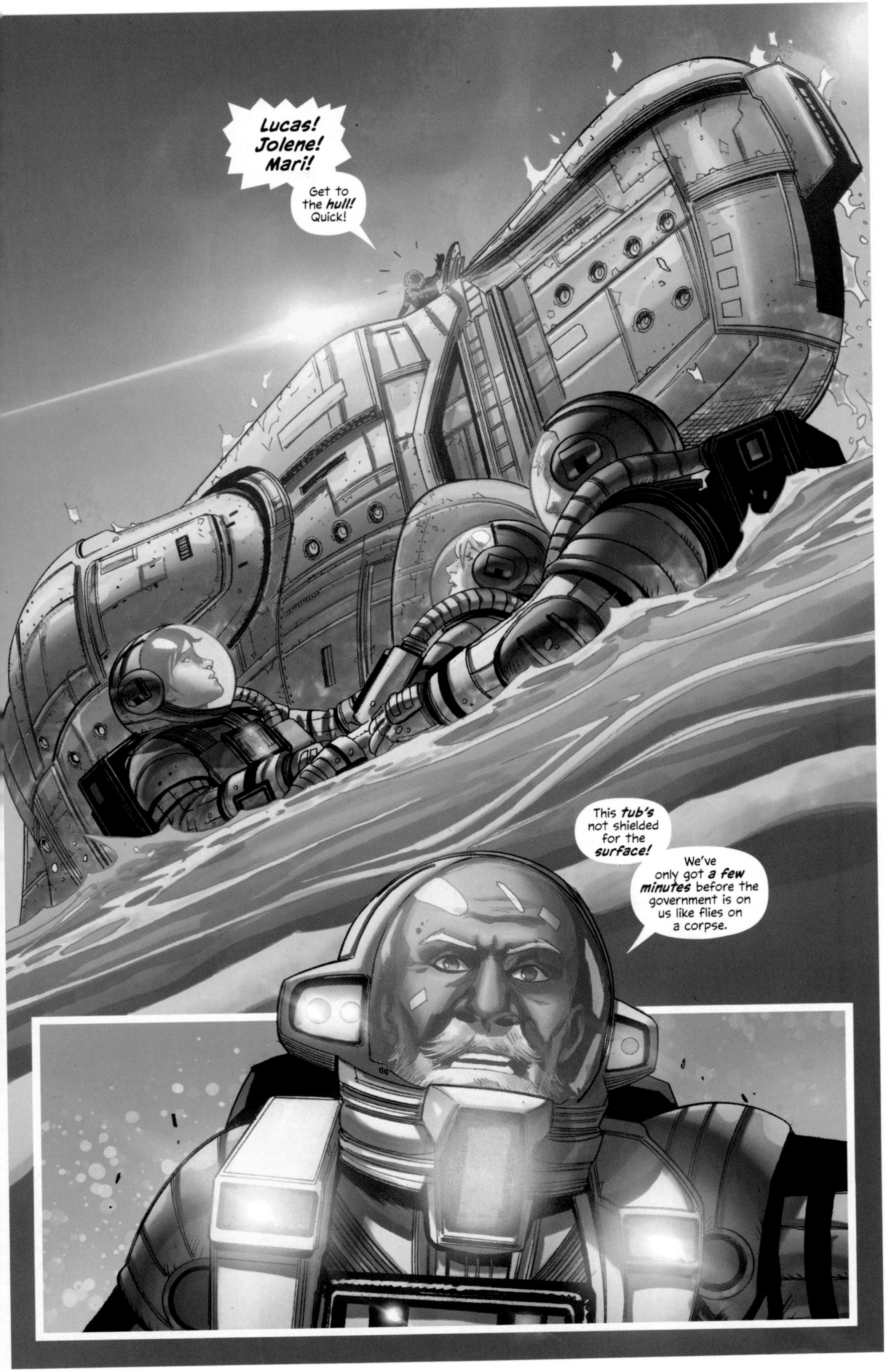
Lucas! Jolene! Mari!
Get to the hull! Quick!
This tub's not shielded for the surface!
We've only got a few minutes before the government is on us like flies on a corpse.

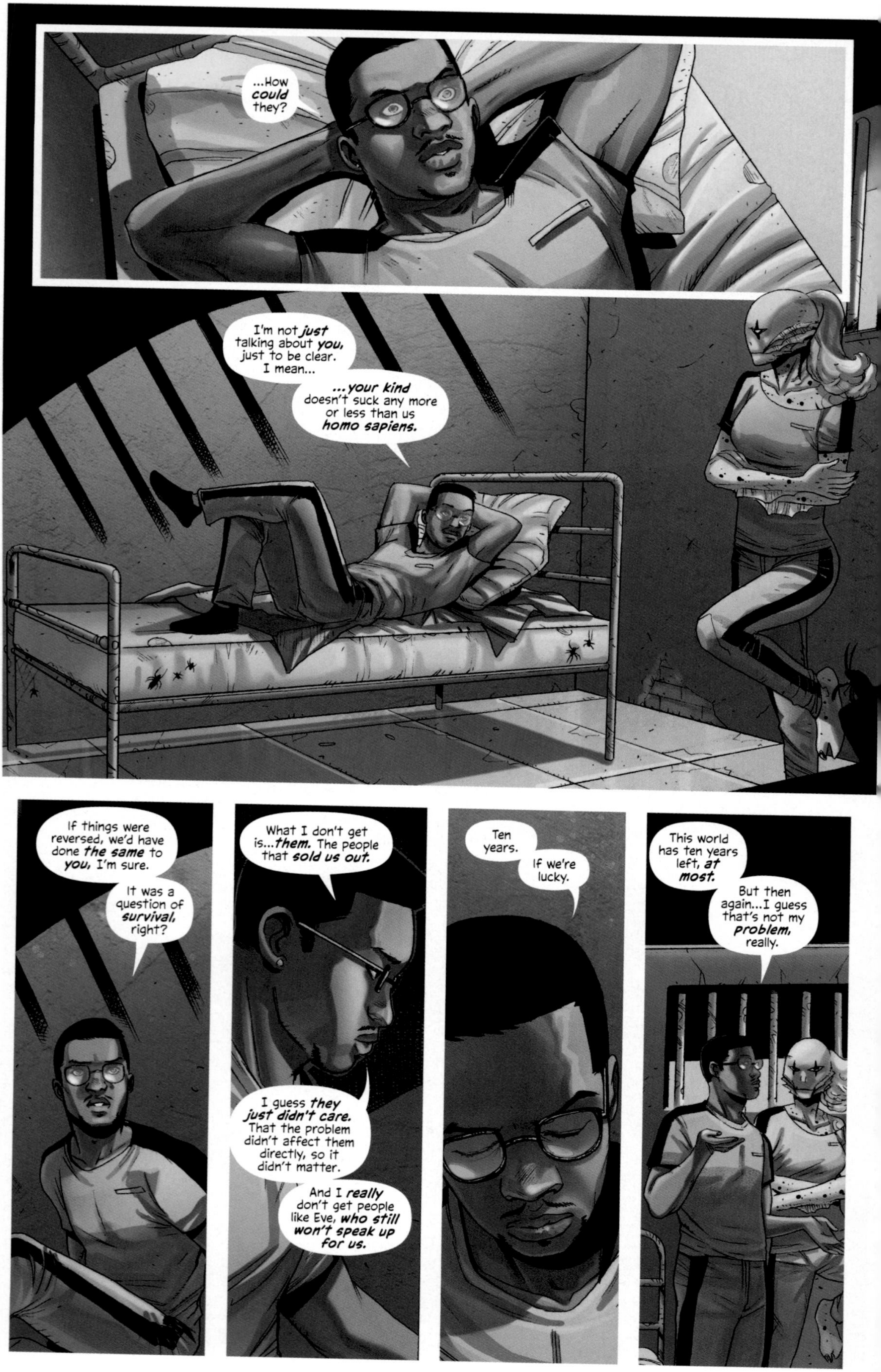
...How could they?
I'm not just talking about you, just to be clear. I mean...
...your kind doesn't suck any more or less than us homo sapiens.
If things were reversed, we'd have done the same to you, I'm sure.
It was a question of survival, right?
What I don't get is...them. The people that sold us out.
I guess they just didn't care. That the problem didn't affect them directly, so it didn't matter.
And I really don't get people like Eve, who still won't speak up for us.
Ten years.
If we're lucky.
This world has ten years left, at most.
But then again...I guess that's not my problem, really.

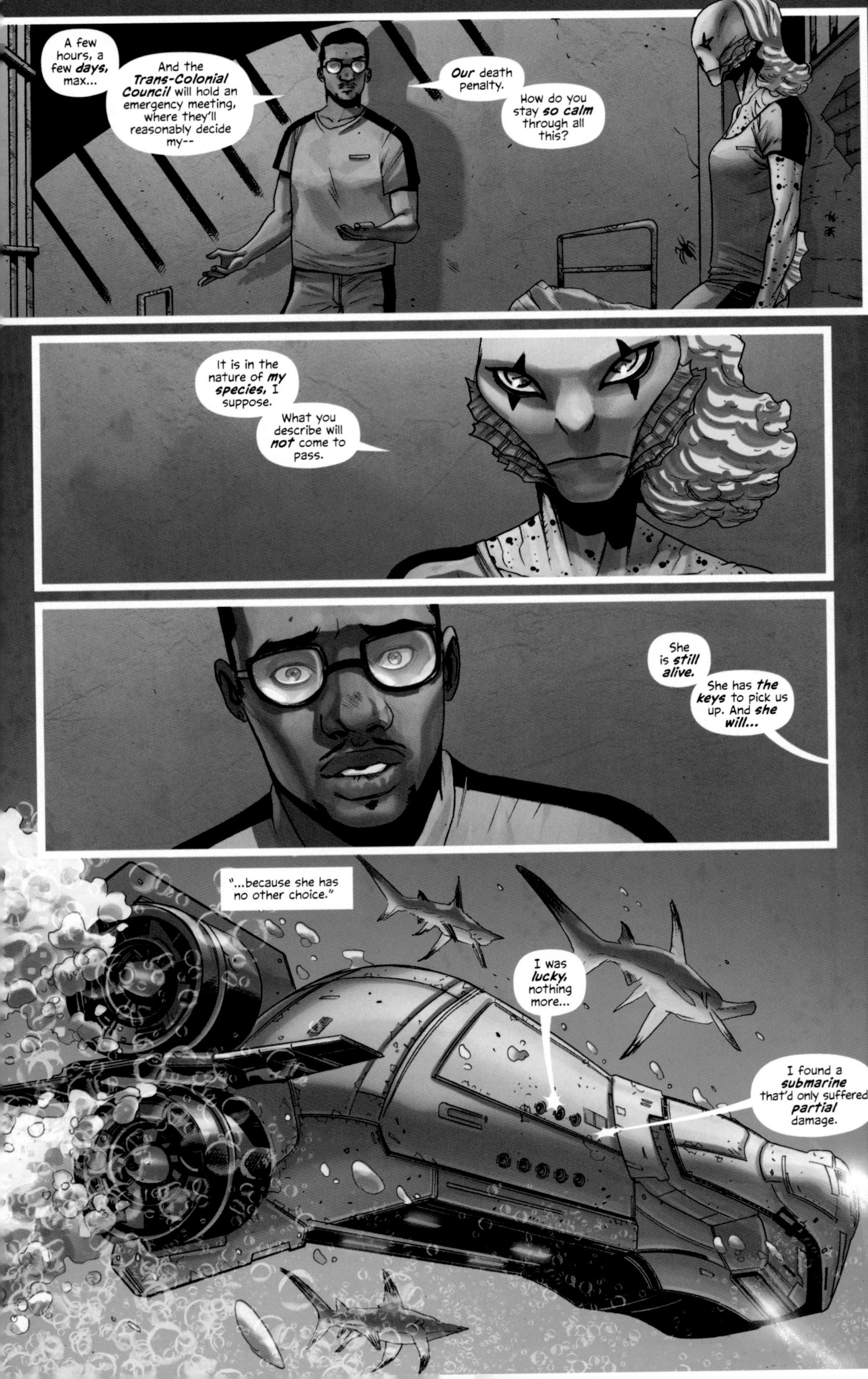
A few hours, a few *days,* max...
And the *Trans-Colonial Council* will hold an emergency meeting, where they'll reasonably decide my--
Our death penalty.
How do you stay *so calm* through all this?
It is in the nature of *my species,* I suppose.
What you describe will *not* come to pass.
She is *still alive.*
She has *the keys* to pick us up. And *she will...*
"...because she has no other choice."
I was *lucky,* nothing more...
I found a *submarine* that'd only suffered *partial* damage.

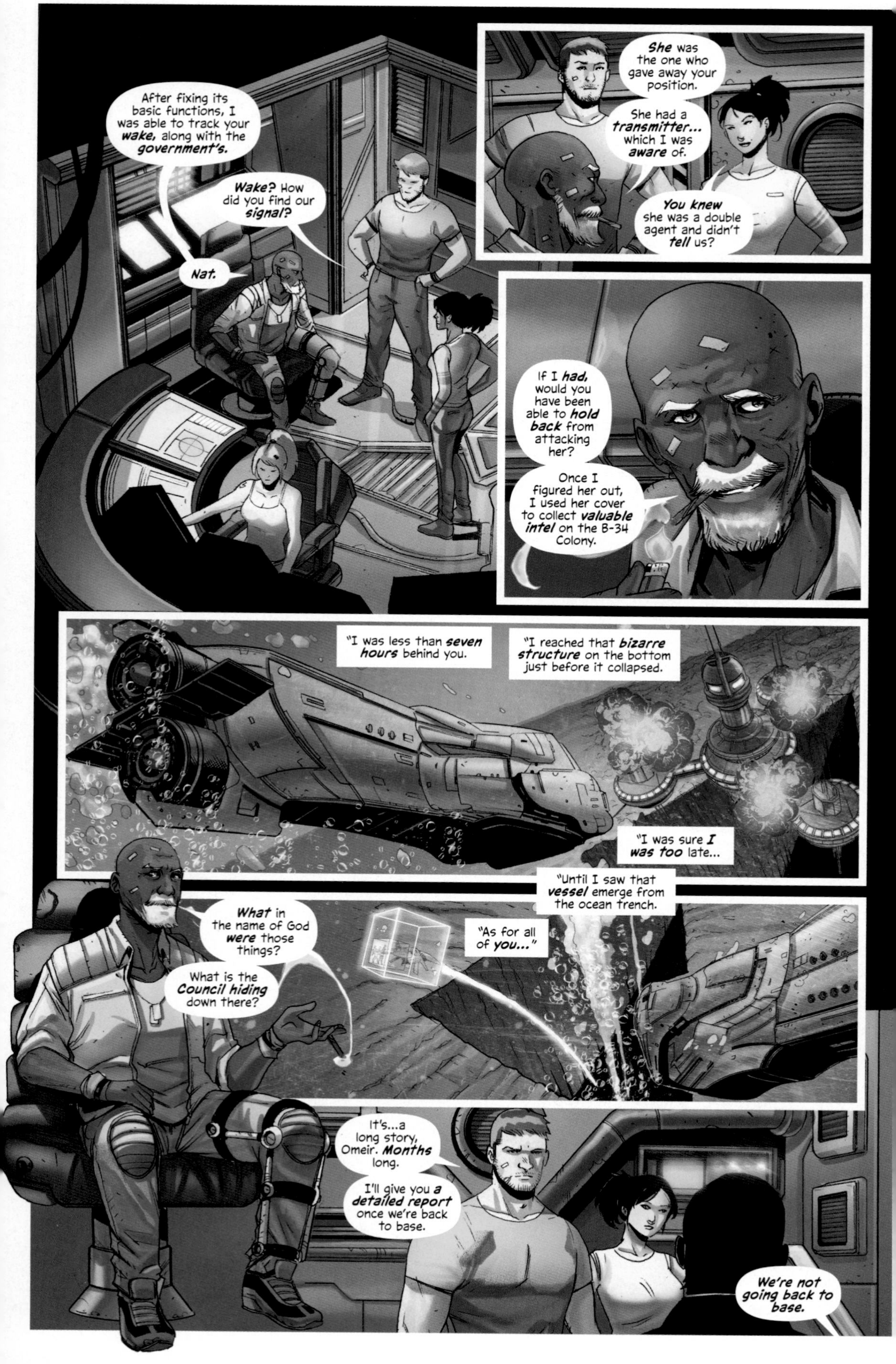
After fixing its basic functions, I was able to track your wake, along with the government's.
Wake? How did you find our signal?
Nat.
She was the one who gave away your position.
She had a transmitter... which I was aware of.
You knew she was a double agent and didn't tell us?
If I had, would you have been able to hold back from attacking her?
Once I figured her out, I used her cover to collect valuable intel on the B-34 Colony.
"I was less than seven hours behind you.
"I reached that bizarre structure on the bottom just before it collapsed.
"I was sure I was too late...
"Until I saw that vessel emerge from the ocean trench.
"As for all of you..."
What in the name of God were those things?
What is the Council hiding down there?
It's...a long story, Omeir. Months long.
I'll give you a detailed report once we're back to base.
We're not going back to base.

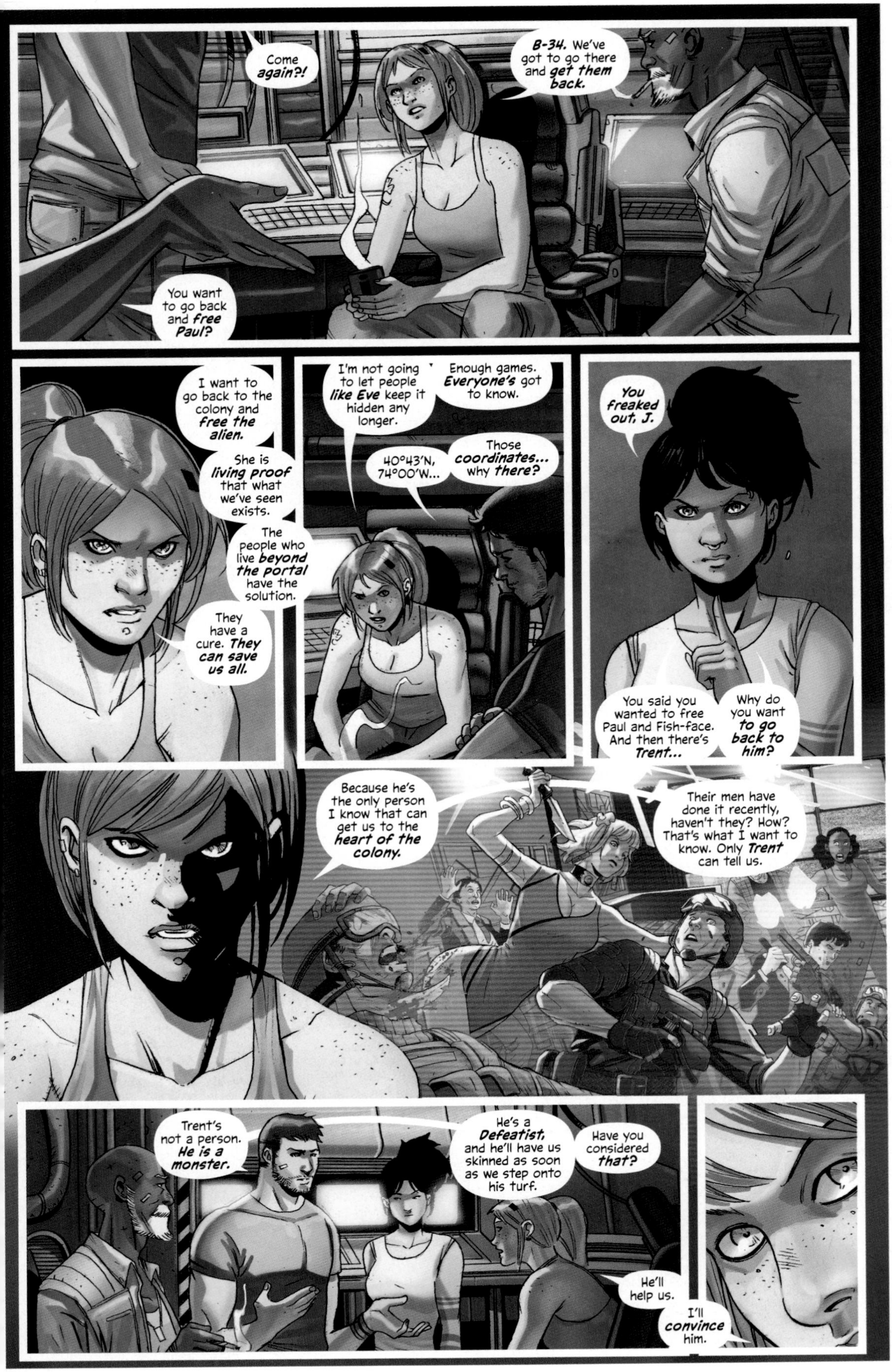

Come again?!
B-34. We've got to go there and get them back.
You want to go back and free Paul?
I want to go back to the colony and free the alien.
She is living proof that what we've seen exists.
The people who live beyond the portal have the solution.
They have a cure. They can save us all.
I'm not going to let people like Eve keep it hidden any longer.
Enough games. Everyone's got to know.
40°43'N, 74°00'W...
Those coordinates... why there?
You freaked out, J.
You said you wanted to free Paul and Fish-face. And then there's Trent...
Why do you want to go back to him?
Because he's the only person I know that can get us to the heart of the colony.
Their men have done it recently, haven't they? How? That's what I want to know. Only Trent can tell us.
Trent's not a person. He is a monster.
He's a Defeatist, and he'll have us skinned as soon as we step onto his turf.
Have you considered that?
He'll help us.
I'll convince him.

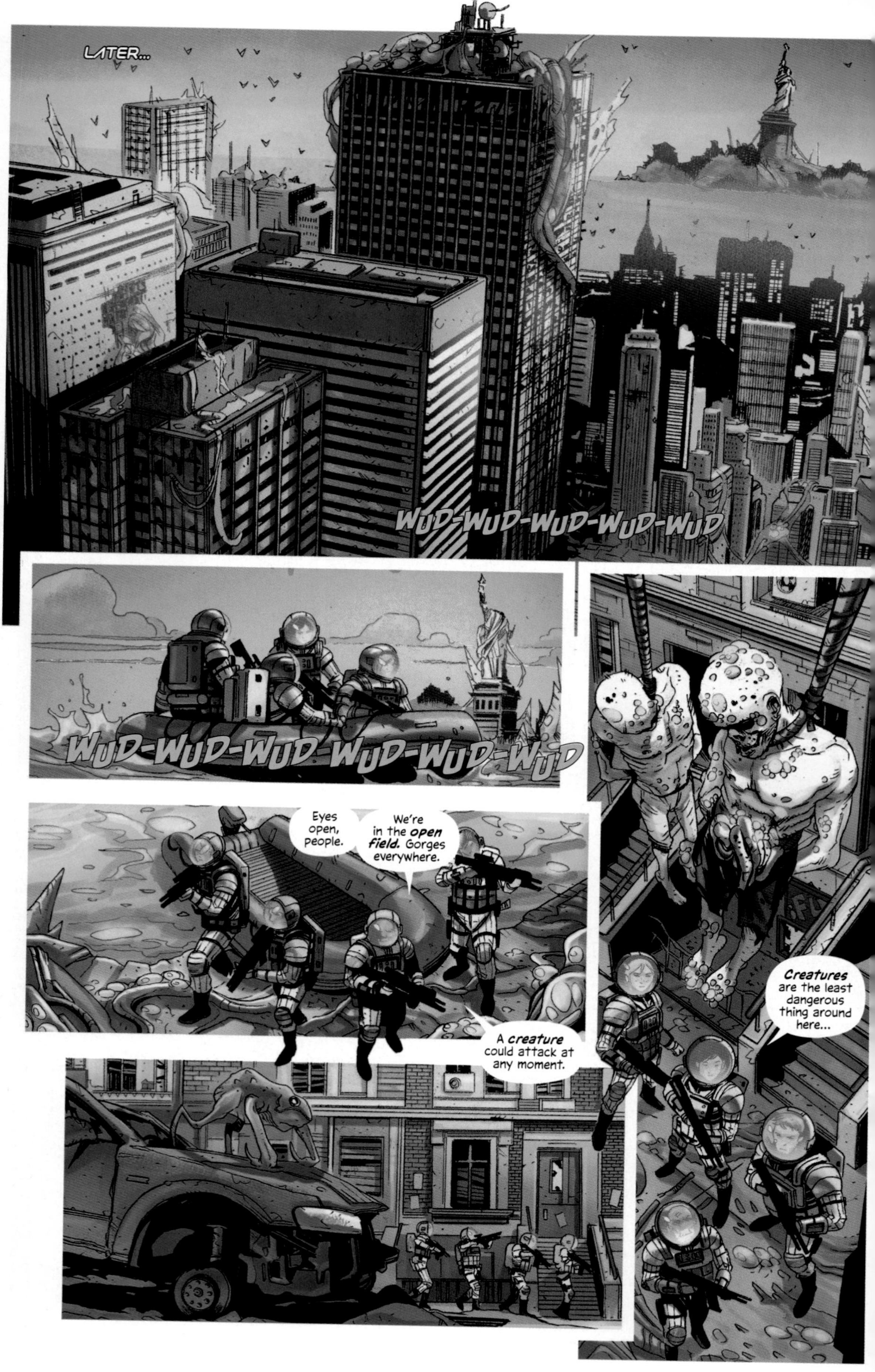

LATER...
WUD-WUD-WUD-WUD-WUD
WUD-WUD-WUD WUD-WUD-WUD
Eyes open, people.
We're in the *open field.* Gorges everywhere.
A *creature* could attack at any moment.
Creatures are the least dangerous thing around here...

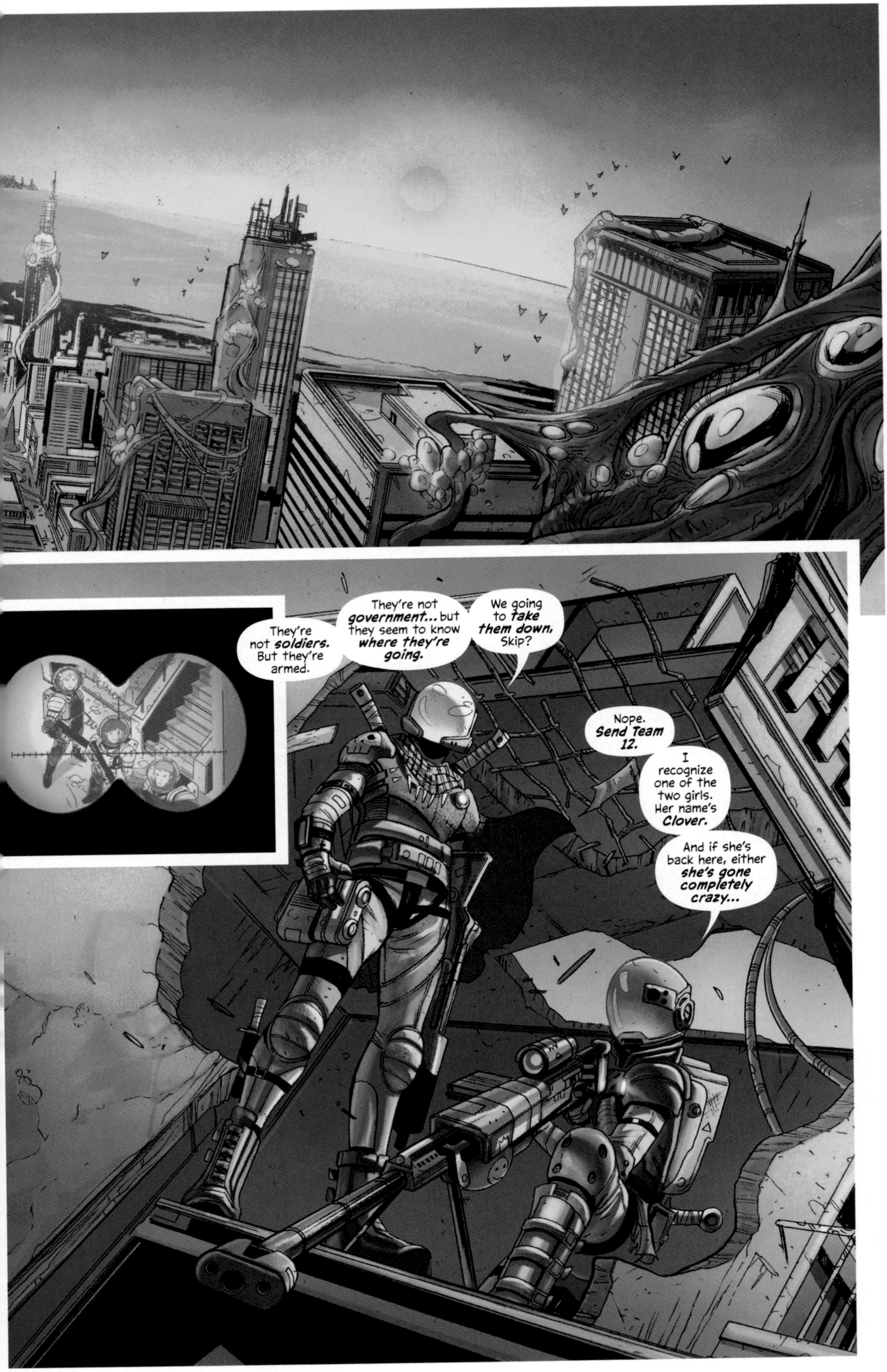
They're not *soldiers.* But they're armed.
They're not *government...* but they seem to know *where they're going.*
We going to *take them down,* Skip?
Nope. *Send Team 12.*
I recognize one of the two girls. Her name's *Clover.*
And if she's back here, either *she's gone completely crazy...*

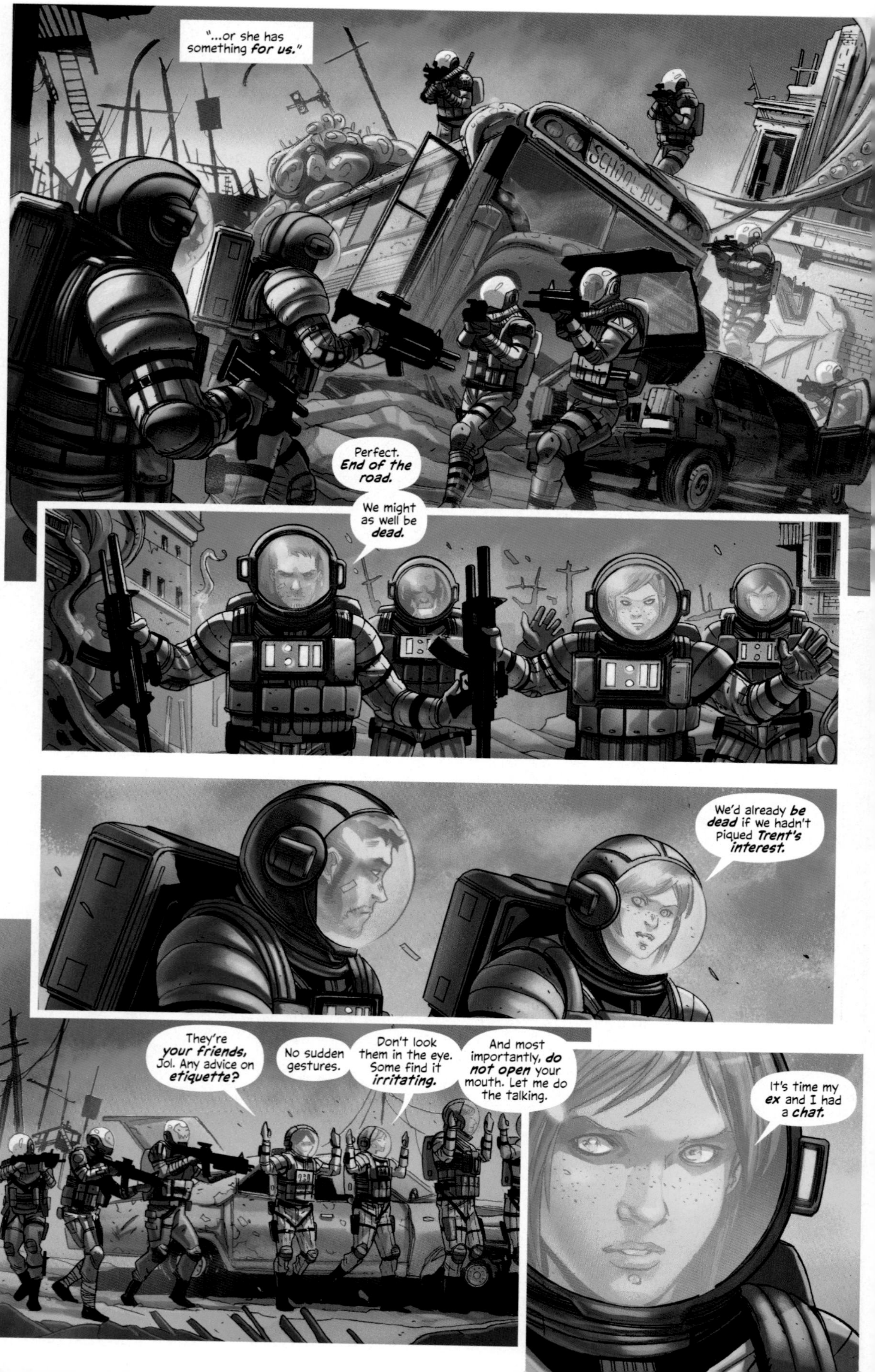
"...or she has something *for us.*"
Perfect. ***End of the road.***
We might as well be ***dead.***
We'd already ***be dead*** if we hadn't piqued ***Trent's interest.***
They're ***your friends,*** Jol. Any advice on ***etiquette?***
No sudden gestures.
Don't look them in the eye. Some find it ***irritating.***
And most importantly, ***do not open*** your mouth. Let me do the talking.
It's time my ***ex*** and I had a ***chat.***

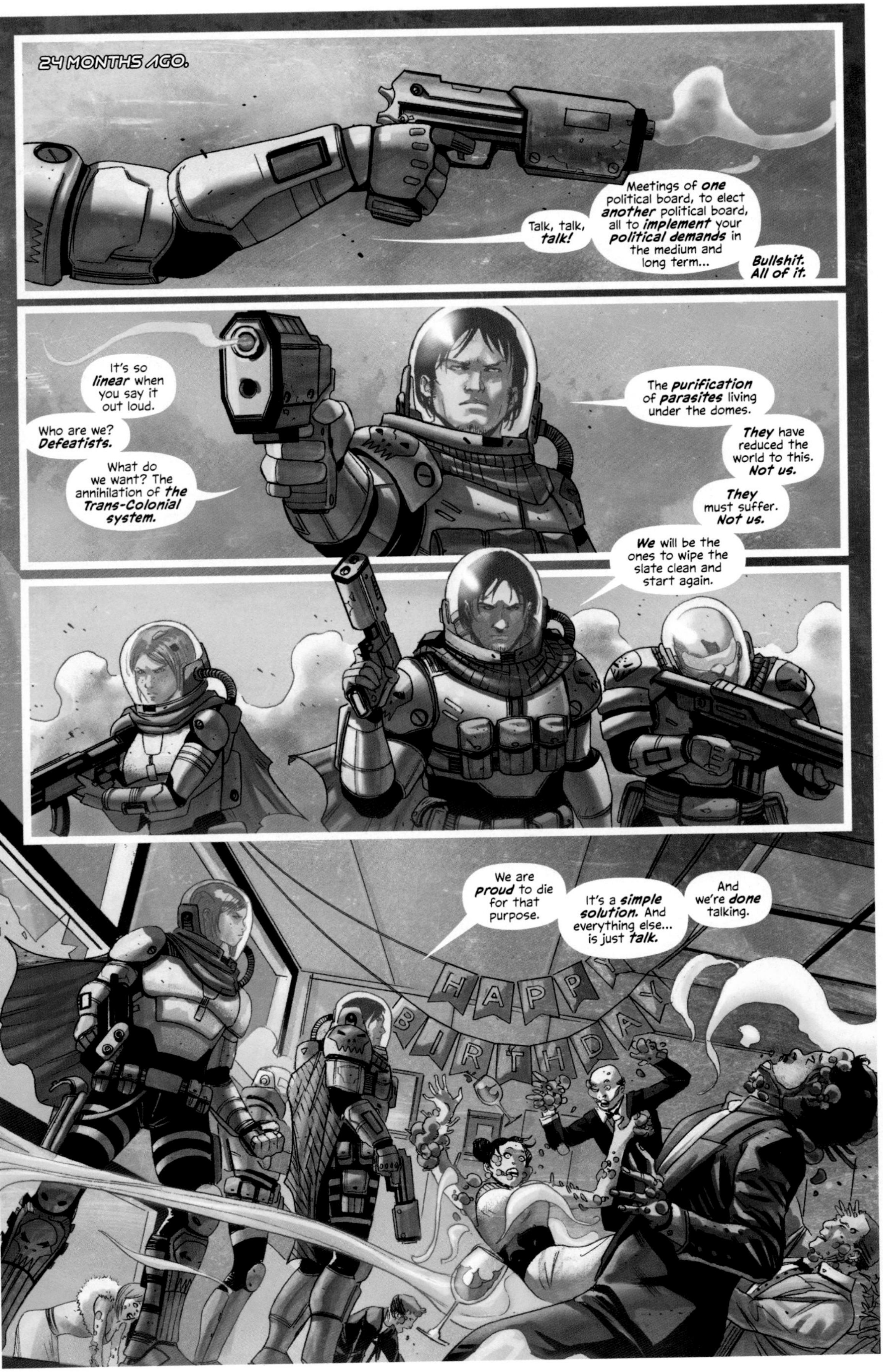
24 MONTHS AGO.
Talk, talk, talk!
Meetings of one political board, to elect another political board, all to implement your political demands in the medium and long term...
Bullshit. All of it.
It's so linear when you say it out loud.
Who are we? Defeatists.
What do we want? The annihilation of the Trans-Colonial system.
The purification of parasites living under the domes.
They have reduced the world to this. Not us.
They must suffer. Not us.
We will be the ones to wipe the slate clean and start again.
We are proud to die for that purpose.
It's a simple solution. And everything else... is just talk.
And we're done talking.
HAPPY BIRTHDAY

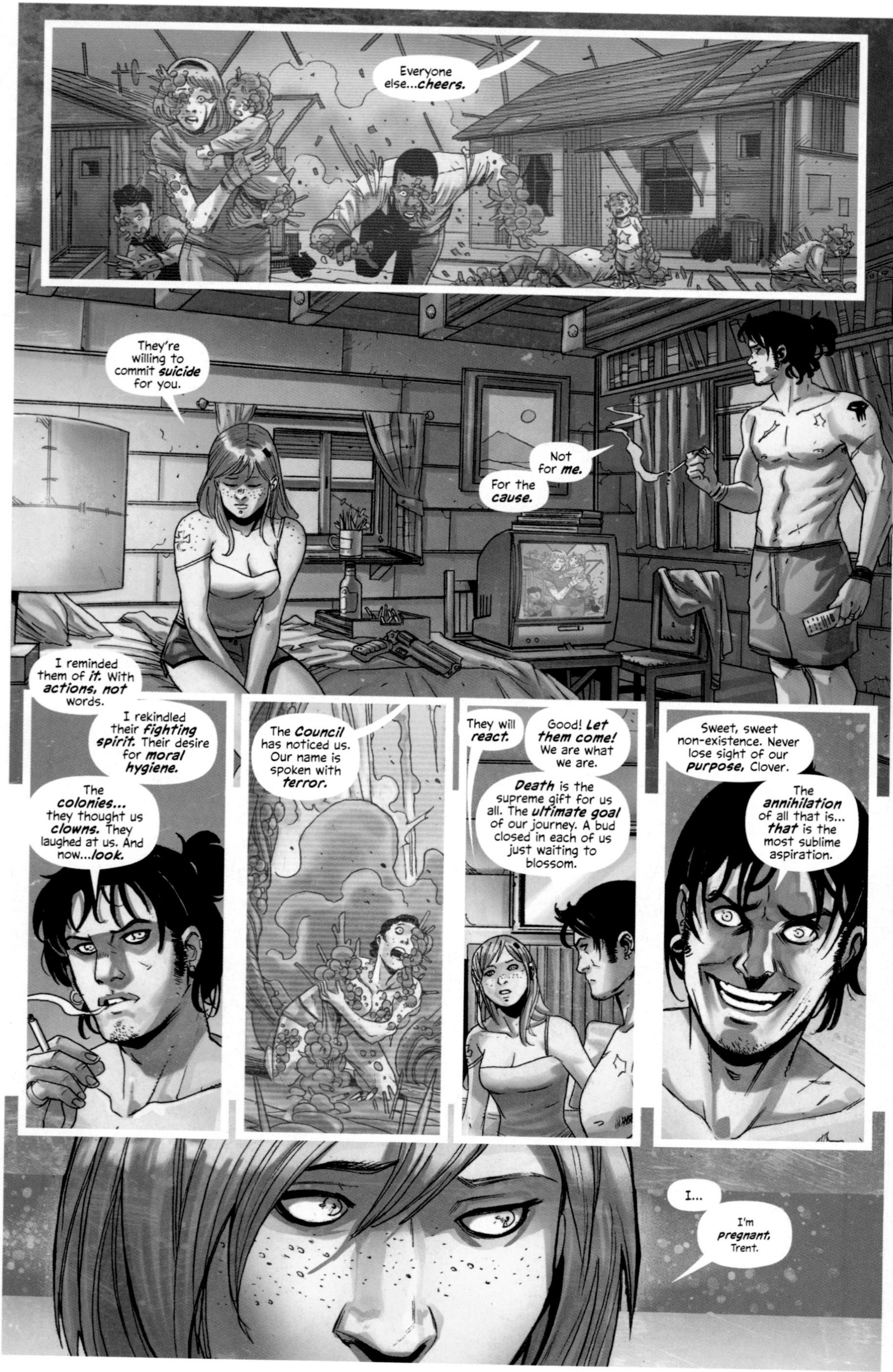
Everyone else...*cheers.*
They're willing to commit *suicide* for you.
Not for *me.*
For the *cause.*
I reminded them of *it.* With *actions, not* words.
I rekindled their *fighting spirit.* Their desire for *moral hygiene.*
The *colonies...* they thought us *clowns.* They laughed at us. And now...*look.*
The *Council* has noticed us. Our name is spoken with *terror.*
They will *react.*
Good! *Let them come!* We are what we are.
Death is the supreme gift for us all. The *ultimate goal* of our journey. A bud closed in each of us just waiting to blossom.
Sweet, sweet non-existence. Never lose sight of our *purpose,* Clover.
The *annihilation* of all that is... *that* is the most sublime aspiration.
I...
I'm *pregnant,* Trent.

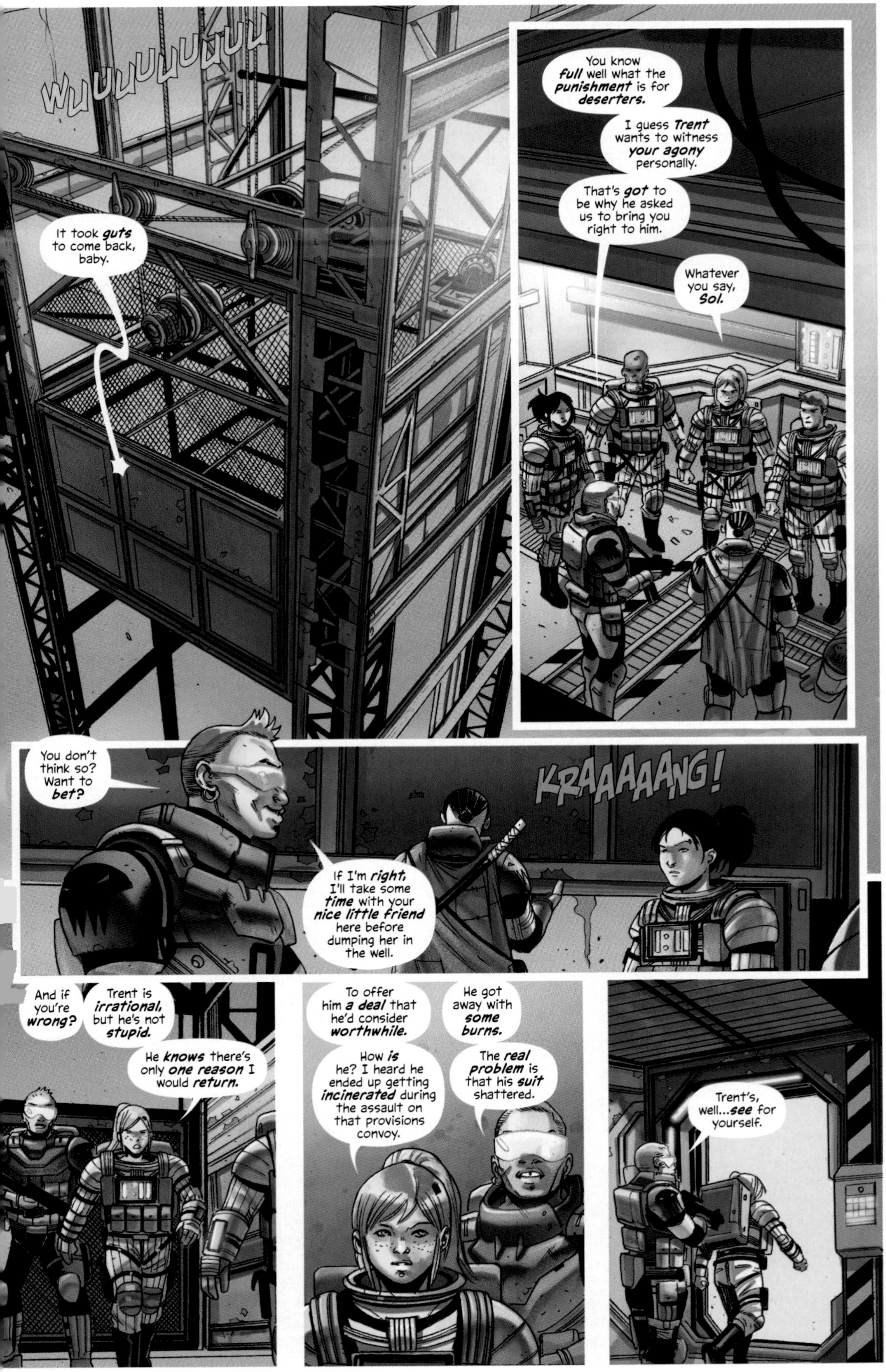
WUUUUUUUUU
It took guts to come back, baby.
You know full well what the punishment is for deserters.
I guess Trent wants to witness your agony personally.
That's got to be why he asked us to bring you right to him.
Whatever you say, Sol.
You don't think so? Want to bet?
KRAAAAANG!
If I'm right, I'll take some time with your nice little friend here before dumping her in the well.
And if you're wrong?
Trent is irrational, but he's not stupid.
He knows there's only one reason I would return.
To offer him a deal that he'd consider worthwhile.
How is he? I heard he ended up getting incinerated during the assault on that provisions convoy.
He got away with some burns.
The real problem is that his suit shattered.
Trent's, well...see for yourself.

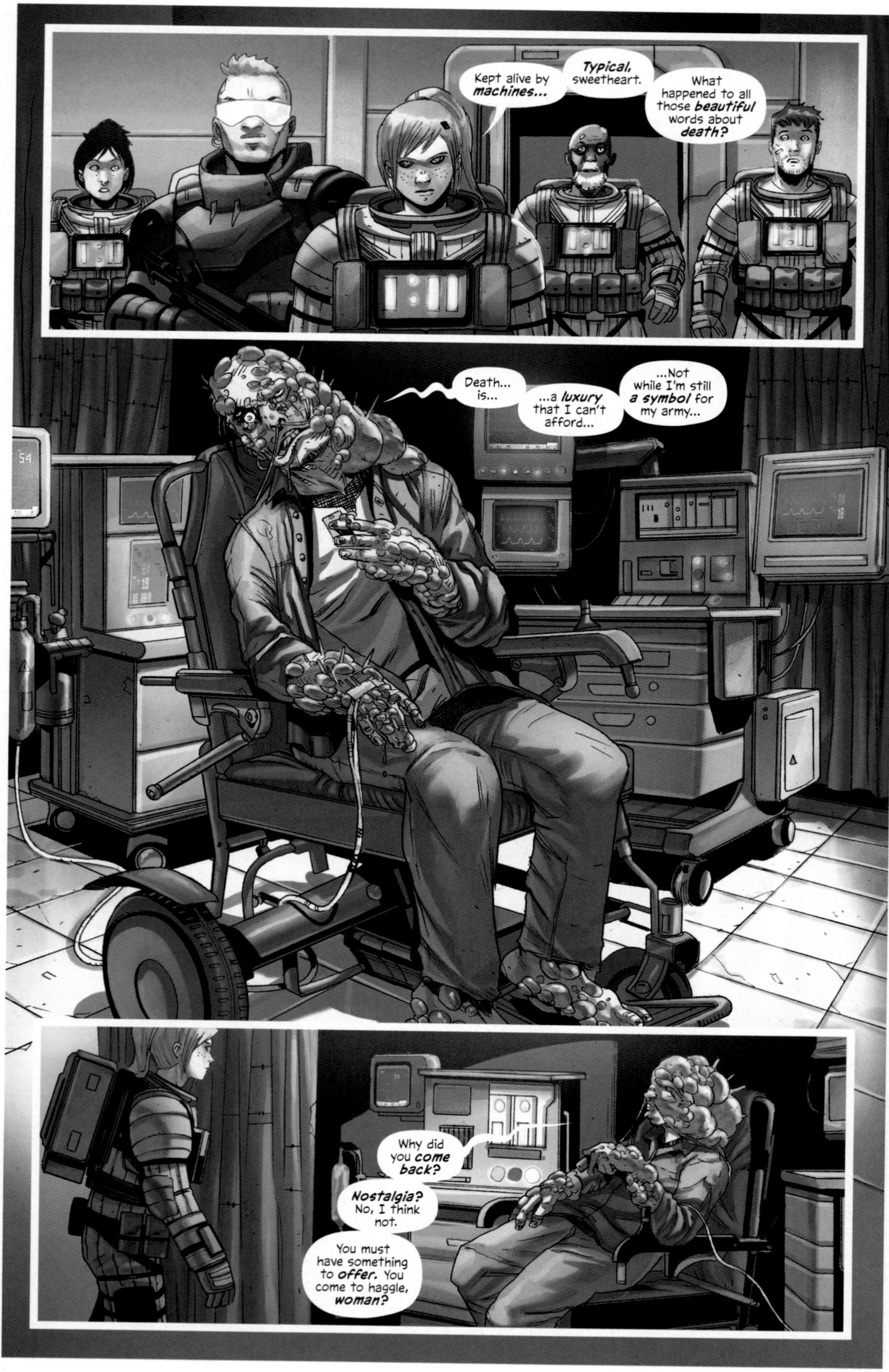
Kept alive by *machines...*
Typical, sweetheart.
What happened to all those *beautiful* words about *death?*
Death... is...
...a *luxury* that I can't afford...
...Not while I'm still *a symbol* for my army...
Why did you *come back?*
Nostalgia? No, I think not.
You must have something to *offer.* You come to haggle, *woman?*

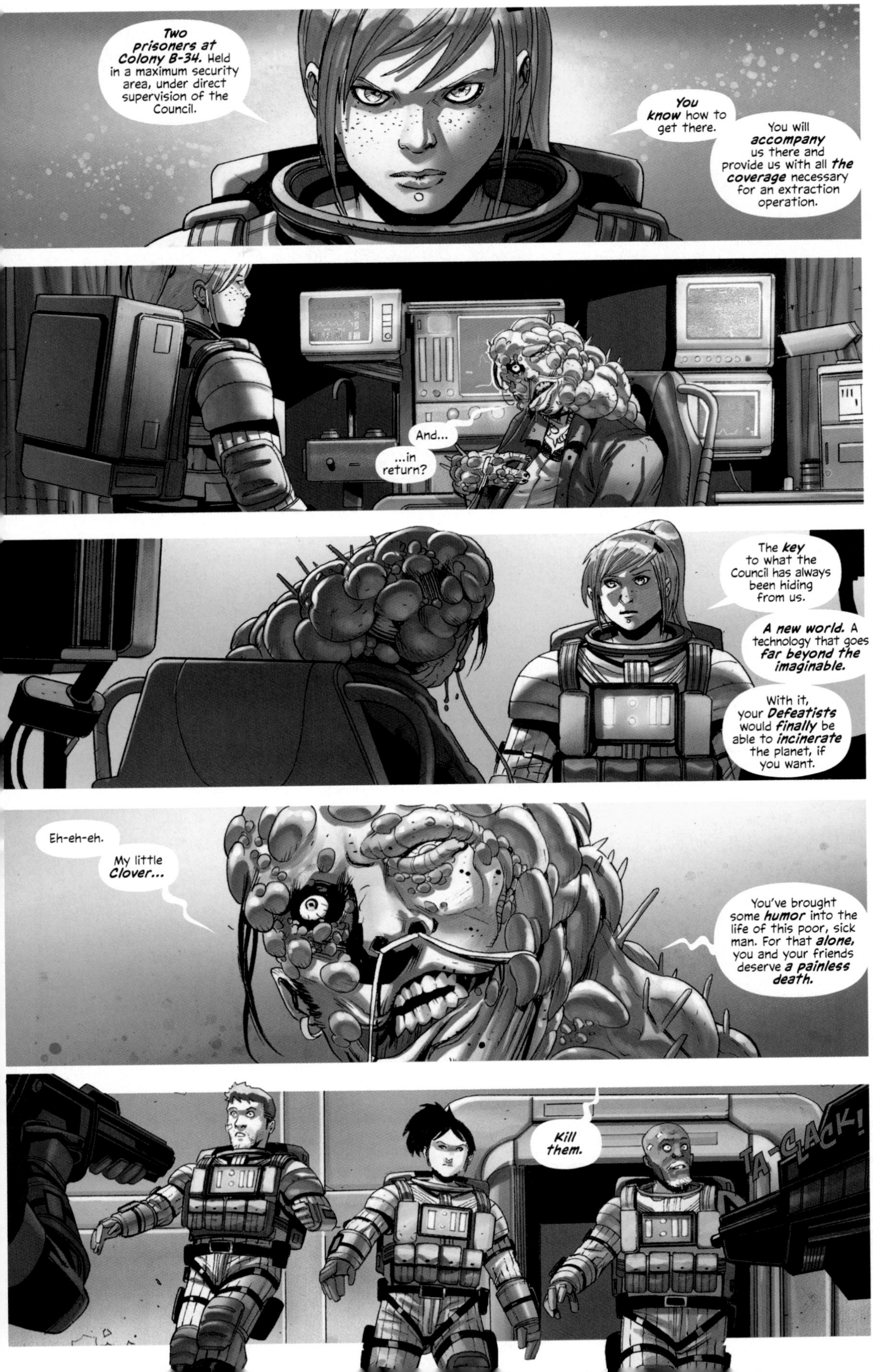
Two prisoners at Colony B-34. Held in a maximum security area, under direct supervision of the Council.
You know how to get there.
You will accompany us there and provide us with all the coverage necessary for an extraction operation.
And...
...in return?
The key to what the Council has always been hiding from us.
A new world. A technology that goes far beyond the imaginable.
With it, your Defeatists would finally be able to incinerate the planet, if you want.
Eh-eh-eh.
My little Clover...
You've brought some humor into the life of this poor, sick man. For that alone, you and your friends deserve a painless death.
Kill them.
TA-CLACK!

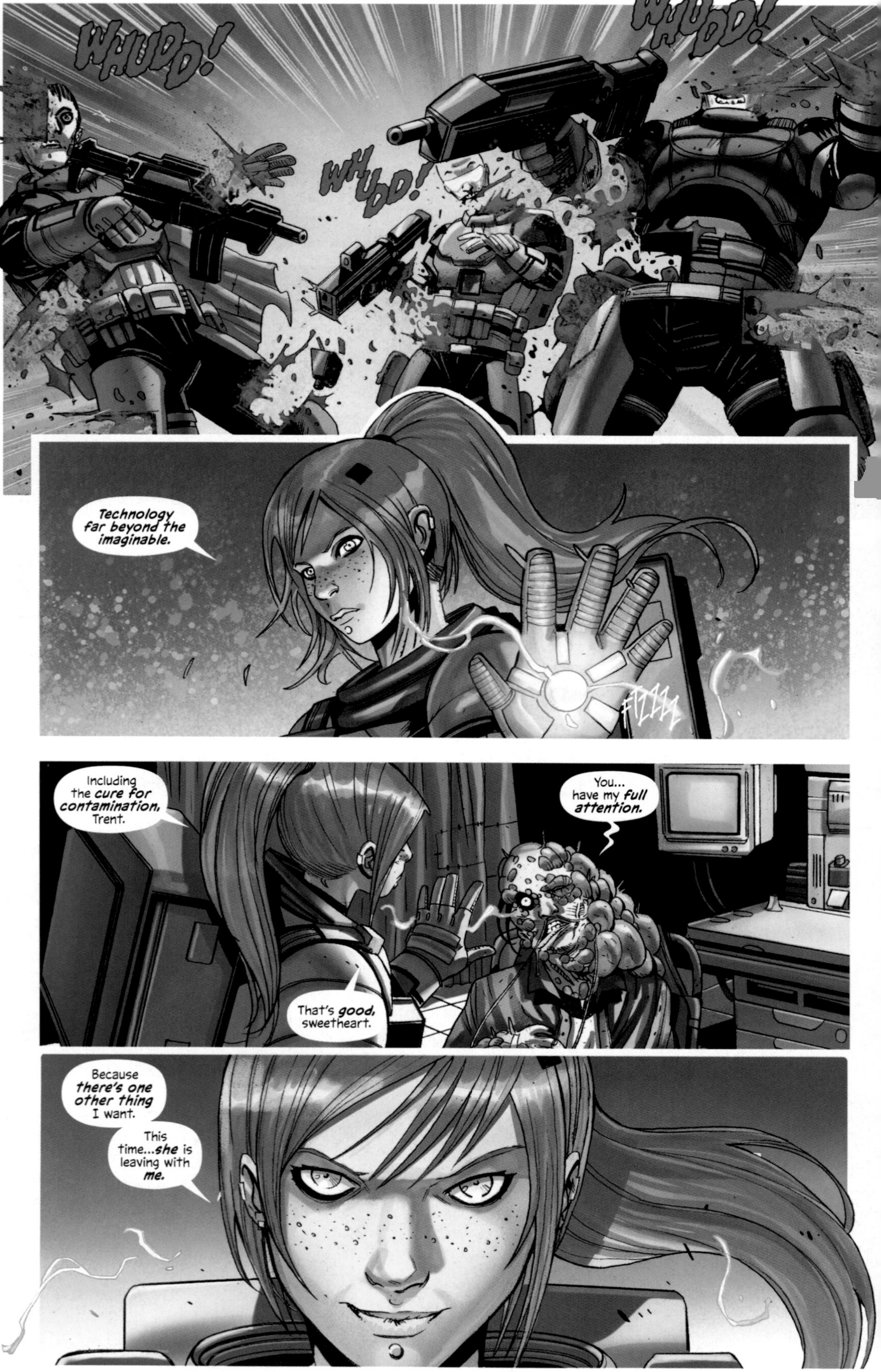
WHUDD!
WHUDD!
WHUDD!
Technology far beyond the imaginable.
FZZZZ
Including the cure for contamination, Trent.
You... have my full attention.
That's good, sweetheart.
Because there's one other thing I want.
This time...she is leaving with me.

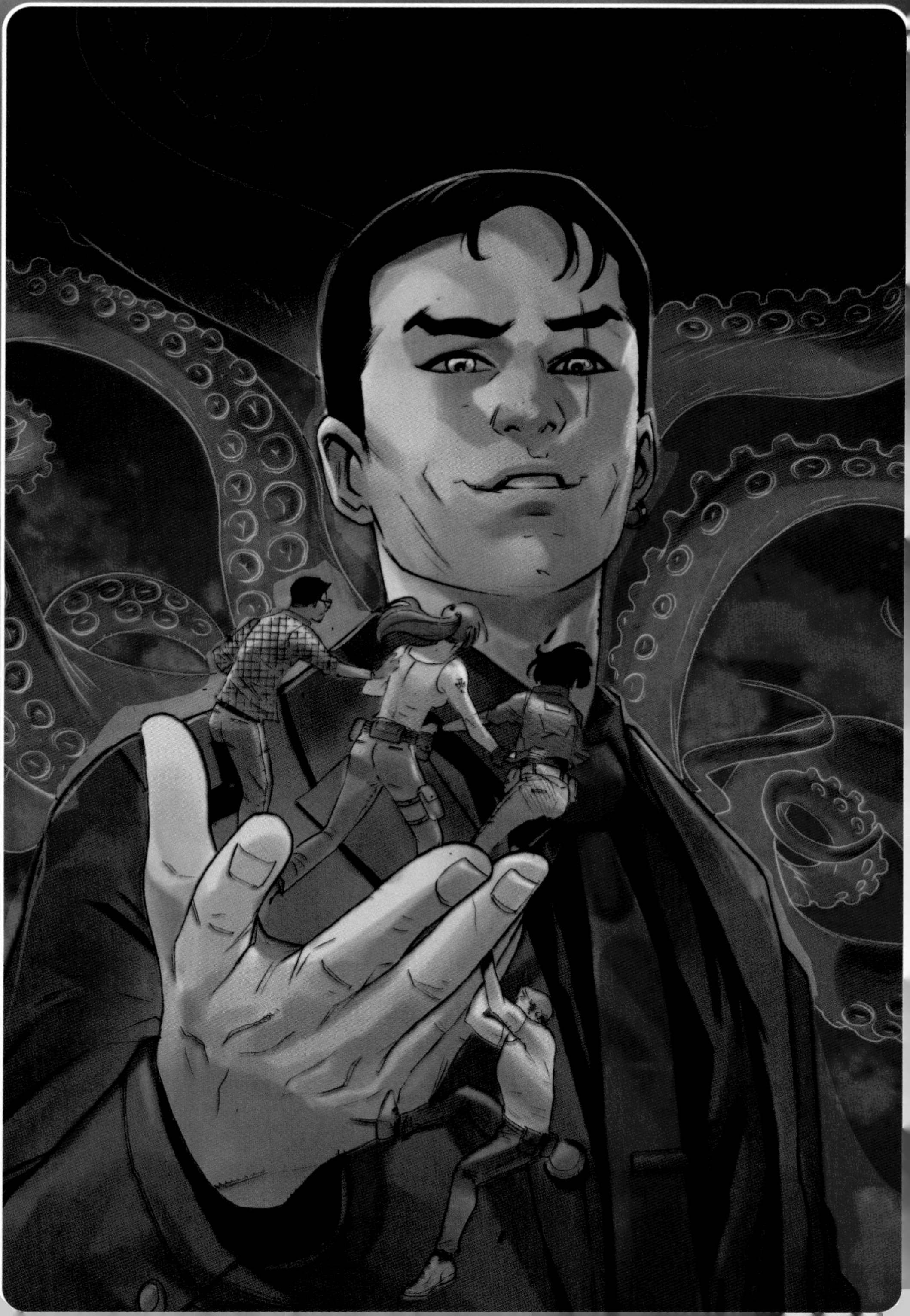

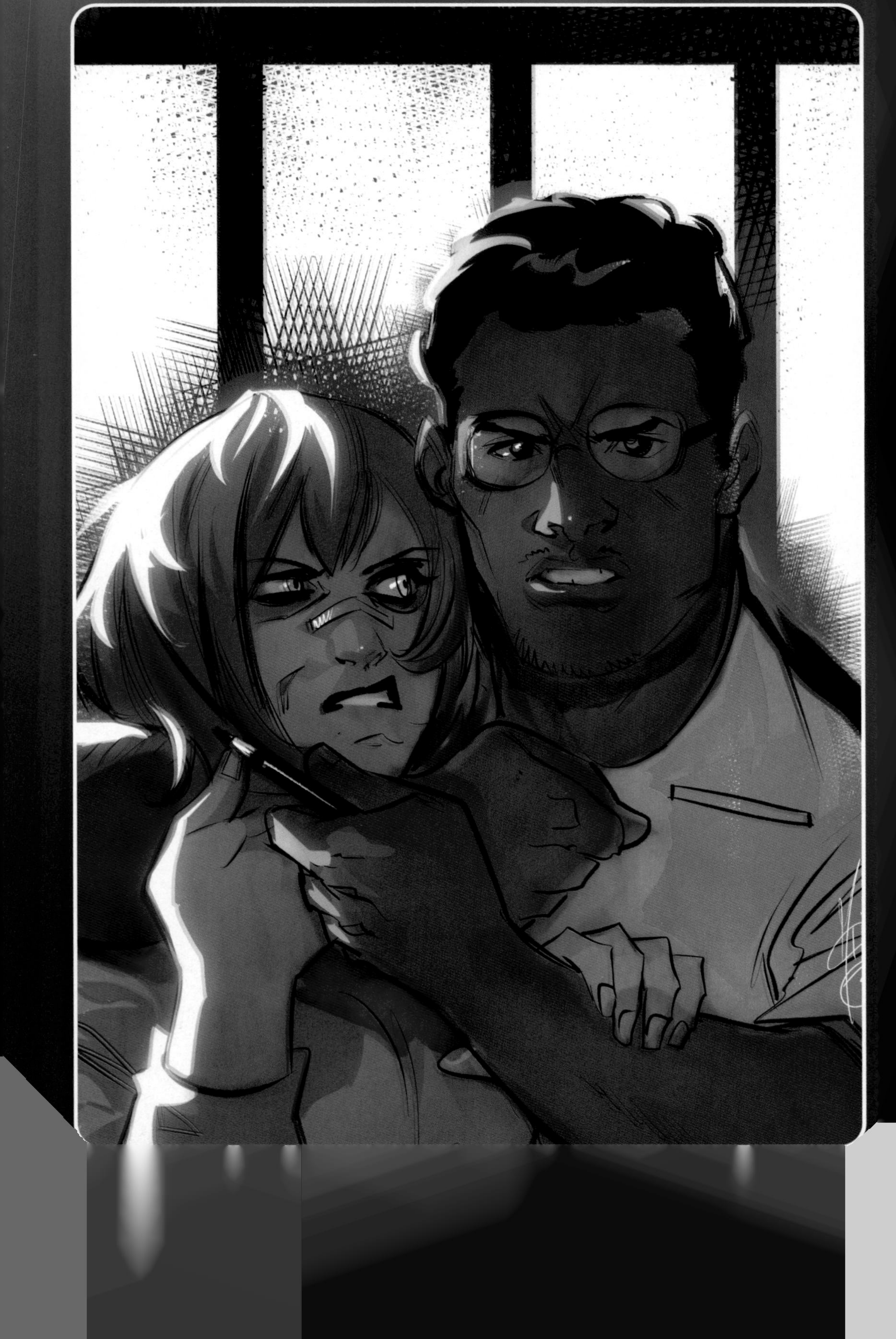

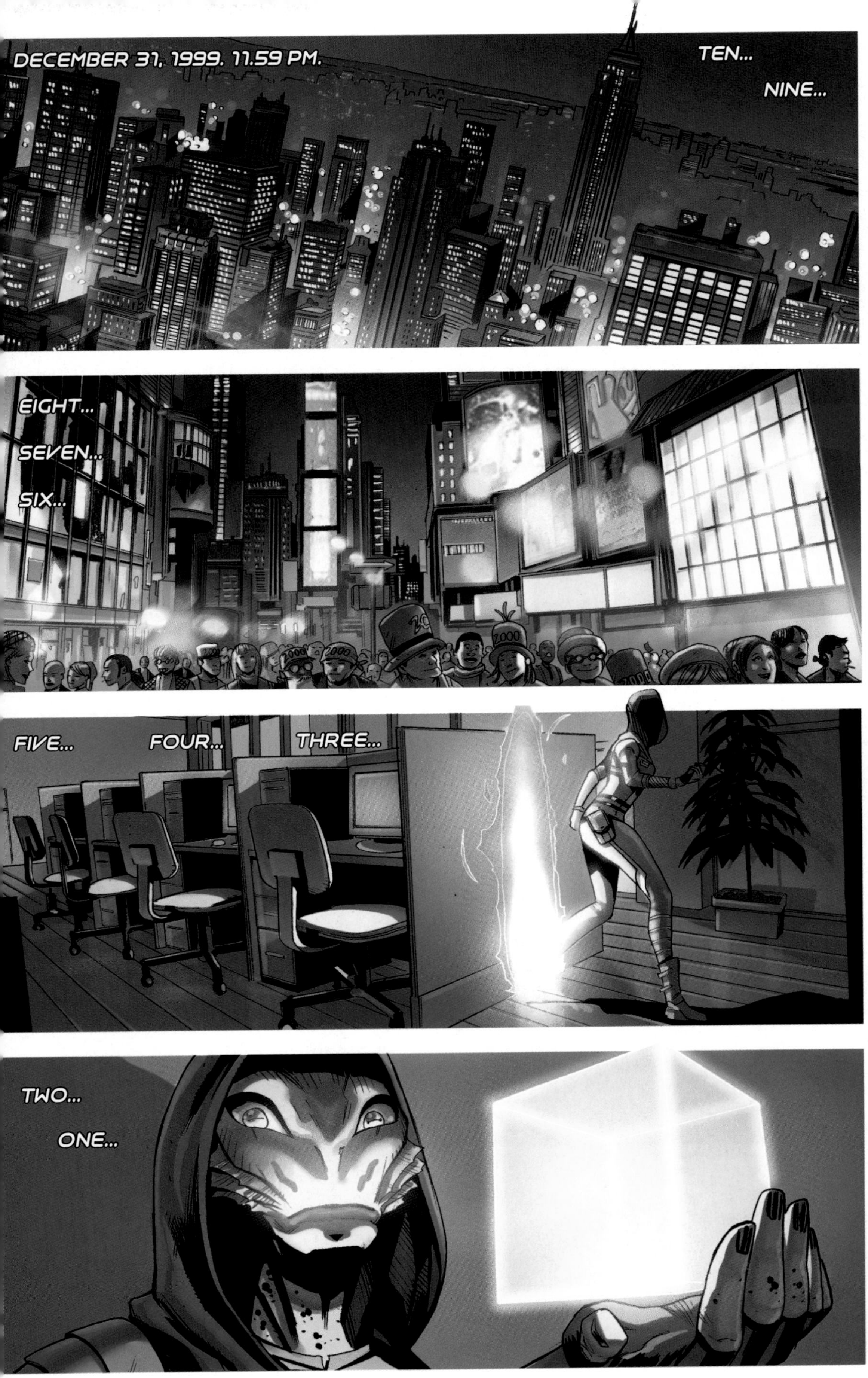
DECEMBER 31, 1999. 11.59 PM.
TEN...
NINE...
EIGHT...
SEVEN...
SIX...
FIVE...
FOUR...
THREE...
TWO...
ONE...

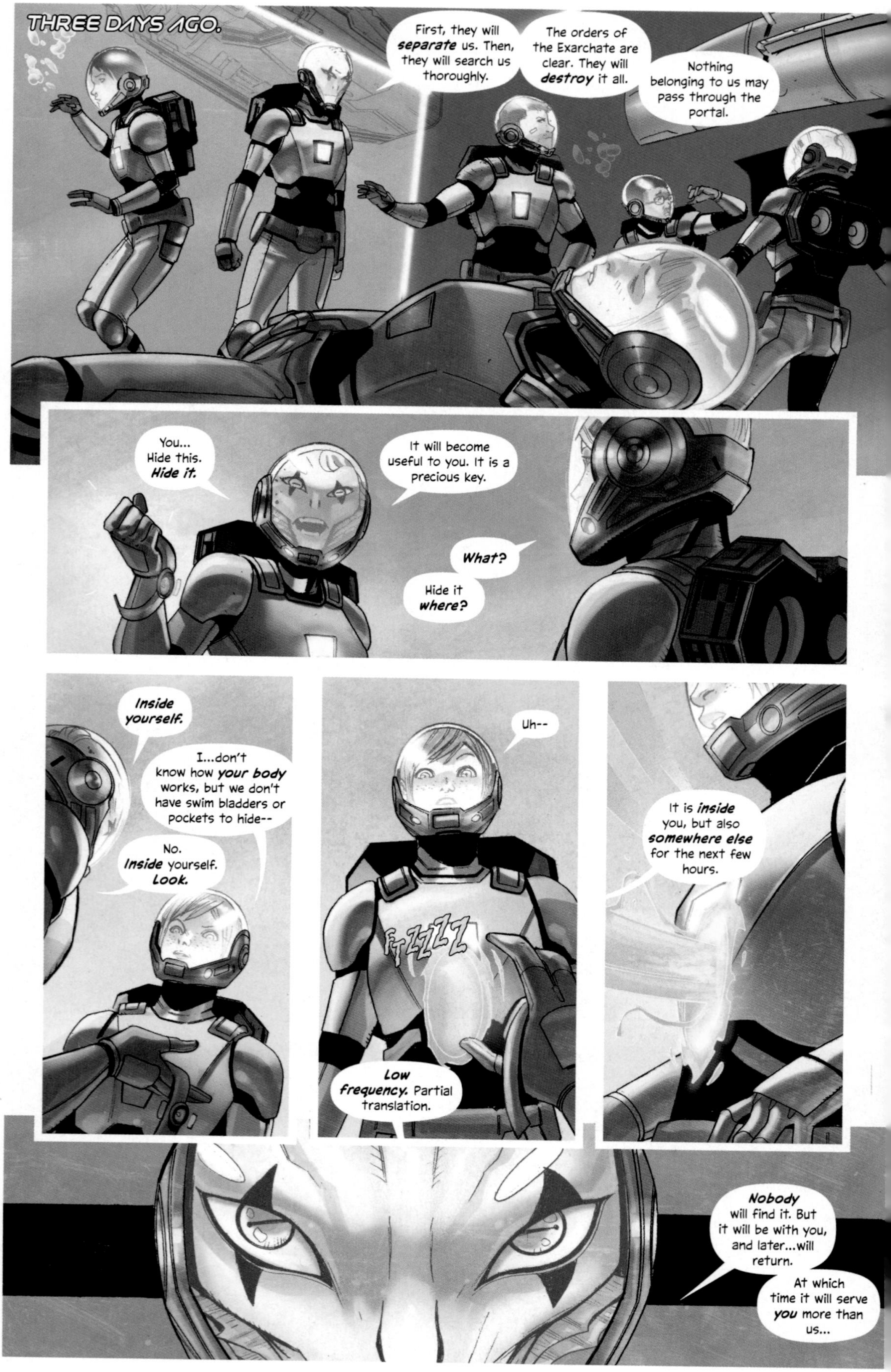
THREE DAYS AGO.
First, they will *separate* us. Then, they will search us thoroughly.
The orders of the Exarchate are clear. They will *destroy* it all.
Nothing belonging to us may pass through the portal.
You... Hide this. *Hide it.*
It will become useful to you. It is a precious key.
What?
Hide it *where?*
Inside yourself.
I...don't know how *your body* works, but we don't have swim bladders or pockets to hide--
No. *Inside* yourself. *Look.*
Uh--
FTZZZZ
Low frequency. Partial translation.
It is *inside* you, but also *somewhere else* for the next few hours.
Nobody will find it. But it will be with you, and later...will return.
At which time it will serve *you* more than us...

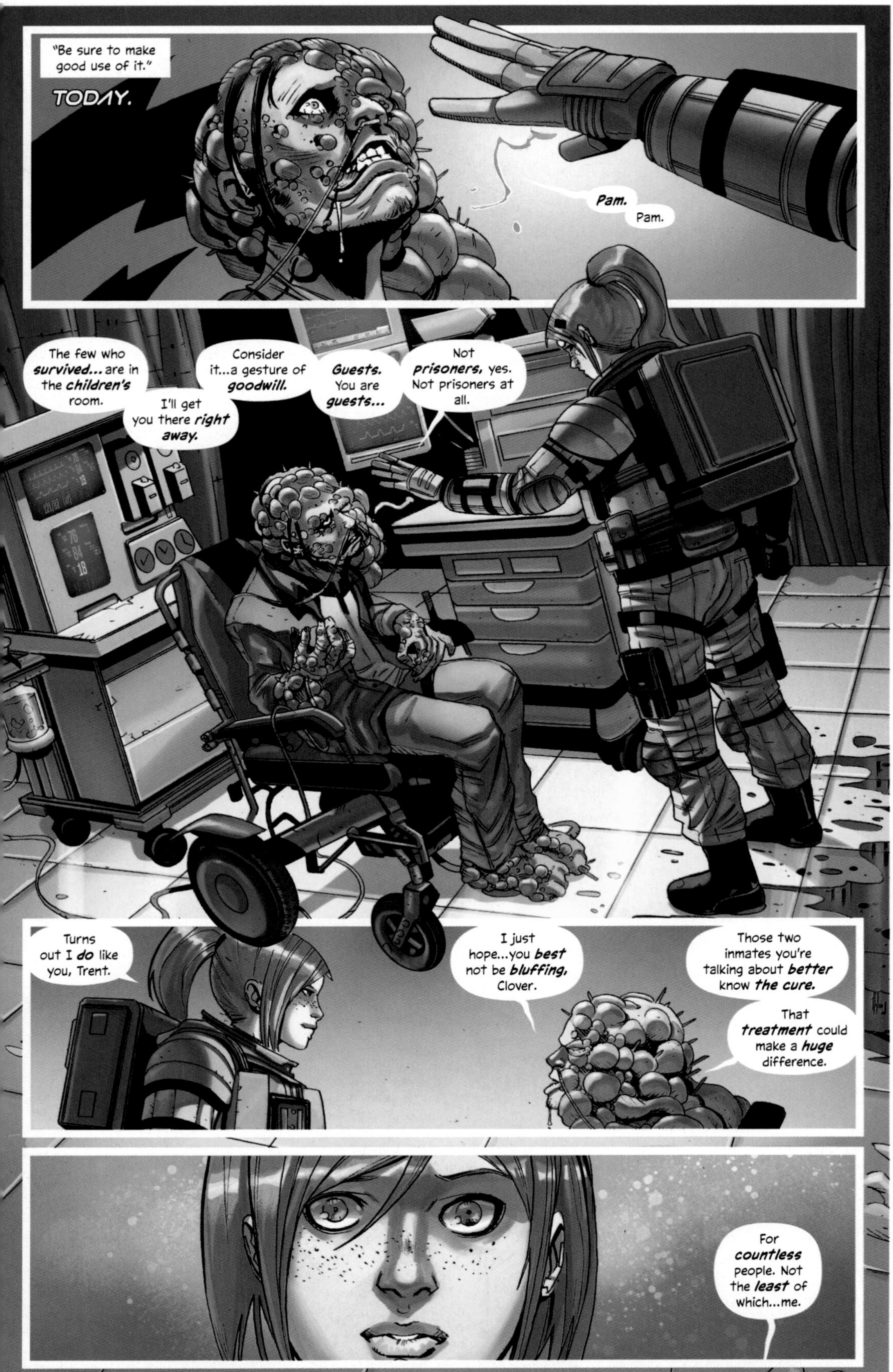

"Be sure to make good use of it."
TODAY.
Pam.
Pam.
The few who survived... are in the children's room.
I'll get you there right away.
Consider it...a gesture of goodwill.
Guests. You are guests...
Not prisoners, yes. Not prisoners at all.
Turns out I do like you, Trent.
I just hope...you best not be bluffing, Clover.
Those two inmates you're talking about better know the cure.
That treatment could make a huge difference.
For countless people. Not the least of which...me.

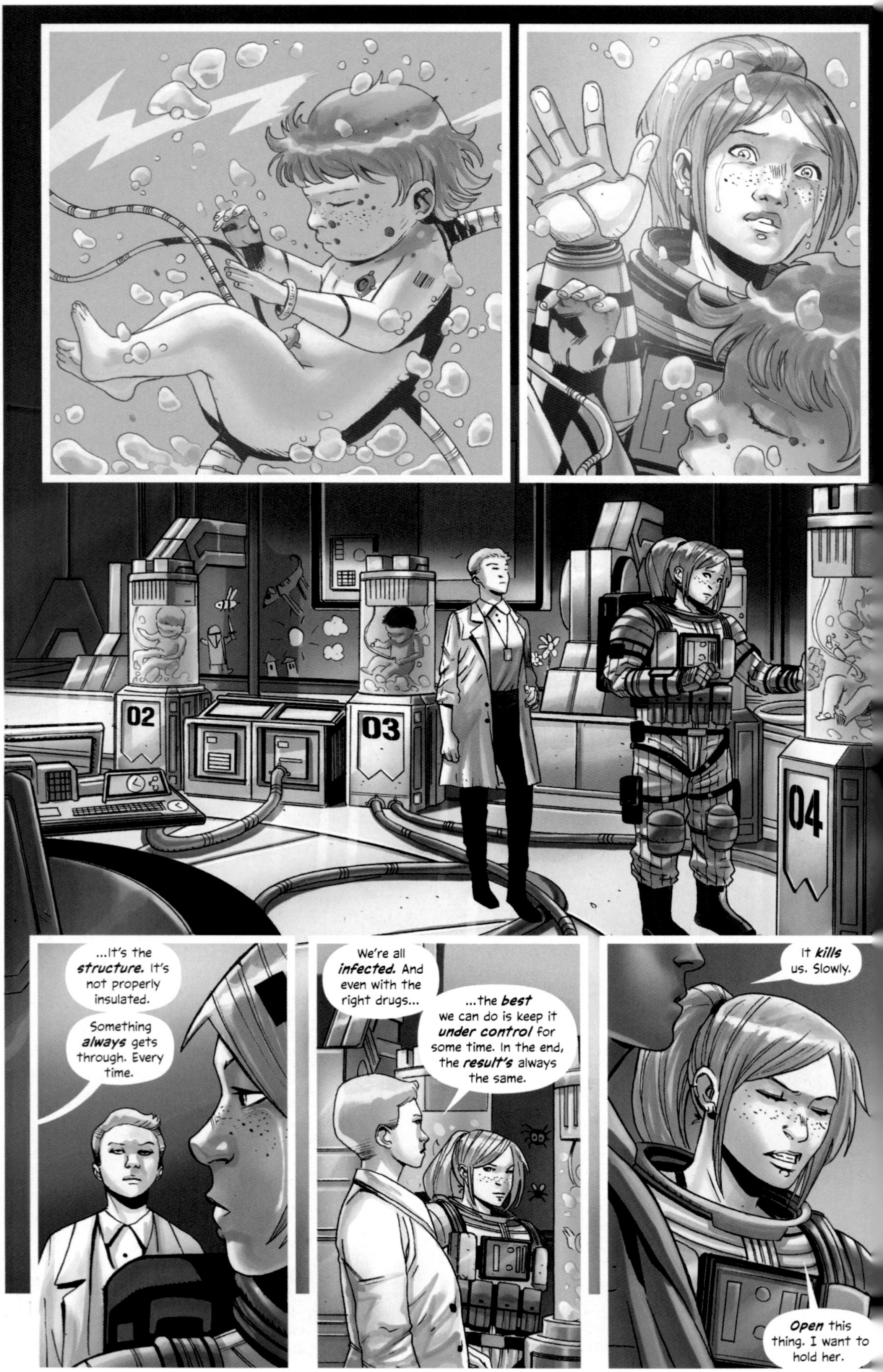
02
03
04
...It's the structure. It's not properly insulated.
Something always gets through. Every time.
We're all infected. And even with the right drugs...
...the best we can do is keep it under control for some time. In the end, the result's always the same.
It kills us. Slowly.
Open this thing. I want to hold her.

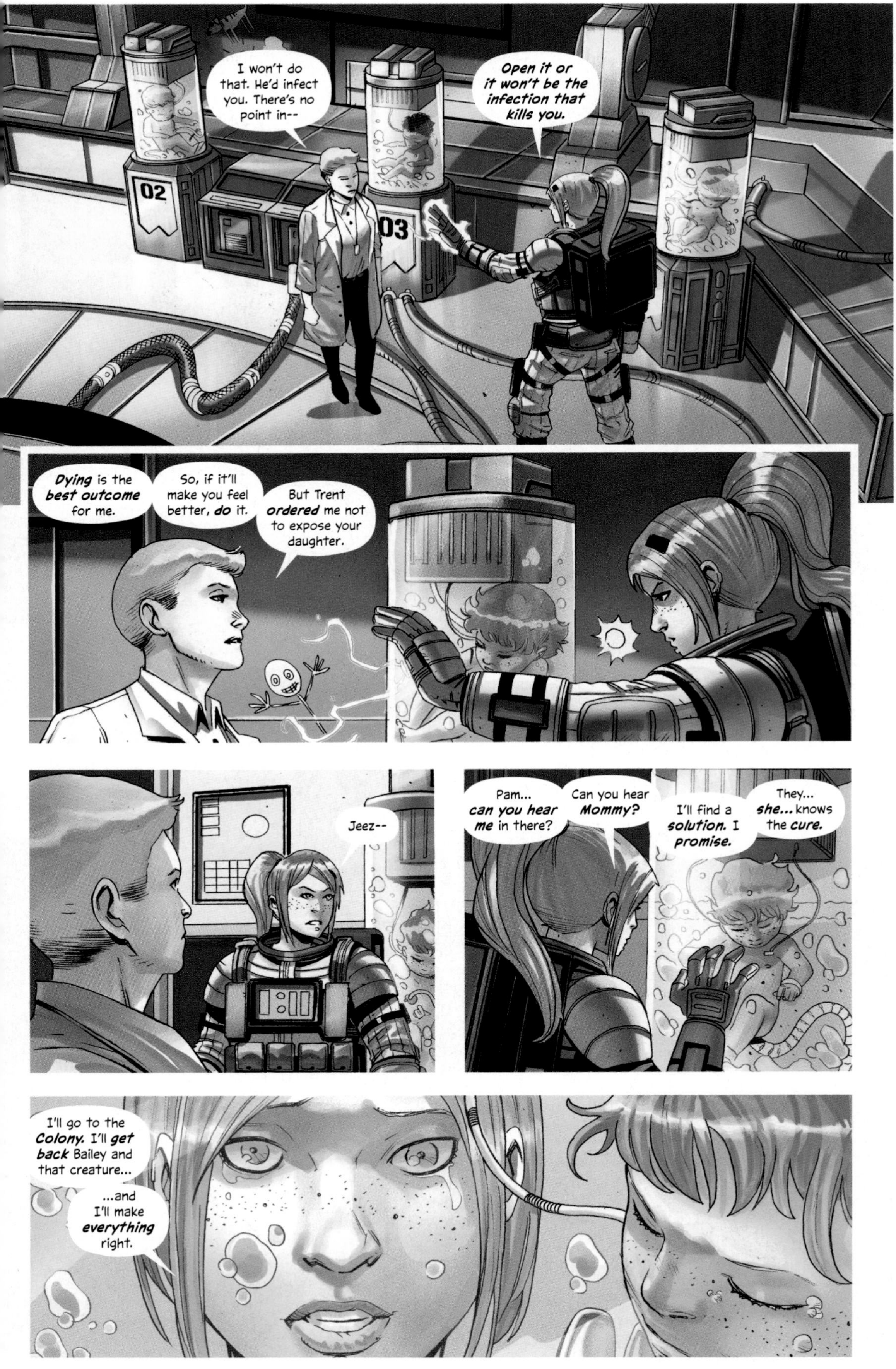

I won't do that. He'd infect you. There's no point in--
Open it or it won't be the infection that kills you.
02
03
Dying is the best outcome for me.
So, if it'll make you feel better, do it.
But Trent ordered me not to expose your daughter.
Jeez--
Pam... can you hear me in there?
Can you hear Mommy?
I'll find a solution. I promise.
They... she... knows the cure.
I'll go to the Colony. I'll get back Bailey and that creature...
...and I'll make everything right.

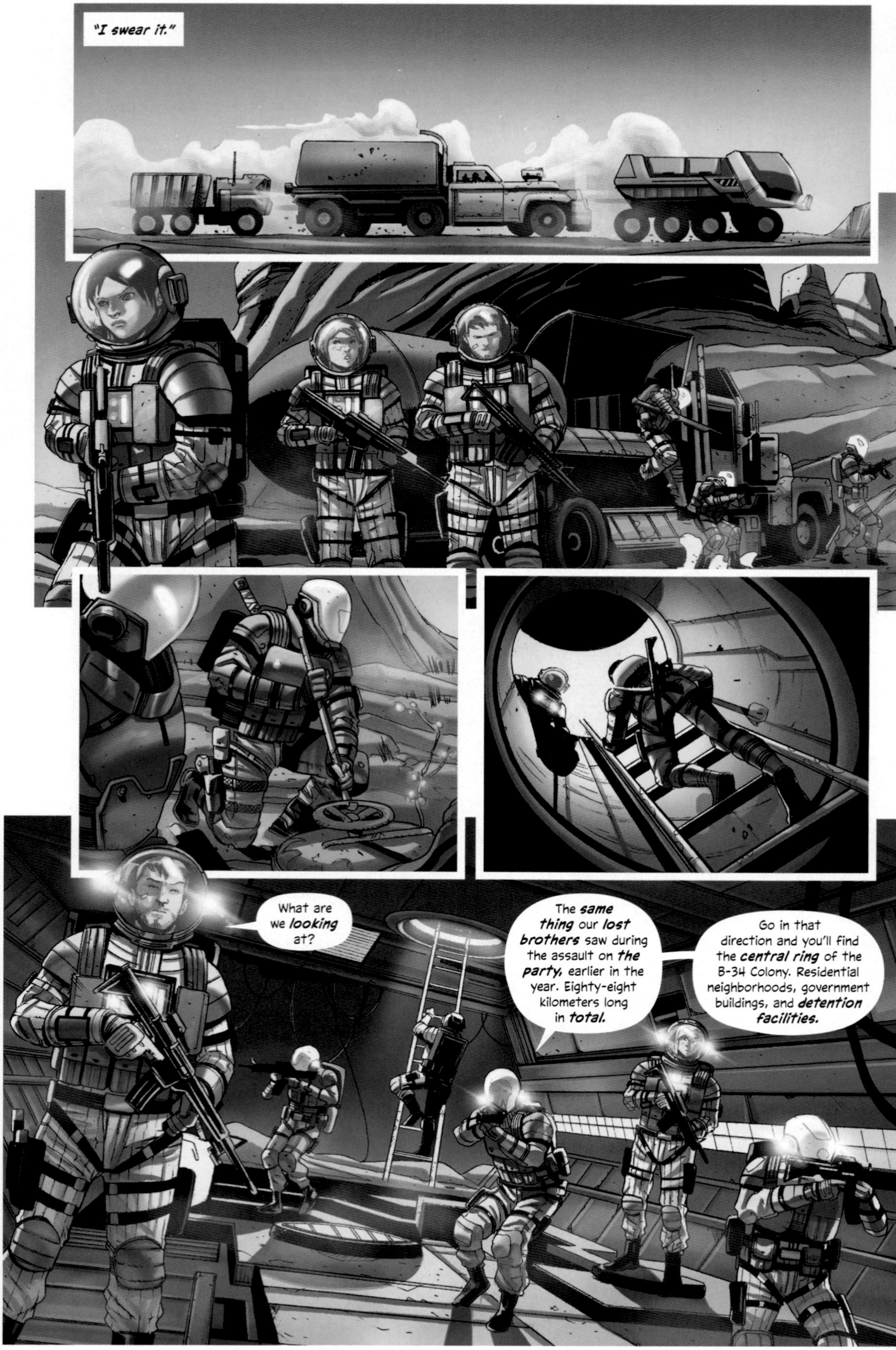
"I swear it."
What are we *looking* at?
The ***same thing*** our ***lost brothers*** saw during the assault on ***the party,*** earlier in the year. Eighty-eight kilometers long in ***total.***
Go in that direction and you'll find the ***central ring*** of the B-34 Colony. Residential neighborhoods, government buildings, and ***detention facilities.***

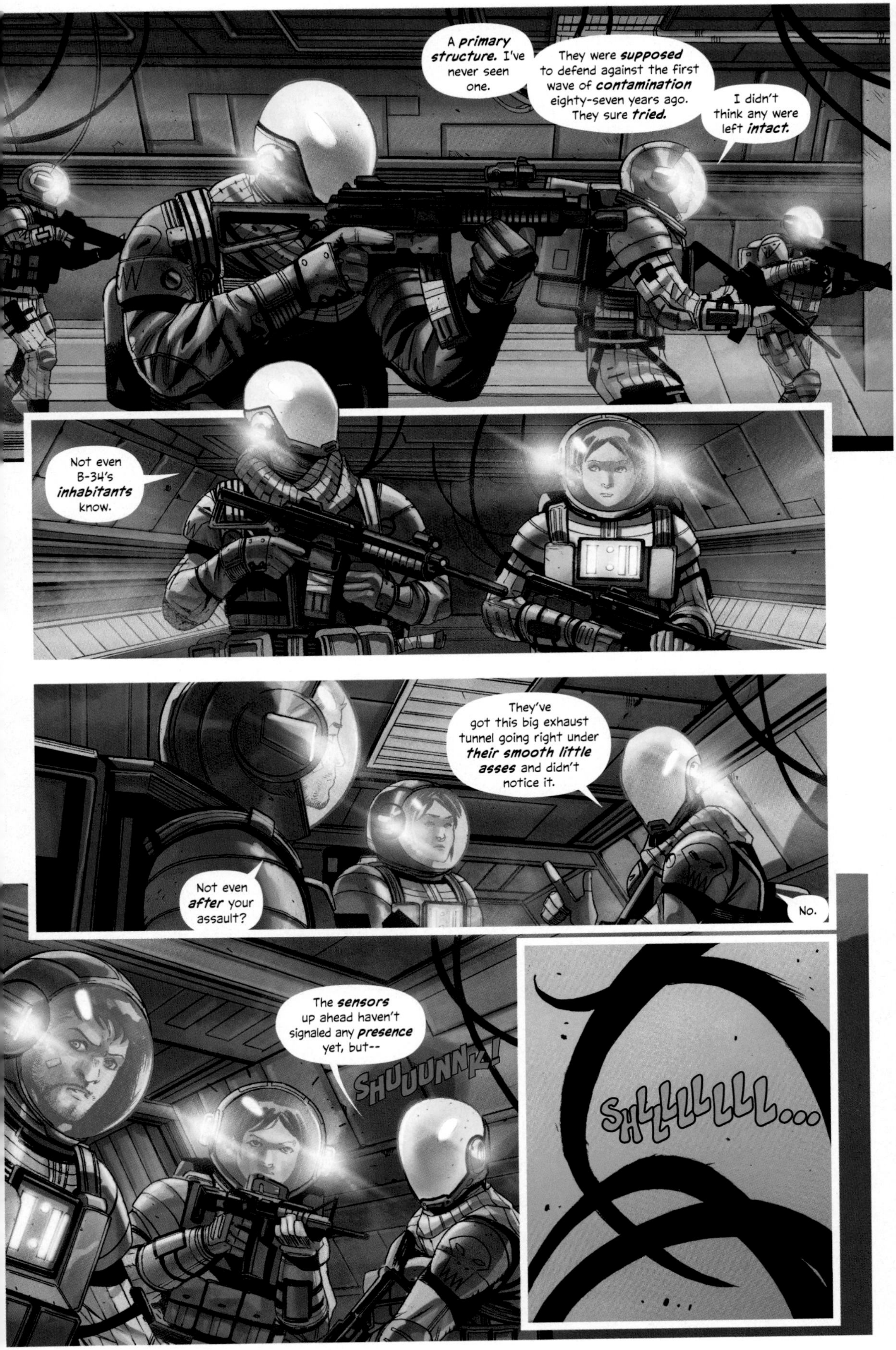

A primary structure. I've never seen one.
They were supposed to defend against the first wave of contamination eighty-seven years ago. They sure tried.
I didn't think any were left intact.
Not even B-34's inhabitants know.
They've got this big exhaust tunnel going right under their smooth little asses and didn't notice it.
Not even after your assault?
No.
The sensors up ahead haven't signaled any presence yet, but--
SHUUUNNK!
SHLLLLLL...

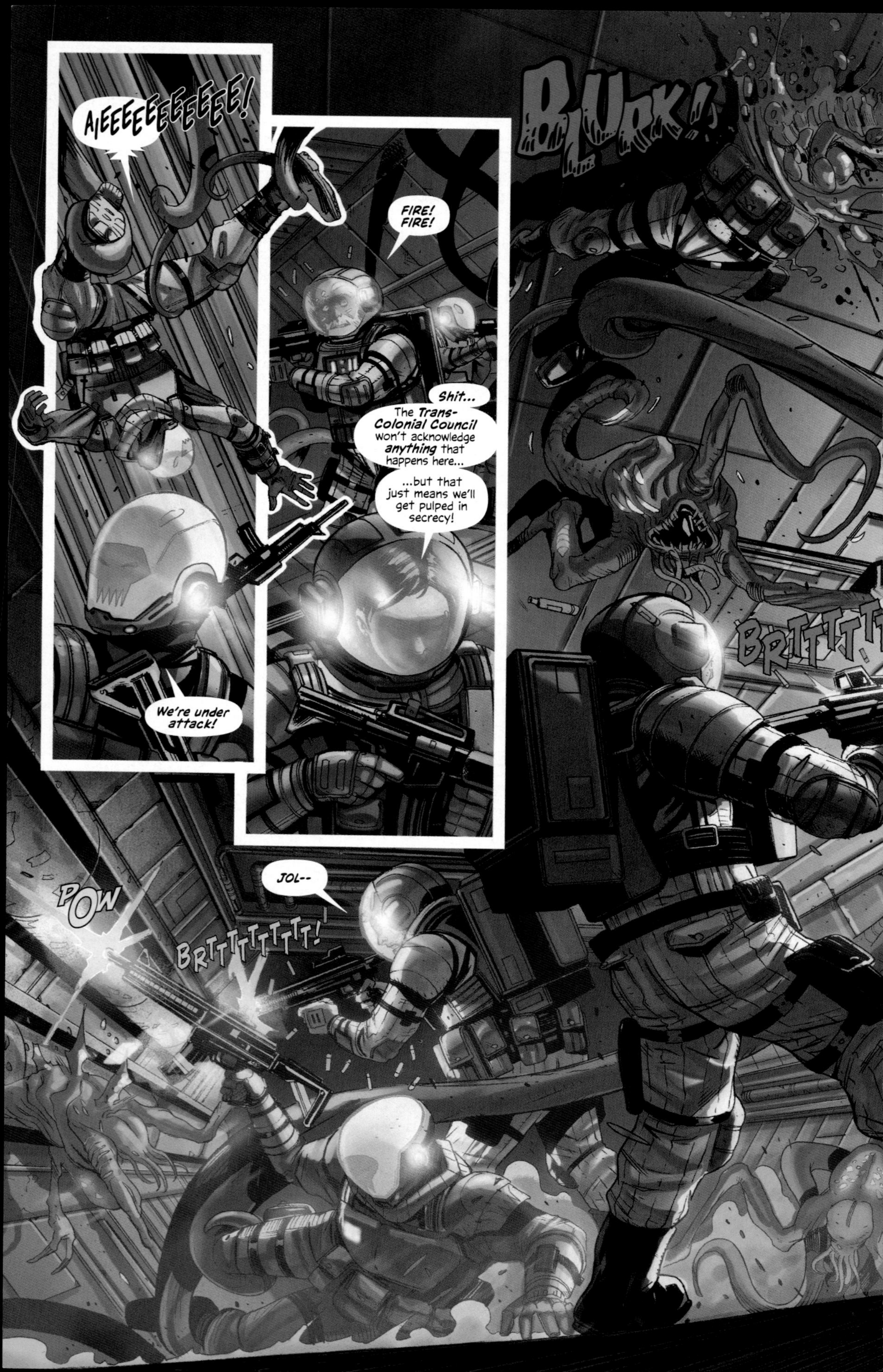

AIEEEEEEEEEEEE!
We're under attack!
FIRE! FIRE!
Shit...
The Trans-Colonial Council won't acknowledge anything that happens here...
...but that just means we'll get pulped in secrecy!
BLURK!
BRTTTTT
JOL--
POW
BRTTTTTTTTT!

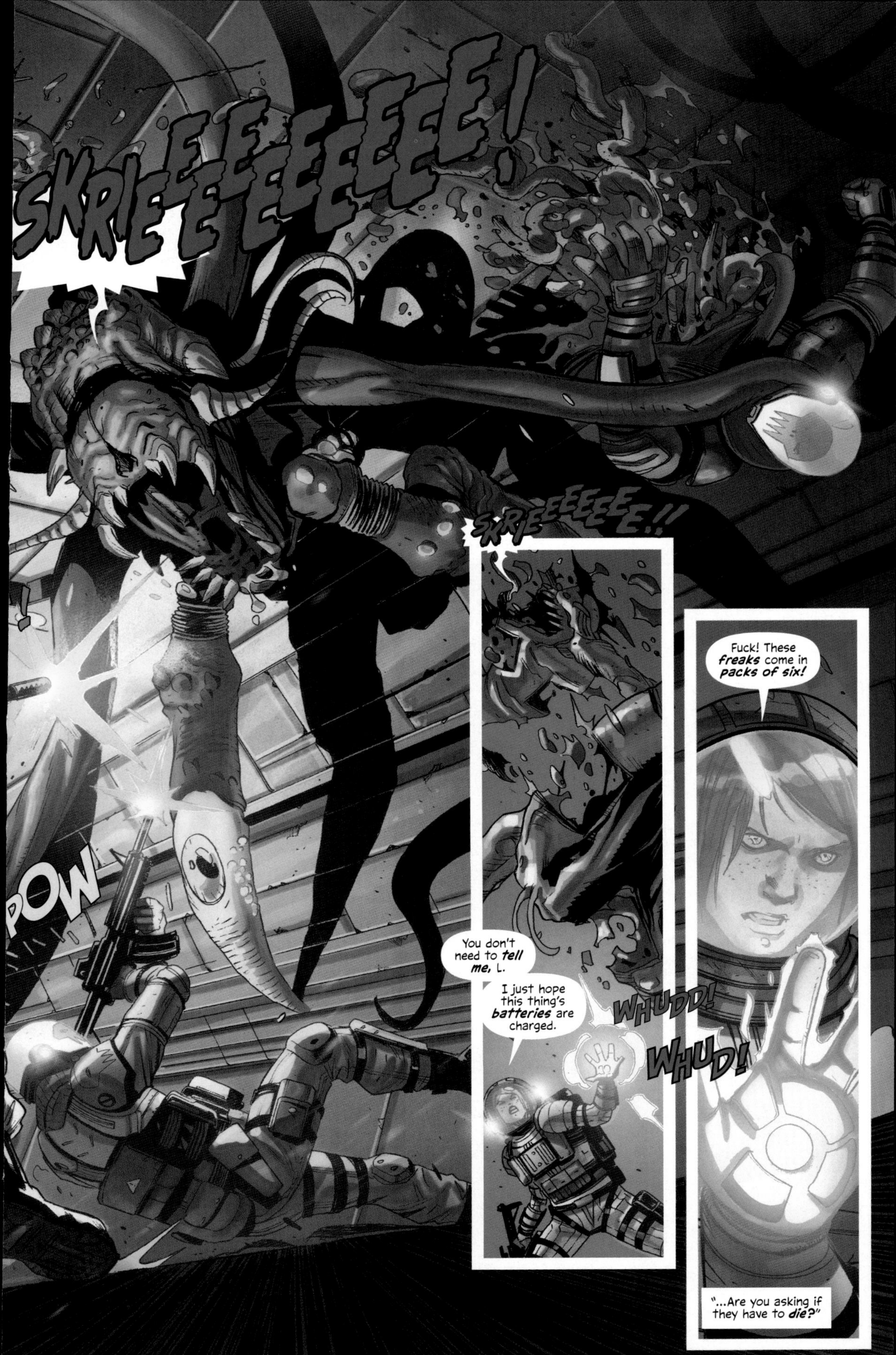
SKRIEEEEEEEEEE!
!
POW
SKRIEEEEEEEEEE!!
Fuck! These freaks come in packs of six!
You don't need to tell me, L.
I just hope this thing's batteries are charged.
WHUDD!
WHUD!
"...Are you asking if they have to die?"

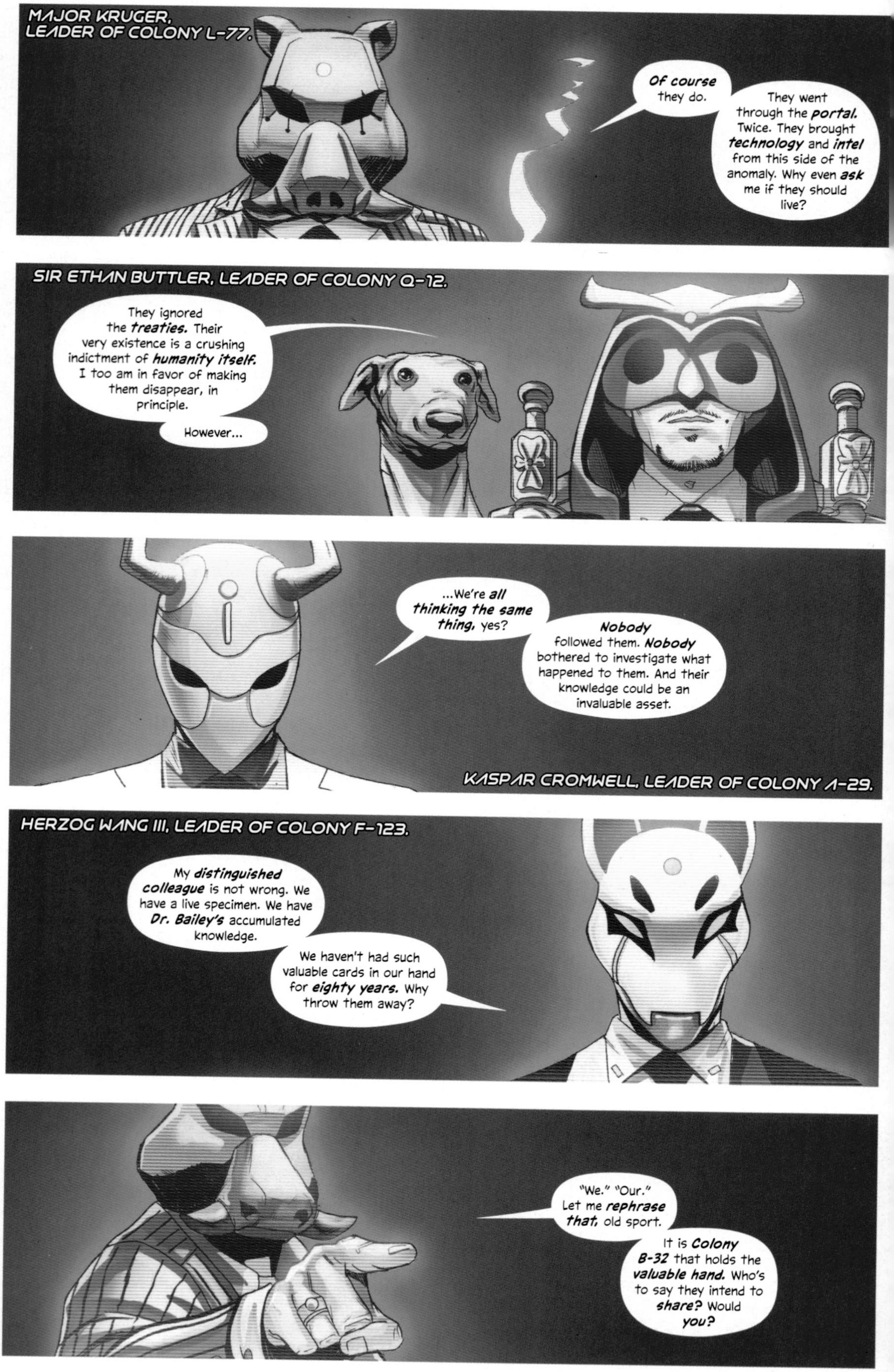
MAJOR KRUGER, LEADER OF COLONY L-77.
Of course they do.
They went through the portal. Twice. They brought technology and intel from this side of the anomaly. Why even ask me if they should live?
SIR ETHAN BUTTLER, LEADER OF COLONY Q-12.
They ignored the treaties. Their very existence is a crushing indictment of humanity itself. I too am in favor of making them disappear, in principle.
However...
...We're all thinking the same thing, yes?
Nobody followed them. Nobody bothered to investigate what happened to them. And their knowledge could be an invaluable asset.
KASPAR CROMWELL, LEADER OF COLONY A-29.
HERZOG WANG III, LEADER OF COLONY F-123.
My distinguished colleague is not wrong. We have a live specimen. We have Dr. Bailey's accumulated knowledge.
We haven't had such valuable cards in our hand for eighty years. Why throw them away?
"We." "Our." Let me rephrase that, old sport.
It is Colony B-32 that holds the valuable hand. Who's to say they intend to share? Would you?

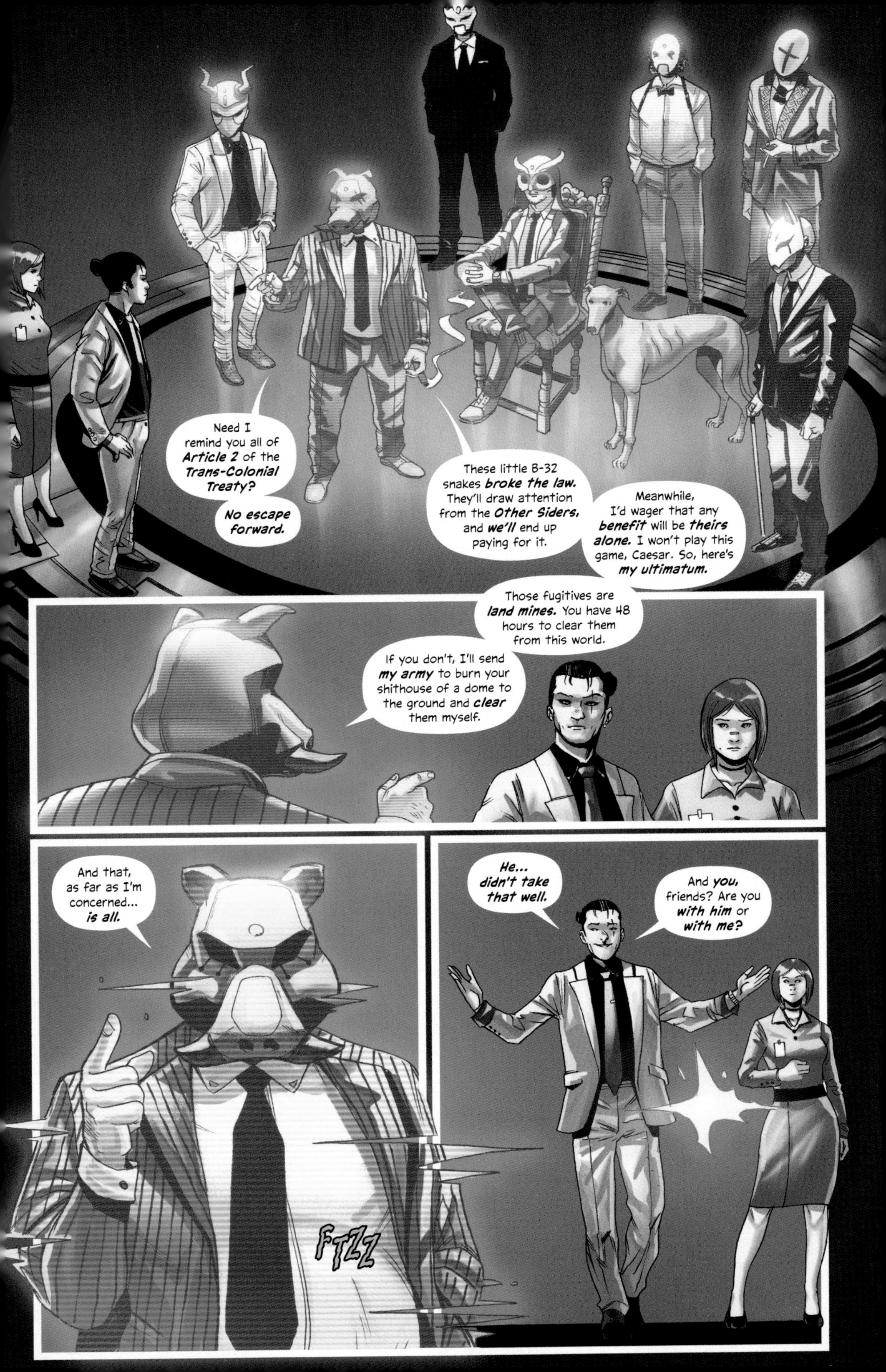
Need I remind you all of Article 2 of the Trans-Colonial Treaty?
No escape forward.
These little B-32 snakes broke the law. They'll draw attention from the Other Siders, and we'll end up paying for it.
Meanwhile, I'd wager that any benefit will be theirs alone. I won't play this game, Caesar. So, here's my ultimatum.
Those fugitives are land mines. You have 48 hours to clear them from this world.
If you don't, I'll send my army to burn your shithouse of a dome to the ground and clear them myself.
And that, as far as I'm concerned... is all.
FTZZ
He... didn't take that well.
And you, friends? Are you with him or with me?

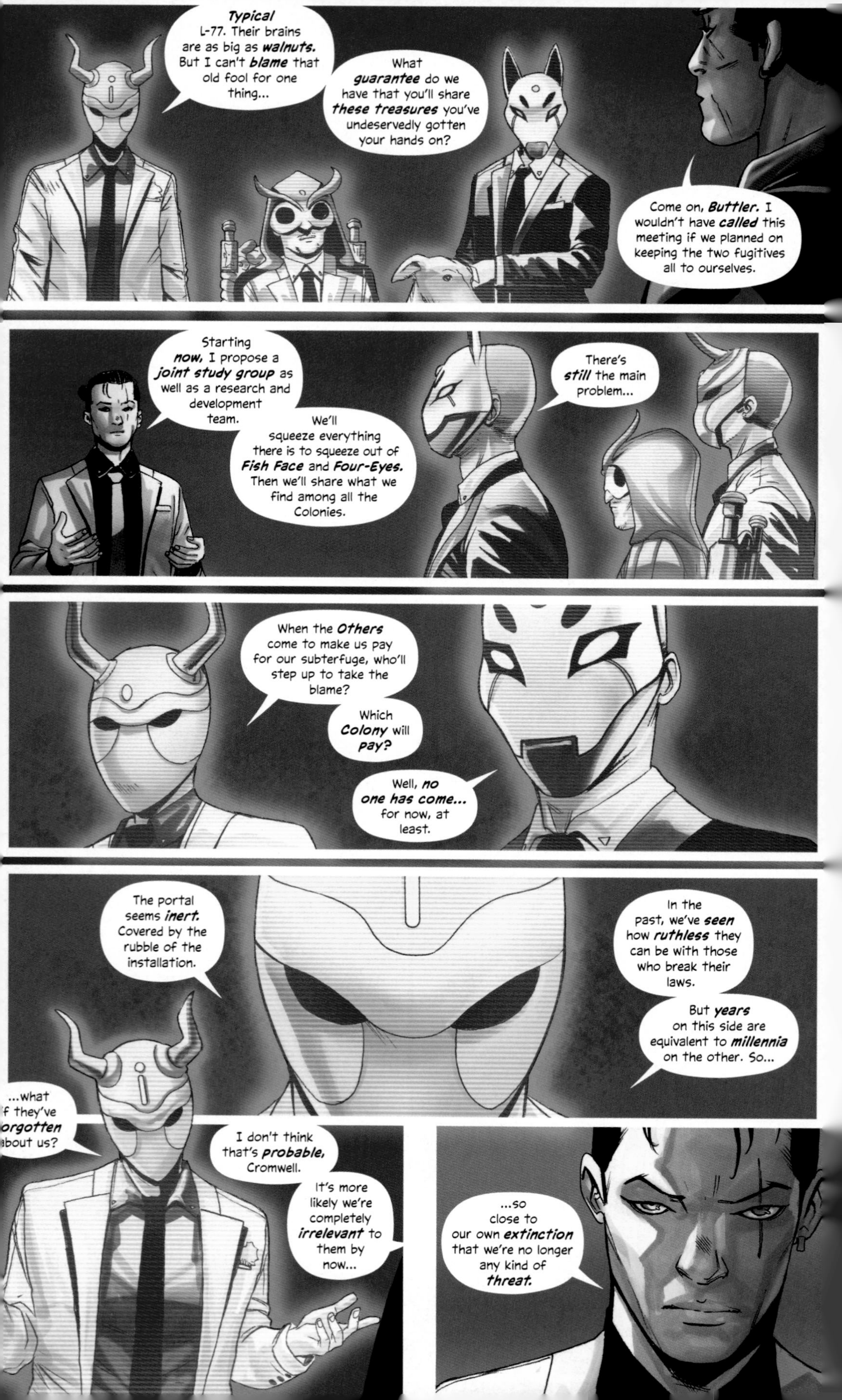
Typical L-77. Their brains are as big as walnuts. But I can't blame that old fool for one thing...
What guarantee do we have that you'll share these treasures you've undeservedly gotten your hands on?
Come on, Buttler. I wouldn't have called this meeting if we planned on keeping the two fugitives all to ourselves.
Starting now, I propose a joint study group as well as a research and development team.
We'll squeeze everything there is to squeeze out of Fish Face and Four-Eyes. Then we'll share what we find among all the Colonies.
There's still the main problem...
When the Others come to make us pay for our subterfuge, who'll step up to take the blame?
Which Colony will pay?
Well, no one has come... for now, at least.
The portal seems inert. Covered by the rubble of the installation.
In the past, we've seen how ruthless they can be with those who break their laws.
But years on this side are equivalent to millennia on the other. So...
...what if they've forgotten about us?
I don't think that's probable, Cromwell.
It's more likely we're completely irrelevant to them by now...
...so close to our own extinction that we're no longer any kind of threat.

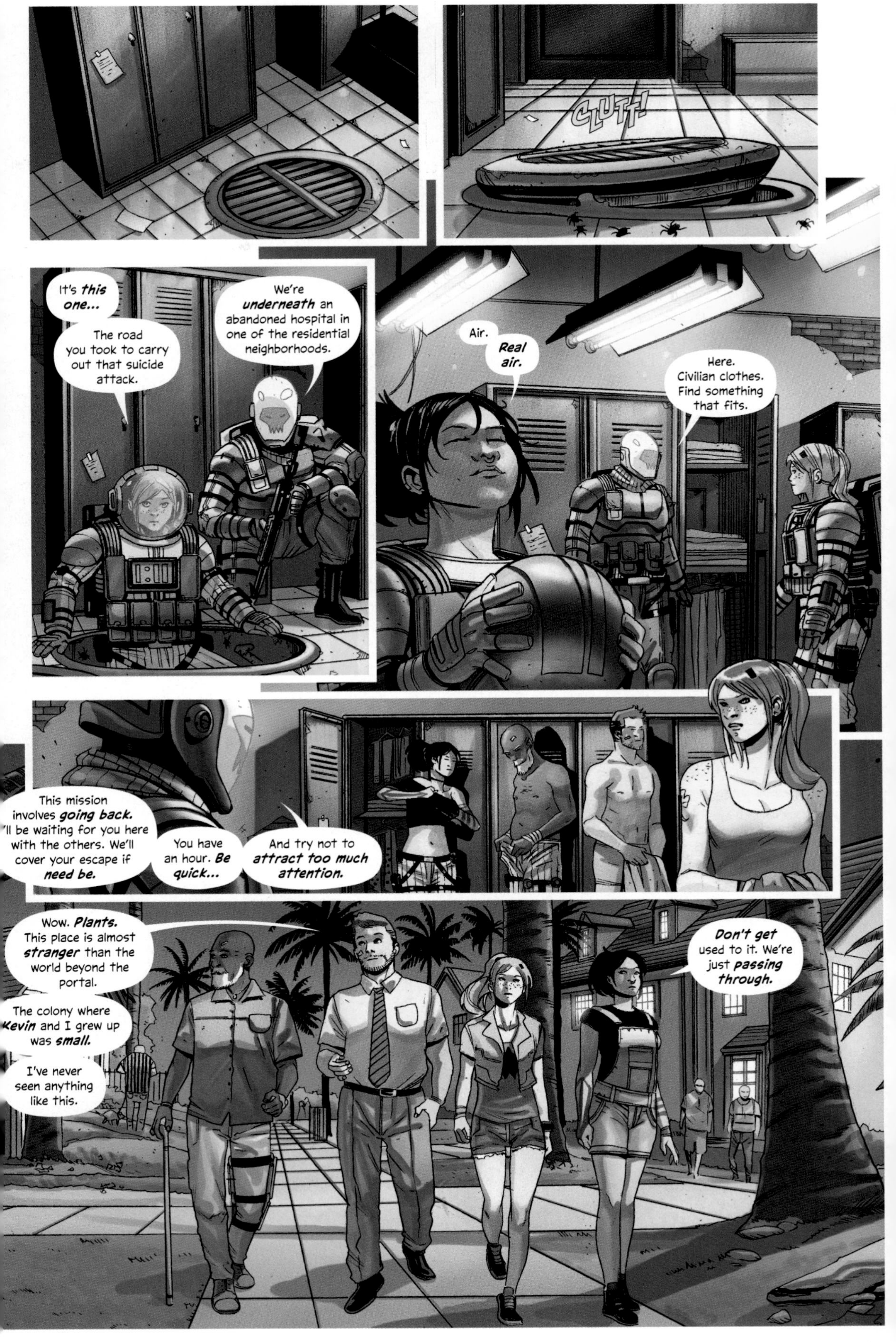
CLUTT!
It's this one...
The road you took to carry out that suicide attack.
We're underneath an abandoned hospital in one of the residential neighborhoods.
Air. Real air.
Here. Civilian clothes. Find something that fits.
This mission involves going back. 'll be waiting for you here with the others. We'll cover your escape if need be.
You have an hour. Be quick...
And try not to attract too much attention.
Wow. Plants. This place is almost stranger than the world beyond the portal.
The colony where Kevin and I grew up was small.
I've never seen anything like this.
Don't get used to it. We're just passing through.

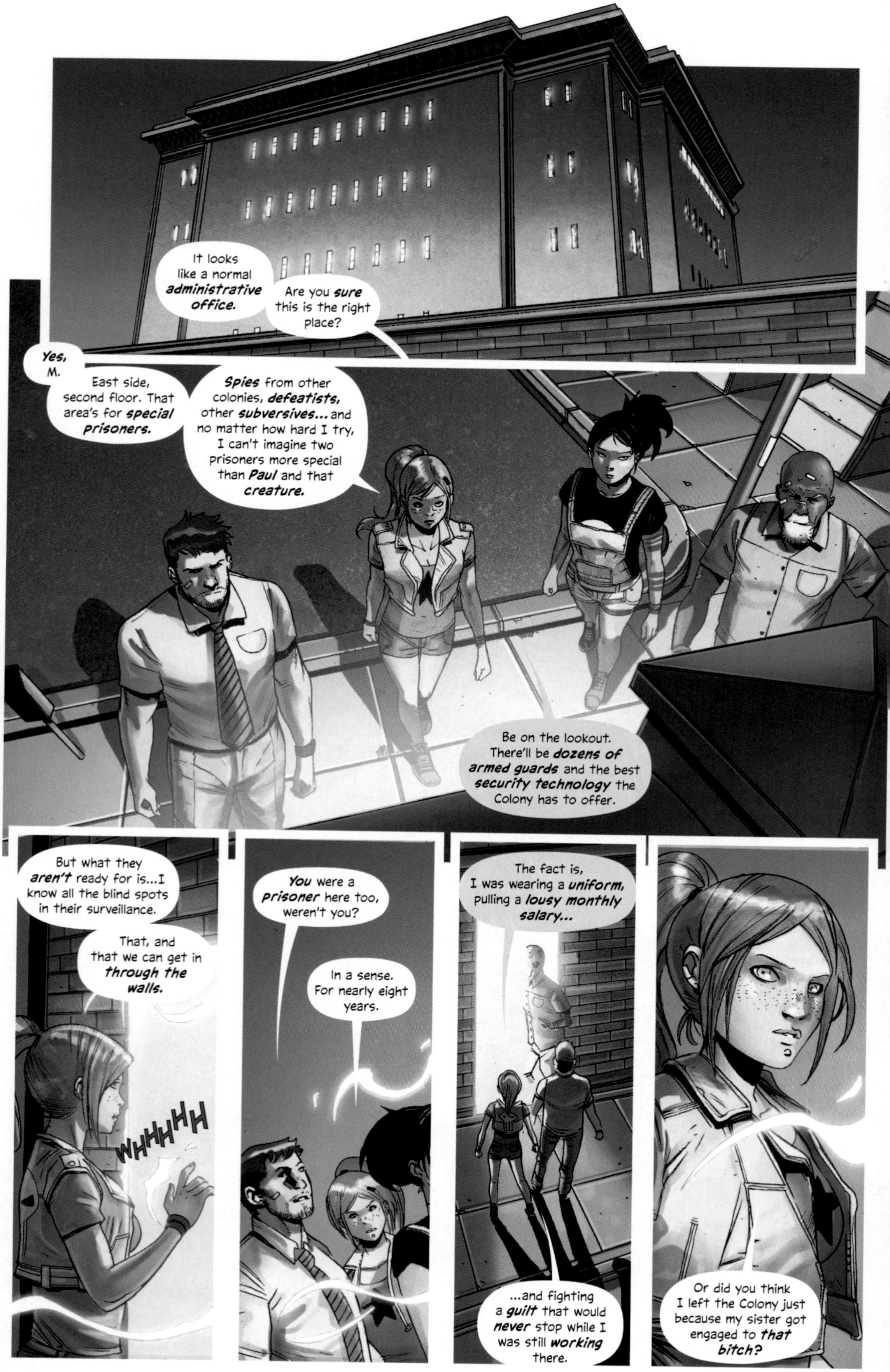
It looks like a normal administrative office.
Are you sure this is the right place?
Yes, M.
East side, second floor. That area's for special prisoners.
Spies from other colonies, defeatists, other subversives... and no matter how hard I try, I can't imagine two prisoners more special than Paul and that creature.
Be on the lookout. There'll be dozens of armed guards and the best security technology the Colony has to offer.
But what they aren't ready for is...I know all the blind spots in their surveillance.
That, and that we can get in through the walls.
WHHHHHH
You were a prisoner here too, weren't you?
In a sense. For nearly eight years.
The fact is, I was wearing a uniform, pulling a lousy monthly salary...
...and fighting a guilt that would never stop while I was still working there.
Or did you think I left the Colony just because my sister got engaged to that bitch?

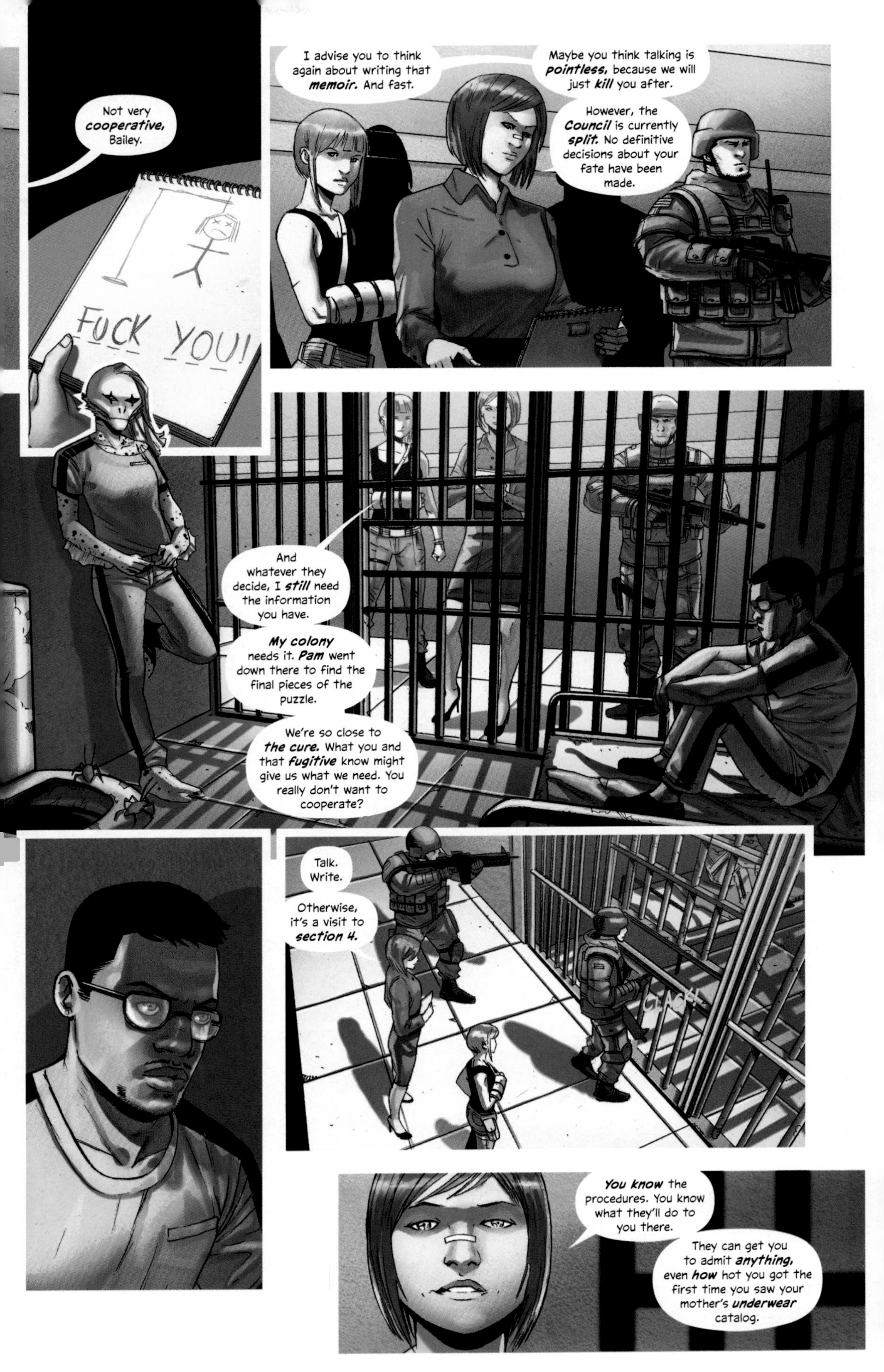

Not very *cooperative,* Bailey.
FUCK YOU!
I advise you to think again about writing that *memoir.* And fast.
Maybe you think talking is *pointless,* because we will just *kill* you after.
However, the *Council* is currently *split.* No definitive decisions about your fate have been made.
And whatever they decide, I *still* need the information you have.
My colony needs it. *Pam* went down there to find the final pieces of the puzzle.
We're so close to *the cure.* What you and that *fugitive* know might give us what we need. You really don't want to cooperate?
Talk. Write.
Otherwise, it's a visit to *section 4.*
CLACK!
You know the procedures. You know what they'll do to you there.
They can get you to admit *anything,* even *how* hot you got the first time you saw your mother's *underwear* catalog.

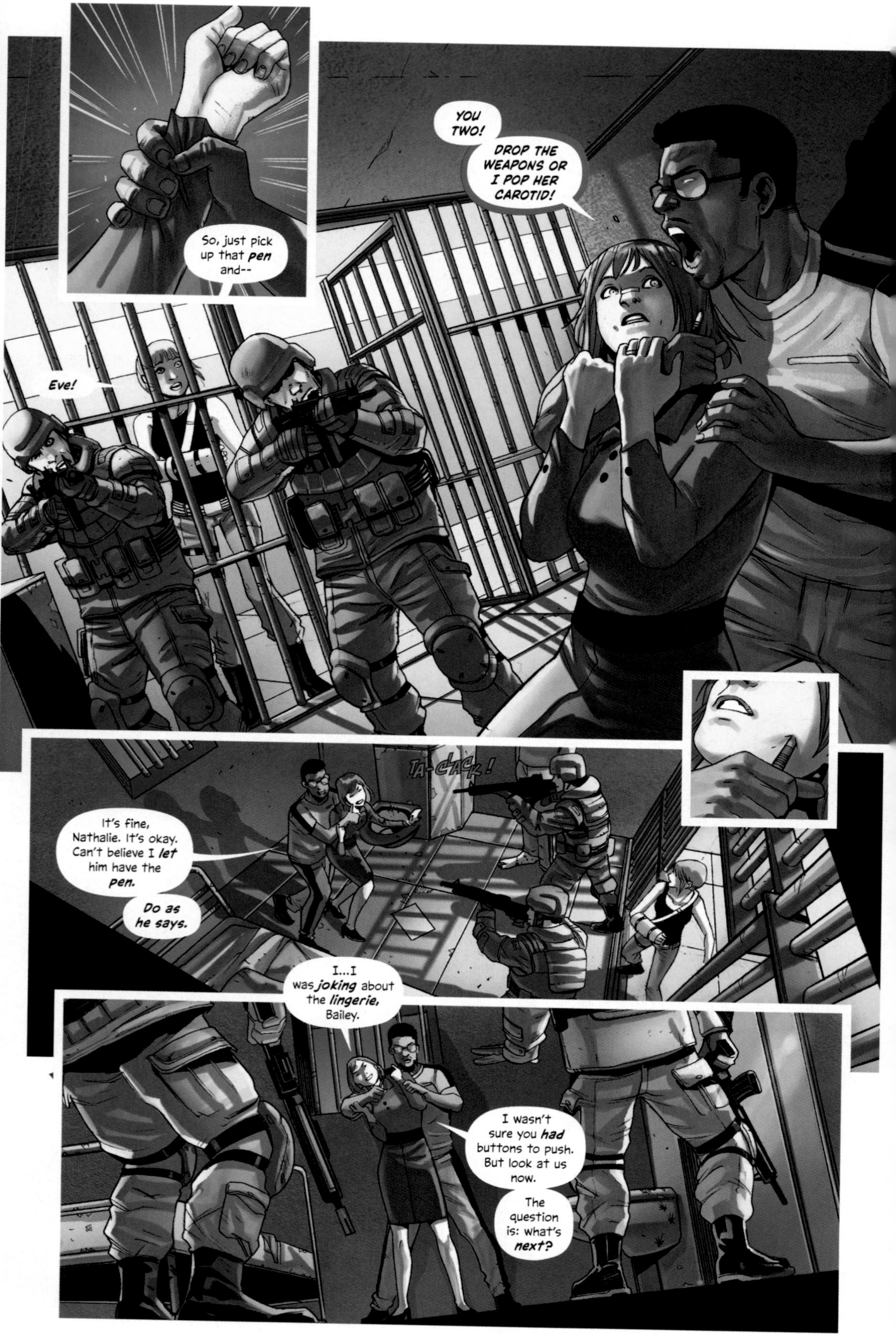

So, just pick up that *pen* and--
YOU TWO!
DROP THE WEAPONS OR I POP HER CAROTID!
Eve!
TA-CLACK!
It's fine, Nathalie. It's okay. Can't believe I *let* him have the *pen.*
Do as he says.
I...I was *joking* about the *lingerie,* Bailey.
I wasn't sure you *had* buttons to push. But look at us now.
The question is: what's *next?*

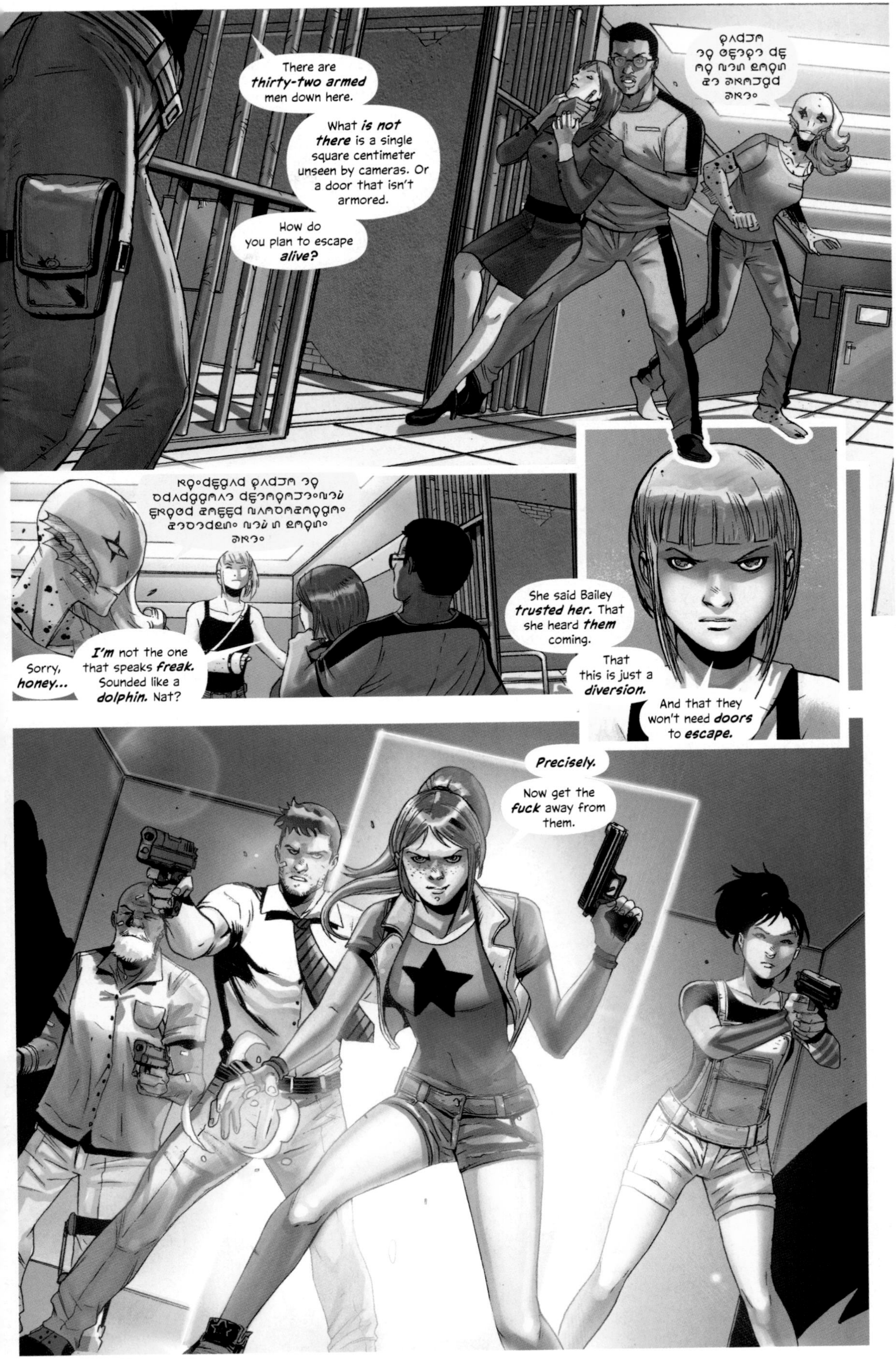
There are thirty-two armed men down here.
What is not there is a single square centimeter unseen by cameras. Or a door that isn't armored.
How do you plan to escape alive?
Sorry, honey...
I'm not the one that speaks freak. Sounded like a dolphin. Nat?
She said Bailey trusted her. That she heard them coming.
That this is just a diversion.
And that they won't need doors to escape.
Precisely.
Now get the fuck away from them.

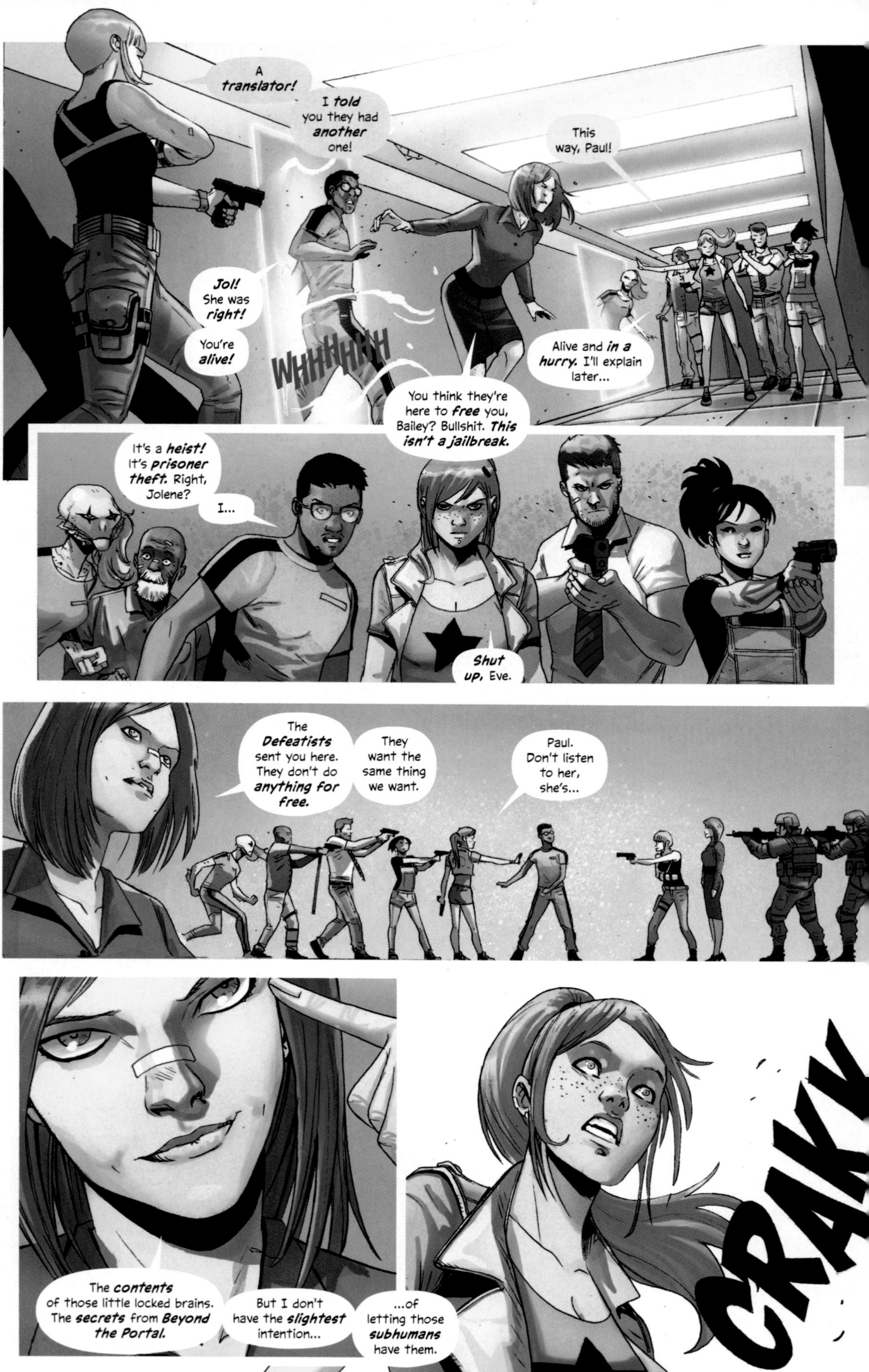
A *translator!*
I *told* you they had *another* one!
This way, Paul!
Jol! She was *right!*
You're *alive!*
WHHHHHHH
Alive and *in a hurry.* I'll explain later...
You think they're here to *free* you, Bailey? Bullshit. ***This isn't a jailbreak.***
It's a *heist!* It's *prisoner theft.* Right, Jolene?
I...
Shut up, Eve.
The *Defeatists* sent you here. They don't do *anything for free.*
They want the same thing we want.
Paul. Don't listen to her, she's...
The *contents* of those little locked brains. The *secrets* from *Beyond the Portal.*
But I don't have the *slightest* intention...
...of letting those *subhumans* have them.
CRAK

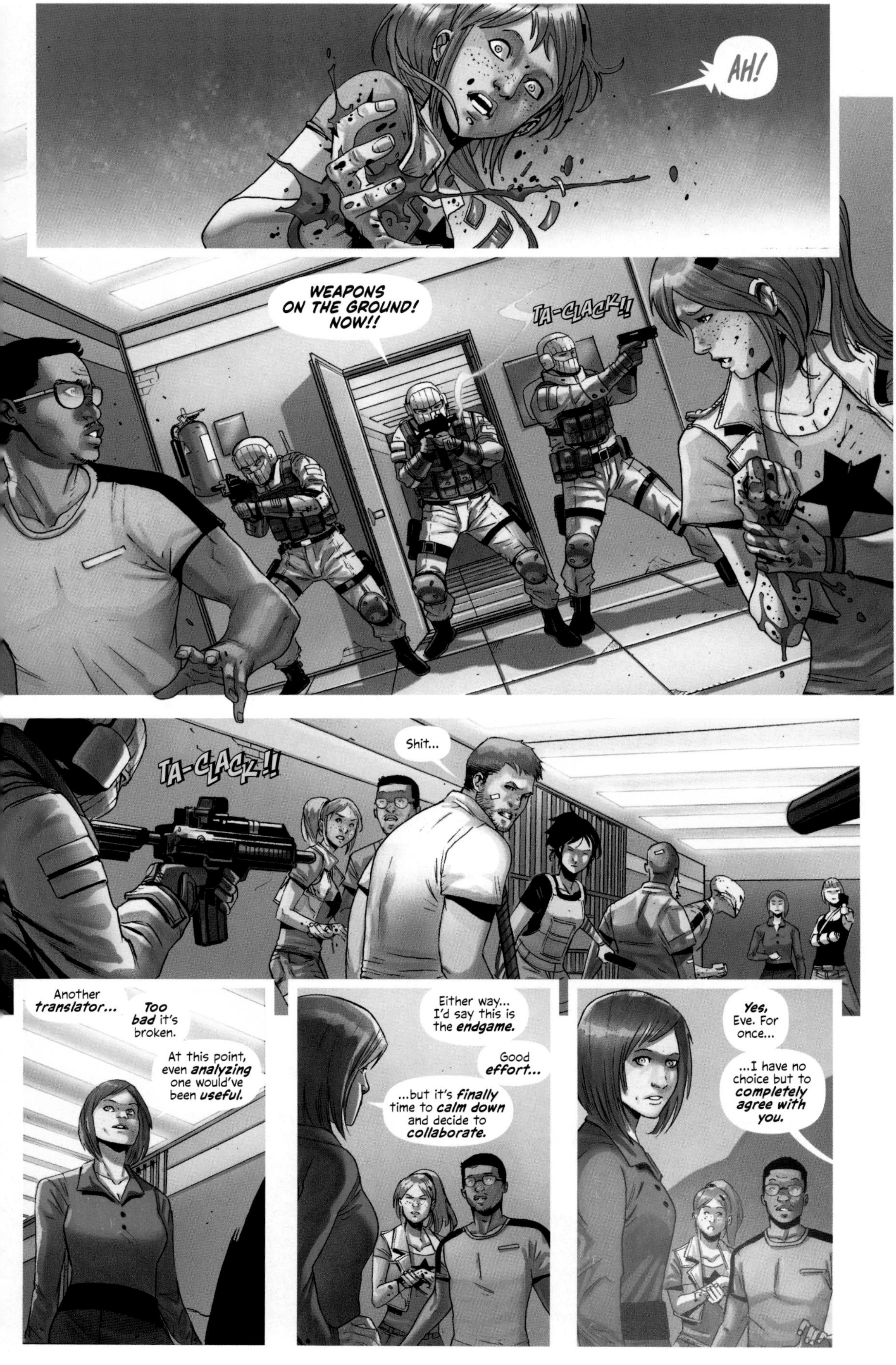
AH!
WEAPONS ON THE GROUND! NOW!!
TA-CLACK!!
TA-CLACK!!
Shit...
Another translator... Too bad it's broken.
At this point, even analyzing one would've been useful.
Either way... I'd say this is the endgame.
Good effort...
...but it's finally time to calm down and decide to collaborate.
Yes, Eve. For once...
...I have no choice but to completely agree with you.

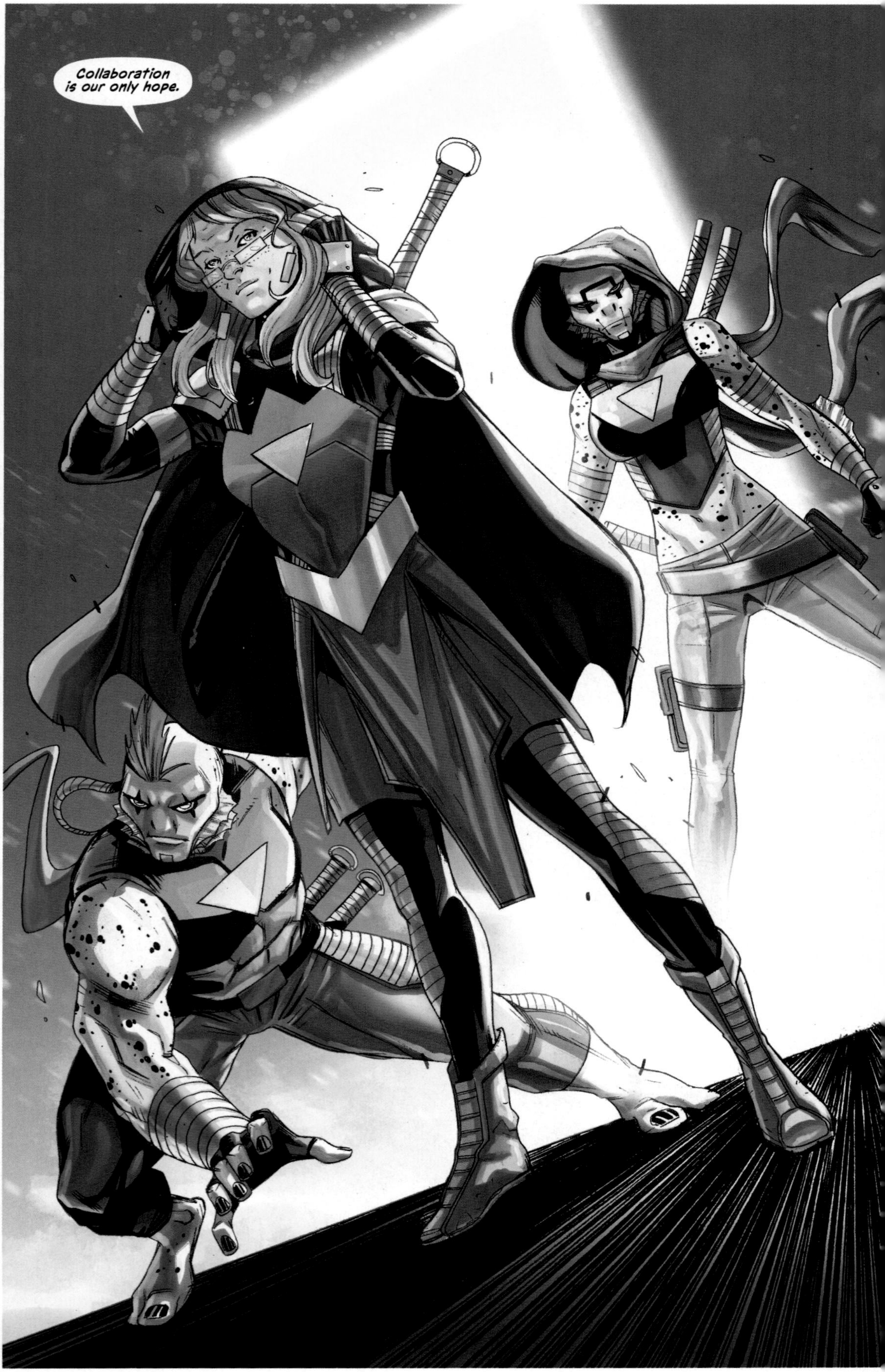
Collaboration is our only hope.

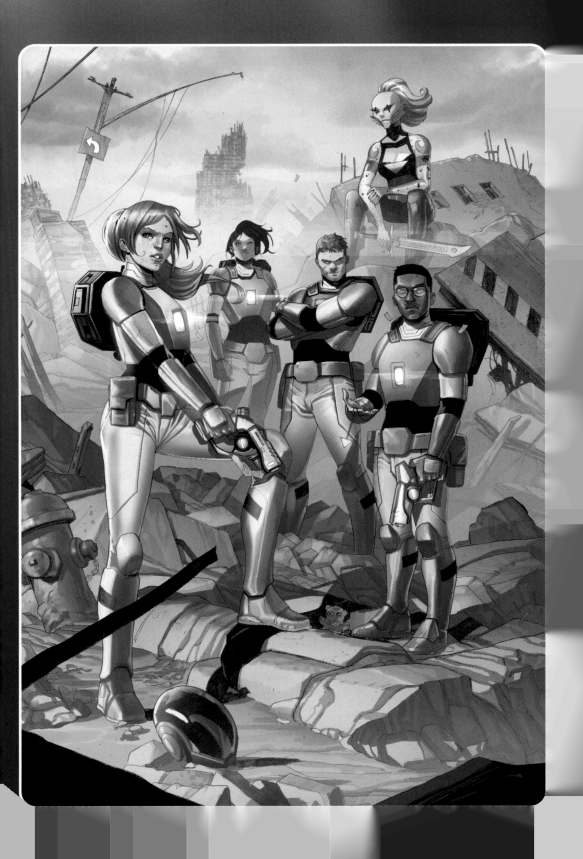

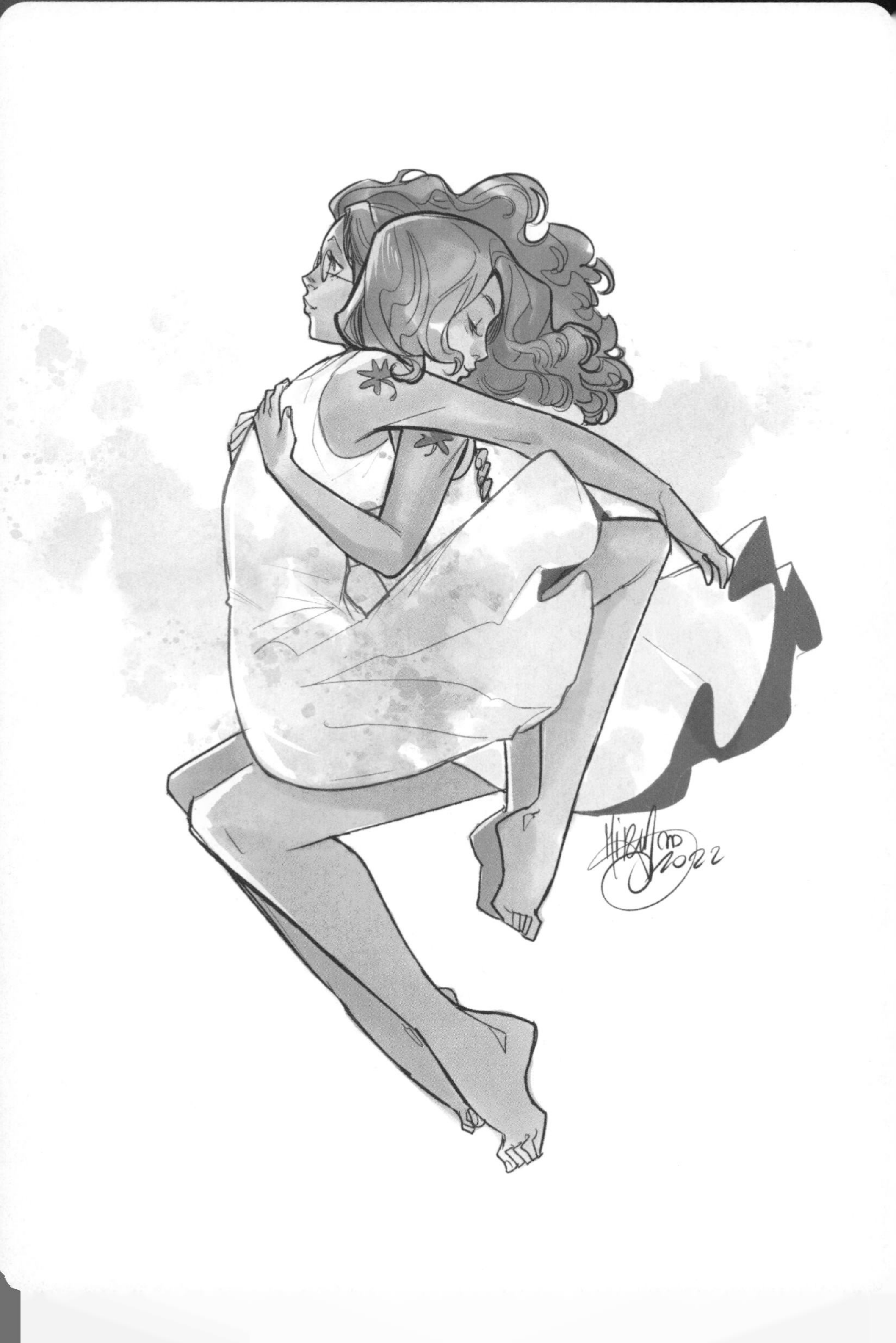

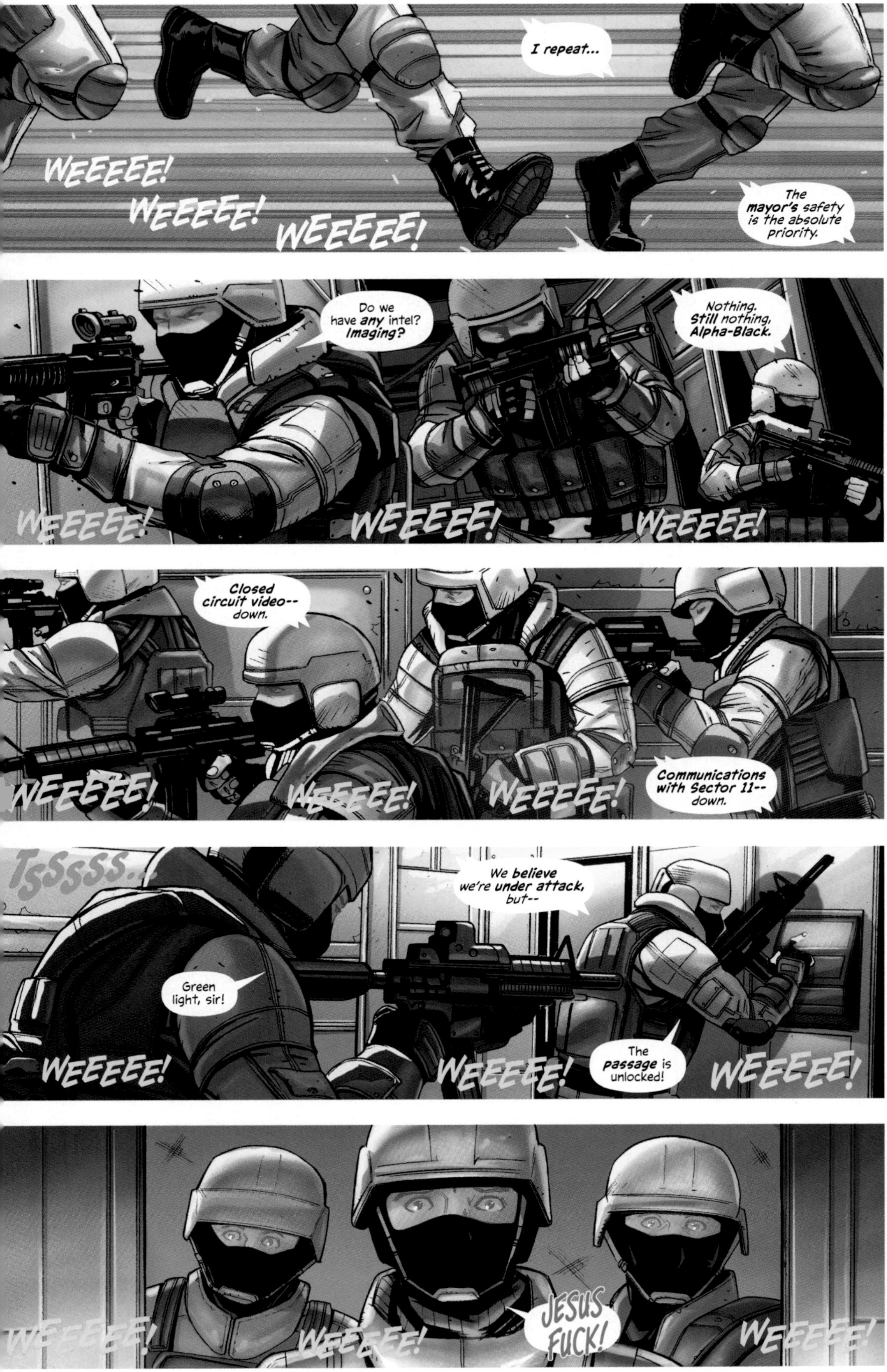
I repeat...
WEEEEE!
WEEEEE!
WEEEEE!
The mayor's safety is the absolute priority.
Do we have any intel? Imaging?
Nothing. Still nothing, Alpha-Black.
WEEEEE!
WEEEEE!
WEEEEE!
Closed circuit video-- down.
Communications with Sector 11-- down.
WEEEEE!
WEEEEE!
WEEEEE!
TSSSSS...
We believe we're under attack, but--
Green light, sir!
The passage is unlocked!
WEEEEE!
WEEEEE!
WEEEEE!
JESUS FUCK!
WEEEEE!
WEEEEE!
WEEEEE!

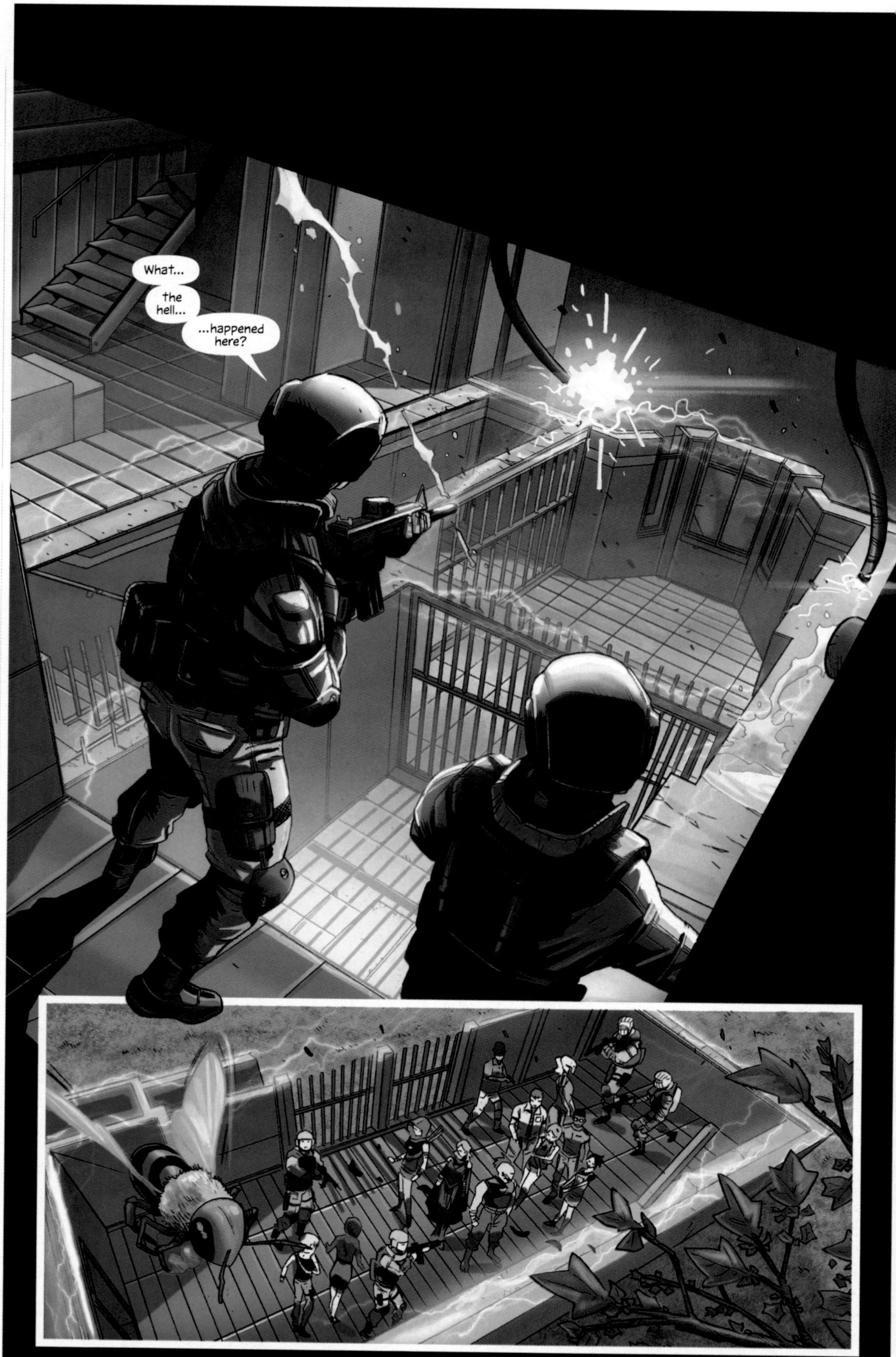
What...
the hell...
...happened here?

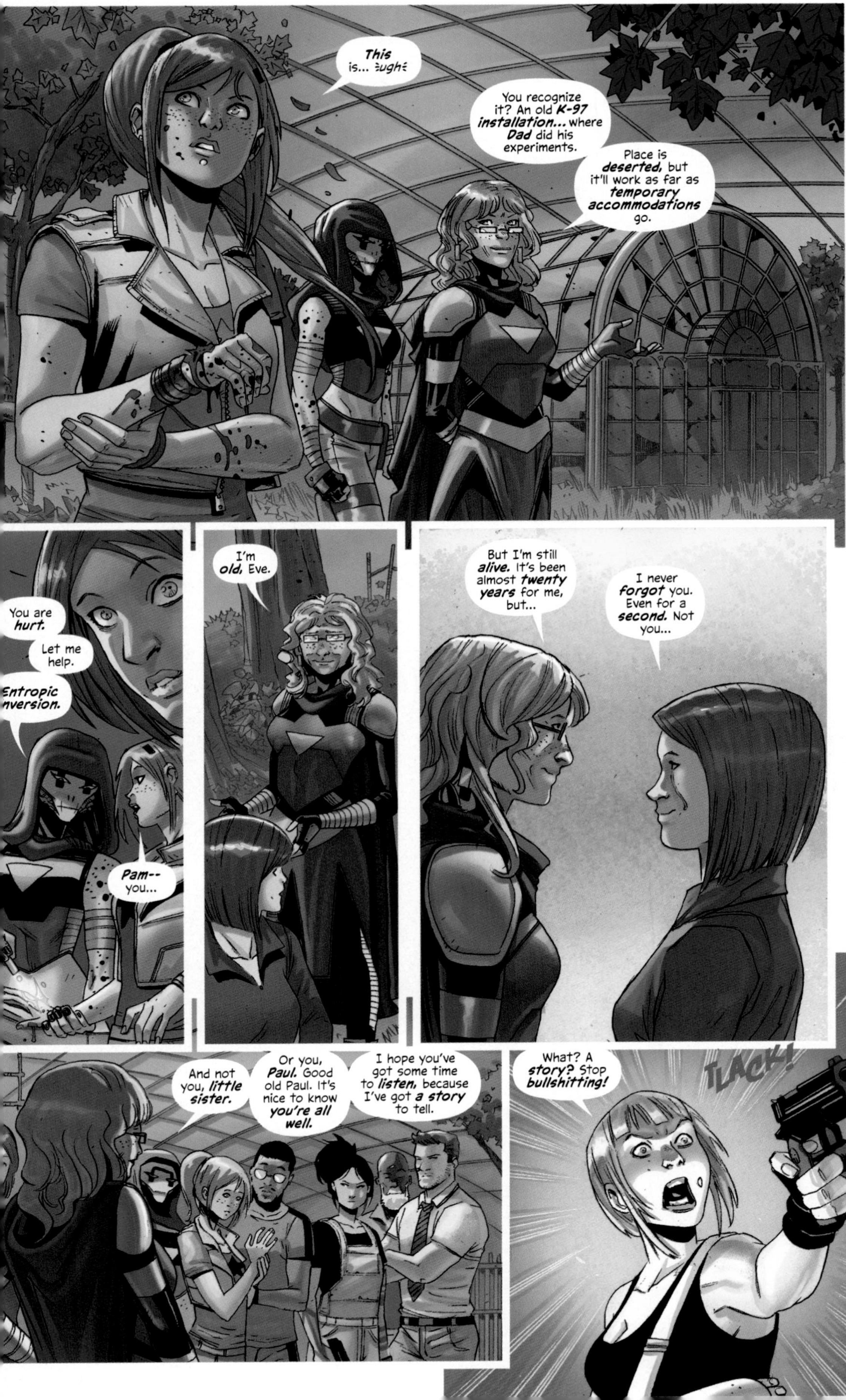

This is... *ugh*
You recognize it? An old ***K-97 installation...*** where ***Dad*** did his experiments.
Place is ***deserted,*** but it'll work as far as ***temporary accommodations*** go.
You are ***hurt.***
Let me help.
Entropic inversion.
Pam-- you...
I'm ***old,*** Eve.
But I'm still ***alive.*** It's been almost ***twenty years*** for me, but...
I never ***forgot*** you. Even for a ***second.*** Not you...
And not you, ***little sister.***
Or you, ***Paul.*** Good old Paul. It's nice to know ***you're all well.***
I hope you've got some time to ***listen,*** because I've got ***a story*** to tell.
What? A ***story?*** Stop ***bullshitting!***
TLACK!

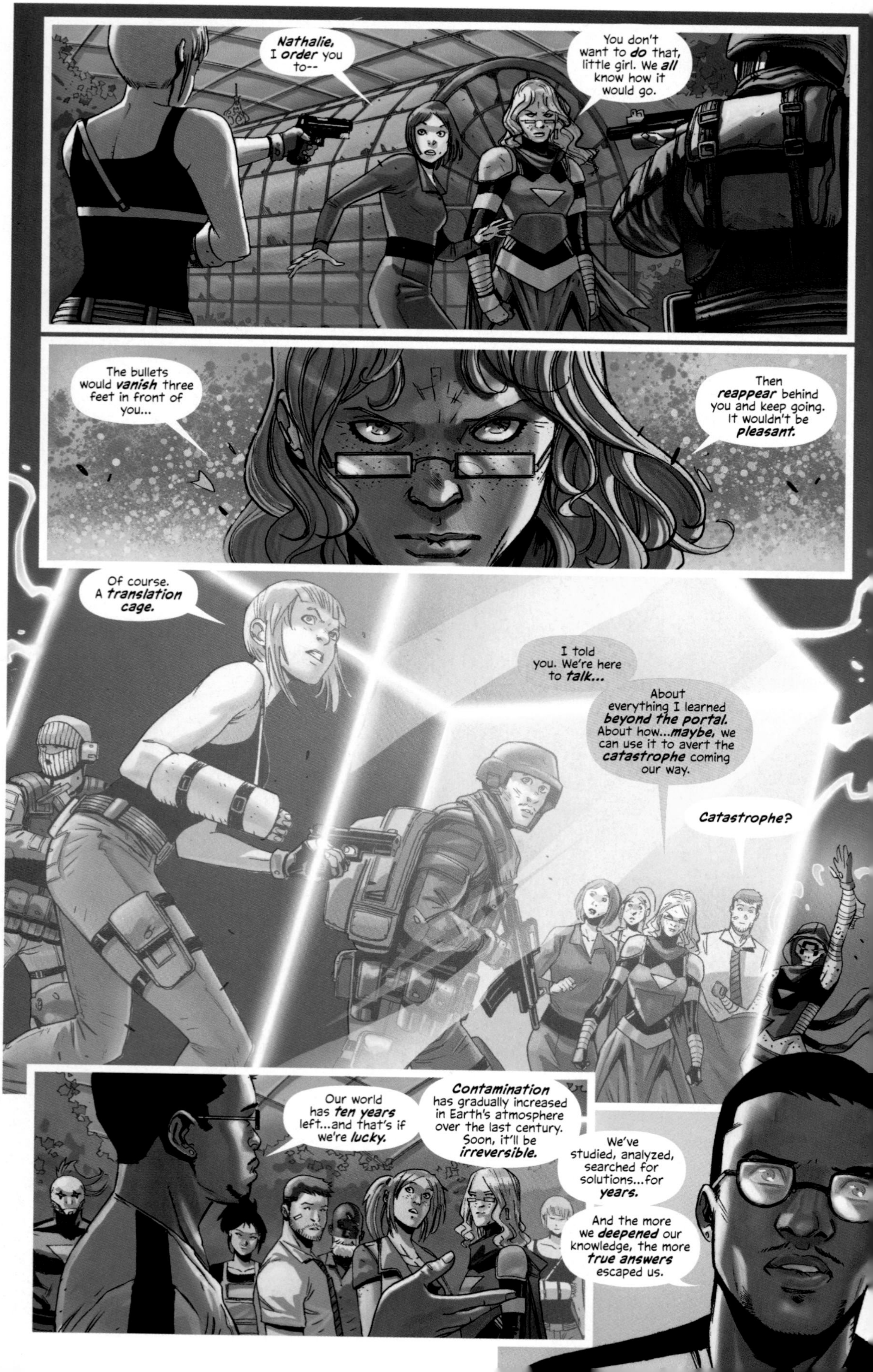
Nathalie, I order you to--
You don't want to do that, little girl. We all know how it would go.
The bullets would vanish three feet in front of you...
Then reappear behind you and keep going. It wouldn't be pleasant.
Of course. A translation cage.
I told you. We're here to talk...
About everything I learned beyond the portal. About how...maybe, we can use it to avert the catastrophe coming our way.
Catastrophe?
Our world has ten years left...and that's if we're lucky.
Contamination has gradually increased in Earth's atmosphere over the last century. Soon, it'll be irreversible.
We've studied, analyzed, searched for solutions...for years.
And the more we deepened our knowledge, the more true answers escaped us.

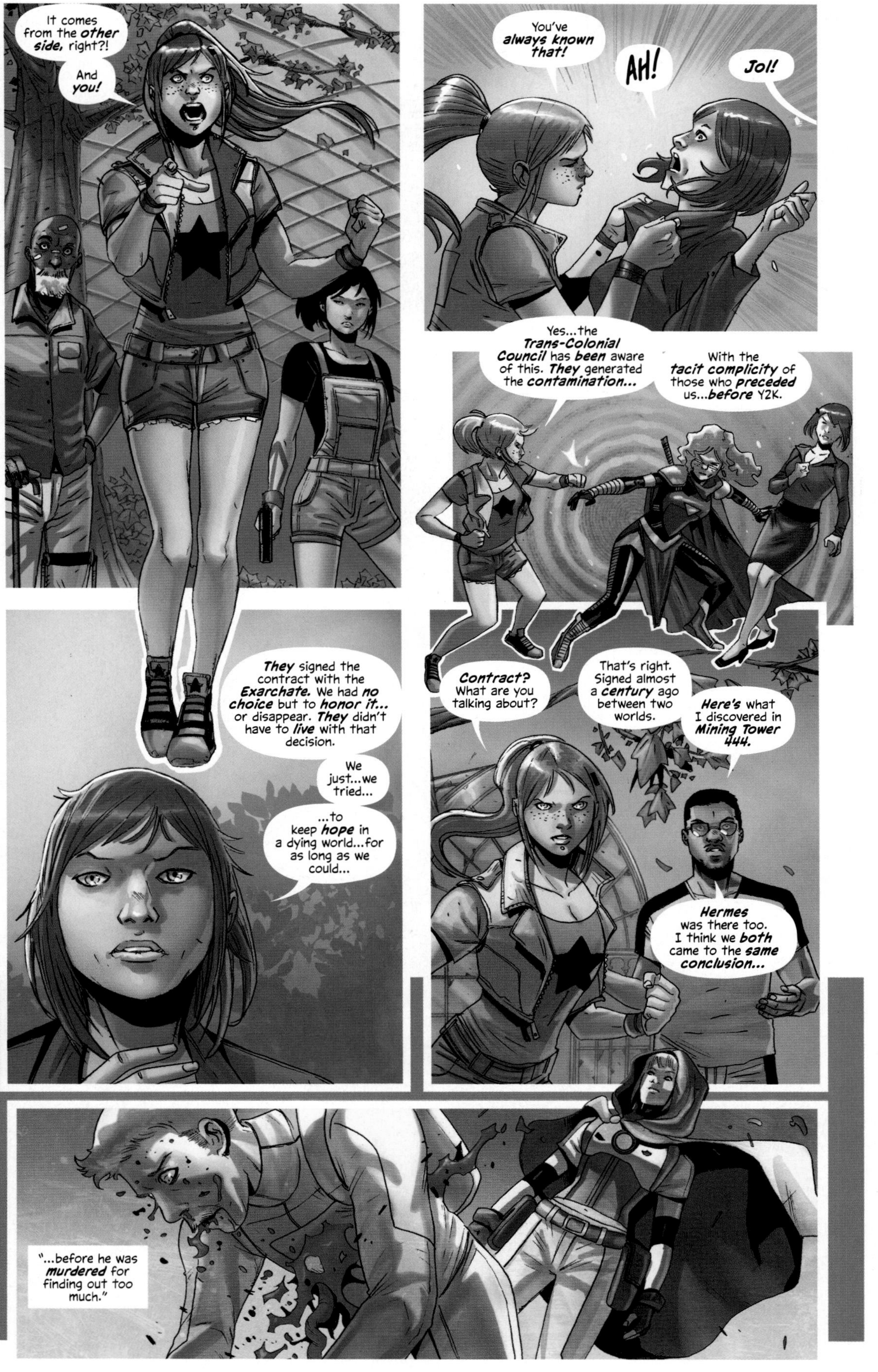
It comes from the other side, right?!
And you!
You've always known that!
AH!
Jol!
Yes...the Trans-Colonial Council has been aware of this. They generated the contamination...
With the tacit complicity of those who preceded us...before Y2K.
They signed the contract with the Exarchate. We had no choice but to honor it... or disappear. They didn't have to live with that decision.
We just...we tried...
...to keep hope in a dying world...for as long as we could...
Contract? What are you talking about?
That's right. Signed almost a century ago between two worlds.
Here's what I discovered in Mining Tower 444.
Hermes was there too. I think we both came to the same conclusion...
"...before he was murdered for finding out too much."

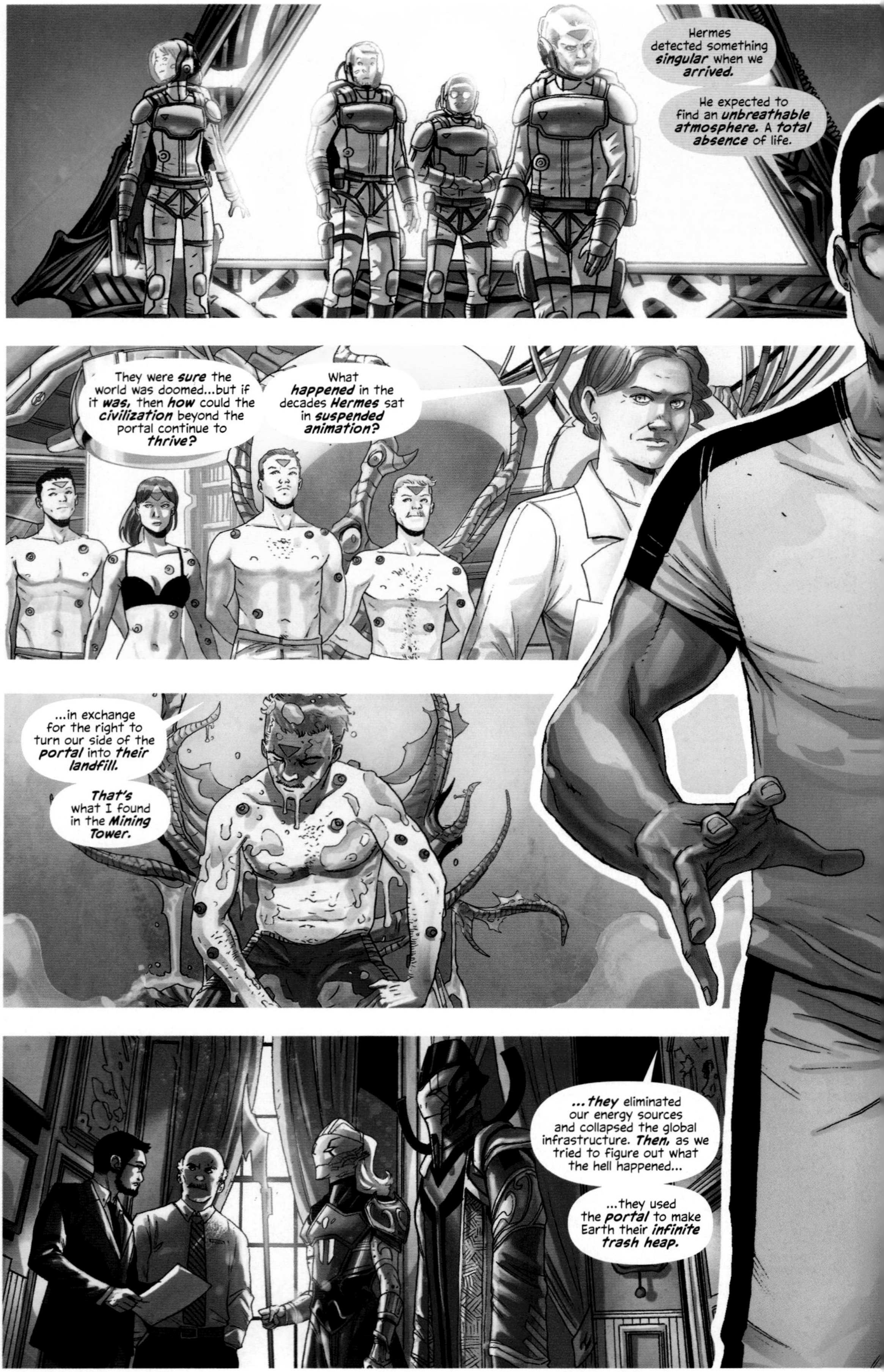
Hermes detected something *singular* when we *arrived.*
He expected to find an *unbreathable atmosphere.* A *total absence* of life.
They were *sure* the world was doomed...but if it *was,* then *how* could the *civilization* beyond the portal continue to *thrive?*
What *happened* in the decades *Hermes* sat in *suspended animation?*
...in exchange for the right to turn our side of the *portal* into *their landfill.*
That's what I found in the *Mining Tower.*
...they eliminated our energy sources and collapsed the global infrastructure. *Then,* as we tried to figure out what the hell happened...
...they used the *portal* to make Earth their *infinite trash heap.*

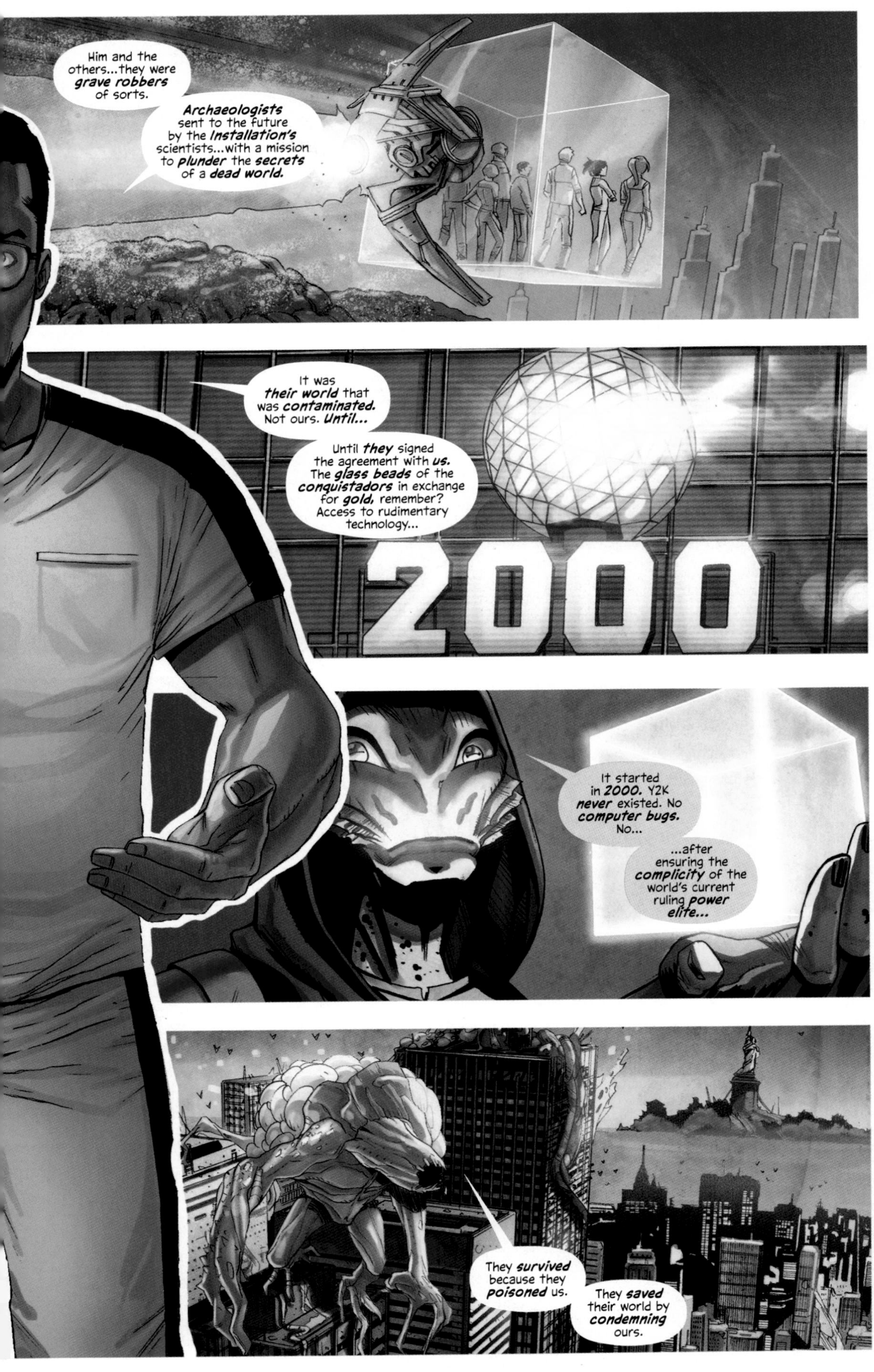
Him and the others...they were grave robbers of sorts.
Archaeologists sent to the future by the Installation's scientists...with a mission to plunder the secrets of a dead world.
It was their world that was contaminated. Not ours. Until...
Until they signed the agreement with us. The glass beads of the conquistadors in exchange for gold, remember? Access to rudimentary technology...
2000
It started in 2000. Y2K never existed. No computer bugs. No...
...after ensuring the complicity of the world's current ruling power elite...
They survived because they poisoned us.
They saved their world by condemning ours.

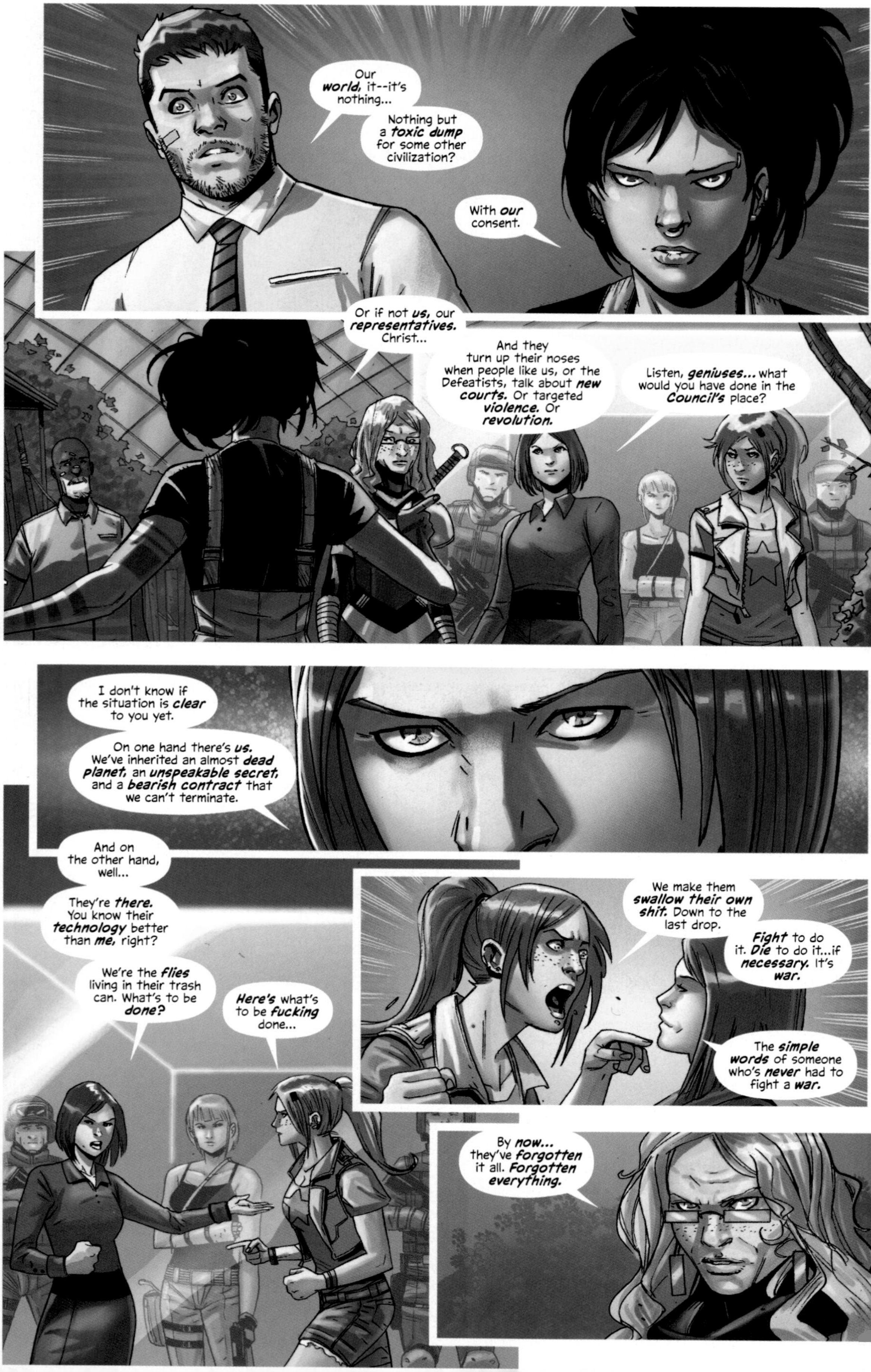

Our world, it--it's nothing...
Nothing but a toxic dump for some other civilization?
With our consent.
Or if not us, our representatives. Christ...
And they turn up their noses when people like us, or the Defeatists, talk about new courts. Or targeted violence. Or revolution.
Listen, geniuses... what would you have done in the Council's place?
I don't know if the situation is clear to you yet.
On one hand there's us. We've inherited an almost dead planet, an unspeakable secret, and a bearish contract that we can't terminate.
And on the other hand, well...
They're there. You know their technology better than me, right?
We're the flies living in their trash can. What's to be done?
Here's what's to be fucking done...
We make them swallow their own shit. Down to the last drop.
Fight to do it. Die to do it...if necessary. It's war.
The simple words of someone who's never had to fight a war.
By now... they've forgotten it all. Forgotten everything.

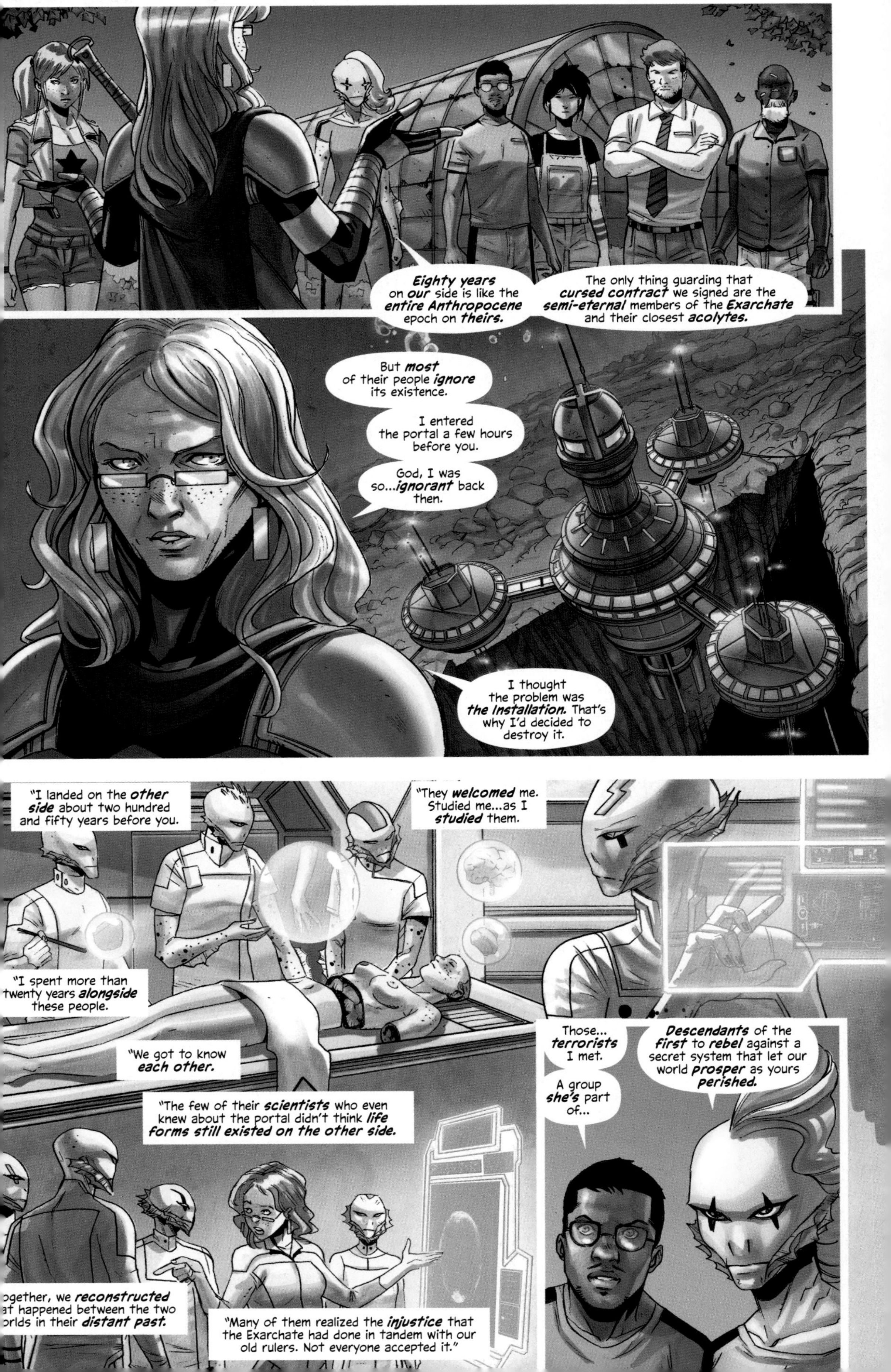

Eighty years on our side is like the entire Anthropocene epoch on theirs.
The only thing guarding that cursed contract we signed are the semi-eternal members of the Exarchate and their closest acolytes.
But most of their people ignore its existence.
I entered the portal a few hours before you.
God, I was so...ignorant back then.
I thought the problem was the Installation. That's why I'd decided to destroy it.
"I landed on the other side about two hundred and fifty years before you.
"They welcomed me. Studied me...as I studied them.
"I spent more than twenty years alongside these people.
"We got to know each other.
"The few of their scientists who even knew about the portal didn't think life forms still existed on the other side.
ogether, we reconstructed at happened between the two orlds in their distant past.
"Many of them realized the injustice that the Exarchate had done in tandem with our old rulers. Not everyone accepted it."
Those... terrorists I met.
A group she's part of...
Descendants of the first to rebel against a secret system that let our world prosper as yours perished.

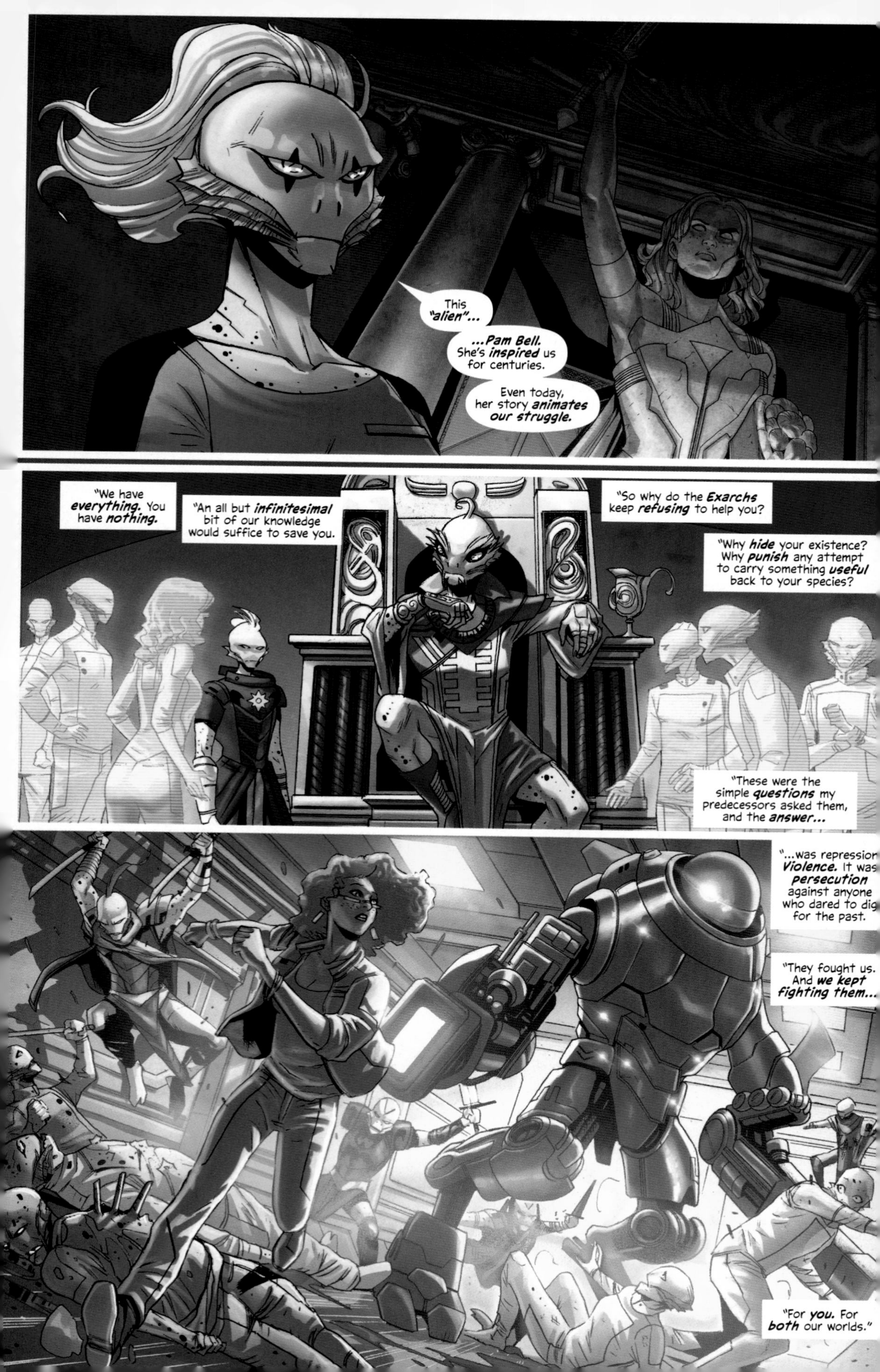
This "alien"...
...Pam Bell. She's inspired us for centuries.
Even today, her story animates our struggle.
"We have everything. You have nothing.
"An all but infinitesimal bit of our knowledge would suffice to save you.
"So why do the Exarchs keep refusing to help you?
"Why hide your existence? Why punish any attempt to carry something useful back to your species?
"These were the simple questions my predecessors asked them, and the answer...
"...was repression. Violence. It was persecution against anyone who dared to dig for the past.
"They fought us. And we kept fighting them...
"For you. For both our worlds."

And I thought *I* was the **revolutionary**.

Ironic, isn't it? But since that *war*, as we **expected**...

We've been hopelessly **persecuted, hunted down**, and **executed**...

"We took refuge **underground**, on the edge of their asthenosphere...deep enough to evade detection.

"There, we became aware of a **horrible truth**.

"We could **never** have reversed the **status quo**...not without **your help**.

"I went back through the **portal** in the opposite direction, just over **twenty years** after I had entered.

"*This* is why, *accompanied* by some of *them*...

"I decided to try to **go back**.

"I suppose *my* journey was similar to *yours*.

"I had *no idea* that just as I was leaving the *Installation* behind...

"...You were on a **collision course** with it."

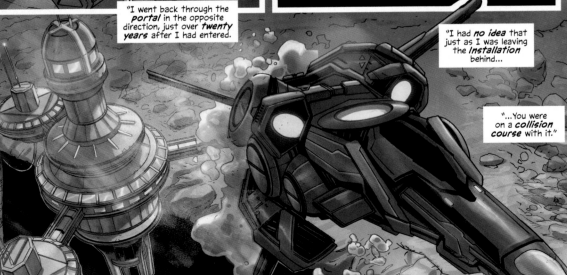

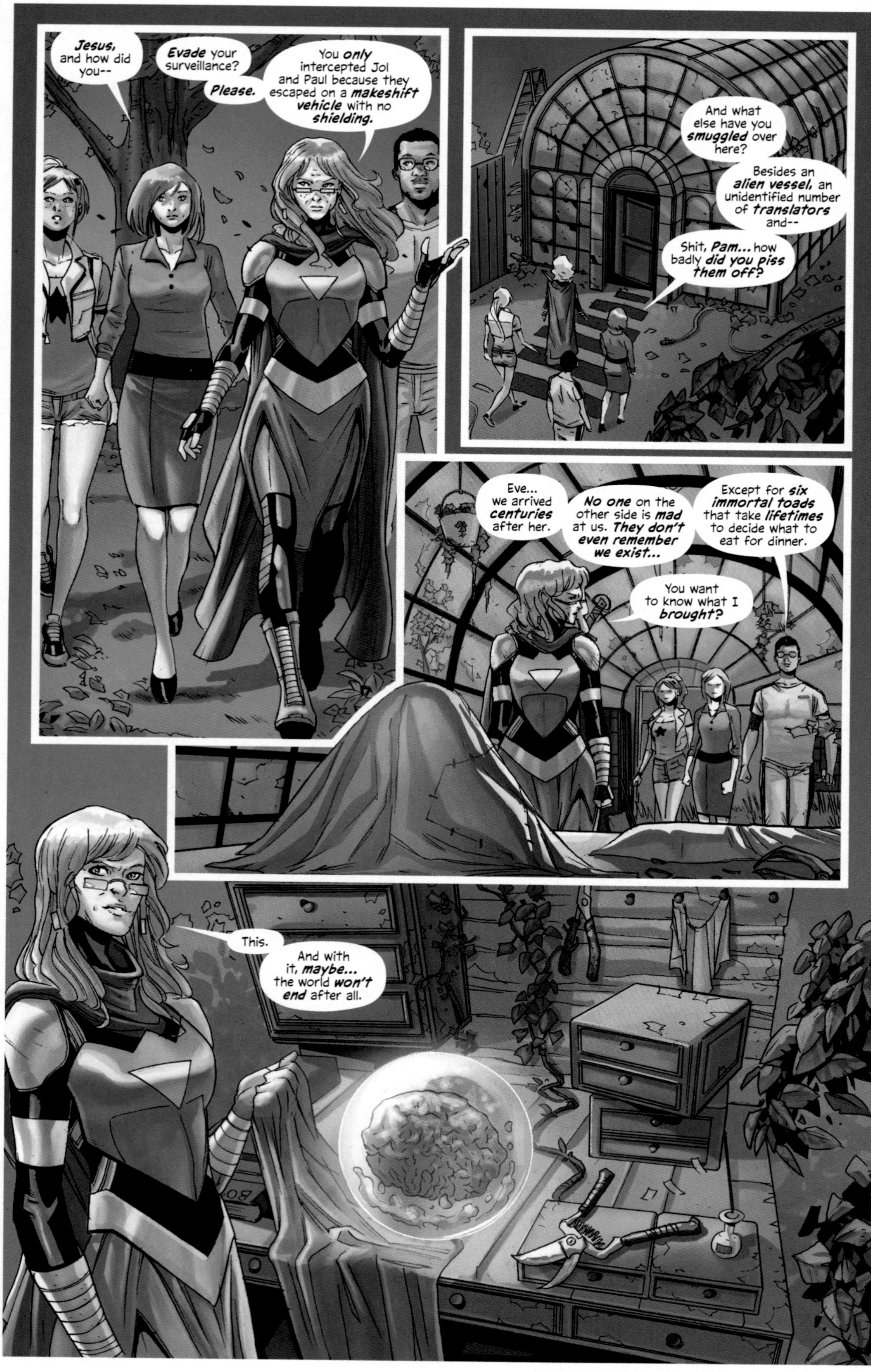

Jesus, and how did you--
Evade your surveillance?
Please.
You only intercepted Jol and Paul because they escaped on a makeshift vehicle with no shielding.
And what else have you smuggled over here?
Besides an alien vessel, an unidentified number of translators and--
Shit, Pam... how badly did you piss them off?
Eve... we arrived centuries after her.
No one on the other side is mad at us. They don't even remember we exist...
Except for six immortal toads that take lifetimes to decide what to eat for dinner.
You want to know what I brought?
This.
And with it, maybe... the world won't end after all.

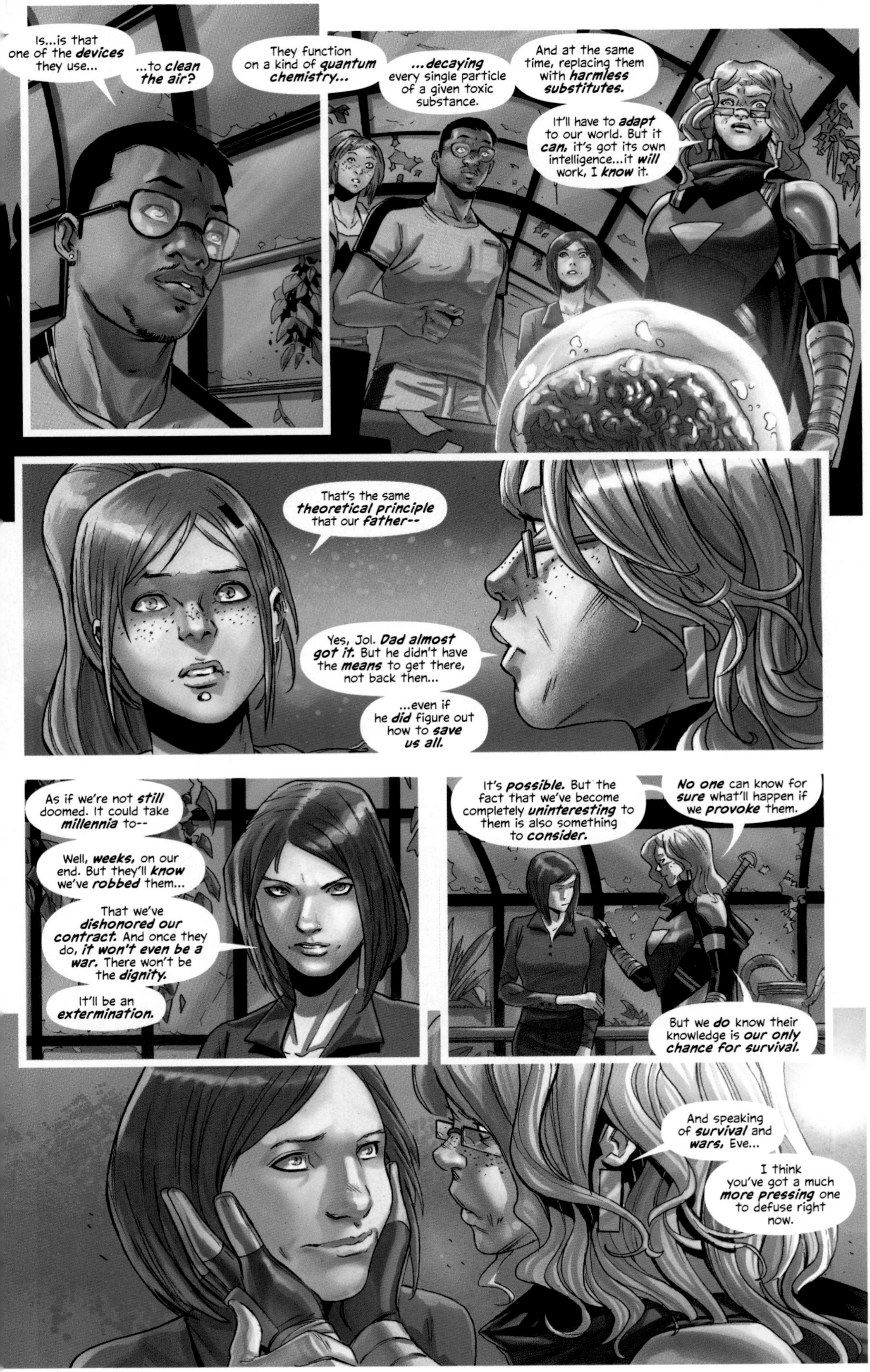
Is...is that one of the devices they use...
...to clean the air?
They function on a kind of quantum chemistry...
...decaying every single particle of a given toxic substance.
And at the same time, replacing them with harmless substitutes.
It'll have to adapt to our world. But it can, it's got its own intelligence...it will work, I know it.
That's the same theoretical principle that our father--
Yes, Jol. Dad almost got it. But he didn't have the means to get there, not back then...
...even if he did figure out how to save us all.
As if we're not still doomed. It could take millennia to--
Well, weeks, on our end. But they'll know we've robbed them...
That we've dishonored our contract. And once they do, it won't even be a war. There won't be the dignity.
It'll be an extermination.
It's possible. But the fact that we've become completely uninteresting to them is also something to consider.
No one can know for sure what'll happen if we provoke them.
But we do know their knowledge is our only chance for survival.
And speaking of survival and wars, Eve...
I think you've got a much more pressing one to defuse right now.

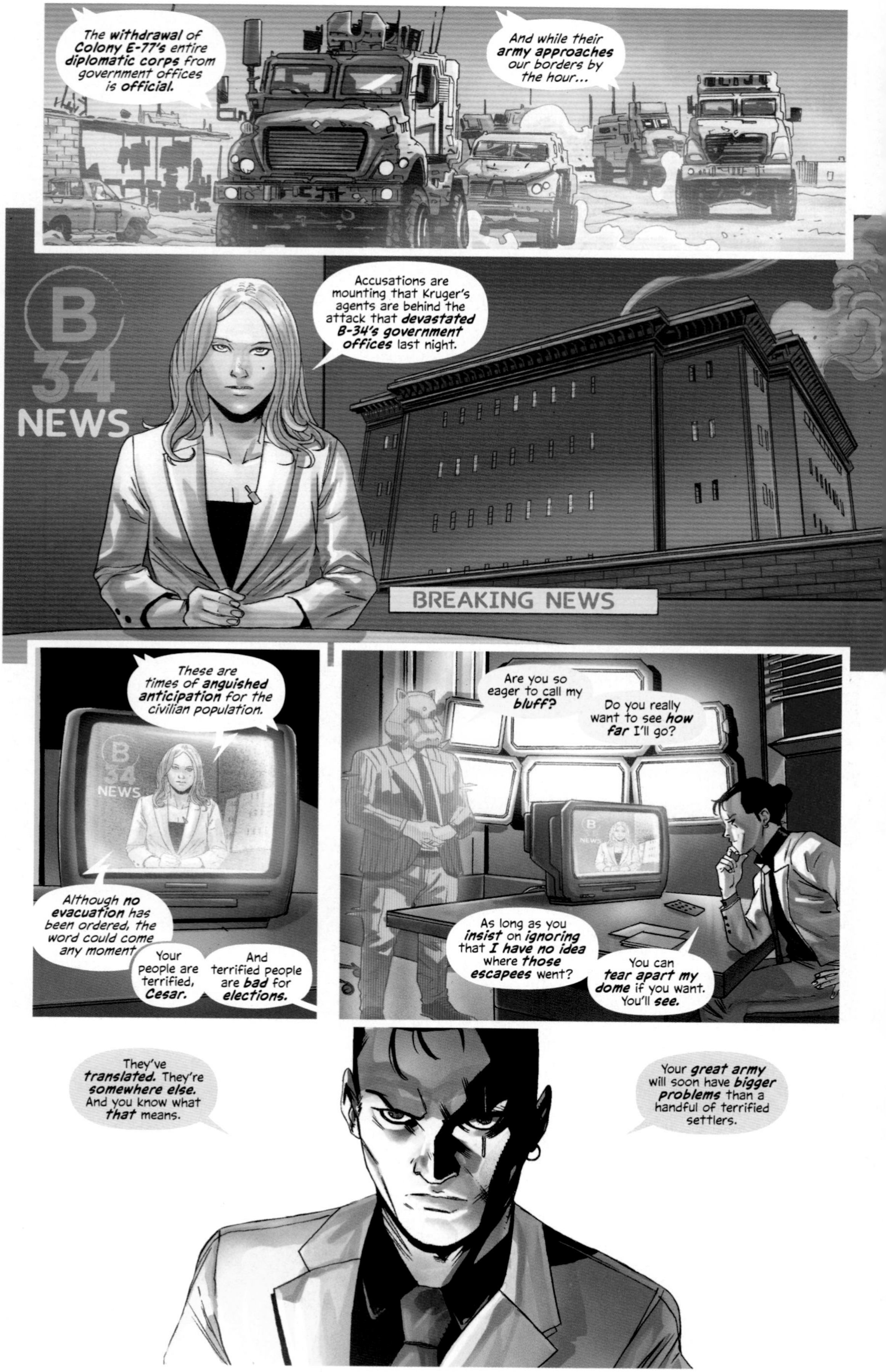
The withdrawal of Colony E-77's entire diplomatic corps from government offices is official.
And while their army approaches our borders by the hour...
B 34 NEWS
Accusations are mounting that Kruger's agents are behind the attack that devastated B-34's government offices last night.
BREAKING NEWS
These are times of anguished anticipation for the civilian population.
B 34 NEWS
Although no evacuation has been ordered, the word could come any moment.
Your people are terrified, Cesar.
And terrified people are bad for elections.
Are you so eager to call my bluff?
Do you really want to see how far I'll go?
As long as you insist on ignoring that I have no idea where those escapees went?
You can tear apart my dome if you want. You'll see.
They've translated. They're somewhere else. And you know what that means.
Your great army will soon have bigger problems than a handful of terrified settlers.

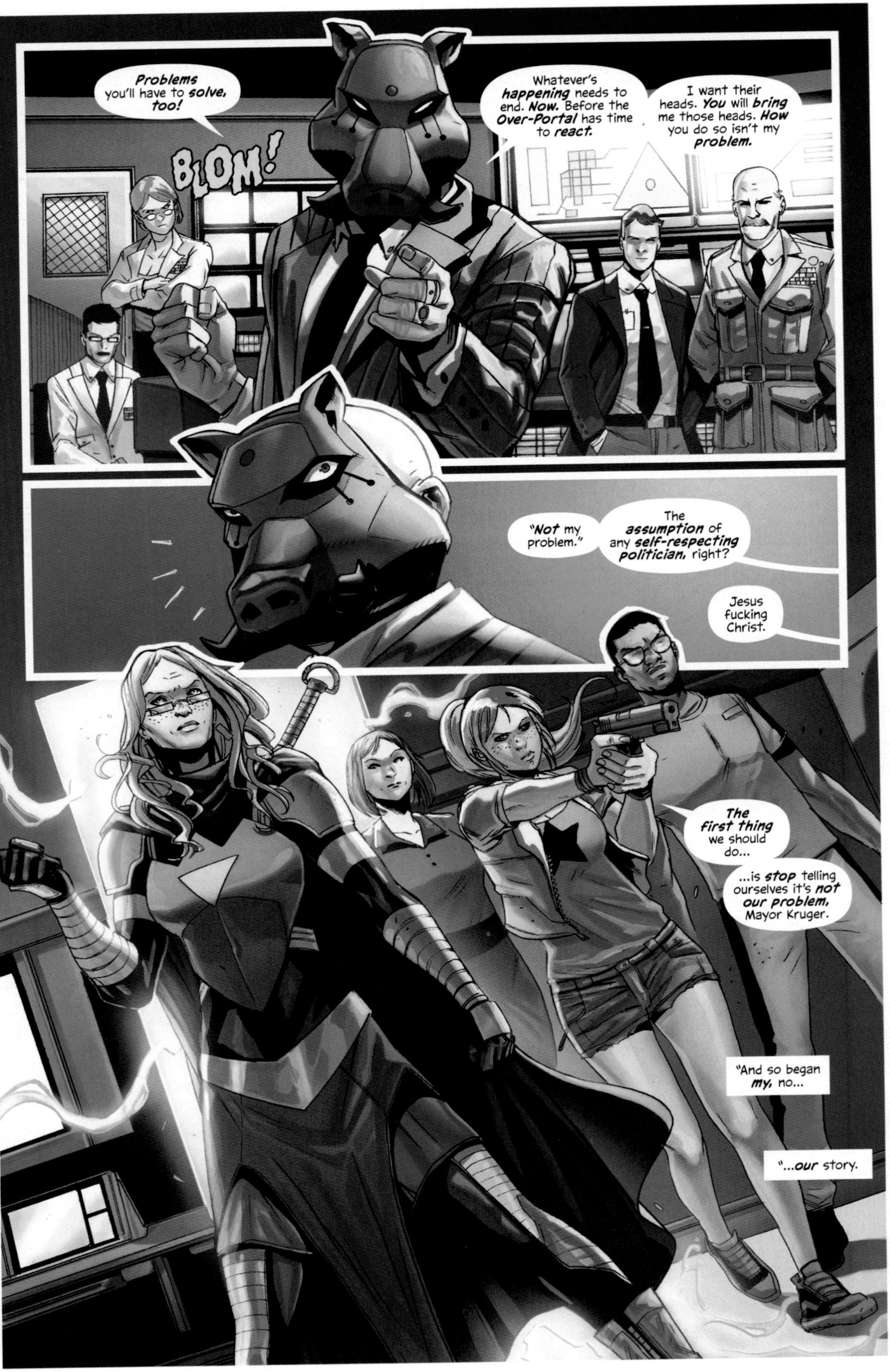
Problems you'll have to solve, too!
BLOM!
Whatever's happening needs to end. Now. Before the Over-Portal has time to react.
I want their heads. You will bring me those heads. How you do so isn't my problem.
"Not my problem."
The assumption of any self-respecting politician, right?
Jesus fucking Christ.
The first thing we should do...
...is stop telling ourselves it's not our problem, Mayor Kruger.
"And so began my, no...
"...our story.

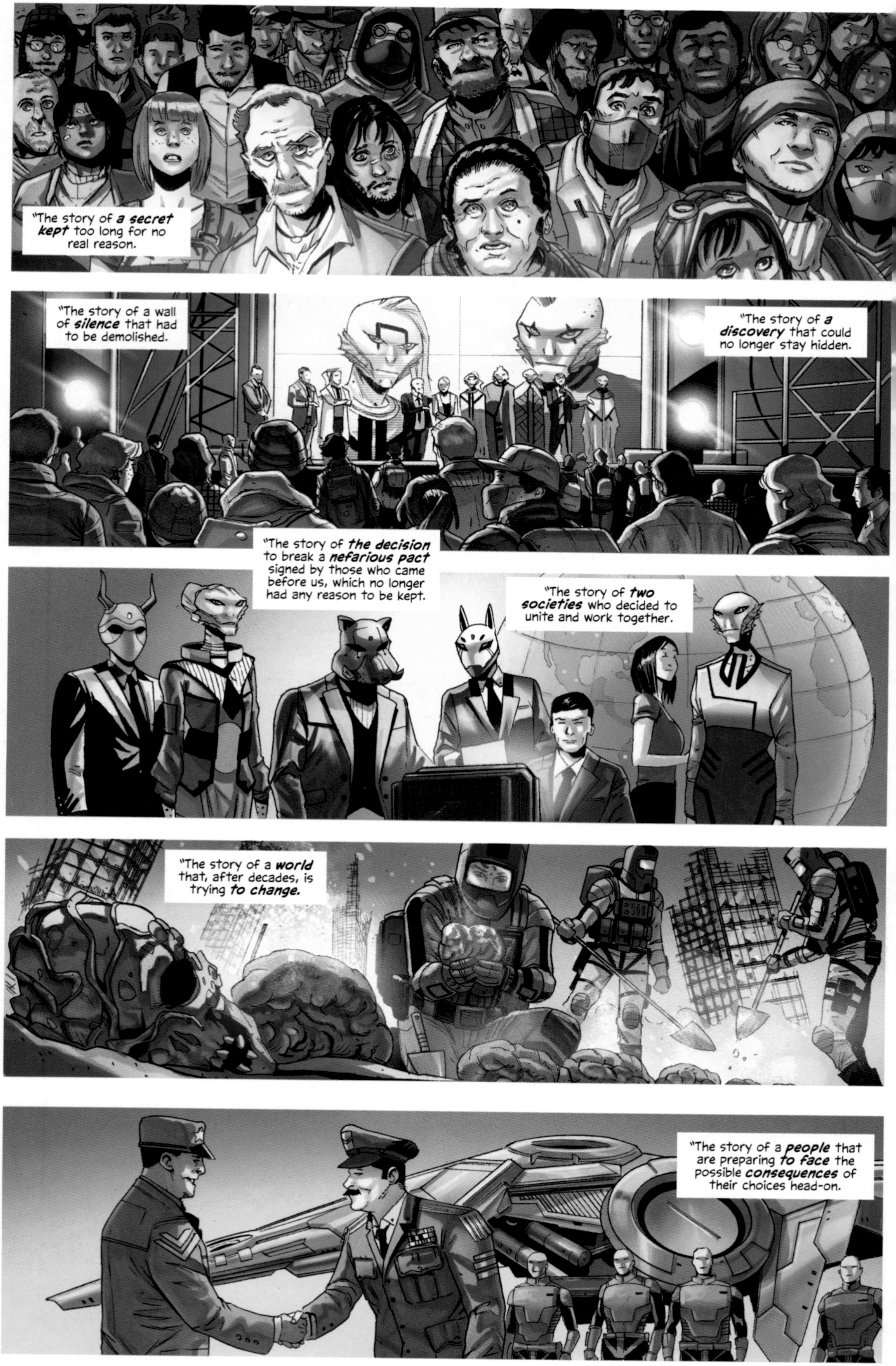
"The story of a secret kept too long for no real reason.
"The story of a wall of silence that had to be demolished.
"The story of a discovery that could no longer stay hidden.
"The story of the decision to break a nefarious pact signed by those who came before us, which no longer had any reason to be kept.
"The story of two societies who decided to unite and work together.
"The story of a world that, after decades, is trying to change.
"The story of a people that are preparing to face the possible consequences of their choices head-on.

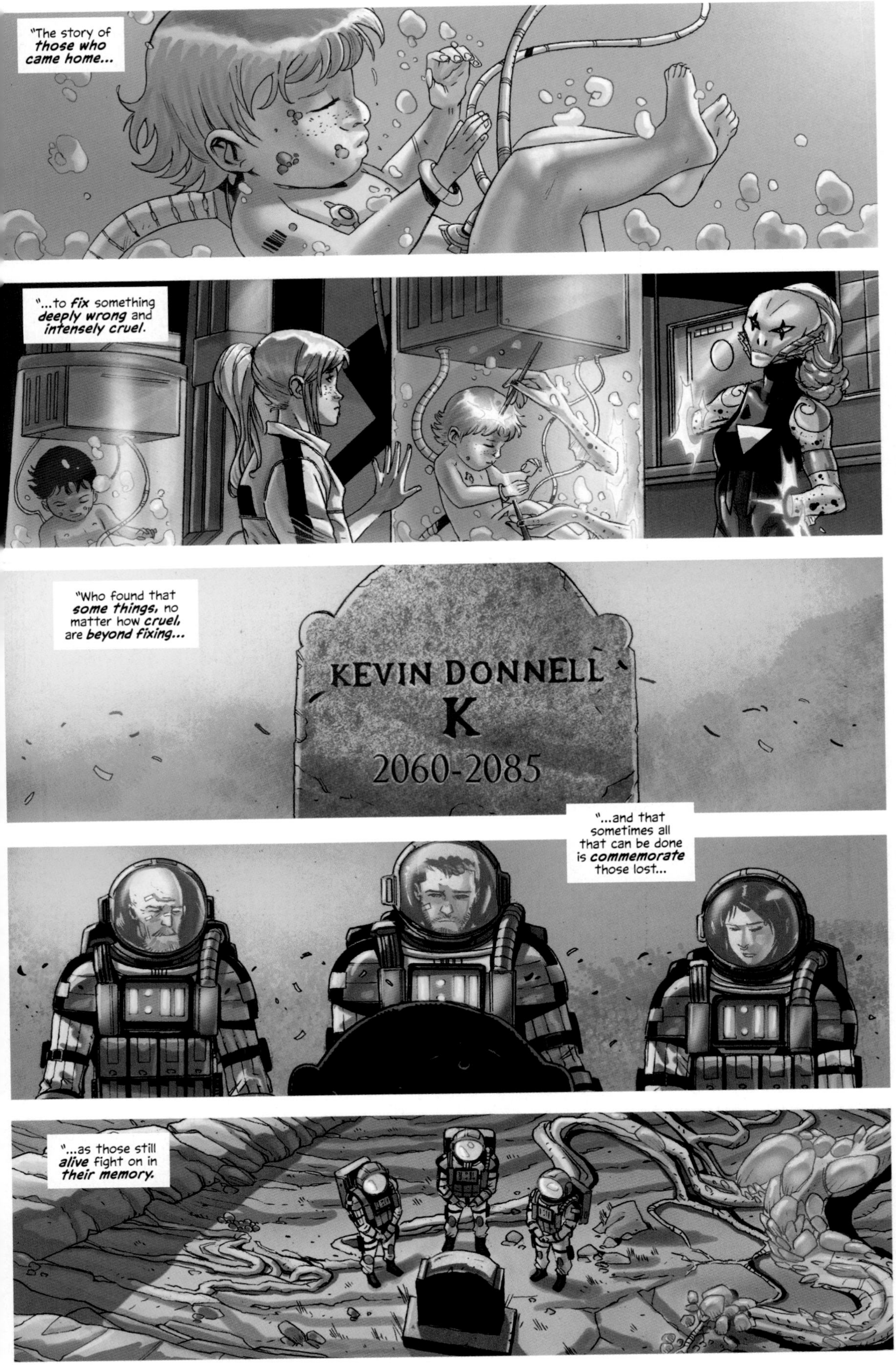
"The story of those who came home...
"...to fix something deeply wrong and intensely cruel.
"Who found that some things, no matter how cruel, are beyond fixing...
KEVIN DONNELL
K
2060-2085
"...and that sometimes all that can be done is commemorate those lost...
"...as those still alive fight on in their memory.

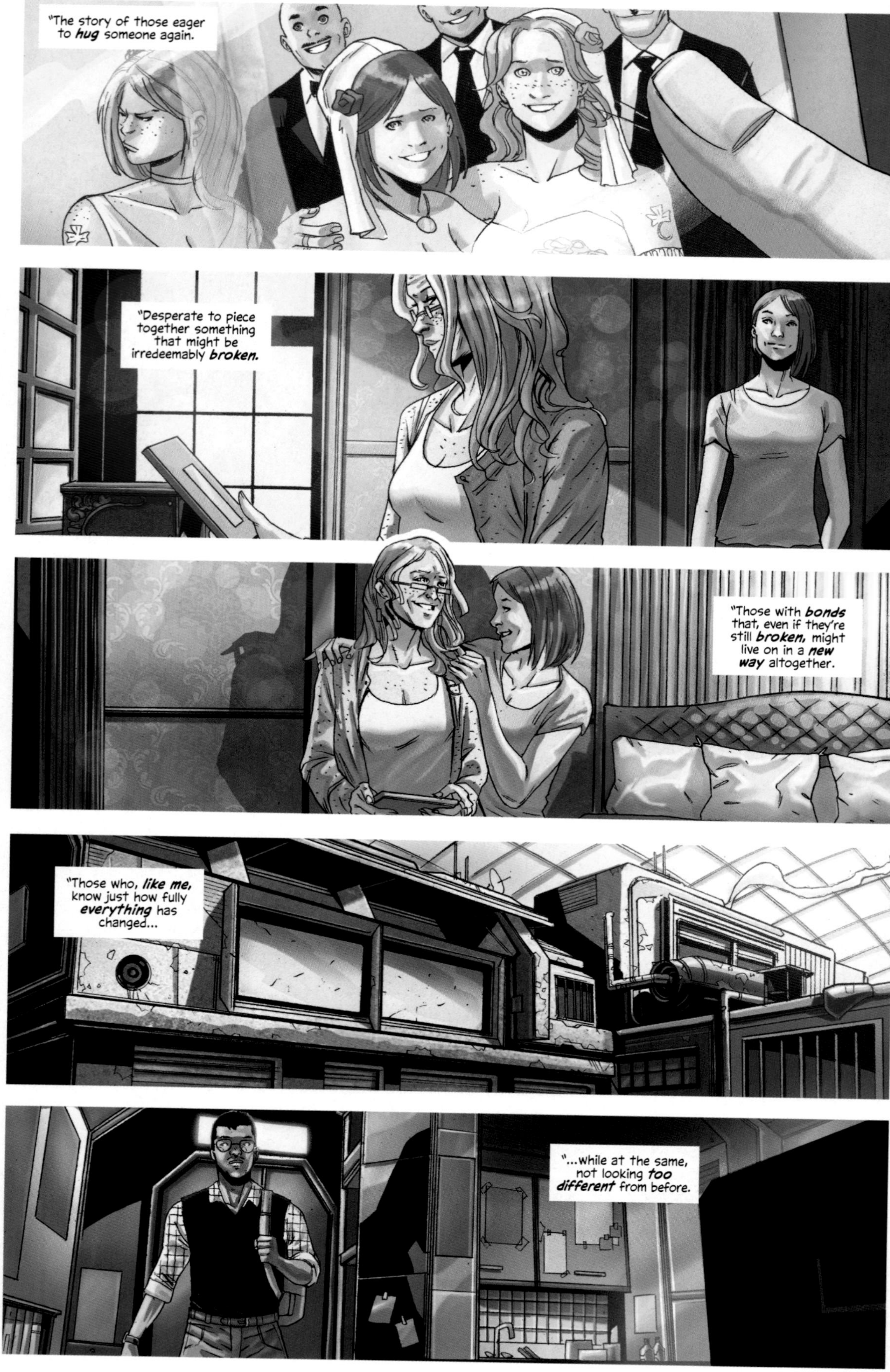
"The story of those eager to ***hug*** someone again.
"Desperate to piece together something that might be irredeemably ***broken.***
"Those with ***bonds*** that, even if they're still ***broken,*** might live on in a ***new way*** altogether.
"Those who, ***like me,*** know just how fully ***everything*** has changed...
"...while at the same, not looking ***too different*** from before.

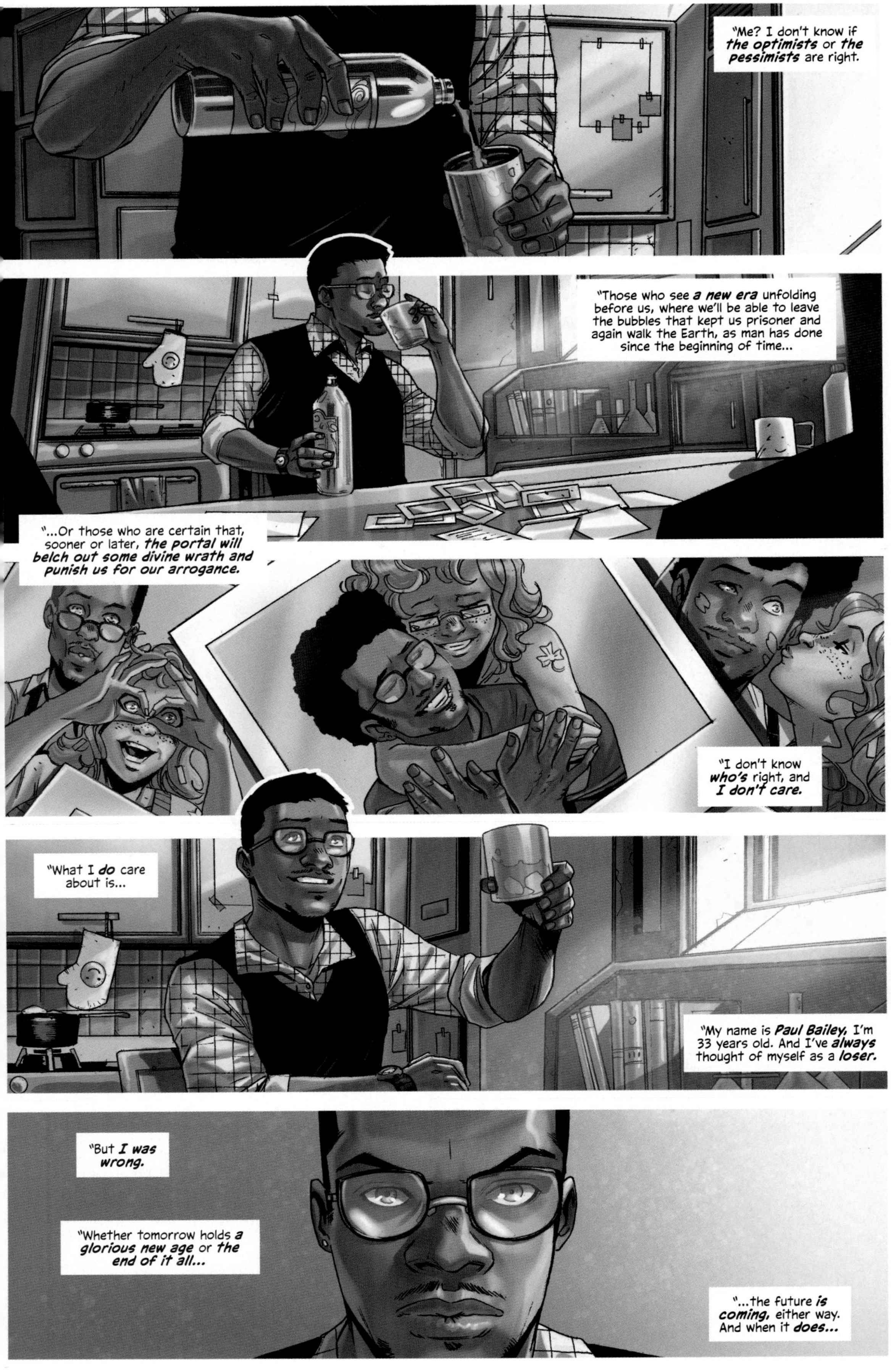
"Me? I don't know if *the optimists* or *the pessimists* are right.
"Those who see *a new era* unfolding before us, where we'll be able to leave the bubbles that kept us prisoner and again walk the Earth, as man has done since the beginning of time...
"...Or those who are certain that, sooner or later, *the portal will belch out some divine wrath and punish us for our arrogance.*
"I don't know *who's* right, and *I don't care.*
"What I *do* care about is...
"My name is *Paul Bailey,* I'm 33 years old. And I've *always* thought of myself as a *loser.*
"But *I was wrong.*
"Whether tomorrow holds *a glorious new age* or *the end of it all...*
"...the future *is coming,* either way. And when it *does...*

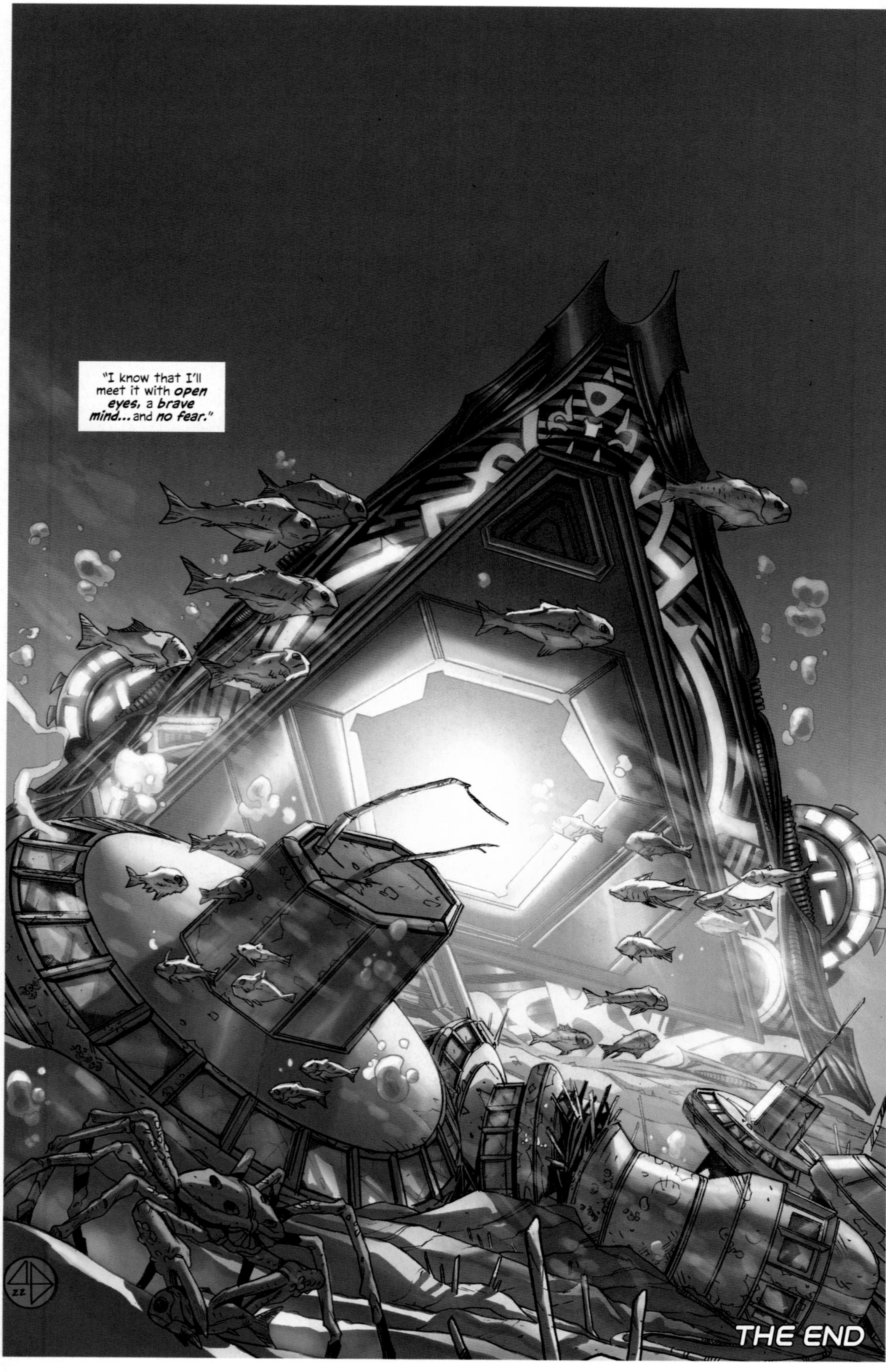
"I know that I'll meet it with *open eyes*, a *brave mind*... and *no fear*."
THE END

COVER GALLERY

`-,-`

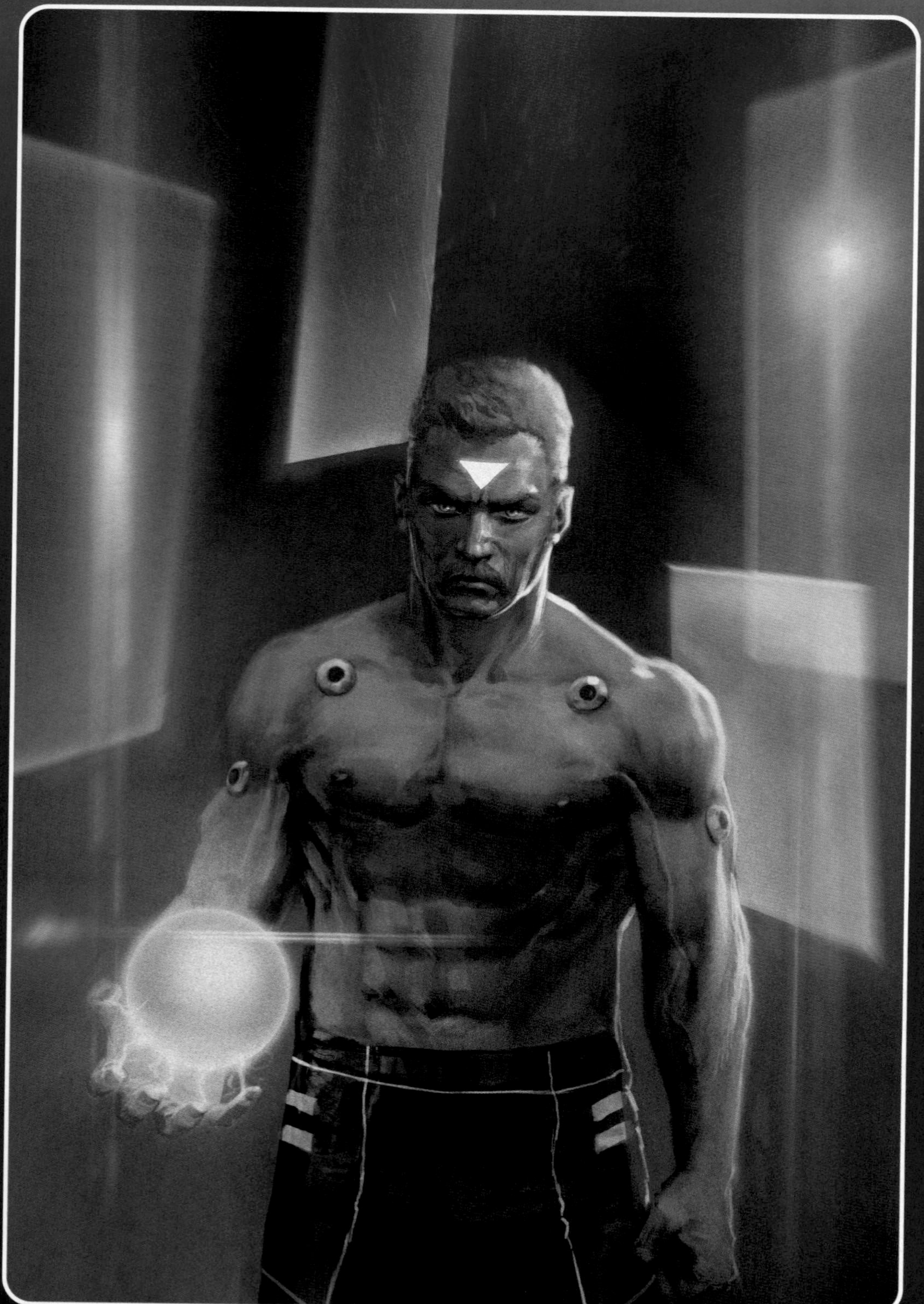

ANDREA MELONI

ISSUE 07

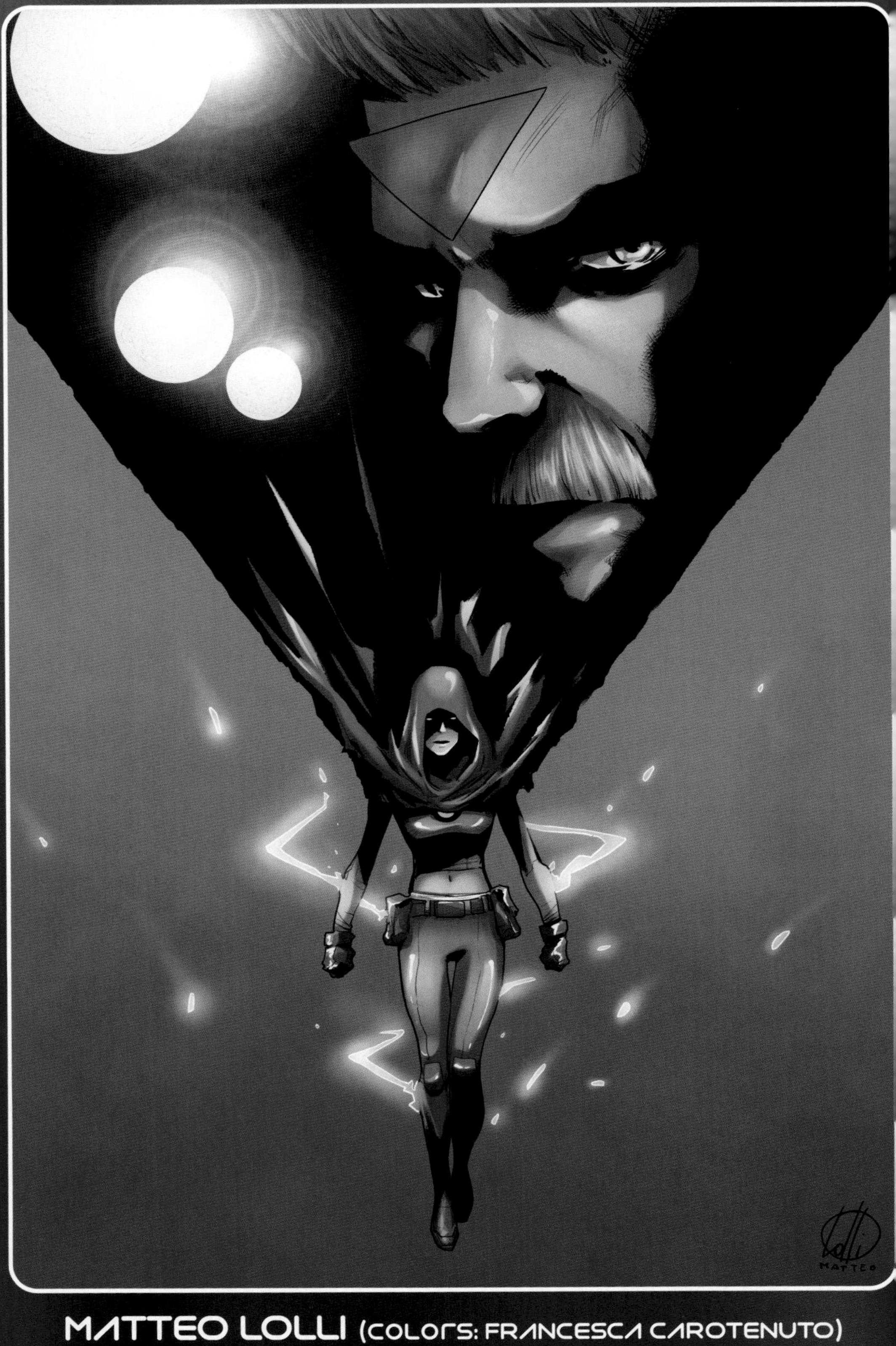

MATTEO LOLLI (colors: FRANCESCA CAROTENUTO)

ISSUE 07

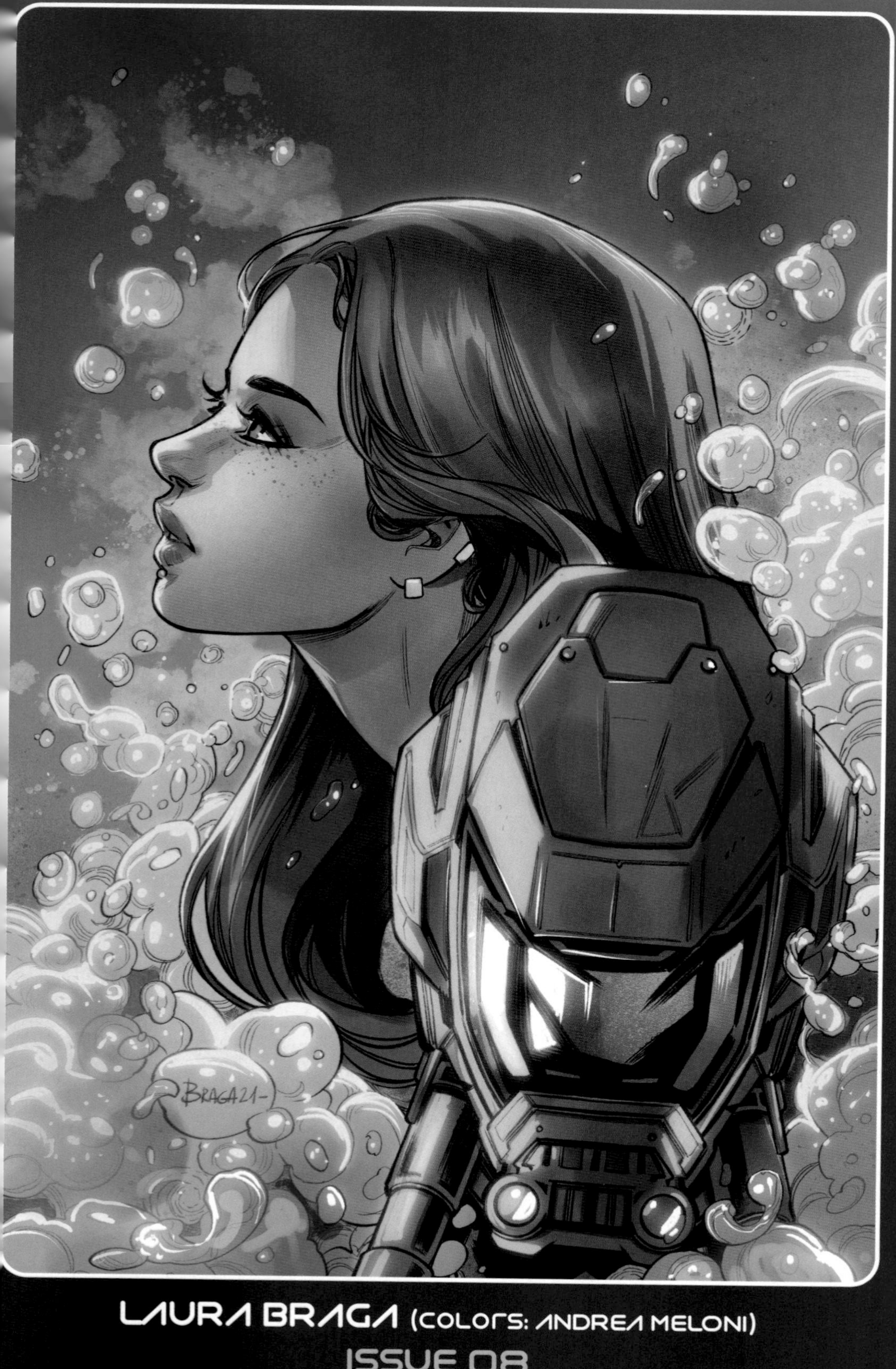
BRAGA21-

LAURA BRAGA (colors: ANDREA MELONI)

ISSUE 08

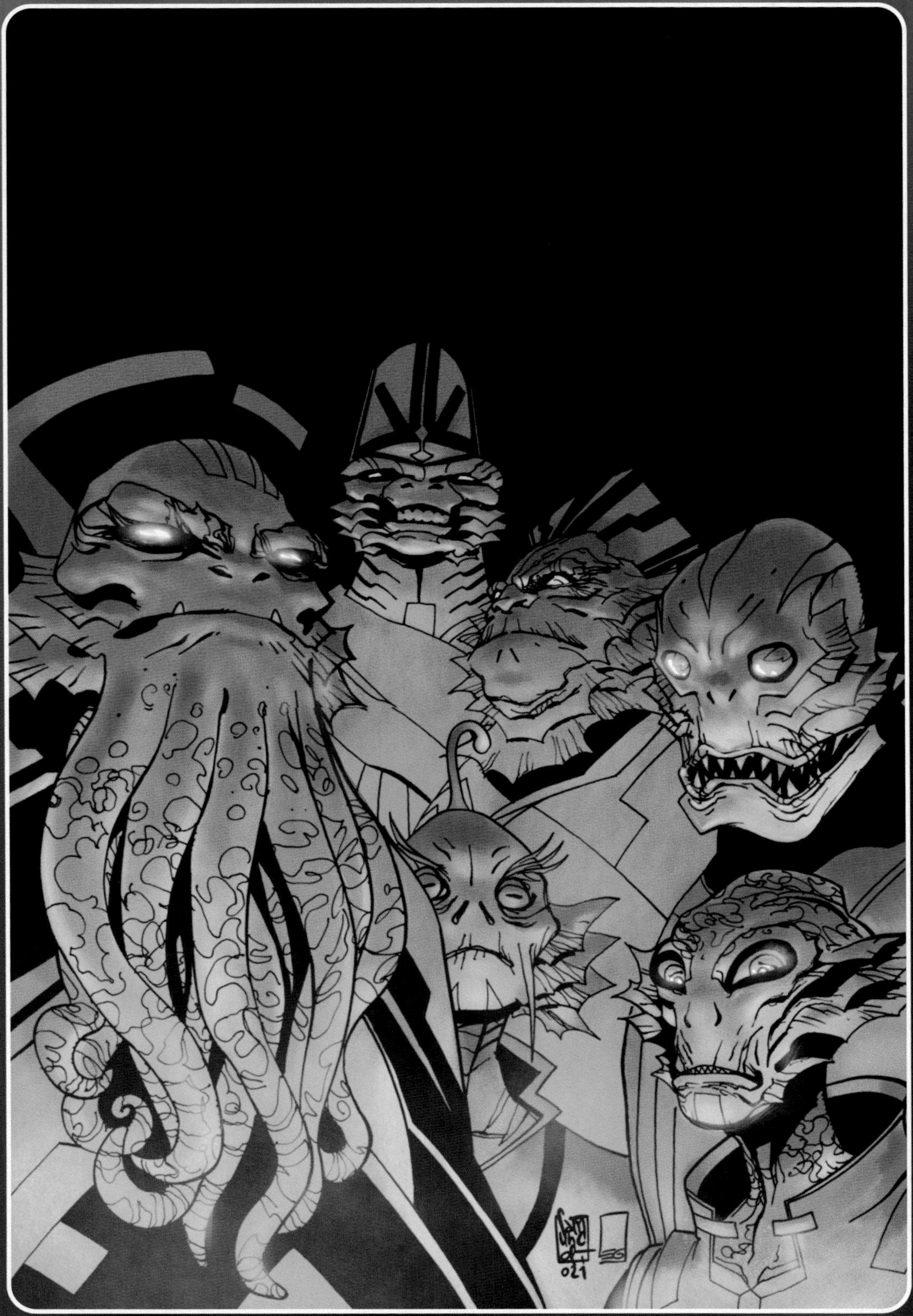

GIUSEPPE CAMUNCOLI (INKS & COLORS: LEONARDO M. GRASSI)

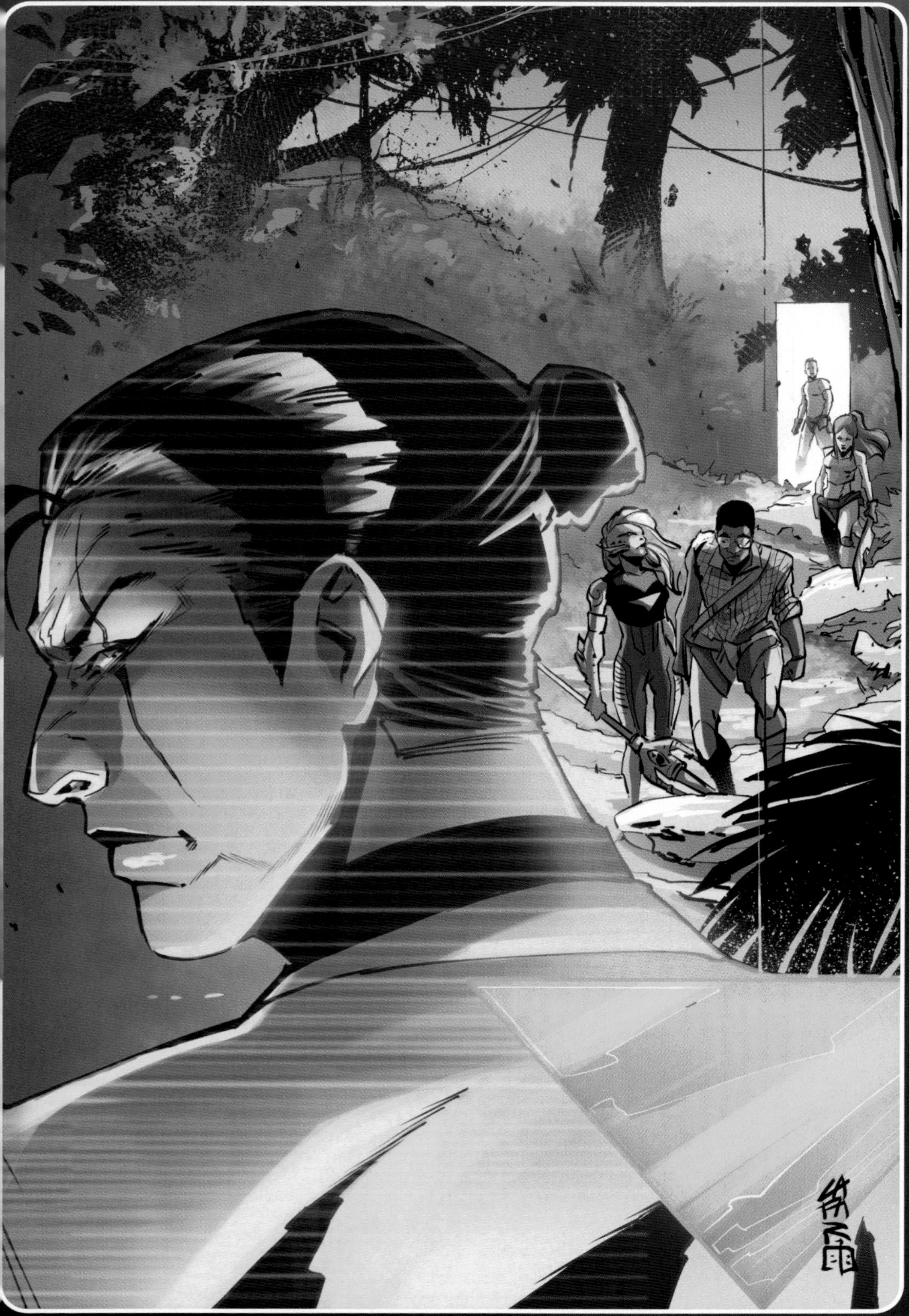

GIUSEPPE CAFARO (colors: FRANCESCA CAROTENUTO)

ISSUE 09

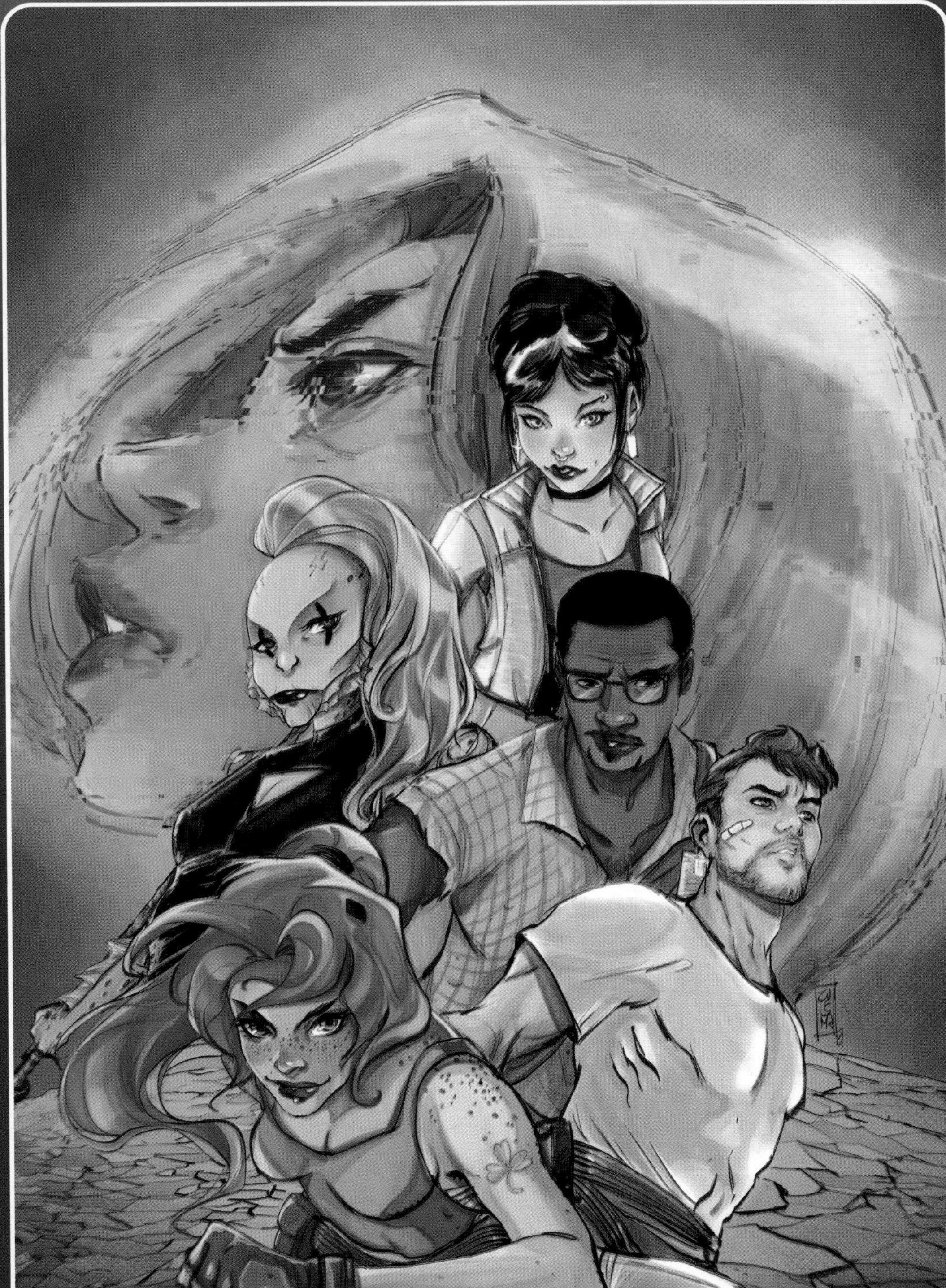

ZULEMA SCOTTO LAVINA
ISSUE 09

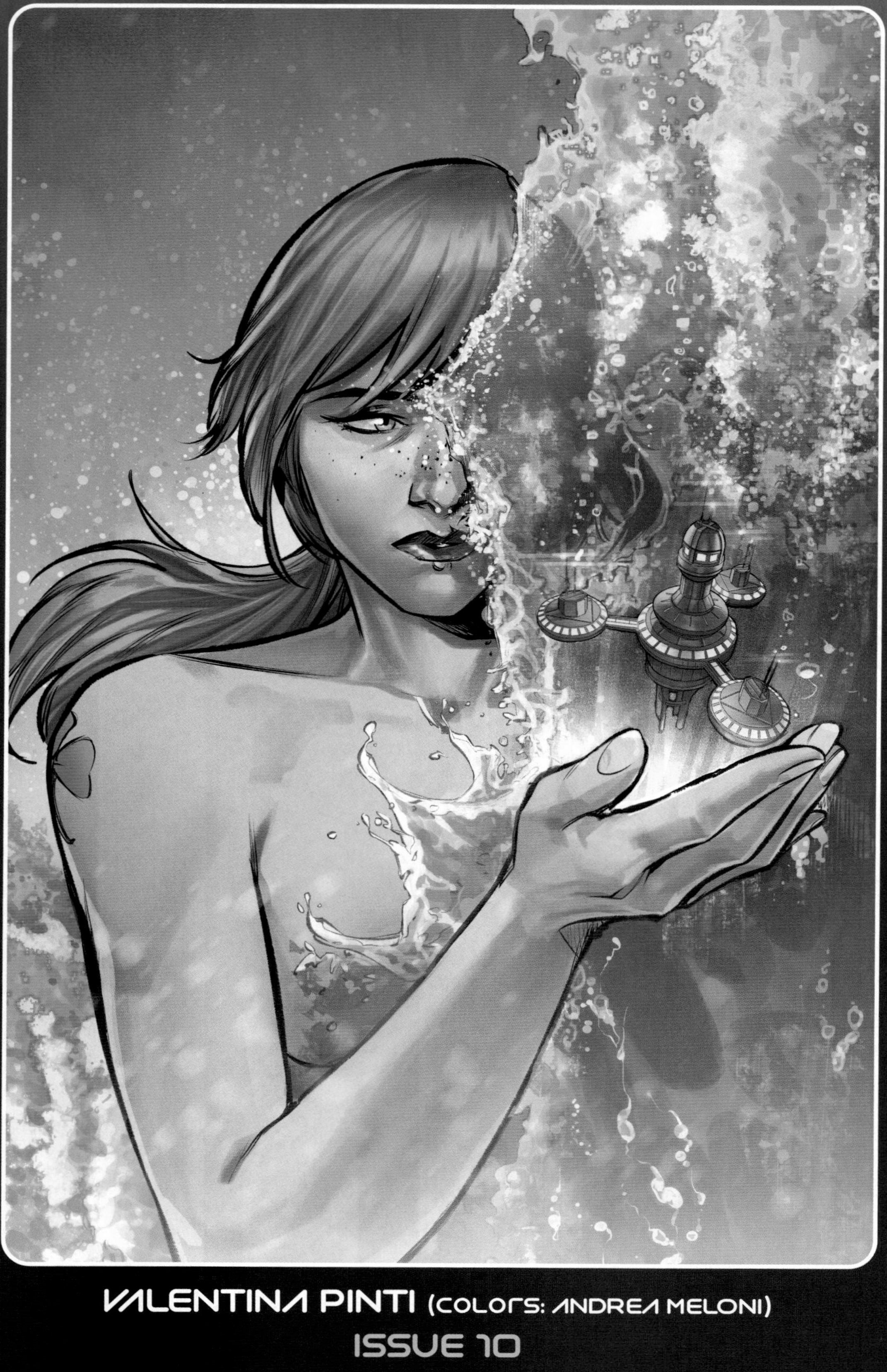

VALENTINA PINTI (Colors: ANDREA MELONI)
ISSUE 10

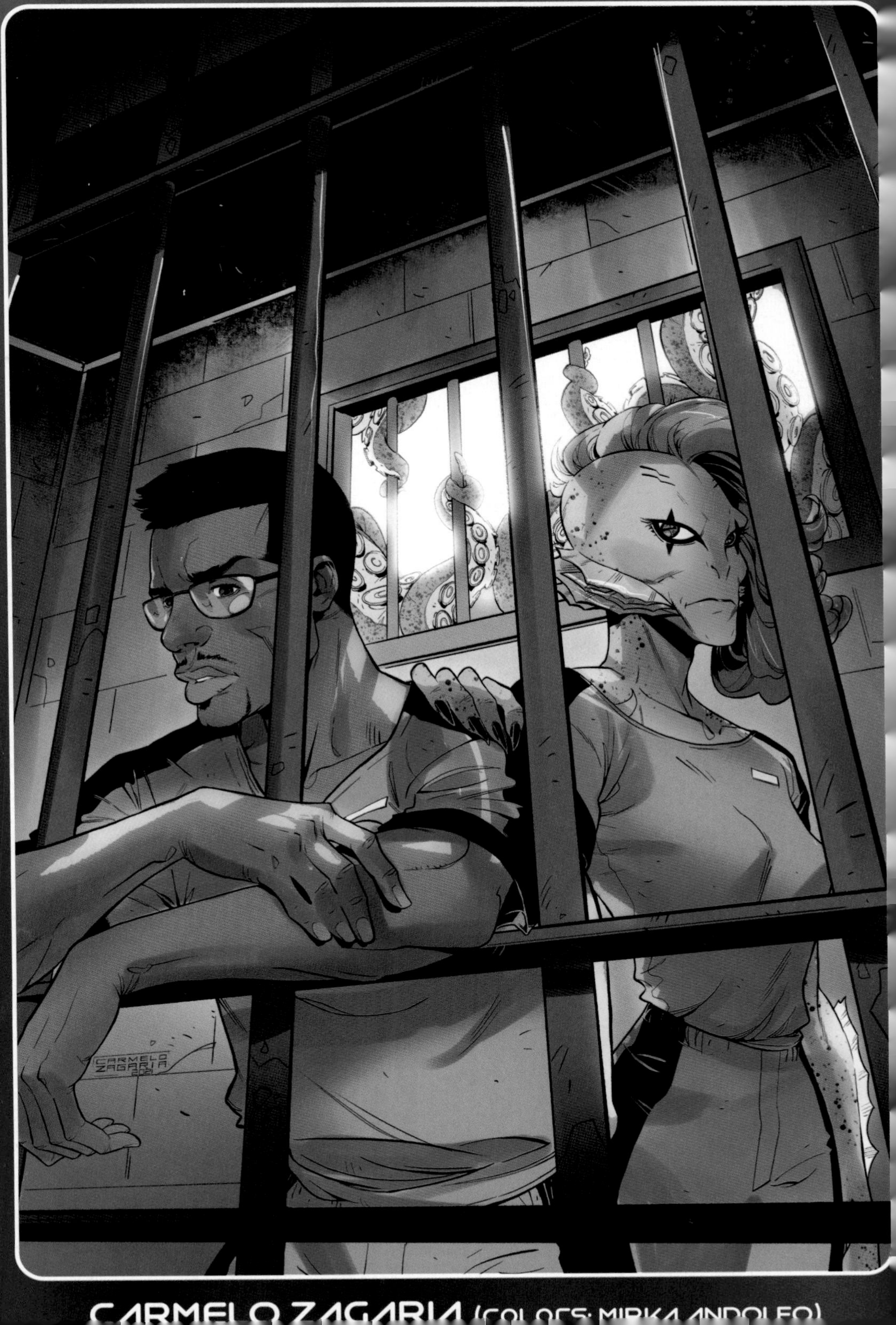
CARMELO ZAGARIA

CARMELO ZAGARIA (COLORS: MIRKA ANDOLFO)

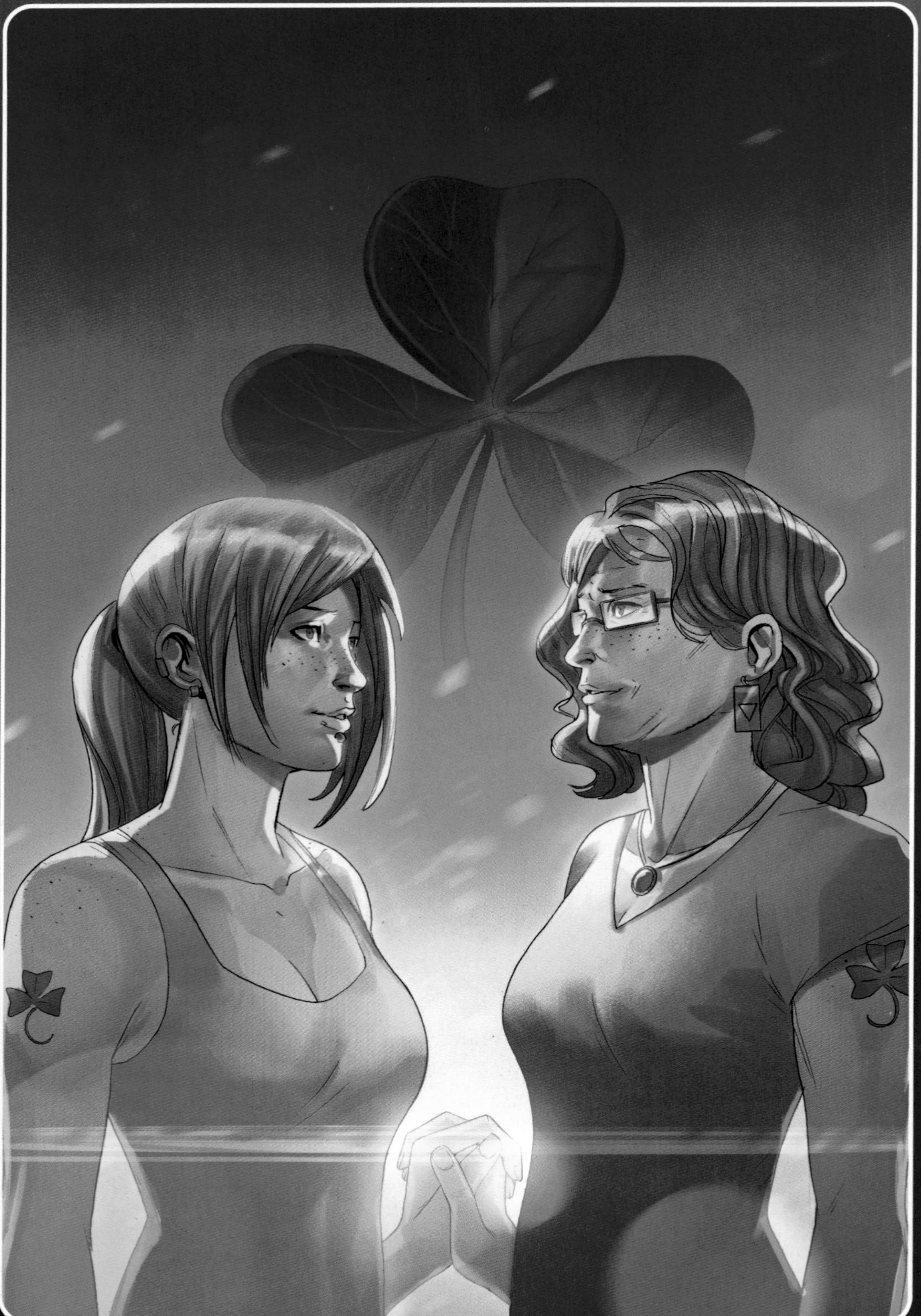

ANDREA BROCCARDO (colors: ANDREA MELONI)
ISSUE 12